THE CLEVER ADULTERESS

THE CLEVER ADULTERESS
& Other Stories

A Treasury of Jain Literature

Edited by Phyllis Granoff

mosaic press

Library and Archives Canada Cataloguing in Publication

Granoff, P. E. (Phyllis Emily), 1947-
The clever adulteress & other stories : treasury of Jain literature / by Phyllis Granoff.

Adapted and translated from Sanskrit Jain literature.
Includes bibliographical references.
ISBN 978-0-88962-889-2

1. Jaina literature, Sanskrit--India--Translations into English. 2. Didactic literature, Sanskrit--India--Translations into English. 3. English literature--Translations from Sanskrit. 4. Didactic literature, English--Translations from Sanskrit. I. Title.

PS8563.R362C54 2008 891'.2080382 C2008-901878-8

Publishing by Mosaic Press, offices and warehouse at 1252 Speers Rd., units 1 & 2, Oakville, On L6L 5N9, Canada and Mosaic Press, PMB 145, 4500 Witmer Industrial Estates, Niagara Falls, NY, 14305-1386, U.S.A.

info@mosaic-press.com

ISBN 978-0-88962-889-2

Second Printing © 2008

Mosaic Press in Canada:
1252 Speers Road, Units 1 & 2,
Oakville, Ontario
L6L 5N9
Phone/Fax: 905-825-2130
info@mosaic-press.com

Mosaic Press in U.S.A.:
4500 Witmer Industrial Estates
PMB 145, Niagara Falls, NY
14305-1386
Phone/Fax: 1-800-387-8992
info@mosaic-press.com

www.mosaic-press.com

INTRODUCTION

This book is a collection of translations of Jain stories that were originally written either in Sanskrit or in one of the older vernacular languages related to Sanskrit. The Jains trace the history of their religion back through a series of twenty-four teachers, Jinas or "Conquerors," the last of whom, Mahāvīra, was a contemporary of the Buddha. From the very beginning Jains told stories to illustrate their religious teachings. Stories fill their existing canon, and many of the commentaries to canonical texts are veritable treasure houses of stories. Indeed in later medieval times some of these stories from the canon and the commentaries were gathered together with other popular tales into large and often very diverse collections that were aptly called "treasure houses of stories."

Early in its history the Jain community split into two groups, the Śvetāmbaras, who were concentrated mainly in the north of India, and the Digambaras, who were concentrated primarily in the south. While most of the translations in this volume are of stories in the Śvetāmbara Jain tradition, the Digambara Jains also told and collected stories in Sanskrit and other Indian languages. It is in all of these Jain writings that much of medieval Indian story literature as a whole has been preserved, and without them we would know much less than we do of popular culture in medieval India.

The material in the Jain canon, its commentaries, and the story collections that grew from this older tradition is often didactic. Part I of the present book is a selection of Jain didactic stories. It begins with Dr. Bollée's translation of a parable from one of the eleven *aṅgas*, which takes us back to the very starting point of Jain story literature. This is followed by a long section from the story tradition that is preserved in the commentaries to the *Āvaśyakasūtra*. The prominence given to the Āvaśyaka stories here is an accurate reflection of their importance within the Jain tradition. The Āvaśyaka commentaries are the life-blood of the didactic story tradition in Śvetāmbara Jainism; they preserve an enormous number of stories and were one major source for many later collections of stories. By translating a block of stories Dr. Balbir has given the English reader the unique opportunity to see the range of stories that the commentarial tradition preserves, and to understand how the stories functioned in their original setting. The section on didactic stories continues with examples from later didactic story collections, some of which are rooted in the Āvaśyaka tradition. Dr. P.S. Jain, who has translated the story of the faithful wife Rohiṇī, has chosen to retain much of the verse form of the original, which gives the reader the chance to see just how varied in style Jain stories can be. I have translated several stories on a single theme, making gifts to monks and nuns. The section on didactic stories concludes with a story that illustrates karmic retribution. It comes from the Digambara tradition and is translated by Dr. Friedhelm Hardy.

Part II offers selections of another significant group of stories that were told throughout the history of Jainism. In addition to avowedly didactic stories, Jains also recounted the lives and deeds of people who were important to their tradition. They also collected and told stories about their holy places. The boundary line between Jain "biographies" in particular and the didactic story is admittedly fluid; on the one hand, biographies may incorporate didactic stories or be used as didactic stories. At the same time biographies could be preserved in didactic story collections and yet lack a clear didactic purpose. Jain biography collections also from time to time include stories about famous poets and kings who were not specifically connected with the Jain tradition. Collections of the deeds of monks and nuns, pious laymen and women, appear regularly from the 12th century on. Biographies of the Jinas, the founding teachers of Jainism, have a longer history, but they continued to be a popular subject in medieval times.

In chapter 1 of Part II of this book I have translated biographies from a number of major Jain biography collections. For chapter 2 I have given two accounts of lay devotees who became demi-gods. These accounts come from a text on Jain holy places. In chapter 3 Dr. Lefeber has translated the humorous account of the minister Cāṇakya, whom Jain, Hindu, and Buddhist sources alike celebrate as the power behind the throne of India's first great empire. Chapter 4 contains three chapters from the Digambara *Ādipurāṇa* that have been translated by Dr. Ralph Strohl. The chapters describe the conflict between the two brothers Bharata and Bāhubali, and between secular and religious authority. Chapter 5 is a selection of translations from the same pilgrimage text that records the deeds of the lay devotees become gods translated in chapter 2. Here Dr. Cort has selected several accounts of medieval holy places. Some of these are miracle stories or stories of the origins of a holy site; others are more descriptive in nature and still others belong more properly to the class of literature we would call hymns. By providing samples of all these types, Dr. Cort has given the English reader the chance to see the kind of religious world his stories inhabit.

The title of the book, "The Clever Adulteress and the Hungry Monk," was taken from one story in Part I and one in Part II. In Part I Dr. Bablir has translated a tale of a clever woman who outwits both her husband and the divine being who tests her chastity. In Part II I have translated a story about a Jain monk who is too eager for food and so converts to Buddhism.

In the original each of the stories that are translated in this collection has an unmistakable and unique stamp; Jain story literature as a whole is characterized by a plurality of styles and a freedom of invention that surely contributed to its lasting appeal. Some stories read like simple folk-tales; others read more like the bare framework for a sermon while still others seem more like courtly romances. In addition, although they all appear here in English, these stories in the original are not even in the same language. A single story may even be in more than one language, for it is not unusual for stories to switch from one language to another, using Sanskrit and the vernaculars side by side. Some of the stories that appear here were written entirely in prose, while others were in verse or in mixed prose and verse. The stories have been translated by several scholars, and no attempt has been made to achieve a uniform translation style. This was a deliberate decision; the originals themselves exhibit great diversity and it was hoped that at least an impression of that richness might be conveyed by the strikingly different translations that each scholar has made. The freedom of the translators included the choice of adding footnotes or incorporating necessary background information into the text. The originals themselves exhibit the same wide range of tone, from scholarly and erudite to popular and easily accessible. Several translators kept to the popular vein; others have added notes that will be of great interest to specialists as well as general readers. These translations offer only a brief glimpse into what is an enormous body of literature. Hopefully the availability of these stories in English will help stimulate interest in this warm and lively literature.

I take this opportunity to thank the Dean of Social Sciences at McMaster for assistance in having the manuscript typed.

Phyllis Granoff

List of Contributors

Dr. Nalini Balbir is a member of the Centre National de la Recherche Scientifique in Paris. She has published numemous articles on Jainism. Her book *Dānāṣṭakakathā* was published in 1982.

Dr. Willem B. Bollée teaches the literature of the older Indian religious traditions at the South Asia Institute of Heidelberg University. His publications include *The Kunāla Jātaka* (1970) and *Studien zum Sūyagaḍa I and II* (1977, 1988), and "Traditionell indische Vorstellungen uber die Fusse in Literature und Kunst," 1983.

Dr. John Cort received his Ph.D. from Harvard University in religion and is teaching there. His thesis was on Jainism. In addition to articles on Jainism and Gujarati religion he has published translations of the Sanskrit poetry of Bhartṛhari and Yogeśvara.

Dr. Phyllis Granoff teaches Sanskrit and Indian religions at McMaster University . Her publications include *Philosophy and Argument in Late Vedānta* (D. Reidel, 1974) and the book, *Monks and Magicians: Religious Biography in Asia* (Mosaic Press, 1988, which she recently edited with Dr. K.Shinohara.

Dr. Friedhelm Hardy teaches at the University of London. He has a long-standing interest in Jain narrative literature and numerous scholarly publications on a wide range of subjects in Indian religions, including the book *Virahabhakti*, on South Indian devotional literature.

Dr. Prem Suman Jain is head of the Department of Prakrit and Jainology at Sukhadia University in Udaipur in Rajasthan. His scholarly publications include a discussion and translation into Hindi of the story that he has translated for this volume.

Dr. Rosalind Lefeber teaches Sanskrit at McMaster University. Her publications include a translation of the *Kiṣkindha Kāṇḍa* of the *Rāmāyaṇa* which is soon to appear from Princeton University Press.

Dr. Ralph Strohl received his Ph.D. from the University of Chicago. He wrote his thesis on the stories that he has translated for this volume. He currently works in the Development Office of the University of Chicago.

Table of Contents

Part I

Of Manners and Morals: A selection of didactic stories

The Peacock Egg: a parable of Mahāvīra (Nāyādhammakahāo 1,3)

Translated by Willem Bollée

Introduction

The Nāyādhammakahāo is the sixth text in the canon of the Śvetāmbara Jains. It consists of two books containing parables and sermons respectively. The parable of the Peacock Egg tells how monks ought to respect the rules that govern them. It is formulaic in style, as is much of the Śvetāmbara canon, and contains strings of stock phrases that may be found elsewhere. I have indicated in my translation where such stock descriptions are to be supplied, and the source from which they have been taken. Mahāvīra, the founder of Jainism, here answers a question by his disciple Goyama Suhamma, who in his turn reports to us.

The Peacock Egg

50. [97a 5] Thus indeed, Jambū, in those days, at that time, there was a city named Campā[1] — description (after Aup § 1).[2] Outside this city of Campā, to the north-east of it, there was a park called Subhūmi-bhāga ('beautiful place') rich in flowers and fruits of every season, delightful like the Nandana-wood (in Indra's heaven), provided with a pleasantly fragrant and cool shade. Now at a place to the north of this Subhūmi-bhāga park there was a *māluyā*[3] thicket — description (after Nāyā 1,2; cf. Aup § 3). At that place a jungle peahen[4] laid two plump peacock eggs that were produced at the right time[5], pale like a dumpling, not yet showing cracks, unspoilt, in size larger than a fist, and when she had laid them she sat (there) protecting, keeping and

covering them with her own feathers which she spread over them (*pakkha-vāeṇaṃ*).

Now in the city of Campā there lived two sons of caravan leaders, Jiṇadatta-putta and Sāgaradatta-putta. Born on the same day,[6] they grew up and played in the sand box together, married at the same time, were attached to and trailed after each other, [97 b] living in compliance with each other's wishes, fulfilling each other's heart's desires and performing all duties that came up in each other's houses.

51. [98a] Then, one day, these caravan leaders' sons met, encountered each other and sat together, and entered upon the following conversation: "Dear friend (*devāṇu-ppiya*), whatever pleasant or unpleasant (thing), leaving home to become a monk or travelling abroad, may fall to our share, that we must experience together."[7] With these words they promised each other co-operation and continued to go about their own business.

52. [98a 5] In the city of Campā there lived at that time a courtesan Devadattā[8] by name, rich, proud, famous, owning spacious and vast palaces, dwellings, chariots and draught animals, possessing much wealth, gold and silver, lending out money on interest and making investments, and offering food and drink liberally,[9] skillful in the sixty-four arts,[10] provided with the sixty-four good qualities of a courtesan,[11] flirting in twenty-nine ways,[12] excelling in the twenty-one sexual qualities,[12] able to serve a man in thirty-two ways,[12] having awakened from sleep the nine senses of her body[13] (i.e. a woman in her prime of youth), conversant with the eighteen vernaculars, elegantly dressed in her boudoir (?), of proper gait, mode of laughing,[14] speech, behaviour, sporting, conversation; with perfectly fitting manners,[15] holding high the banner (of conceit),[17] taking a thousand as a fee,[17] (a woman) whom a sunshade and various chowries had been granted (by the king) and who moved about in a litter.[18] She exercised and held sovereign power,[19] preeminence, mastery, ownership, strength and military command over many thousands of courtesans and was enjoying various pleasures under the great din[20] of repeated[21] dancing, singing, instrumental music, strings,[22] beating of time, clapping the hands, *tūya*-music, and the sounds of big (i.e., deep)[23] and clear drums.

Then, one day, these sons of caravan leaders came together after having had breakfast[24] and lunch together at the proper time;[26] they had purified themselves, were perfectly clean and were sitting at their ease; they began the following conversation: "Dear friend, it would be very good to have much food, drink, sweets and seasonings prepared tomorrow, when[26] the night lets daybreak appear and the morning, pale then, fully opens the soft (? *komala*) blue and pink lotus flowers, when the sun shining intensely red like the Jonesia aśoka or the open Butea frondosa flower, like a parrot's beak or the (red) half of the Gunjā berry, the Pentapets phoenicea, the feet and eyes of a pigeon, the Koīl's red eyes, like a mass of Chinese roses or vermilion — when the sun has arisen waking up the clusters of pink lotuses, when the thousand-rayed day-maker glows in his radiance.[27] (It would be very good) to take this abundance of food (etc.), incense, flowers, perfume, clothes, wreaths and ornaments and to enjoy for a while (*viharittae*) the pleasure grove beauty of the Subhūmi-bhāga park in the company of the courtesan Devadattā." With these words they agreed on this point with each other and thereupon sent the next day, when the night (...up to) [98 b] radiance, for their servants, and told them thus: "Go, good people, cook abundantly food (etc.), take incense (...), set out for the Nandā pond in the Subhūmi-bhāga park and near that pond erect a pavilion on posts. (then) sprinkle it, cleanse it, smear it with cow-dung,[28] provide it with an arrangement of fresh and fragrant cut flowers in groups of five colours,[29] make it highly delightful[30] with the fragrantly rising smell of burning aloe, choice *kundurukka*, *turukka*[31] and incense, scent it well with fine perfumes and turn it into a fragrant bottle, so to speak, and stay waiting for each of us." (The servants...) did so.[32]

Thereupon the sons of caravan leaders gave further (*doccaṃ*) orders and told their servants: "As quickly as possible,[33] as soon as it is yoked bring a carriage which you have had dexterous people (?) yoke[34] with excellent young bullocks matching each other in hoofs and tails, and the end of whose sharp horns have been cut level with each other;[35] who are steered by nose ropes having thread-strings with silver bells and that are exquisitely intertwined with gold;[36] they should carry garlands made of blue lotuses. The carriage should be overspread with a network of various jewels and silver and gold bells, and endowed[37] with auspicious marks."[38] They (i.e., the servants) for their part (*vi*) brought (a carriage) exactly as they were told.

After that the sons of caravan leaders bathed,[39] performed a food sacrifice and expiatory rites for good luck, adorned themselves with few but very valuable ornaments, entered the carriage, went to Devadattā's house, got out of the carriage again and entered Devadattā's house.

The courtesan Devadattā saw the caravan leaders' sons approach, became glad and joyful, rose from her seat, went seven or eight steps[40] to meet them and spoke as follows: "The gentlemen should say what they have come hither for." Thereupon the caravan leaders' sons spoke thus: "Dear lady, we should like to enjoy the Subhūmi-bhāga park for a while in your company." Devadattā then complied with this request of the caravan leaders' sons, bathed (etc. as above) and joined them in beautiful dress. [99 a] Then the caravan leaders' sons ascended the carriage with the courtesan Devadattā, drove right across the centre[41] of the city of Campā to the Subhūmi-bhāga park and the Nandā lotus pond, got out of the carriage, went into the pond, plunged into the water, splashed one another, and after bathing in the company of Devadattā went out again and, betaking themselves to the pavilion on posts, entered it. After putting on all their ornaments, taking a rest and recovering on a comfortable seat they tasted, enjoyed, shared and ate the many foods (etc. as supra) and thus stayed in the company of Devadattā. After the meal they enjoyed for a while with Devadattā the many human pleasures of the senses.

53. [100a 2] When they had breakfast and lunch the caravan leaders' sons left the pavilion on posts again holding hands[42] with the courtesan Devadattā and stayed in the Subhūmi-bhāga park enjoying the pleasure grove beauty in the many bowers of *ālis*,[43] bananas, creepers, bowers to abide in (? *acchna-ghara*),[46] scenic bowers, bowers for dressing up (? *pasāhaṇa-ghara*) labyrinths,[45] bowers of boughs/ Śāl tree bowers,[46] net-like (?) bowers[47] and flowering bowers.

54. Then the caravan leaders' sons proceeded to the *māluyā* thicket. The jungle peahen saw them coming, left the *māluyā* thicket scared and trembling, squawking loudly and repeatedly screaming "*kekā*" and standing on a branch of a tree remained looking at the caravan leaders' sons and the *māluyā* thicket with steady gaze. The caravan leaders' sons addressed each other saying: "Dear friend, as soon as this jungle peahen saw us coming, she left (...) gaze.[48] There must be a reason for this." With these words they entered the *māluyā* thicket. There they saw two plump (etc. as above in *sūtra*[49]) peacock eggs, addressed each other and said: "Dear friend, it would be very good for us to have these two jungle peacock eggs placed among the eggs of our own pure-bred fowl. The latter, then, [100 b] shall watch over and protect these eggs with their own feathers which they spread over them and we shall have two young peacocks to play with." With these words they agreed on this point with each other; each sent for his own servants and told them thus: "Go, good people, take these eggs and place them among the eggs (...)." They did so.

The caravan leaders' sons, after enjoying for a while the pleasure grove beauty of the Subhūmi-bhāga park in the company of the courtesan Devadattā, ascended their carriage and drove to her house in the city of Campā, entered, gave her a lavish present of money (*pīīdāṇam*) befitting her social rank, paid their respects and honored her, returned from her house each to his own house and engaged themselves once more in their own business.

55. The next day, the caravan leader Sāgaradatta's son, when the night (...as above, *sū* 52 up to) radiance, went to his peacock egg and afraid, anxious, doubtful, divided, unclear in his thoughts [50] (asked himself) "Shall I be able to play with this peacock chick or not?" Thinking thus he threw the egg up again and again, turned it round, stirred it slightly,[50] shook it thoroughly, moved it to and fro, made it palpitate, knocked against it, bashed it and made it tick over and over again at his ear. Thereupon the peacock egg became addled.[51]

Sāgaradatta, the caravan leader's son, one day [101 a] went to his egg, saw that it was addled and exclaimed: "Helas, now I shall not have a young peacock to play with." In consequence of this he became dejected[52] and despondent, placed his head between his hands, was overcome by tormenting thoughts and became pensive.

In exactly the same way, venerable monk(s), whosoever of our male or female ascetics parted with his or her hair[53] in the presence of an *āyariya* and an *uvajjhāya*,[54] left his family for the life of a religious wanderer and is afraid (...as above up to) unclear in his thoughts as to the five major vows (or) the six groups of souls[55] in the doctrine of the Jainas, he or she should in this existence be despised, reproached, blamed, censured and treated with contempt by many monks, nuns, male and female lay followers. Moreover, in the next world,[56] such people will undergo many punishments, will often have their hair pulled out, be rebuked, hit, put in irons, be tormented, suffer the death of their parents, brothers and sisters, wife,[57] sons, daughters and daughters-in-law.[57] Much poverty, misfortune, association with unpleasant people, separation from loved ones, bad luck and distress will be their share. Again and again they will err through the jungle of *saṃsāra* which has neither beginning nor end, and extends[58] in all four directions.

45. Then Jiṇadatta's son went to his peacock egg and, not worried about it (...as above), thinking: "It is clear/surely[59] I shall have a young peacock to play with here" he did not throw it up again and again (...as above up to) his ear and the egg, left in peace, one day broke open and out came a young peacock. Jiṇadatta's son saw it and, glad and joyful, he addressed the peacock-breeders and told them: "You, good people, watch over this young peacock, protect it, raise it by and by with the many things suitable for peacock breeding and teach it to dance." Thereupon the peacock-breeders promised this to Jiṇadatta's son, took the young peacock, went to their dwelling and raised (...as above up to) dance.

The young peacock grew up[60] with auspicious marks, signs and qualities. Its wings and mass of tail feathers[61] were full-sized, it had a hundred eyes on its many-coloured tail, a blue neck and was able to dance. At one snapping of the fingers it could be made to make hundreds of dancing steps and *kekā* calls. The peacock breeders seeing the young peacock grown up (...as above up to) calls took it and brought it to Jinadatta's son. He, seeing (...up to) calls, was glad and joyful, presented them with a lavish present of money corresponding to their social rank and dismissed them. Then, at one snapping of his fingers, the young peacock danced, bowing its neck like a tail;[62] the corners of its eyes were white,[63] and it let its wings droop as if they were detached(?)[64]; the many eyes of its tail stood up and it uttered a hundred times its call. In the city of Campā, at squares, cross-roads, intersections, highways and paths Jinadatta's son earned (? *jayaṃ karemāṇe*) for a long time hundreds, thousands and hundreds of thousands in goods[65] through this young peacock.

In exactly the same way, venerable monk(s), whosoever (...as in *sū.* 55 up to) wanderer and is trustful, free from doubts and firm, he or she should in this existence be treated with respect,[66] greeted, saluted, worshipped , honored, revered by many monks, nuns,[67](...as above) and humbly[68] worshipped as being something excellent, auspicious, divine and sacred.

Thus you should know, Jambū, the contents of the third lecture of the Parables as told by the Venerable Ascetic Mahāvīra, the founder[69] (sc. of the Doctrine), the Tīrthakara (...as in Nāyā 1, 1,7 up to) who has reached the placed called *Siddhagai* ('Condition of Salvation'). — Thus I say.

A Note on the Translation

As the older prints mentioned in Schubring's *Lehre der Jainas* (§ 46) were not available to me for my translation, I have used the text published in the Ānandacandra-granthābdhi (Bhāvnagar, 1951) with Abhayadeva's 11th century commentary. I also adopted its *sūtra* numbers beginning with 50 on fol. 97a. Walther Schubring gave us a free adaptation in German which, after his death, was edited from his unpublished works by J. Deleu (Wiesbaden, 1978). I further used the text critically edited by Muni Nathmal in the Anga Suttāni Series III (Lādṇūn 1974/ V.S. 2031). Abbreviations follow the system stated in my *Studien zum Sūyagaḍa I* (Wiesbaden, 1977) and II (Stuttgart, 1988), hereafter BSS. I and II respectively. Nathmal's text concludes with five *āryās* which in the Bhāvnagar *pothī* belong to the commentary.

Notes

1. For the capital of ancient Anga, ca. 6 km to the West of modern Bhagalpur in Bihar, see N.L. Dey, *The Geographical Dictionary of Ancient and Mediaeval India* (1927), repr. New Delhi, 1979.

2. See L.D. Barnett's translation of the *Antagada-dasão and Aṇuttarovavāiya-dasāo*. London, 1907, p. 1 et passim.

3. *Māluyā*, Pāli *māluvā*, probably is a creeper, Bauhinia vahlii, for which see BSS. II, p. 103.

4. The *pavo cristatus* Linn. "Inhabits dense scrub and deciduous jungle (...) always excessively shy and alert. Slinks away through the undergrowth on its legs, and flies only when suddenly come upon (...). Eggs: 3-5, glossy pale cream or café-au-lait colour" (Sàlim Ali, *The book of Indian birds*. 11th ed. Bombay, 1979, p. 36, no. 71).

5. Sch(ubring) renders *pariyāgae* by 'fast aufbruchreif' which seems to be logically impossible for freshly laid eggs, and in view of what will be done with them in the course of the story. *Paryāyeṇa-prasava-kāla-krameṇāgate paryāyāgate prākṛtatvena ya-kāra-lopāt pariyāgae* (Abh.). MW gives 'revolved, elapsed, passed (as years); finished, done' for *paryāgata* and 'to go round, elapse, last, live' for *paryāgacchati*.

6. For the bond of congeniality see the present author's article "The Indo-European Sodalities in ancient India", in ZDMG 131, 1 (1981), p. 187 sqq. As a literary motif it is used in India up to the present day, e.g. in S. Rushdie's *Midnight's Children*.

7. For the lectio facilior *samecca* of the text read Abhayadeva's variant *saṃhicca* or, perhaps better still, *saṃhiccāe*, see G. Roth, *Mallī-Jñāta*. Wiesbaden, 1983, p. 157.

8. Literally, 'God-given,' but in fact equivalent to our 'Miss So-and-so.' On Indian courtesans see Moti Chandra, *The world of courtesans*. Delhi, 1973; J.C.Jain, *Life in Ancient India as Depicted in the Jain Canon and Commentaries*. Delhi, 1984, p. 216 sqq.

9. Up to this point, the description is taken from Aup (*apātika*) § 11, see Bollée, "On royal epithets in the Aupapātikasūtra," JOIB 27, 3-4 (1978), p. 97.

10. "These were a stock list, which included not only music, dancing and singing, but also acting (...), sorcery, archery (...), and clay modelling" (A.L. Basham, *The Wonder that was India*. London, 1954, p. 183). See Kāmasūtra (Bombay, 1934) 1, 3, 15 (p. 87 sq.). — Vivāgasutta, 2, describing the courtesan Kāmajayā, mentions 72 arts.

11. See Kāmasūtra 2, 2, 3 (p. 275 sq.).

12. According to the scholiast, these are also well-known from the Kāmasūtra, a glossary of which together with Yaśodhara's commentary would be more useful and urgent than further translations, to facilitate finding such details.

13. These are, in Abhayadeva's enumeration, the ears, eyes, nostrils, tongue, skin and mind which *suptānīva yauvanena pratibodhitāni*.

14. Omitted in Vivāga 2.

15. The text, which has *saṃgaya-gaya-hasiya* only, has been supplied after L, but Abhayadeva has the compound go on in a slightly different way. The scholiast (99b 1) mentions as a variant *sundara-thaṇa-jaghaṇa-vayaṇa-caraṇa-nayaṇa-lāvaṇṇa-rūva-jovvaṇa-vilāsa-kaliyā*.

16. For the metaphorical use of "banner" in the sense of "conceit" see K.R. Norman, *Elders' Verses I*. London, 1969, note on Theragāthā 424 (*ussita-ddhaja*). Sanskrit lexicographers mention 'pride' as a meaning of *dhvaja* (MW).

17. On courtesan's fees see W. Bollée, *Kuṇālajātaka*. London, 1970, p. 110.

18. The *karṇī-ratha*, according to Mallinātha ad Kālidāsa, *Raghuvaṃśa* 14, 13, was a small chariot to be used by women (*strī-yogyo'lpa-rathaḥ*), and only by the wealthy, as Abhayadeva explains (99b 3).

19. The following stock phrase has been supplied after Aup § 53, but it occurs also in Kappa (see next note) and Sūy 2, 2, 55.

20. Following Jacobi's rendering of Kappa Jinac 14 *in fine*. As to *mahayā* see the present author's article "Die Geschichte vom Frosch (Nāyādhammakahāo 1, 13]" in K. Watanabe (ed.), Volume in Honour of J. Deleu. Tokyo, 1990 (in preparation).

21. Jacobi, l.c. translates *āhaya* by 'uninterrupted story-telling' which I do not understand. Sa. *āhanti* means 'to sound (a musical instrument; to repeat' (MW).

22. *Tantī*, apparently *pars pro toto*. Jacobi's translation does not exactly follow his text.

23. Or: percussion instruments (like cymbals, *ghaṇa*) and drums. Jacobi takes *ghaṇa* to mean 'great.'

24. Also, e.g., Vivāga 1, 19.

25. Also, e.g., Kappa 105 and Vivāga 1, 18 and 19.

26. The following cliché has been supplied after Kappa 59. It occurs also in Nāyā 1, 1 and 1, 13, 15 (see above my paper "Die Geschichte vom Frosch").

27. See Roth, op. cit., p. 121, note 63.

28. Hardly as a reverential adornment, as Barnett, op. cit., p. 3 thought.

29. The Jain stock list of colours consists of black, blue, red, green and white (e.g. Ṭhāṇanga 5), whereas the Pāli Buddhist one contains blue (*nīla*), yellow, crimson, blood-red and white (*odāta*), e.g., MN I 509, 15 sqq. and Vinaya I 25, 32 (with *phalikavaṇṇa* instead of *odāta*). In Pāli, flowers of five colours are mentioned, e.g., Sv 140, 10 (PED). — this and the next stock phrases also occur in Aup § 32.

30. Thus Jacobi at Kappa § 32 for *uddhuyābhirāma*.

31. *Kundurukka* is olibanum, i.e., the aromatic gum resin of Boswellia thurifera tree (Barnett, op. cit., p. 3 note 4); *turukka* is also olibanum (MW) or the resin of other trees (Barnett, l.c.).

32. As in Nāyā 1, 8, 46, (ed. Roth).

33. Hereafter Nathmal may be right in supplying *bho devāṇu-ppiya*, cf. Uvās 7, 206.

34. See Hoernle's discussion of *lahu-karaṇa-jutta-joiyaṃ*, which has a variant *°juttehiṃ joiyaṃ*, in his Uvāsaga-dasāo translation, p. 134. Sa. *laghū-karaṇa* means 'lessening, diminishing' (MW), Pāli *lahuṃ karoti* 'to be frivolous' (PED); Roth (op. cit., § 48) renders the compound by 'Geschicklichkeit.'

35. *Same-tulye likhite-Śastreṇāpanīta-bāhya-tvakke tīkṣṇe śṛṅge yayos tau tathā* (T 99b 8). Here the scholiast mentions another word — *jambūṇayamaya-kalāva-jutta-paivisiṭṭhaehiṃ* — which he apparently did not consider canonical, though he comments upon it, but which is actually found in the text at Uvās 7,206 and rendered by Hoernle as 'adorned with neck-ropes (set) with golden tassels' (see also H.'s note 194 on this). In this way bullocks are still decorated for festive occasions, e.g., for the last day of Saṃkrānti/ Pongal and for the Royal Ploughing ceremony in Thailand.

36. *Sūtra-rajjuke-kārpāsika-sūtra-davarakamayyau varakanakākhacite ye naste-nāsikā-nyasta-rajjuke tayoḥ pragraheṇa-raśminā avagṛhītakau-baddhau yau* (Ṭ 99b 11).

37. *Uvaveya* — Sa. *upeta*. Neither Pischel nor Geiger mentions such reduplication in their grammars, but see Leumann, Aup glossar, s.v., where, however, there is no reference to Hoernle's note, op. cit., p. 136.

38. Ṭ 99b 13 mentions another additional epitheton *sujāta-jugga-jutta-ujjuga-pasattha-suviraiya-nimmiyaṃ*, for which see Hoernle, l.c.

39. The following cliché has been supplied from Aup § 17.

40. See Bollée, "Traditionell-indische Vorstellungen Über die Füße in Literatur und Kunst", VAVA 5 (1983), p. 229.

41. The background of this striking yet frequent expression is not clear to me. The centre is the most distinguished part of the ancient Indian city.

42. *Hattha-saṃgellīe*. For the second part of the rare compound, which Ṭ 101b 13 is explained by *hastāvalambanena*, see Leumann's Aup Glossar, Bühler's *Pāiyalacchi Nāmamālā*, vs. 221 and Jacobi's *Bhavisattakaha*, Glossar s.v. *saṃgiliya*.

43. Apparently a *hapax legomenon* denoting a *vanaspati-viśeṣa* (Ṭ, l.c.).

44. *Acchaṇaṃ ti āsanaṃ* (Ṭ 101b 14), c.f. Pāli *acchati* (CPD) and R.N. Shriyan, *A critical study of <the> Mahāpurāṇa of Puṣpadanta*, Ahmedabad, 1969, p. 98 no. 269.

45. See G. Roth, op. cit., p. 202-220. I do not see why in our passage this should not be a bower, but a "stattliches Gebäude" (Roth, p. 202).

46. Rendered 'Zweiglauben' by Roth, l.c., after the scholiast's ambiguous explanation *sālāḥ śākhāḥ, athavā śālā vṛkṣa-viśeṣāḥ* (Ṭ 102a 1 sq.).

47. 'Maßwerkgehäuse' (Roth, l.c.).

48. 'Trembling' is followed by two more participles: 'upset' and 'running away.'

49. *Kalusa-samāvanne: mati-mālinyam upagataḥ* (Ṭ 102a 6).

50. *Āsārei: īṣat-sva-sthāna-tyājanena* (Ṭ 102a 7).

51. *Poccadaṃ: a-sāraṃ*. (Ṭ 102a 10); for this rare word's (Dravidian ?) etymology see Turner, CDIAL, no. 8395.

52. This cliché occurs also in Nāyā (L) 1, 1, 46 and resembles the one in Kappa Jinac § 92 which is used of Tisalā fearing the death of Mahāvīra in her womb.

53. *Muṇḍe agārāo aṇ-agāriyaṃ* not in the Bhāvnagar *pothī*. Cf. in L1, 1, 101 and see BSS. II, p. 92.

54. For these kinds of teachers see Schubring, *Doctrine*, § 141.

55. Such as have earth-, water-, fire-, wind-bodies belong to the vegetable kingdom. These five do not move of their own, are *ṭhāvarā*, as against the sixth group — *tasā* — who are self-moving, such as animals and mankind. See Schubring, op. cit., § 118 and Dasav 4 (*chaj-jīvaṇiyā*) and, for the form *chaj-jīva-nikāya*, Leumann's Aup Glossar, s.v.

56. The following cliché is also found in Sūy 2, 2, 81 where, however Śramaṇas and Brāhmaṇas who in their sayings do not propagate *ahiṃsā* are threatened with these punishments in the future (*āgantu*, § 80) which is more suitable.

57. As in the beginning also nuns are addressed, one would expect also *pai-maraṇāṇi* and *jāmāuya-mo*.

58. Cf. Suttanipāta 740 *puriso dīghaṃ addhānā saṃsaraṃ*.

59. *Su(v)vattae*: Sa. *su + vyakta + kaṃ* ?

60. The next words of this stock phrase, viz., *vinnaya-pariṇaya-mette* 'as soon as he had reached the years of discretion' and *jovvaṇagaṃ aṇupatte* 'having reached puberty' I pass over as being not applicable to an animal. In fact, these and the next compounds up to *pehuṇa-kalāve* are used of the child Mahāvīra at Kappa, §§ 51 and 52.

61. For the rare noun *pehuṇa* which Shriyan (op. cit., no 1122) classes as a pure Deśī word see also Turner's (CDIAL 8991) connection with Sa. *prekṣaṇa* 'show.' Up to *paḍipuṇṇa*, the *veḍha* is identical with Kappa § 9 and 51, where it becomes metrically irregular afterwards, and continues in our text adapted to a bird and metrically regular but for the last syllable of *kalāve*.

62. *Nangolābhanga-siro-dhare: lāṅgulābhaṅgavat-siṃhādi-puccha-vakrī-karaṇam iva* (Ṭ 102b 1f.).

63. *Seyāvange*: probably to show its positive feelings as opposite to Sa. *lohita-nayana* 'red-eyed, having eyes reddened with anger or passion' (MW). The scholiast did not understand this and mentions *śvetāpāṅga* only as an alternative to *svedāpanna* which makes no sense. Cf. Sa. *sitāpāṅga* 'peacock' (MW), a compound Dave takes to mean 'having the orbital skin of a white colour' (K.N. Dave, *Birds in Sanskrit literature*. Delhi, 1985, p. 270 sq.). — The pothī adds *ginhai* after *seyāvange*.

64. *Avayāriya-painna-pakke* (or, with L. *oyāriya-paiṇṇaō*): *avatāritau-śarīrāt pṛthak-kṛtau prakīrṇau-vikīrṇa-picchau pakṣau yasya sa tathā, tataḥ pada-dvayasya karma-dhārayaḥ* (Ṭ 102b 3).

65. *Paṇiehim: paṇitaiḥ-vyavahārair hoddādibhir* (?) *ity arthaḥ* (Ṭ 102b 5).

66. The following cliché which stems from Aup § 2, is also found, e.g., at Uvāsagadasāo § 187 (see Hoernle, op. cit., II p. 127).

67. Here the Bhāvnagar text reads *jāva vītivatissati. Evaṃ khalu, Jambhū* (...), whereas L continues as at Sūy 2, 2, 82 and at the end of Nāyā 1,2 which does not at all fit our story.

68. *Viṇayeṇa* ~ Sa. *vinatena*.

69. This is not true, of course. At Sūy 2, 2, 80 *āigara dhammāṇaṃ* is used of the founders of the 363 philosophical schools.

Stories from the Āvaśyaka commentaries

Translated by Nalini Balbir

Introduction

The *Āvaśyakasūtra* is one of the most important texts of the Śvetāmbara Jain canon. Written in Ardhamāgadhī, the *Āvaśyaka* starts with the fivefold homage to the Teachers (*pañcanamokkāra*) and then proceeds to describe the six necessary duties which a monk or layman is to perform every day. These six required duties, the "*āvaśyaka*," are as follows. 1) The cultivation of equanimity (*sāmāiya*), 2) praise of the 24 Jinas (*cauvvisatthaya*), 3) showing respect to the religious teacher (*vandana*), 4) repentance (*paḍikkamaṇa*), 5) undisturbed abandonment of the body (*kaussagga*), and 6) renouncing specific things such as particular food items (*paccakkhāṇa*). The *Āvaśyakasūtra* may seem short by comparison to other Jaina *sūtras*, but its brevity is hardly an indication of the important position that it occupies in the Śvetāmbara Jain tradition. The *Āvaśyakasūtra* became the centre around which a vast corpus of exegetical literature developed over the course of time. The translations I have done here are of stories that occur in these commentaries. I have given further information about the tradition of commentaries to the *Āvaśyaka* in an appendix for those who may be interested. The appendix also includes some brief remarks on the stories that I have translated and a brief bibliography.

Table of contents

A. How can *sāmāyika* be gained?

*1. By compassion (*aṇukampā*): the two doctors (*ĀvC *I 460,91-461,13).*

In the city of Dvāravatī lived the Vāsudeva Kṛṣṇa.[1] He had two doctors, Dhanvantari and Vaitaraṇi. Vaitaraṇi was destined for Emancipation, but not Dhanvantari. Vaitaraṇi used to talk gently to the sick monks. He used to tell them all that should be done and to instruct them about what was pure and permissible for monks. He used to prescribe for them pure and permissible cures. If he himself had the necessary medicinal plants, he used to give them to them. Dhanvantari, on the other hand, used to prescribe for them reprehensible cures, which were not suitable at all for monks. When they said, 'How can we use such things?,' Dhanvantari used to answer that he had not studied medical treatises meant for religious people. So the two of them practiced their medical art in the whole of Dvāravatī, doing much harm and making much money.[2]

One day the Vāsudeva Kṛṣṇa asked the Tīrthaṃkara Nemi, 'Having harmed so many poor souls, where will those two men be reborn?'

Then the Lord explained:

'That Dhanvantari will be reborn in the part of the seventh hell called Apratiṣṭhāna, and that Vaitaraṇi will be reborn as a monkey on the Kālañjara, between the great river Ganges and the Vindhya mountains. When he is grown up, he will make himself the head of a troop of monkeys. Then, one day, some monks will pass that way along with a caravan. One of the monks will get a thorn stuck in his foot. His fellow monks will say, 'We shall wait for you.' But he will answer, 'There is no reason for us all to die. You please go on. I shall give up all food, preparing myself for a pious death.'[3] Then they will insist on helping him, but they will not be able to remove the thorn. They will lead the monk to a pure and shady place and go on.

Then the head of the troop of monkeys will come to the place where the monk will be. Those of the monkeys who see him first will utter shouts of joy. When the head of the troop sees them shouting like that he will be furious until he sees the monk. When he sees him, he will think intensely,[4] 'Where have I seen such a person?' Thanks to the positive ripening of his actions, he will remember his former birth. He will remember all that happened in Dvāravatī. Then he will bow down to this monk. He will see the thorn in his foot. He will remember all his medical art. He will climb the mountain and will bring down medicinal plants fit for extracting thorns. He will apply those plants to the monk's foot. Then the thorn will fall out and lie at the side of monk's foot. Thanks to this cure, the monk will be fit. Then the monkey will write the following words in front of him, 'In my former birth in Dvāravatī, I was the doctor Vaitaraṇi.'

The monk had heard about him.[5] Then he told him the Law and the monkey gave up all food, preparing himself for a pious death. After three days he went to the sixth heaven called Sahasrāra.

"Thanks to the compassion he showed to a monk in a forest, the head of a troop of monkeys became a Vaimānika god with a beautiful and bright body." (=*ĀvN* 847)

That god made use of *avadhi*-knowledge[6] until he could perceive forms. He then saw this monk. And when he saw him he came and showed him his heavenly glory, saying, 'I owe this to you. Tell me what I can do.'

The monk had reached the place where the other monks were. They asked, 'How did you manage to come here?' The monk told them the whole story.

This is how, thanks to compassion (*anukampae*), the monkey, formerly the doctor Vaitaraṇi, had access to the Scriptures and to the sāmāyika of the right faith, and how he gained Emancipation. His former behaviour had only made him fit for hell. When he has exhausted his birth as a god, he will get the sāmāyika of right conduct and Emancipation.

2. By involuntary expulsion of karman (**akāmanijjarā**)*: the elephant-driver (*ĀvC *I 461,13-465,6).*[7]

There was the city of Vasantapura. There lived the young wife of a rich man. She was taking a bath in the river. A young man saw her and said:

1. "This river is asking you whether you have enjoyed your bath, O you whose thighs are like the trunk of an elephant in rut! The trees of the river ask you also, and we do too, bowing down at your feet!"

Then she also answered him:

"Happy may these rivers be! Long life to these trees on the river. We shall try our best to please those who ask whether we have enjoyed our bath."

But he did not know who she was or where she lived.

3. "A child can be captivated with food and drinks, a girl of marriageable age with ornaments, a courtesan with skillful speech, and an old woman with harsh service."

The girl had children with her to help her. They were sitting on a tree and looking at the scene. The youth gave them flowers and fruit and asked, 'Who is she? Whose daughter is she?'

'She is the daughter-in-law of so and so.' Clearly he could not resort to bad conduct to get her. He thought over the matter. Then came a nun in search for alms.

4. "She looks as bright as the saffron flower and full of grace with her monastic robe; anointed with fresh Aloe wood, she resembles the new crescent of the autumnal moon. Since the nun bursts out laughing playfully when she is spoken to by handsome youths, surely, she goes in search of love while in search of alms."

He served her. So she was pleased and asked, 'What can I do for you?'

'Speak to the daughter-in-law of so and so on my behalf.'[8]

The nun went there and said, 'My lady, a young man full of so many fine qualities asks for you.'

The girl was washing some dishes. She became angry, and with her hand smeared with lamp-black she stamped the mark of her five fingers on the nun's back. Then she threw her out by the back-door. The nun went back to the youth and reported, 'She has not even said her name.' But the boy understood that the five fingers meant a rendezvous on the fifth day of the dark fortnight. Then, on that fifth day, he again sent the nun in order to find out the place for their meeting. The girl shamefully hit her and threw her into a clump of aśoka-trees by a gap in the fence. Again the nun went to the youth and reported, 'She has not even said her name. She has hit me and thrown me out by a side-door.' The boy understood that she had indicated the place of their meeting. So by the side-door he went to the clump of aśoka-trees. There they slept together until they were seen by the father-in-law. He realized that this boy was not his son. So he took an anklet from the girl's foot. She had been conscious of what he did. So she said to her lover, 'Go away, quickly. You will have to help me.'

Then she went in to her husband and said, 'It's very warm here. Let us go to the clump of aśoka-trees.' Both of them went and slept there. When her husband was asleep, she woke him up, saying, 'Do people in your family always do things like this? My father-in-law took an anklet from my foot while I was asleep.'

'Go to sleep,' he said. 'You will get it back in the morning.'

The old man told the husband what he had seen. The husband, very angry, said to him, 'Are you mad, old man?'

'I saw a man that was not you,' the father said.

Then, as they quarreled, the girl asked, 'Shall I clear myself of this accusation?'

'You should indeed.'

And so she took a bath and went to the temple of a yakṣa. (It was like this: a guilty person could not walk between the legs of the yakṣa without being trapped between the yakṣa's testicles. An innocent person would be released). That girl went running. At that moment her lover appeared, disguised as a demon, and caught her by her sari. So she[9] said to the yakṣa, 'I swear that I have not known the touch of anyone other than the man who was given to me by my parents and this demon. You be the judge.'

5. The yakṣa was baffled and pondered, 'Look at the type of things she thinks up. Even I am deceived by her. There is indeed no decency in this rogue of a woman!'

And while the yakṣa was thus pondering, the lady beat a quick retreat.

Then the old man was rebuked by everybody. Because of his anxieties about her, he could not sleep any more. That came to be known by the king, who appointed him as a watchman of the harem.

The royal elephant used to stand under the window of a sleeping-room: one of the queens was in love with the elephant-driver. So in the night the elephant used to stretch its trunk through the window. The queen used to go down on it. In the morning she used to come back up in the same way. So time passed.

One day the elephant-driver struck her with the elephant's chain because she had taken a long time to come. She said, 'There is a certain an old man, who does not sleep. Don't be angry.'

The old man saw her and thought, 'When even such royal ladies behave like this, what is one to expect from others?' So he decided to sleep. In the morning everybody got up, but not that old man. The matter was reported to the king who said, 'Let him sleep.' On the seventh day he finally got up. The king asked him what had happened. The old man said, 'There is one of the queens, I don't know which one, who behaves in a very bad way.'

So the king got an elephant made of *bhiṇḍa*-flowers. All the ladies of the harem were asked to step over this elephant in order to worship him. All agreed to do so, except that one, who said, 'I am afraid.'

6. "To avoid a chariot one stays at a distance of five fore-arms, at ten for a bull, for an elephant at a hundred; a bad person can be avoided only by exile."

So the king hit her with a lotus stalk. She pretended to faint and fell to the ground. Thus he knew that she was the culprit. He said:

7. "You are used to climbing on a maddened elephant, but you are afraid of an elephant made of *bhiṇḍa*-flowers. You faint now that you are hit by a lotus stalk. You did not faint then, when you were beaten by a chain."

Her back was uncovered, and the marks of the chain could be seen. Then the king put those three (the elephant, the elephant-driver and that lady) in secluded quarters.

The elephant-driver was asked to make his elephant play a stunt. The king posted people with bamboo sticks in their hands on either side of the elephant. The elephant raised one leg.

'Is that what this animal can do?,' people said. 'Let these two be killed.' The king was still very angry. Then the animal raised two legs, then, the third time, three legs and stood on only one. People then shouted in applause, saying to the king, 'How can you destroy such a jewel?' So the king calmed down slightly and said to the elephant-driver, 'Can you make him come back to his initial position?'

'If you give us your assurance of safety.' The king did. Then by means of the hook the elephant was made to come back to his initial position. He turned around and stood on the ground.

Then the elephant-driver and the lady were made to dismount and were sentenced to exile.

They stayed in a deserted house in some secluded place in a border village. Then, at night, a thief who had done harm to the village people entered that house. The villagers said, 'We have surrounded the house. Let nobody go inside. We shall catch him at dawn.' The thief was lying down and somehow came near that lady. She felt his touch. He came nearer and she asked, 'Who are you?'

'I am a thief.'

'Be my husband,' she said. 'We shall say that he is the thief.'

And at dawn the elephant-driver, who had been pointed out by her, was seized. He was impaled on the stake which pierced right through him.

The lady went on along with the thief. Then they came to a river. The thief told her, 'Wait in this thicket of reeds until I cross over with these clothes and ornaments.' He left her and crossed over hurriedly. She said:

8. "The river appears full of water. It is full to the brim. All my belongings, my friend, are in your hands. As you wish to cross over to the other side, surely you wish to abscond with my things."

He replied:

9. "You have exchanged a man who has been your intimate for a long time for one you made your intimate by lying, a reliable one for an unreliable one. Knowing your real nature, what wise man would trust you?"

'Where are you going?,' she asked.

'As you caused that elephant-driver's death, so could you equally find some means to cause mine too.'

As for the elephant driver, pierced by the stake, he was asking people for water. Then a Jain devotee said, 'If you utter the *mantra* to the five entities (*pancanamokkara*)[10], I shall give you some.' He went to bring water. In the meantime, while uttering the formula, the elephant-driver died. He became a Vyantara. That Jain devotee was caught by the policemen.

The Vyantara made use of his *avadhi*-knowledge until he could perceive forms. He then saw this Jain being sentenced to death. He magically produced a rock and released him. Then he saw that lady in the thicket of reeds and felt pity for her. By magic he took on the shape of a jackal. That jackal went about on the bank of the river, holding a piece of meat, until it saw a fish. Leaving aside the piece of meat, it ran towards the fish. The piece of meat was snatched away by an eagle and the fish slipped into the water. The jackal lamented.

She said:

10. "Having left aside the piece of meat, you are longing for the fish, you jackal. Having lost the fish and the meat you lament miserably, O jackal."

11. He answered, "O you, who are covered by a cloth of leaves in your thicket of reeds, deprived of your husband! Having lost your husband and your lover you lament miserably, you hussy."

She was ashamed. Then the god assumed his real appearance. He told her to give up worldly life and he threatened the king, who allowed her to come back to the city. She gave up worldly life with the respect of others and went to the world of gods.

Thus the elephant-driver gained sāmāyika by involuntary expulsion of karman.

***3. By a fool's penance* (bālatava)*: Indranāga* (ĀvC *I 465,7-466,9*).**

There was the city of Jīrṇapura. The house of a merchant had been destroyed by plague. There was in that city a young boy called Indranāga. He was hungry and ill and was looking for water. What did he see? All had died and the people had fastened their doors with thorns. So the child went out through a hole. He wandered in the city with a bowl searching for alms. People used to give him something because they had heard about him. He grew up in that manner, with people always giving him something out of compassion.

One day a merchant came from Rājagṛha. Wishing to go back there the merchant had a proclamation made in the city. Indranāga heard that proclamation and set out with the caravan. There he got some cooked rice which he ate. The next day he took no food. There he remained without eating. The merchant observed all that and he understood that the boy was keeping fasts: He was an ascetic whose marks were not visible. On the following day, while he was wandering for alms, the boy was given abundant and rich food by the merchant. He remained without food for two days, leaving that food uneaten. The merchant understood that the boy was keeping a three days' fast. He began to feel some regard for the boy. On the third day, while wandering for alms, Indranāga was addressed by the merchant, 'Why didn't you come yesterday?' The boy remained silent. The merchant understood that he had kept a six meals' fast. Then he offered him abundant and rich food, and with that he remained for another two days. So other people too felt respect towards him. Even if somebody other than the merchant invited the boy, he did not take anything. (According to others Indranāga used to take food once a day and thereby reached Mt.Aṣṭāpada.)[11]

Indranāga was told by the merchant not to take anything from anybody until they reached the town. They went to the town. The merchant had a monastery built in his own house. Then he shaved the boy's head and had ascetic robes made for him. Indranāga became very famous, but even then he did not want any food. Then on the day of his fast-breaking people came with food and he accepted some, but it was not known from whom. In order to find out, the people resorted to the town crier, 'Whoever had offered food, let him hit the drum!' The people would come. So time passed.

The Lord held his general preaching.[12] To the monks who were talking together about alms, he said, 'Wait a moment. It is not time for food.' After he had had his food, the Lord said to them, 'Come down.' To Gotama he said, "Go and tell Indranāga on my behalf: 'You, eater of several rations a day, an eater of only one ration wants to see you."

Gotama did so. The boy angrily replied, 'You are the ones who eat several hundred rations. I eat alone; therefore I am a single eater.' Then he calmed down and after a while said, 'This monk surely does not lie. How can what he says be so?'

He finally got the knowledge of the Scriptures, 'I am indeed an eater of several hundred meals, since on the day of my fast-breaking several meals were prepared. These monks eat only one ration which has not been especially prepared for them. So Gotama is right.'

After intense thoughts he remembered his former births. He became a Pratyekabuddha and uttered the chapter, 'The Perfect Indranāga had said.'[13] He was Emancipated.

Thus sāmāyika can be gained by a fool's penance.

4. By charity (**dāṇa**)*: Kṛtapuṇya* (ĀvC *I 466,10-469,4).*

There was the son of a cowherd-woman. On the occasion of a festival people cooked some milk-rice. There were children in the neighborhood. The boy saw them eating. So he addressed his mother, 'Give me some milk-rice too.'

'I don't have any,' she replied worriedly, and she burst out in tears.

The neighbors asked what the matter was. As they insisted, the woman told them. Full of compassion, one after the other they brought some milk and some rice grains. The old woman cooked some milk-rice. The child was bathed and a plate full of milk-rice with melted butter and honey was served to him.

Then came a monk who was at the end of a month's fast. While the old woman was busy inside the house, the boy thought, 'Let me do some pious act,' and he gave the monk one third of his plate. Then he thought that it was too little, and gave a second third. Then again thinking that something else, such as sour milk, would not be good with this, he finally gave the monk the last third. (Here the purity of this gift, from the points of view of the thing given, etc. should be described).[14]

His mother thought that he had eaten the whole plate, so she filled it again[15], and the boy filled his stomach very greedily. The following night he died from serious intestinal disorders. He went to the world of gods.

He fell down from there and was again born in Rājagṛha as the son of the wealthy Dhanavāha and Bhadrā. While he was still in his mother's womb, people used to say, 'The soul who will be born there has done good deeds.' Therefore, when he was born, he was given the name Kṛtapuṇya. He grew up, learnt the arts and was married. His mother and some friends took him to a courtesan. After twelve years his family was completely ruined. However, he did not leave the courtesan. His parents died. Finally his wife sent her own ornaments and a thousand coins. The chief-courtesan understood that the boy was penniless. So she sent back the ornaments and another thousand coins. Then she gave orders to throw the boy out, but the courtesan did not want to obey her. So the chief-courtesan herself threw him out, accusing him of theft, and saying, 'The house is going to be repaired. Go away.' He left, but he lingered just outside. A servant then shouted at him, 'You have been thrown out and still you stay here!' So he went back to his own house. His wife got up hurriedly. He told her all the story, and overcome by grief, he asked, 'Is there anything with which I can travel elsewhere and do business?' So she showed him the ornaments and the thousand coins the chief-courtesan had acquired in exchange of the cotton she had spun,[16] and that she had given her. On that very day a caravan was about to leave. Kṛtapuṇya took his possessions and went along with it. He spread his bed outside a temple and spent the night there.

A certain mother had learnt from some merchant or other that her son had died in a shipwreck, and she had given this man some money, telling him,

'Don't disclose this news to anybody.' She feared that her possessions would fall to the king's lot if she had no heir.

That very night she went there thinking to adopt some parentless boy. Then she noticed Kṛtapuṇya. She woke him up and adopted him. She took him home, crying, 'My son, who had disappeared for so long!' To her four daughters-in-law she said, 'Here is your young brother-in-law who had disappeared for so long.' They became very fond of him. In that house, too, he spent twelve years. He got five children from each of these four girls. Then the old lady said, 'Let us now throw him out.' The girls could not bear that. They prepared some sweets for him for the trip and filled them with precious stones, thinking that they might be of some use. Then they made him drunk, carried him to that same temple, placed the provisions by his head and went back home. A cool wind woke him up. It was morning. That very day the caravan returned and his wife sent somebody to look for him. And so that person took him back home. His wife got up hurriedly. She took the provisions. He entered the house. His body was rubbed with unguents and so on. At that time, when he had left home, his wife was pregnant. They now had a son eleven years old.

The boy came back from school, crying, 'Give me some rice, so that the schoolmaster does not beat me.' His mother gave him one of those sweets. He went out eating it, and saw the jewel inside. His school-mates saw it too. From that time on every day they would give the jewels to the cake-seller, telling him to give them cakes in exchange. Kṛtapuṇya, too, ate those sweets. He opened them and saw the jewels. He said, 'I had hidden them there out of fear of the customs officers.' Thanks to these jewels he was able to expand his business.

Secanaka, the best of King Śreṇika's elephants, had been caught in a river by a water-snake. The king was deeply distressed, but his minister Abhaya[17] said, "He will only be released if we find a rock crystal. But there are so many precious stones in the royal treasury that it would take too long to find one.' So the drum was beaten, 'Whoever gives a rock crystal will be given half the kingdom and the king's daughter.'

The cake-seller brought one. The water was dried up. The snake realised that it was going to be cast on to dry land. The elephant was released.

The king wondered how the cake-seller could have gotten this jewel. So he asked him, 'Where did you get it?'

As the questions became insistent, he finally answered, 'The son of Kṛtapuṇya gave it to me.'

The king was happy, saying, 'How could have I married my daughter to anybody else?' He called Kṛtapuṇya and gave him his daughter. He gave him a territory, too. Kṛtapuṇya then enjoyed life.

Later on that courtesan came. She approached him, saying, 'I have been waiting for you for so long! I kept my hair twisted into a single plain braid and I searched for you through all the small streets. Only now have I seen you!'

Then Kṛtapuṇya told Abhaya, 'I have four other wives in this city. But I do not know where.'

So a Jain temple was built. A yakṣa, who looked exactly like Kṛtapuṇya, was made out of clay. Its solemn inauguration was proclaimed. Two doors were arranged, one for entry, the other for exit. Kṛtapuṇya and Abhaya were sitting together on high seats placed near the doors. The Fullmoon festival was proclaimed, 'Take the image inside. Perform the inauguration.' It was announced in the city that all the women should come with their children. People came, and among them these four wives. Their children came to sit on the yakṣa's knees saying, 'It's daddy!' Thus the wives were recognised. Abhaya rebuked the old lady.[18] Kṛtapuṇya's wives were made to come and stay with him. Then they all enjoyed life together. So Kṛtapuṇya was now in possession of numerous pleasures.

The Lord Vardhamāna came there to hold his general preaching. Then Kṛtapuṇya asked the Master, 'What is the reason for my success and failures?' 'The gift of milk-rice you offered,' the Master said. Full of indifference for worldly life, Kṛtapuṇya gave it up. Thus, Enlightenment can be gained by charity too.

***5. By humble behaviour* (vinaya)*: Puṣpaśāla's son* (ĀvC *I 469,5-11*)**

There was in Magadha the village of Gobbara. There lived the householder Puṣpaśāla, and his wife Bhadrā. They had a son whom they called Puṣpaśāla-suta. The child asked his parents, 'What is my duty?' 'You should obey your parents. For

1. "There are only two gods in the world of souls, the father and the mother. The more important is the father, in whose power the mother is."

So the child used to wash his parents' feet and mouths. (The full description is to be supplied). He used to serve them like gods.

One day the village-head came to their house. The parents surrounded him in great haste to offer hospitality. Then the boy thought, 'For them, he is the god. So if I worship him, I shall do my duty.' Thus he showed him obedience. Another time, the head's head came, then the latter's head and so on. Finally, the boy started serving king Śreṇika himself.

The Lord Mahāvīra held his general preaching. Śreṇika went out with great pomp and bowed down to the Lord. The boy said to the Lord, 'I wish to serve you.'

The Lord said, 'As for me, I am to be served merely with a broom and a begging-bowl.'[19]

Having heard that, the boy was Enlightened. So much for humble behaviour.

[*6. By the knowledge called* vibhaṅga*: the ascetic Śiva* (ĀvC *I 469,12-472,10*). Story in Canonical prose identical to *Viyāhapannatti* XI 9]

7. By ownership and loss* (samyoga—viyoga)*: the two merchants from the two Mathurās* (ĀvC *1 472,11-474,4).

There were two cities with the name Mathurā. A merchant went from northern Mathurā to southern Mathurā. There, there was a merchant of equal status who offered him hospitality. They both became intimate friends. They thought, 'Our friendship will become even more solid if we arrange a union between our son and daughter.' So the southern one asked the northern one for his daughter as a bride for his son, and the northern one promised her. (They were still children). In the meantime, the merchant from southern Mathurā died. His son took his place.

One day he took a bath. Golden pitchers were placed in the four directions. Beyond them were placed silver pitchers. Beyond those were placed copper pitchers and beyond those earthenware pitchers. On another day he prepared everything needed for his bath. The golden pitchers which had been placed in the eastern direction vanished in the sky, and likewise for all four directions. In this way all the pitchers vanished. When he got up from his bath, the bath-stool also vanished. He became anxious. He sent away the dancing girls. Then he went back home. The table was laid. Dishes made of gold and silver had been prepared. One after the other they began to vanish. The merchant stared at them as they vanished. As his main plate was about to vanish too, he took hold of it. Only the piece he seized with his hand remained. The rest vanished. Then he went to the treasure-house and what did he see? It was also empty. All that he had deposited there had vanished. Not a single ornament was left. All his interest too vanished.

People said, 'We don't know you.' His male and female servants, too, vanished.

The merchant thought, 'Let me give up worldly life.' And he went forth at the feet of the monk Dharmaghoṣa. He studied sāmāyika, the eleven Aṅgas (of the Jaina Canon) and so on.

He still had the piece of the plate with him and, out of curiosity to see if he would be recognised, he went to northern Mathurā in the course of his religious wanderings. All his jewels had gone to his in-laws, and the pitchers too. While the merchant from northern Mathurā was bathing and being praised in song, the pitchers had come. He had used them to bathe. Then at lunch time, all the food-implements had come to him, and had arranged themselves in due order.

The monk entered the house. The caravan-leader's daughter was there, young and lovely, holding a fan in her hand. The monk noticed all the food-implements. The caravan-leader brought him some alms. Though the monk took the alms, he remained there.

So the caravan-leader said, 'What, Venerable monk! Are you looking at this girl?'

'I don't care about the girl,' the monk replied. 'I am looking at the implements.' And he asked, 'How did you get them?'

'They have been passed down from my ancestors.'

'Tell the truth.'

'While I was taking my bath, all these bath-implements came to me, just like that. The same happened with all the other things. At lunch time, all the food implements just came here. Then the treasure-houses were filled up. Deposits could be seen. Some debtors I had never seen before brought them and gave them to me.'

'All that was mine.'

'How?'

Then the monk told him everything, about the bath and so on. 'If you don't believe me,' he added, 'look at this piece of plate.' And he produced it. It immediately stuck to the rest of the plate. The monk told him his father's name and the merchant realised that the monk was his son-in-law. He got up and while embracing him he burst into tears, saying, 'All this is yours. Stay here. This is the girl who was promised to you earlier.'

But the monk said, 'If a man does not give up worldly pleasures first, then the pleasures will leave him first.'

Then the merchant, too, felt disgusted towards worldly pleasures, 'Will they leave me, too, as they left him?' So he decided to give them up.

So, one gained sāmāyika because of union with what was his, the other one because of separation from it.

8. By misfortune* (vasaṇa)*: the two brothers [Vāsudeva and Baladeva]* (ĀvC *I 474,5-475,5).

Two brothers were going in a cart. A *yamaluṇḍī*-snake was writhing about at the side of the road. The elder brother said, 'Turn the cart back.' But the other one drove on. That snake was a conscious being and understood their talk. Then it was cut by the wheel. It died and was reborn as a woman in the city of Hastināpura.

The elder brother died first and was reembodied in her womb. He was born as her son. He was cherished. The other brother also died. He was reembodied in the womb of the very same woman. As soon as he was conceived, his mother thought, 'Let me leave him aside as I would a stone.' But, in spite of the attempted abortion, the foetus did not die. So a baby was born. The mother gave him to one of her servants, asking her to leave him somewhere. The baby was covered and taken away. While he was being carried away, his father, a merchant, saw him. The servant told him what had happened. So he gave the baby to another servant and the boy was brought up there. The elder boy was called Rājalalita and the other one, Gangadatta. Whatever the elder one received, he used to give to the other boy who was not loved by his mother. Whenever she saw him, she used to hit him with a stick or a stone.

Then, later on, it was the Indramaha festival. The father told his elder son, 'Bring your brother secretly. He will eat something.' The boy brought Gangadatta. He was hidden under a seat and fed. Somehow or other the mother happened to notice him. She seized him and threw him out. He fell into a dirty pool. He cried. His father bathed him.

In the meantime, a monk happened to pass by to collect alms. The father asked him, 'Venerable monk, can there be a son who is not loved by his mother?'

'Yes, indeed.'

'Why?'

The monk explained:

1. "The one, the sight of whom makes anger increase and affection become less, should be known to have been a foe in a former birth.

2. The one, the sight of whom makes affection increase and anger become less, should be known to have been a relation in a former birth."

'Venerable monk,' the father asked, 'Will you accept him as your disciple?'

'Yes.'

So Gangadatta gave up worldly life. Out of affection towards him his brother too gave up worldly life and became the disciple of that same teacher. They were very careful monks (*Īriyāsamitā*). They used to practice asceticism without hindrance (*aṇissitaṃ tavam*). Then Gangadatta expressed the following wish as a reward for his penance, 'If all this bears fruit may I be a source of joy for people in my future births!' Such was the wish he expressed. He practiced severe penance. Then after death he went to the world of gods. When he again fell from there and came down to earth he was born as Vāsudeva, the son of Vāsudeva. The other one was Baladeva.[20]

Thus as a consequence of misfortune he got sāmāyika.

9. By attending a festival* (ussava)*: the conversion of the Ābhīras* (ĀvC *I 475,6-11).

There were Ābhīras who lived on the borders of civilization. They listened to the Law from a monk who described to them the world of the gods. In that way they properly understood the Law.

One day, perhaps at the occasion of the Indra festival, or some other festival, they went to the town. (It should be described as Dvāravatī is). There they saw people fully attired with ornaments, wearing shimmering and perfumed clothes. They said to each other, 'Here is the world of the gods which the Jain monk described earlier. If we go there, we shall do good, since we too shall be reborn in the world of the gods.'

Thus they went and told the monk, 'That world of the gods you described to us, we have seen it for real.'

'The world of the gods is not like that,' the monk said. 'It's otherwise. It has innumerable qualities different from what you saw.'

Thoroughly excited with joy, the Ābhīras gave up worldly life.[21]

Thus sāmāyika can be gained on the occasion of a festival.

[10. By seeing magnificence (**iḍḍhi**)*: the king Daśārṇabhadra see section C, story No. 4].*

11. By respect shown or not shown (**(a)-sakkāra**)*: the acrobat Ilāputra (***ĀvC** *I 484,11-485,13).*

After hearing the Law from an authentic elder, a brahmin and his wives gave up worldly life. They led a very rigorous religious life, but their love for each other did not leave them.[22] One of the ladies still had some pride: she was a brahmin indeed! After death they went to the world of the gods and enjoyed life for the life-time they had.

There was, on the other hand, the city of Ilāvardhana which had Ilā as its tutelary deity. The wife of a caravan-leader who had no child worshipped her. The former brahmin fell from the world of the gods and was born as this lady's son. He was therefore given the name of Ilāputra. He studied the arts. As for the brahmin's former wife, she was born in an acrobat's family.

Both the boy and the girl had now reached marriageable age. One day the boy fell in love with the girl's beauty. Though he asked for her, he did not get her. Her parents said, 'We shall give you the equivalent of her weight in gold. She is our imperishable treasure. But if you set off on tour with us[23] and learn our art, we shall give her to you.'

So Ilāputra set off on tour with them and learned their art. Then he was asked to give a show in front of the king on the occasion of a wedding-ceremony. The company went to Beṇṇātaḍa. The king attended the show together with his harem. Ilāputra was on the stage, but the king had eyes only for the girl. The king did not give any money. There was loud applause: 'Acrobat,' people said to Ilāputra, 'Do a falling stunt.'

On the top of a bamboo there is a piece of wood. Two nails are fixed on it. The acrobat wears shoes which are pierced at the bottom. Then, holding a sword and a shield in his hands, he jumps into the sky. The nails should be fitted into the holes of the shoes by seven jumps forwards and backwards. If the acrobat fails, he falls down and is broken into pieces.[24]

That was the feat Ilāputra did. The king went on gazing at the young girl. People created an uproar. Nobody gave any money since the king did not give anything. The king thought, 'If this acrobat dies, the girl will be mine.' So he said to Ilāputra, 'I did not see. Do it again.' The boy did it again, but again the king did not see. He did it a third time. A fourth time he was asked to do it again. The audience was disgusted. Standing on the top of the bamboo, Ilāputra thought, 'Enough of worldly pleasures! This king is not even satisfied with so many wives. He wants to attach himself to this actress, and in order to fulfill his desire he wants to kill me.' He was ready to give up worldly life.

One day in a merchant's house he saw some monks who were receiving alms from fully adorned ladies. He noticed that the monks looked very peaceful, and said, 'Happy are those who have no more desire for sexual enjoyments. I was a merchant's son. See what condition I have reached after having left my family!'

In that very place, having achieved indifference for worldly objects, he got Omniscience. The indifference of the girl too should be fully described, and also that of the chief-queen. The king, too, felt remorse. All four became Omniscient and Emancipated.

So much for respect.

Or there is the case of Marici who gained sāmāyika after having seen the respect shown by the gods and the demons to the Tīrthaṃkara Ṛṣabha.[25]

B. Definitions and illustrations of repentance (*paḍikkamaṇa*).

Here are eight illustrations pertaining to the synonymous designations of repentance (*paḍikkamaṇa*)

***1. Stepping back* (ĀvC *II 53,6-54,8*).**

Stepping back (*paḍi-kkamaṇa*) is sixfold: from the point of view of designation, position, substance, place, time, and religious meaning.[1] [...] Stepping back from the point of view of religious meaning is the stepping back of the one who is endowed with right faith and other qualities. It is illustrated by the example pertaining to the distance (*addhāna*).

A king wanted to build a mansion outside a city. On the auspicious day he set out the measuring lines and appointed a guard with the warning, 'If somebody comes inside, he is to be killed. He alone is not to be killed, who, when asked to do so, does not walk on the measuring lines, but steps back into the same footsteps: he may be released.' That was the warning he gave.

The place was divided into eighty-one parts. How then? The place was a square which was divided into three parts, then again into three parts, thus into nine parts. Each of these nine parts was in turn divided twice into three, that is to say eighty-one parts. In each of the nine main parts four deities (Soma, Varuṇa, Yama and Vaiśravaṇa) were installed in the four directions, and one was installed in the centre. Thus there were forty-five deities in all.[2]

While the guards were inattentive, two wretched villagers happened to arrive. The guards saw them only as they were stepping forward. With their swords in their hands they shouted, 'Stop, you bastards, how did you come inside?'

'What's the harm?,' one of them, an insolent rogue, said and he started running here and there. He was killed on the spot by the guards. The other one said, 'I came inside without knowing that it was wrong. Don't kill me. I shall do exactly what you say.'

The guards helped him up and said, 'If you do not move away elsewhere than into your own footprints, you will at least be able to escape.'

The poor man was very scared and stepped back into his own footprints. He was released and was able to have his share of happiness in this world. The other one was deprived of it.

That is the parable. Here is its interpretation. The king is the Tīrthaṃkara. The place for the mansion is self-control which is respected or not. The guards are the dangers of the world of transmigration. The villagers are the monks: the one who stepped back behaved in accordance with the Scriptures, but the other one did not. His death is the world of transmigration. Such is the religious meaning. When one has gone astray due to some negligence caused by the sense-organs and so on, he must immediately recite the mea culpa formula.

2. Taking care **(ĀvC *II 54,9-55,2*).**

Taking care (*paḍiyaraṇā*) too is sixfold and should be fully described in the same way as stepping back. It is illustrated by the example of the mansion (*pāsāda*).[3]

In a certain city there was a wealthy merchant. He possessed a newly built mansion complete with all good characteristics and full of jewels. He instructed his wife how to look after the mansion and left for a trip. She was concerned only with herself and when a part of the mansion was broken or destroyed, she would say, 'What does such a small thing matter?' One day a shoot of *pippal* started growing. Again she said, 'What does such a small shoot matter?' But when the shoot grew it cracked the mansion. The merchant came back and saw that it was destroyed.

He threw his wife out and had another mansion built. He married another wife and said to her, 'If this mansion is destroyed, you too will meet with the same fate.' Then he went away. As soon as she saw a small crack, she used every means to have it repaired. Similarly, she used to examine all the painting and the panelling three times a day, so that the house remained exactly as it was. The husband came back and was delighted. He made his wife the owner of all their wealth. That is the parable.

The merchant is the teacher. The mansion is self-control. The merchant's wives are the monks. The one who destroys self-control or despises it has bad fortune. But the one who gives it its full meaning or who carries out an atonement whenever he has failed and puts it right again has perfectly pure behaviour.

3. Avoiding of negative points **(ĀvC *II 55,3-11*).**

Avoiding of bad points (*pariharaṇā*) too is sixfold. It is illustrated by the example of the carrying-pole for milk (*duddha-kāya*).

There was a son of a noble family. He had two sisters who lived in different villages. He had a daughter, and his sisters had sons. All grew up. The two sisters came simultaneously to ask for their niece in marriage[4] Their brother said, 'Which is the dearer of two eyes? Go away and send me your sons. I shall give her to the one who is more thoughtful.' They went away and sent their sons. Their uncle gave both of them the same pots, saying, 'Bring back some milk from the cow-house.' They went, filled up the pots with milk and hung them on the extremities of a bamboo-pole to carry them.[5]

There were two ways. One was winding but was smooth. The other was straight but full of tree stumps and therefore rough. One boy went by the straight road. He stumbled and the two pots were broken. The other boy wandered along the other way but eventually arrived. Their uncle said, 'I told you to bring some milk. I did not say anything about coming slowly or quickly.' The first boy was thrown out. The other one got the girl.

That is the parable. Here is its interpretation at the spiritual level. This son of a noble family is the Tīrthaṃkara. His daughter is the goal of Perfection. The boys are the monks. The milk-pots are moral conduct. Just as the ways can be rough or smooth from the point of view of matter, place, time and mental disposition, in the same way the negative points should be avoided, viz. matter, place, time and mental disposition.

***4. Warding off* (ĀvC *II 55,12-56,3*).**

Warding off (*vāraṇā*) too is sixfold. It is illustrated by the example of the avoidance of poisoned food (*visa-bhoyaṇa*).

A certain king went to besiege another king's city. The latter king poisoned the water.[6] The caravan set up its camp. Learning that food and drink were not far away but had been poisoned, and thus would cause the death of his men, the other king had a proclamation made, 'Whoever drinks water here or eats fruit will die. There may be some who are eager for food. Let those people resort to tasteless waters or tasteless fruit.' And the king went away. Those who avoided food survived. Those who did not died.

Here is the interpretation. The kings represent the Tīrthaṃkaras. The poisonous drinks are the occasions where self-control is not observed. The men are the monks. Similarly, at the spiritual level, the one who avoids evil deeds is saved from the world of transmigration.

***5. Turning back* (ĀvC *II 56,4-57,6*).**

Turning back (*niyatti*) too is sixfold.

a. Here is the example of the first of two girls (*do kannāo*)[7] . In a certain town there was a weaver. Some rogues used to weave in his workshop. This weaver had a daughter. One of the weavers used to sing with a very melodious voice. She became infatuated with him and they had sexual intercourse. The man said, 'Let us go away.'

'I have a friend,' she said. 'I cannot leave without her.'

'Let us take her with us,' he agreed.

The weaver's daughter told her friend what was happening, and she agreed. It was early in the morning when they ran away. And because it was so early they waited for some time. Then somebody sang:

1. "If the karṇikāra-trees are in blossom ..."

The girl went on singing, 'This mango-tree is scolded by the spring:

"If the karṇikāra-trees are in blossom, it is not proper for you, mango-tree, to blossom. Have you not heard the proclamation of your intercalary month?"

The karṇikāras are the worst trees.[8] 'If the weaver's daughter behaves like this,' she thought, 'is it any reason for me to do the same? She is a harlot who has squandered her substance. Bad language does not affect her, nor anything else. After all she is a weaver's daughter. But in my case, it would affect my family's reputation for seven generations, and the whole city would reproach me.' Then she pretended to have forgotten her jewelry-box and by this trick she went back.

Here is the interpretation at the spiritual level. The young girls represent the monks. The rogues represent the sense-objects. The song represents the teacher. The *gīti*-stanza works as an incentive. Similarly, in the religious meaning, one should turn back from the sense-objects.

b.[9] The second illustration pertains to turning back in the literal and the religious meaning. In a group of monks there was a novice. Thinking that he was able to grasp the meaning of the Scriptures and to remember them, his teacher sent him forth as a mendicant. One day, because of the rise of bad karman, he ran away thinking that he would come back later. While he was going out he heard the sound of a song. This song gave him a warning for his benefit. Some young warriors were singing the following piece:

1. "In a battle, the able man should keep his promises or die. A man born in a good family should not bear the insults of a man of inferior status."[10]

Here is the real meaning of this song. On a battle-field some soldiers who had gained glory and had been congratulated by their master had stopped fighting. As they were about to take to flight, one who clung on to the glory of his side shouted, 'You will look bad receiving blows in the back as you go away!' Having heard this, they went back, and remained firm. They rushed against the enemy's army and defeated it. Their master congratulated them and afterwards, bearing the title of good warriors, they looked fine.

When the novice heard the meaning of this song, he became worried: 'Similarly, the battle represents the life of a monk. If I take flight, I shall be blamed by people of an inferior rank who will say, 'this man is a backslider.' So he went back. He confessed, repented and fulfilled his teacher's desires. Thus the stanza was an incentive at the religious level.

***6. Self-reproach* (ĀvC *II 57,7-60,12*).**

Self-reproach (*nindā*) too is sixfold. Here is an illustration. The second of the two girls (*do kannāo*)[11] was a painter's daughter.

A certain king asked his messenger, 'What do I not have that other kings have?'

'You have no hall of paintings.'

It was ordered and begun to be built. The work was shared out among the corporation of painters. The daughter of one of the painters went to bring food to her father. The king was coming along the road on his horse, which ran at full speed. She drew aside and somehow was saved. Her father left the food and went to relieve himself. In the meantime the girl took the paints and drew the picture of a peacock's feather on the paved ground. The king happened to go there. The girl was standing there, her thoughts being elsewhere. The king's eyes fell on the feather and he stretched his hand in order to take it. He hurt his nails. The girl burst out laughing and said, 'My fools' chair cannot stand on three legs, and I was just looking for the fourth one. You indeed are the fourth one!'

'How?,' the king asked.

She said, 'I was bringing rice to my father when a man came riding his horse in the middle of the town. He felt no pity at the thought that he might kill somebody somehow. My own merits kept me alive! The second leg is the king who shared out the hall of paintings among the painters. In every family there are several persons who paint. As for my father, he paints alone. The third leg is my father. While painting the hall of paintings he has spent much of what he acquired before . Now he must make do with whatever food he gets. What kind of a fool is he! And when the food is brought to him, he goes to relieve himself! The fourth leg, it's you. How? Everybody surely thinks, 'What is a peacock's feather doing in a place like this?' And even if someone had chanced to bring one from somewhere, it would have, in any case, not escaped notice.'

'True. All these people are fools,' the king agreed, and he went away. The girl's father took his meal. She went back home. The king sent persons to ask for her in marriage. She told her parents to give her to the king. But they said, 'We are poor. How can we treat the king and his retinue properly?' So the king gave them money and they gave him the girl.

The girl instructed her servant in the following way, 'When you are massaging me and the king, you should ask me to tell a story.'

When the king was ready to sleep, the servant said, 'Mistress, the king tarries with us. Tell some story.'

'I shall,' the girl said.

First Riddle

"Somebody had a daughter. Her parents and brothers gave her to three suitors, because they were not the type of people one could refuse. The time for the wedding arrived. In the night, the girl was bitten by a snake and died. One suitor ascended the funeral pyre with her. The other one undertook fasting unto death. The third one strove to obtain a favour from a deity who gave him a magic formula capable of bringing the dead back to life. Those on the pyre were restored to life. The three dead persons got up. To which of the three should she be given? Is it possible that a single girl be given to two or three husbands?"

" Explain."

"I am feeling sleepy. I want to sleep. I shall explain tomorrow."

Out of eager interest for this story, the next day, too, the king said that it should be this lady's turn. Again she was asked and gave the answer, "The one who brought her back to life could be her father. The one with whom she came back to life could be her beloved brother. So she should be given to the one who undertook fasting unto death."

" Tell me another story."

Second Riddle

She said: "The goldsmiths of a certain king were in an underground chamber from where they could not go out. They had as lights jewels and precious stones. They were making ornaments for the harem.

One of them asked, 'What's the time now?'

Another one answered, 'It's night.'

How can he know, since he sees neither the moon nor the sun?

I am feeling sleepy."

The next day she explained, " He is blind at night. Therefore he knows."

"Tell me another story."

Third Riddle

She said: "There was a king. He punished two thieves. He put them in a basket and threw it into the sea. For some time, it bobbed up and down. Somebody noticed the basket, took it and saw the men.

That person asked them, 'How many days is it since you have been abandoned like this?'

'It's the fourth day,' one of them said.

How did he know?"

The next day she explained, " He suffered from quartan fever. Therefore he knew."

"Tell me another story."

Fourth Riddle

"There were two co-wives. One possessed some jewels. She did not trust the other one, fearing that she might take them from her. She decided to put the jewels in a pot and put the pot in a place where she could see it while going out and coming in. The pot was sealed. The other one learnt about her secret and took the jewels away. She sealed the pot exactly as it had been before. But the other one knew that the jewels had been taken away.

How did she know since the pot had been sealed?"

The next day she explained, "This pot was made of glass. So when they were there, the jewels shone. When they had been taken away, they did not."

"Tell me another story."

Fifth Riddle

She said: "A certain king had four excellent men:

1. An astrologer, a chariot-maker, a champion-fighter and also a doctor. His daughter was given to the four. To one only was she married.

How? This king had a very lovely daughter. She was taken away by some vidyādhara. Nobody knew where she had been carried away. The king said, 'Whoever brings this girl back will have her.'

The astrologer said, 'She has been taken in such and such a direction.'

The chariot-maker made a chariot which could go through the sky. The four men sat in the chariot and flew away. They followed the vidyādhara. The champion-fighter killed him. While killing him he also beheaded the girl. The doctor brought her back to life with the help of life-giving medicinal herbs and she was led back home. The king gave her to all four men. The girl said, 'How could I belong to four men?' Let me enter the fire. I shall be the wife of the one who enters it with me.'

'All right.'

Which one of them will enter the fire with her? Whose wife will she be?"

The next day she explained: " The astrologer knew with the help of a sign that she would not die. Therefore he followed her in the fire. The others refused. Under the place of the fire the girl had had an underground passage dug. Pieces of wood of the type suitable for a funeral pyre were placed there. When the fire was lit, the astrologer and the girl went out through the underground passage. She became the astrologer's wife."

" Tell me another story."

Sixth Riddle

" A woman of wicked disposition, who wanted to go to a ceremony, borrowed some bangles. She pledged some money as surety. She gave the bangles to another lady's daughter. When the ceremony was over, she did not give the bangles back. Several years passed like this. The owners of the bangles asked for them. The lady said, 'I shall give them back.' And so it went on until the girl had grown up and could not take off the bangles any more. Then she said to the owners, 'Give up the matter. I shall give you some more money.' But they were not willing.

'Can we then cut the girl's hands off?'

She proposed, 'I shall have exactly the same bangles made and I shall give those to you.' Then, too, they were unwilling: 'You should give us those very same ones,' they insisted.

How could the matter be solved? How should they be answered so that the girl's hands are not cut off?"

She explained, " They should be told, 'If you can give me those very same coins which I gave you, I shall give you back those same bangles.'"

Since that painter's daughter kept on telling similar stories every day, the king called for her for six months. Her co-wives started seeking weak-points in her. She used to enter her private apartments alone, and putting in front of her her old jewels and her old clothes, she used to reproach herself, 'You are a painter's daughter. These clothes and so on belong to your father. This glory belongs to the king. Having left aside the others, who are royal daughters born in high families, the king attends upon you. Do not get a sense of pride from it. Do not behave in a wrong way.' That's what she used to do every day when she had locked herself inside. Somehow the co-wives came to know about that. They fell down at the king's feet saying, 'May you not die because of her! She is doing black magic.' But the king investigated, heard and was delighted. He invested her with the turban of the chief-queen.

It is the same with self-reproach, like this, 'Soul, wandering in the world of transmigration, in animal and infernal births, you have somehow come to human birth and acquired faith, right knowledge and right conduct. Thanks to them you now deserve to be respected and worshipped by all. Do not take a sense of pride there from, thinking that you are very learned and so on. Do not behave in a wrong way. If you happen to behave in a wrong way, you will have to suffer from it.'

*7. **Blame*** *(*ĀvC ***II 60, 13-61,9).***

Blame (*garahā*) too is sixfold. It is illustrated by the example of the lady who killed her husband (*pai-mariyā*).

There was an old brahmin professor and his wife, who was young. While giving oblations to all the gods, she used to say that she was afraid of crows so that, every day, pupils appointed by their professor used to guard her, holding bows in their hands. One of the pupils noticed, 'This girl is not innocent. She is an expert.' Then he started spying on her.

One day, she went to visit a mendicant and crossed the Narmadā river with a pot. One of those crossing the river with her was seized by an alligator. He started to hit the animal.

'Close his eyes,' she advised. He did so and was released.

'Why did you cross at a bad ford?,' she asked him.

The pupil turned back reflecting on all that. The following day she again gave oblations and it was this pupil's turn to guard her. He said:

1. "In the daytime you are afraid of crows. At night you cross the Narmadā. You know the bad fords and you know that alligators' eyes should be closed."

So she understood that he had seen her. She started hanging around him.

'What! In front of my professor?,' he said. So she killed her husband. She threw the corpse in a basket and went to the forest in order to leave it there. She was stopped by a Vyantarī deity. She began to roam around in the forest and was unable to bear the hardships of hunger. The corpse which she was carrying on her head started dripping. She was blamed by the people: 'It's a husband-killer who roams around like this.' She was smitten with remorse and asked them, 'Please give some alms to a husband-killer.'

2. "Addicted to love, I killed my old husband. Longing for a young man, I forgot family and virtue."

For a long time she kept falling at their feet, and at the feet of others likewise. When she fell at our feet, her basket fell down. She gave up worldly life. Thus, bad behaviour must be censured.

8. Cleaning

Cleaning (*sohī*) means annihilation of faults. It is sixfold, and should be fully described. It is illustrated by two examples: the example of the clothes (*vattha*) and the example of the antidote (*agaa*).

a. Here is the example of the clothes (*ĀvC* II 61,11-13)

In Rājagṛha reigned king Śreṇika. He gave a pair of linen clothes to the launderer. It was the period of the fullmoon festival (= Holi). The launderer gave the clothes to his two wives who were going with him. Śreṇika and his minister Abhaya went incognito for a stroll to the fullmoon festival. They saw the clothes: they had been dyed with betel! The launderer's wives came back and were rebuked by their husband who cleaned the clothes with saline earth. Next morning he brought them back. He was asked to tell the truth, and told it. Śreṇika was pleased, thinking, 'What a skillful person he is!'

Similarly, the monk should cleanse himself of all faults by confession and other means.

b. For the example of the antidote, see the section called *Namaskāra*, above (*ĀvC* I 554,9-13)

Seeing that an enemy army was coming to besiege his town, a king thought that he had better pollute the water. He summoned the poison-maker. Poison balls were made. The doctor came with only a very small quantity of poison. The king was angry, but the doctor explained, 'It can affect a hundred thousand people.'

'How?,' the king asked.

An elephant whose life was coming to an end was brought. A hair on his tail was raised up. Just through the tip of that one hair the poison was given to him. It could be seen making him colorless. The whole animal became poison: whoever eats this poison becomes poison. Such is the poison which can pierce a hundred thousand people.

Is there any means to stop its effect? Indeed. A strong antidote was applied exactly at the same place. The effect of the poison was diminished and disappeared.

Similarly, the monk, too, should cross over the poison of spiritual mistakes with the help of such antidotes as self-reproach and so on.

For all illustrations, the lesson is to be developed accordingly. Thus, the various synonymous designations of "repentance" (*paḍikkamaṇa*) have been made clear.

C. A collection of thirty-two catchwords defining "Jain Yoga."

1. Confession* (āloyaṇā)*: about two wrestlers* (ĀvC *II 152,9-153,12).

The city was Ujjayinī and the king Jitaśatru. He had a wrestler called Aṭṭana, whom no one in any kingdom could defeat. On the other hand, on the seashore there was the city of Sopāraka, the king of which was Siṃhagiri. He used to reward very well the wrestler who won. Aṭṭana used to go to his contest, and year after year, he used to win the flag of victory. The king thought, 'This man who comes from a foreign kingdom always wins. For me it is an humiliation.' Then he went in search of a rival competitor.

He saw a fisherman who was drinking some melted fat. He ascertained his strength. When he had realized it he fed him. Aṭṭana came back again. (Thinking that there would be wrestling-contests in the future he had left his town with an ox[1] loaded with supplies, travelled without any difficulty and reached Sopāraka). He was defeated in the contest by the fisherman turned wrestler. He went back to the place where he lived, thinking, 'This man has the strength of a young person. I am now unfit.' So he went in search of another wrestler. He heard that there were some in Saurāṣṭra.

While he was on the way, he happened to see a ploughman in the surroundings of Bhṛgukaccha, in the village Dūrullakūviyā. With one hand he was handling the plough, and with the other one he was pulling up the cotton-plants. Aṭṭana stood looking at him, wishing to examine the ploughman's diet. The oxen were unyoked. The ploughman's wife came with food for her husband. Aṭṭana looked: there was a bowl of rice and a pot of vegetables. The ploughman took his meal and went to relieve himself. Even then, Aṭṭana kept on examining his behaviour. He came to know everything. At night he asked for a place to stay in his house. It was granted to him. During the conversation he asked the ploughman what his earnings were. The ploughman told him. The wrestler said, 'I am Aṭṭana. I shall make a master of you.' He gave the lady the price of the cotton. They left for Ujjayinī.[2]

Aṭṭana prepared some emetics and purgatives, and fed them to the ploughman. He taught him hand-to-hand fighting. When the time of the great festival came again, he went there exactly as he used to do. The first day when the fight took place between the two wrestlers, — the former cotton-man and the former fisherman-, neither of the two won or was defeated. The king went away in expectation of the next day, and the two wrestlers went back, each to his own house. Aṭṭana asked the former cotton-man, 'Tell me, my child, where you have been hurt.' The boy told him. Aṭṭana rubbed him and with the help of a massage he made him like new. The king also sent the former fisherman some persons to rub him, but he dismissed them, saying, 'Even the father of this wrestler would not scare me! Not to speak of this poor boy!' On the next day, they again fought and were equal. On the third day the fisherman was standing helpless in the ring, covered in bruises.

'Cotton-man!,' Aṭṭana shouted and the wrestler pulled his opponent's head as he would have seized a cotton-plant and it fell to the ground like a pumpkin. He was congratulated. He went back to Ujjayinī and had his share of all kinds of pleasures. The other one died.

Thus, the flag of victory is the aim to reach. Aṭṭana embodies the teacher. The wrestlers are the monks. The blows are the errors. The one who makes confession to his teacher is devoid of thorns and wins the flag of Emancipation in the ring of the three worlds.

2. Complete discretion (*niravalāva*): about two friends (*ĀvC *II 153,12-154,10).

And now, to what type of person should one make confession? The one who does not repeat it to somebody else, — such is the type of person one should serve. Here is an example.

In the city of Dantapura, there was the king Dantacakra and the queen Satyavatī. She had a pregnancy-longing, 'How might I enjoy myself in a mansion made of ivory?,' she wondered. In order to get ivory the king had a proclamation made, 'A suitable price will be paid. But the king will punish the one who will not give his ivory.'

In the same city lived Dhanamitra, a merchant, and his two wives, Dhanaśrī, the elder one, and Padmaśri, the younger one. He loved the latter more.

One day, a quarrel broke out among the co-wives. Dhanaśrī said, 'Why are you so proud? What do you have more than I have? What? Would a mansion like Satyavatī's be made for you?'

'If it is not made,' Padmaśrī replied, 'I am no more.' She locked the door of her inner-apartments and she remained there. The merchant came back and asked, 'Where is Padmaśrī?' The female servants told him. He went in there and tried to placate his wife but she was not placated: 'If I don't get it,' she said, 'I won't live.'

The merchant had a friend, Dṛḍhamitra, who came to visit him. He asked what was the matter. Dhanamitra explained everything. The friend answered, 'Let the mansion be made. May you not die because of her death; if you die, I shall also die. The king has made a proclamation. So let us manage secretly.'

Then Dṛḍhamitra took clothes, jewels and lacquered-bangles suitable for the tribesmen as payment for ivory, and went to the forest. He got some tusks, made a heap of them, stowed them inside bundles of grass, loaded a carriage and carried them back. At the moment they were entering the city, the load was pulled apart by a bull. Suddenly, a tusk fell down. The policemen saw it. They arrested Dṛḍhamitra and brought him to the king. He was sentenced to death.

When Dhanamitra learnt about this, he came. He fell down at the king's feet and explained, 'I am the one who had these tusks brought.' When Dṛḍhamitra was asked questions, he said, 'I don't know this man. Who is he?'

That is the way they spoke for each other. The king asked them questions under oath, and gave them assurances of safety. Then the whole matter was revealed. The two men were well-treated and sent away.

Similarly, the *ācārya* should abstain from revealing what has been confessed.

3. Firmly keeping to religious orthodoxy in difficult situations* (āvaīsu daḍha-dhammayā)*: about two monks* (ĀvH *667b 1-668a,3)

a. There was the city of Ujjayinī. There lived Vasu, a merchant. As he wished to go to Campā, he made a proclamation (like Dhanna in the Nāyā-dhammakahāo)[3]. A monk called Dharmaghoṣa responded to it. When the caravan had entered far into a forest, it was plundered by tribesmen, and was scattered here and there. Along with other people the monk had gone deep into the forest. They were eating roots and drinking water. He was also invited by them to do so, but he persistently refused food. On one side, sitting on a rock, he renounced food, preparing himself for a pious death. Since he was not depressed but full of endurance, Omniscience came to him, and he was Emancipated.

b. In the city of Mathurā, the king was Yamuna. To the west, there was the garden of Yamunāvakra (there the river Yamunā was making a bend). The monk Daṇḍa was practicing asceticism in that place. The king happened to pass by and saw him. Full of anger, he cut off the monk's head with his sword. (According to others, he struck the monk with a fruit). Then all the king's men made a heap of stones over him. The rising of anger made him suffer. He died and was Emancipated. Then, the coming of the gods, who extolled him, and the coming of Śakra on his celestial car Pālaka should be narrated.

As for the king, he became restless. Śakra threatened him with his thunderbolt, 'If you leave worldly life, you will be released.' The king left worldly life. In the presence of an elder he made the following resolution, 'If, while going for alms, I remember, I shall not eat, and if I have started to eat, I shall leave the rest.'

In this way, it is reported that this Lord did not take food even for one day. He suffered physically. Daṇḍa suffered mentally.

4. Penance observed without support* (aṇissiovahāṇa)*: about the teacher Mahāgiri and others* (ĀvC *II 155,9-157,13).

The monk Sthūlabhadra had two disciples, Āryamahāgiri and Āryasuhastin. Mahāgiri was Suhastin's preceptor. Mahāgiri entrusted his group of monks to Suhastin. Though the Jinas' religious way of life had became obsolete, he did not want to be connected anymore with the Community, and albeit living inside the Community, he used to practice spiritual exercises proper to the Jinas' way of life.[4] During the course of their religious wandering, they reached Pāṭaliputra. There lived the merchant Vasubhūti. After having heard the Law from them, he became a true Jain layman. One day he said to Suhastin, 'Venerable master, you have given me the means to be saved from the world of transmigrations. I have explained it to my relatives, but it does not appeal to them. Maybe you could just happen to go to them and tell them.' Suhastin went there and taught the Law. Then Mahāgiri entered. When he saw him, Suhastin immediately got up. Vasubhūti asked, 'Do you also have another teacher?'

Suhastin answered by praising Mahāgiri's qualities: 'The Jinas' way of life has disappeared, but even so he practices spiritual exercises proper to their rule.' Thus Suhastin spoke at length of Mahāgiri. He gave the layman's vows to Vasubhūti and left.

When Vasubhūti's relatives had taken their food, he said to them, 'Make sure that some food remains left over, in case a monk of this quality comes. A gift of this kind would yield good results.' On the following day, Mahāgiri entered the house for alms. Seeing such an extraordinary happening, he considered the matter to see whether the food was suitable from the four viewpoints.[5] He understood that he had been recognized, and left without taking this food, saying, 'You have made this food not proper for me.'

'How?,' Suhastin asked.

'Because yesterday you got up for me to show me respect. '

Then Mahāgiri and Suhastin left for Vaidiśa. After they had worshipped a Jina image there, Mahāgiri left for Elākākṣa in order to visit the sacred spot Gajāgrapada.

Why was this place named Elākākṣa?

In former times it was the city of Daśārṇapura. A Jain laywoman of this city was married to a non-Jain . When she used to observe the necessary duties prescribed for the evening and to abstain from food, he used to make fun of her, saying, 'What? Would anyone get up at night to eat!' One day he said, 'I shall also abstain from food at night.'

'You will fail,' she replied.

'Have I ever gotten up to eat?,' he said. So she allowed him to take the vow. A deity thought, 'He makes a mockery of this true Jain lady. So let me teach him a lesson today. ' The husband's sister also lived with the couple. At night the deity assumed her appearance and came with a delicacy. The man started to eat it. The Jain lady wanted to stop him, but he said, 'O stop chattering. I don't care a hoot for what you say.' The deity gave him a blow. His eye-balls fell to the ground. Fearing that dishonour would come on her, the Jain lady stood in *kāyotsarga*.[6] At midnight the deity came and asked her why. 'To avoid dishonour coming on me,' she answered. So the eyes of a ram which had just been killed were brought and fitted in. Next morning the people said, 'Your eyes look like those of a ram.' So he told them everything and became a true Jain layman. Out of curiosity people came and asked him. Everywhere in the kingdom the matter came to be known. When people used to ask, 'Where do you come from?,' the reply was, 'From the place where the ram-eyed man lives.' (According to others: it was the king of Daśārṇapura who was ram-eyed). So Daśārṇapura came to be known as Elākākṣa).

In that city of Elākākṣa Mount Gajāgrapada is located. Now, about the origin of this place see the account on magnificence (*iḍḍhi*).[7]

[*ĀvH* 669b,2-670a,1] In this same city of Daśārṇapura lived the king Daśārṇabhadra. He had a harem of five hundred queens. He was so infatuated with his youth and beauty that he thought that nobody else had such youth and beauty. In that period, in that age, the general preaching of Lord Mahāvīra took place on Mount Daśārṇakūṭa. The king thought, 'Tomorrow I shall worship him as he has never been worshipped before by anyone.' Śakra understood what he had in mind and came. As for the king, he went out with great magnificence, and worshipped the Lord in great magnificence. Śakra mounted Airāvaṇa. He magically provided the elephant with eight tusks. On each of the tusks he produced eight ponds, on each of the ponds eight lotuses, on each of the lotuses eight leaves, and on each of the leaves the thirty-two types of dramatic shows. Thus mounted on Airāvaṇa in great pomp he went around the Lord from left to right. Then, thanks to his divine power, the elephant's feet were imprinted on Mount Daśārṇakūṭa. Hence the name of Gajāgrapada ('Mount Elephant's tiptoes'). Seeing such a wonder, Daśārṇabhadra thought, 'How could I acquire such magnificence? Śakra has practiced the Law. I too shall practice it.' And he left worldly life. Such was the origin of Mount Gajāgrapada.

[*ĀvC* II, 157,3] It was there that Mahāgiri renounced all food, preparing himself for a pious death, and became a god. As for Suhastin, he went to Ujjayinī in order to worship an image. He remained in a garden, and told his monks to go and look for a place to stay. Then while in search of alms, a pair of monks entered the house of Bhadrā, a merchant's wife.

'Where are you from, monks?,' she asked.

'We belong to Suhastin,' they said. 'We are looking for a place to stay. She showed them the cart-shed. They stayed there.

One day in the evening, the teacher was reciting the lesson called 'Nalinīgulma.'[8] Bhadrā's son, whose name was Avantisukumāla, had enjoyed himself with his thirty-two wives in his seven-floored mansion. Just as he woke up from sleep he heard something. Thinking that this was not a show, he went down from floor to floor listening at each one. He went outside: 'Where have I heard such things?,' he wondered. Then he remembered his former births, went to the monks' feet and explained, 'I am Avantisukumāla. I was a god in the Nalinīgulma. I am eager to leave worldly life. I am unable to observe ascetic life for a long time, but I shall endure fasting unto death.' Suhastin refused because the boy had not asked permission from his mother. So Avantisukumāla pulled out his hair himself. In order to avoid his taking the ascetic's marks himself, Suhastin finally gave them to him.

In a cremation-ground there was a thicket of *kanthāra*-trees. There the boy renounced all food, preparing himself for a pious death. Attracted by the smell of the blood which was flowing from his tender feet, a female jackal and her young came. The mother ate one leg, the young, the other one. They first ate the knees, then the thighs and the belly. Avantisukumāla died. Perfumed water and showers of flowers poured down from the sky. The teacher made confession. His wives asked questions among themselves. The teacher told them what had taken place. The pious Bhadrā went to the cremation-ground along with her daughters-in-law. All of them left worldly life. One of them who was pregnant drew back. Her son had a temple built in that place. It has now become a Śaiva temple, adopted by the Hindus. This is narrated in the Uttarāculikā.[9]

[5. Learning (*sikkhā*): From the foundation of Rājagṛha to Bhadrabāhu and Sthūlabhadra (*ĀvC *II 157,14-188,10)

[See E. LEUMANN, *Übersicht über die Āvaśyaka-Literatur*. Hamburg,1934, p. 24b, 37-27b,6; Nalini BALBIR, paper to be published in *Bulletin d'Études Indiennes* 6.1988].

6. Not taking care of one's own physical condition (*nippaḍikammayā*): about a young man whose behaviour should not be followed (*ĀvC *II 188,11-189,3).

In the city of Pratiṣṭhāna lived the merchant Nāgavasu and his wife Nāgaśrī. Both were true Jain devotees. Their son Nāgadatta had no taste for sensual pleasures and left worldly life. He observed that the Jinas were worshipped and respected. (This should be fully described. The full description of those monks who were observing *kāyotsarga* is also to be supplied). He said, 'I shall observe the Jinas' religious way of life.'[10] His teacher refused, but the boy did not care and thought that he would observe it without anybody's help. He went away, and observed *kāyotsarga* in some secluded Vyantara-temple. In order to prevent his death a deity endowed with right faith took the appearance of a woman and came to his side with some food. She worshipped the Vyantara and said, 'Take this food, you fasting ascetic.' He took rice with sesamum and various eatables. After having eaten, he again stood in *kāyotsarga*. (Those who follow the Jinas' religious way of life do not sleep). He had dysentery. The deity informed the boy's teacher, 'Your pupil is in such and such a place.' Then some monks were sent to fetch him, and they brought him back. The deity said, 'Give him some *bilva* berries. The dysentery ceased. He was then taught not to treat his body in that way.

7. Not longing after fame (*aṇṇāyayā*): how the monks Dharmaghoṣa and Dharmayaśas practiced penance (*ĀvC *II 189,5-191,6).

There was a city Kauśambī. The king there was Ajitasena and his queen Dhāriṇī. There were the ācārya Dharmavalgu and his two disciples, Dharmaghoṣa and Dharmayaśas, the chief-nun Vigatabhayā and her disciple Vinayavatī. The latter renounced eating, preparing herself for a pious death. The community carried out her funeral with great pomp. (The full description is to be supplied). Dharmavalgu's two disciples carried out the purification rites.

Now, in Ujjayinī lived Pradyota's two sons, Pālaka and Gopālaka. Gopālaka left worldly life. Pālaka was placed on the throne. He had two sons, Rājyavardhana and Avantivardhana. Pālaka chose Avantivardhana as king and Rājyavardhana as crown-prince and left worldly life.

Rājyavardhana's wife was Dhāriṇī; she had a son called Avantisena. One day, the king Avantivardhana suddenly fell in love with the unsuspecting and trusting Dhāriṇī whom he had seen in full beauty in a garden. He sent a female messenger to her. Dhāriṇī refused his advances. He sent the messenger again and again, but she replied contemptuously, 'Don't you even feel any shame in front of your brother?' Then the king killed him. (The full description is to be supplied).

On that evening, she took the jewels belonging to her. A caravan was on its way to Kauśambī. She approached a merchant who was a Jain layman and went along. In Kauśambī she asked Jain nuns for a place to stay. They were standing in *kāyotsarga* in the cart-shed belonging to the king. Dhāriṇī went there and bowed down to them. Since she was considered to be a Jain laywoman, she was allowed to enter monastic life. Inquiry was made: no defect was found in her. In fact, she had recently become pregnant, but fearing that the nuns would not initiate her if they knew about it, she did not inform them. Later on, when it came to be known, she was asked questions by the chief-nun and told the truth, 'I am Rāṣṭravardhana's wife,' she confessed. She was then kept a little aside from the nuns. One night, she gave birth to a baby. In order not to be a source of shame for the nuns, she entered the ladies' apartments. She dug up the seal with her name and her ornaments, placed the baby in the court-yard of the palace, and remained hidden.

Ajitasena, who was on the terrace of the palace, was attracted by the glitter of the jewels. He took the child and entrusted him to the chief-queen. (He himself had no child). When Dhāriṇī was questioned by the nuns, she answered that the child was stillborn, that she had left him, and that he did not exist anymore. She then used to come and go in the ladies' apartments, so that she became friendly with the ladies. The child had been given the name Maṇiprabha. The king died. Maṇiprabha became king. It so happened that he felt love for the nun Dhāriṇī.

Full of remorse after having murdered his brother because he could not obtain his wife, Avantivardhana had given the kingdom to Avantisena,[11] out of affection for his brother, and had left worldly life. This Avantisena asked Maṇiprabha for tribute, but since Maṇiprabha refused to give it Avantisena hastened to Kauśambī with all his forces.

As for the two monks (Dharmaghoṣa and Dharmayaśas), after the completion of the funeral rites, the first one thought, 'Let me also get such glory as Vinayavatī,' and he renounced eating right in the city, preparing himself for a pious death. The second one, Dharmayaśas, who was not longing for splendour, renounced eating in a lonely place, inside a mountain cave, on the bank of the Vatsakā river, between Kauśambī and Ujjayinī.

Avantisena besieged Kauśambī. The population was in distress, so no one went to see Dharmaghoṣa, who finally died without having obtained what he desired. As there was no way out through the gates of the city, he was thrown over the wall. The nun Dhāriṇī then thought, 'Let me disclose my secret so that the people will not suffer.' She entered the ladies' apartments, and taking Maṇiprabha aside she said to him, 'Why are you fighting against your brother?'[12]

'How?," he asked. Then she told him everything in due order. 'If you don't believe me,' she added, 'then ask your adoptive mother.'[13] He asked her. She understood that the secret had certainly been disclosed, and she told him what had happened. She showed him the seal with the name and the ornaments belonging to Rāṣṭravardhana. Now convinced, he said, 'If I draw back, I shall be dishonoured,' and he added, 'Tell the matter to Avantisena too.'

'All right,' she agreed, and went out. Avantisena was informed, 'The nun wants to see you.'

The nun came in. No sooner had her personal servants seen her feet, than they recognized her. They fell at her feet, and burst into tears. Avantisena was told that she was his mother. He too fell at her feet, bursting into tears. Dhāriṇī explained everything, that Maṇiprabha was his brother.

The two kings met outside. They embraced each other and burst into tears. They stayed for some time in Kauśambī. Then the two of them hastened to Ujjayinī. Their mother too was taken there together with the chief-nun. They reached the bank of the Vatsakā river. Seeing the monks of this country climbing up and down to pay their respects to Dharmayaśas, they asked them questions. Then the monk was shown respect by them too. On the next day, the king also hastened to that place. The nuns told him, 'He has completely given up eating, so we shall stay with him.' Then the two kings also stayed. Every day, they worshipped Dharmayaśas. The monk died. Then the kings went away.

Thus, though he was not longing for worship, this monk got it, while the other one, who wanted it, did not get it.

8. Not being greedy (**alobha**)*: about Kṣullakakumāra and others* (ĀvC *II 191,7-192,11).*

There was a city Sāketa. The king there was Puṇḍarīka, the crown prince Kaṇḍarīka. The crown prince's wife was Yaśobhadrā. Puṇḍarīka desired this lady. The crown prince was murdered. The lady went to Śrāvastī. She had just become pregnant.

The religious teacher was Ajitasena, the chief-nun Kīrtimatī. Yaśobhadrā became a nun at her feet. (One should supply here the same full description as in the case of Dhāriṇī[14] except that Yaśobhadrā did not leave her child). She gave him the name of Kṣullakakumāra. He became a monk. When he became a young man, he thought that he would not be able to bear the religious life. He took leave of his mother, 'I am going,' he said. She instructed him. Even then, he did not want to stay. Then she said, 'Come now, for my sake enter the religious life for twelve years.' He agreed to do so. Again, he wanted to take leave. 'Ask leave from the chief-nun,' his mother replied. She told him to stay for twelve years. The preceptor said twelve years. The religious master said twelve years. In all, it made forty-eight years. Still, he did not want to stay. Then they let him go, but his mother said, 'Do not roam here and there. Go directly to your grandfather Puṇḍarīka. See, I took with me this seal with a name which belonged to your father, and also this precious blanket. Take them, and go.' Kṣullakakumāra went to the city. He spent the night in the cart-shed of the king intending to meet the king on the next day.

That very night a dancer was dancing, and Kṣullaka too attended the show with the audience. It so happened that after having danced the whole night, at dawn the dancer fell asleep. Then her manager thought: 'The audience is satisfied. Much money has been earned. If at this point she becomes careless, we shall be offended.' Then he sang the following song:

'You have recited well, you have sung well, you have danced well, O dark nice lady. After having stood firm for long nights, don't become careless through sleep!'[15]

Kṣullakakumāra left her the precious blanket. The crown prince Yaśobhadra was there. He gave her a pair of earrings, worth 100,000. There was also Śrīkāntā, the caravan-leader's wife, who gave a necklace, the minister Jayasandha, who gave a sword, the elephant-driver Karṇapāla, who gave his hook. Whether one was satisfied, displeased or no matter what he paid, everyone was noted down. If the name was known, all the better. If not, a vertical line was written down. In this way, note was taken of everyone.

The next morning Kṣullaka was called and asked, 'Is it you who gave the blanket?' He told all his story, that his father had been murdered, that he was not able to tolerate the right life, that he had come to the king's feet in order to take the kingdom. The king agreed to that, but Ksullaka said, 'Enough of that. The dream is over. When I die, let the self-control which I have previously observed not go to waste.'

The crown prince explained, 'I had a plan to commit a murder. The king is old and I thought he would not give me the kingdom.' He, too, refused the kingdom, though the king was ready to give it to him.

The caravan-leader's wife said, 'As my husband has been absent from home for twelve years and is continuously on the road, I was thinking of taking another man.'

The minister confessed that he was preparing a plot together with some other kings.

The neighboring kings had told the elephant-driver, 'Kill this elephant or bring it to us.' The king told them to do so, but they too refused. They followed the path opened by Kṣullakakumāra and entered the religious life. All of them gave up their greed.

***9. Forbearance* (titikkhā)*: success in a* svayaṃvara *(*ĀvC *I 448,10-450,10).*[16]**

There was a city Indrapura. The king there was Indradatta. His dear and beloved queens gave him twenty-two sons. (According to others, they were all born from only one queen). Each in his individual kingdom was as dear to the king as his own life. The king had also married the only daughter of his minister, but had soon lost interest in her. One day, the king saw her as she had just finished her bath. 'Who is she?,' he asked.

'Your queen,' was the reply. Then he spent a night with her. She normally took a bath following her monthly courses; now she became pregnant. She had been told before by the minister, 'When you are pregnant, you should tell me.' So she informed her father of the day, and also of the hour, the exact moment and what the king had said to her as a welcome. He took note of everything on a tablet, and kept it safe until a boy was born after nine months. On that very day his servants' children Aggiyaa, Pavvayaa, Bahuliya and Sāgaraa[17] were also born. They all shared the same birth day.

The minister took the boy to the schoolmaster, who made him learn the arts of writing, counting and so on. While the schoolmaster was teaching the boy, the servants' children used to annoy him, and because of the lingering effects of their past deeds to beat him too,[18] but he did not care about it a bit, and learned the arts. The twenty-two princes also were made to learn, but they used to butt with their heads the master to whom they were entrusted. And when the master beat them, they would tell their mothers. They would say, 'Is it so easy to give birth to a son?' So these children did not learn anything.

And at that time in Mathurā, the king Jitaśatru had a daughter named Siddhikā. (According to others, her name was Nirvṛti). She was led to the king fully adorned. The king said, 'Whomsoever you like as a husband will be yours.' She considered, 'Let whoever is a brave and valiant hero be my husband. The king will give him his kingdom.' So taking with her a military force and chariots she left for Indrapura.

The numerous sons of king Indradatta were there (Or: a messenger was sent and all the kings were invited to come). Indradatta came to know about the girl's arrival. Flags were erected. An arena was prepared. Eight wheels were irregularly whirling around on the same axle. A puppet was placed in front of them. The challenge was to hit it in the eye.

With full equipment the king came out together with his sons. The princess, beautifully attired, was standing on one side. (The arena and the kings, the tax-collectors, the soldiers, the chiefs are to be fully described following the account of Draupadī[19]). The king's eldest son was a prince called Śrīmālin. He was told, 'My son, you can have this girl and the kingdom provided you hit this target.' The prince was glad, thinking that he was surely more capable than all the other kings. He was invited to hit it. But he was not at all an expert. In the middle of that gathering he was not even able to hold the bow. Somehow he finally held it and shot, 'Be that as it may,' he thought. The arrow broke. Similarly, another one lost one arrow, another one two, another one three. Others even shot outside.

The minister had also informed his grandson. He had brought him on that day and so he was present at the gathering. The king was in complete distress, clasping his hands together, 'Alas, I have been humiliated!' The minister asked, 'Why, my Lord, are you distressed?'

'They have brought dishonour on me,' the king said.

'But you have another son, who is an expert,' the minister replied. 'He is the prince Surendradatta. Let him be tested too.'

'Where does this son of mine come from?,' the king asked.

The circumstances of the boy's birth were explained to him. The king was happy and said, 'If you shoot through these eight wheels you will have the good fortune to get the happiness of the kingdom and the girl Nirvṛti.'

Then the prince took his place, seized the bow and shot an arrow in the direction of the target. The four servants' children were beating him from all sides. The other men were standing at his side with swords in their hands. The twenty-two princes also created especially perverse hindrances. But the boy bowed down to his master, the king and the audience. His master also was frightening him, 'If you miss the target these two men will make your head fall off.' But without caring a bit about these men, the princes or the four servants' children, he estimated the holes of the eight cart-wheels, aimed through the holes when they became as one in line, and with an undeviating eye, not paying attention to anything else, he pierced the puppet in the eye.

There was loud applause and cheer. He won the girl.

To get human birth is as difficult as it was to hit this target.[20]

10. Straightforwardness (*ajjava*): about two pupils (*ĀvC *II 193,2-9)

In Campā there was the teacher Kauśikārya. He had two pupils. One had a handsome body. Therefore he was called Aṅgarṣi. The second one was called Rudraka. He was a pickpocket. The two of them were sent to fetch wood. Aṅgarṣi came back with his load of wood. As for the other one, he enjoyed himself during the day, and in the evening remembered his task. He then hastened to the forest and there saw Aṅgarṣi coming with his load of wood. He thought, 'I am going to be thrown out.'

Now, a female cowherd called Yogayaśā, who had brought her son Panthaka his meal, was coming with a load of wood. Rudraka killed her with a club, took her load of wood and returned by another road, ahead of Aṅgarṣi. Trembling he gave the wood to his teacher saying, 'Your nice pupil has killed the poor Yogayaśā.' (A full description is to be supplied here). Aṅgarṣi came back. The teacher expelled him. He retired to a forest and kept thinking. He conceived good thoughts, remembered his previous births, practiced self-control and reached Omniscience. The gods extolled him. The gods said that Rudraka had accused him wrongly. Then the people blamed Rudraka and he thought, 'It is true that I have wrongly accused Aṅgarṣi.' Through thinking he was Enlightened. He became a Pratyekabuddha. The brahmin and his wife left worldly life. The four of them were Emancipated.

11. About purity or hearing* (sui*: Sk.* śuci/śruti*): about a merchant; then about Nārada.

a. *ĀyvH* 705a,7-705b,3.

There was the city of Saurikapura. There lived the yakṣa Suravara. There also lived the merchant Dhanañjaya and his wife Subhadrā. They bowed down to Suravara. Since they wanted to have a child, they entreated him and promised him a gift. 'If a son is born to us, we shall sacrifice a hundred buffaloes to you.' They were successful. The Lord held his general preaching with the hope of Enlightening the couple. The merchant went to attend it. He was Enlightened. 'If the yakṣa allows me, I shall take the layman's vows.' The yakṣa was appeased.

According to others: when the merchant had taken the vows, the yakṣa asked for the buffaloes. Out of compassion for living beings, the merchant refused to give them. He made a hundred pieces of his own body, and prepared several of them, thinking, 'How lucky I am since I have spared living creatures this pain.' Having put to the test this man's magnanimity, the yakṣa himself was Enlightened. Or: he made flour-bulls[21] and gave them to the yakṣa.

b. *ĀvC* II 193,13-194,12.

The Lord had two disciples, Dharmaghoṣa and Dharmayaśas. They were reciting the Scriptures at the foot of an aśoka tree. They stayed there in the morning, but as in the afternoon the shade did not move, one of them said, 'You have magic power.'

'No, you have,' the other replied. The first one went to a secluded place to relieve himself, and the shadow stayed the same. The second one too, and it stayed the same. Then they realized that neither of them had any magic power. They asked the Lord, who said:

'Here in Saurika in the time of king Samudravijaya, there was a non-Jaina ascetic called Yajñayaśas and his wife Somamitrā. They had a son, Yajñadatta and a daughter-in-law, Somayaśā, who gave birth to a son, Nārada. They lived on the crumbs that they could pick up. They used to eat one day and fast the next day. In the morning they used to leave Nārada at the foot of this aśoka tree and go gathering their crumbs.

Now, it happened that Jṛmbhaka gods attending on Kubera came that way and noticed the boy. Investigating by means of their *avadhi*-knowledge, they understood that the child had fallen from the world of gods, and out of compassion they stopped the shade above him. So much for the question concerning the aśoka tree and the origin of Nārada.

When he was grown up, the Jṛmbhaka gods taught him the magical sciences, the so-called *Prajñapti*-science and the others, so that he was able to wander through the sky with a pot made out of glass and shoes made out of jewels.

One day he went to Dvāravatī, and was asked by Kṛṣṇa, 'What is purity?' He was unable to unravel this question. He delayed giving an answer and making an excuse he left for Pūrvavideha. There the Vāsudeva Yugabāhu was asking the Tīrthaṃkara Sīmandhara, 'What is purity?' and the Tīrthaṃkara answered, 'Purity is truth.' With this one word the Vāsudeva understood everything. Then he went to Aparavideha. The Vāsudeva Mahābāhu was asking exactly the same question of the Tīrthaṃkara Yugandhara,[22] and he too understood everything. Later on, he went back to Dvāravatī and said to Vāsudeva, 'What did you ask me at that time?'

'What is purity?'

'Purity is truth,' Nārada said.

'And what is truth?,' Kṛṣṇa asked. Again, Nārada was confused. Vāsudeva blamed him, saying, 'Where you put that question, you should have put this one too.'

'I have not asked the Master about truth,' Nārada replied. He started thinking. He remembered his former births and was Enlightened. He then pronounced the first lesson, "he says what is worth learning."[23]

12. Right faith* (sammadiṭṭhi)*: about a painting* (ĀvC *II 194,13-195,4).

In Sāketa lived the king Mahābala.

He asked, 'What do I not have that other kings have?'

'A hall of paintings.'

It was caused to be built. Two famous artists were appointed, Vimala and Prabhāsa. They were separated by a curtain as they painted. The first one painted, the other one prepared the floor. The king was happy with the first one and treated him well. When asked, Prabhāsa said, 'I have prepared the floor; at the moment I am not painting.' The king was wondering what that floor looked like. He went to see. The curtain was removed. The painting of the other artist could be seen on the floor. The king became angry. Prabhāsa explained the matter to him, saying, 'The light is reflected here.' The picture was covered. He saw only the plaster and was happy. 'All right,' he agreed.

Similarly, right faith should be practiced with utmost purity.

13. Concentration* (samāhi)*: about the young Suvrata* (ĀvC *II 195, 5-10).

There was the city Sudarśanapura. There lived Susunāga, a householder and his wife, Suyaśā. They were good Jaina devotees. They had a son, Suvrata. His development as an embryo went well. He had an easy birth. He grew up well too. But as he reached marriageable age, he was Enlightened. He took leave of his family and left worldly life. He assumed the rules of the solitary religious life. Śakra praised him. The gods put him to the test in a friendly way. One said, 'May he be lucky, this chaste young man!' Another added, 'Who is unlucky since he has broken the continuity of his family!' But the young Lord remained indifferent. Similarly, the gods showed him his parents being addicted to the objects of the senses or speaking badly of him when they were about to die. Even then, he remained indifferent. Then the gods magically produced the various seasons. A heavenly lady gave him a passionate glance, embraced him and gave long sighs of delight.[24] Even then, he became still more resolute in self-control. He reached Omniscience and was finally Emancipated.

14. Following straight behaviour* (āyārovaga)*: about two brothers* (**ĀvC *II 195,11-195,4).

In Pāṭaliputra lived the brahmin Hutāśana and his wife Jalanaśikhā who were good Jaina devotees. They had two sons, Jalana and Dahana. All four of them left worldly life. Jalana was straightforward, but Dahana was very deceitful. When told to come, he went; when told to go, he came. He died without having repented.

The two brothers were born again in the Saudharma heaven, as members of Śakra's internal assembly. They lived there as gods for five *palyopamas*. The Lord came. His general preaching took place in Āmalakalpā in the park Āmraśāla. The two gods came there and gave a show. One said that he would magically produce something straight and produced something crooked, and vice-versa. The other one said that he would produce something straight and did so, or something crooked and did as he said.

Seeing all these transformations, Gotama asked the Lord. Then the Lord explained that all this was the despicable result of illusion. Jalana, who acted according to straight behaviour, reached Emancipation.

15. Being well-behaved* (viṇayovaga)*: about the young Nimbaka* (**ĀvC *II 196,5-14).

The city was Ujjayinī. There lived the brahmin Ambarṣi and his wife Mālukā who were good Jaina devotees. Mālukā died. Together with his son the brahmin left worldly life. The boy was ill-behaved. He used to throw thorns on the latrines, to sneeze while the monks were reading and studying, or to create disturbances when the exact moment came for them to do something and thus ruin that time for their religious acts. In every matter he used to behave in the way opposite to good conduct. Then the monks said to their superiors, 'Either he goes or we go.' The boy was thrown out. His father, too, followed him. They went to the feet of another teacher. There also the boy was thrown out. It is said that the same thing happened at all the five hundred monasteries of Ujjayinī. He was thrown out of all of them.

The poor father went to relieve himself. He wept.

'Why are you weeping, daddy? ,' the boy asked.

'You really deserve the name of Nimbaka,' the father said. 'Because of your miserable behaviour, I too have no place to stay, and it is not possible for us to return to worldly life!' Then the young boy also became upset, and he said, 'Daddy, let both of us together find some place.'

'We shall not find any place,' the father replied.

Then, when they went to some monks, the monks became very agitated. Their superior said to them, 'Don't be like this, brothers. They will be guests for today. Tomorrow they will go.' But the father and the son stayed. The young novice examined the latrines three times a day.[25] (Here right conduct observed by him is to be fully described). The monks were satisfied. Nimbaka became the best of the novices. He served the five hundred monasteries of Ujjayinī with the utmost zeal. They would not let him go. Thus, later on he became in every way well-behaved.

16. Being of resolute mind* (dhiī maī)*: about Pāṇḍusena's daughters* (ĀvH *708b,g-709a,6).

There was a city Pāṇḍumathurā. There lived the five Pāṇḍavas. They left worldly life and placed their sons on the throne. They hastened to Lord Ariṣṭanemi's feet. They wandered in Hastikalpa looking for alms. While wandering, they came to know about Lord Nemi's death. They rejected the food and the drink they had got, and on Mount Śatruñjaya, they completely gave up eating, preparing themselves for a pious death. They reached Omniscience and were Emancipated.

In their family there was another king whose name was Pāṇḍusena. He had two daughters called Mati and Sumati. As they wanted to visit the Jaina temples in Girnar, they embarked on the boat called "Bull of Waters," going towards Saurāṣṭra. A portent occurred. People prayed to Rudra and Skanda. As for the two girls, they earnestly concentrated on self-control, thinking that death had come. The ship was wrecked. They gained self-control and the state of Omniscient beings. They died and were Emancipated. Their corpses were carried away somewhere. Susthita, the master of the Lavaṇa ocean, extolled them. A divine illumination was produced there. Thus it became the sacred place called Prabhāsa ("Light").

17. Disgust towards worldly life* (saṃvega)*: about Candrayaśā, Sujāta and others* (ĀvC *II 197,8-200,10).

In Campā there lived the king Mitraprabha and his queen Dhāriṇī, the caravan-leader Dhanamitra and his wife Dhanaśrī. After hundreds of prayers to the family deity Dhanaśrī gave birth to a son. People used to say, 'Who is born in such a family which has wealth in plenty has a good birth.' Therefore, after the regular twelve days had elapsed, the boy was named Sujāta (Well-born). It happened that he was as beautiful as a young god. His charm was a subject of conversation. So other people also came to know about it. Our heroes were good Jaina laymen.

In that same city lived the minister Dharmaghoṣa and his wife Priyāṅgu. She heard what Sujāta was like. One day she told her servants, 'When Sujāta happens to pass by, tell me, so that I see him.' Once the boy, surrounded by a group of friends, happened to come by that way. The servants informed Priyāṅgu. She came out, and the other co-wives came too. On seeing Sujāta they said, 'She is lucky whose lover he will be!'

One day the ladies were talking together, 'What charm he has!' Priyāṅgu was providing Sujāta with clothes and ornaments. (They should be fully described). She had a good time with him. So time passed. (The loveliness of his hands should also be fully described). Then came the minister. He walked slowly so that the harem should not suspect anything and he looked through the keyhole. He saw Priyāṅgu engaged in sexual intercourse. He reflected that the harem had been violated, but said to himself, 'Let this matter remain secret in order to avoid the ladies becoming even more unrestrained if the secret is disclosed.' He wanted to murder Sujāta, but he was scared because the boy's father was well treated by the king. Thinking that he should not kill him himself, he looked for a stratagem. He found one.

One day, he managed to have a forged letter written by the spies. The letter was supposed to have come from a feudatory opposed to Mitraprabha. It was addressed to Sujāta and said, 'Kill Mitraprabha. You have his complete confidence. You will get half the kingdom.' The letter was brought. The minister then transmitted it to the king, who was furious. The authors of the letter were sentenced to death, but the minister hid them. Mitraprabha thought, 'If Sujāta's murder comes to be known by the people, there will be unrest among my citizens; and much to my shame that king would see to it that all knew about my act. So I shall kill Sujāta through a stratagem.'

At one border of Mitraprabha's kingdom there was a city named Arakṣurī. The ruler of that place was Candradhvaja. Mitraprabha sent him a letter saying, 'I am sending Sujāta to you. Kill him.' He then called Sujāta and told him, 'Go to Arakṣurī. There become the king's confidant and look into his affairs.' Sujāta went to Arakṣurī. Candradhvaja saw him and thought, 'Let me first make him trust me. Then I shall kill him.' Everyday they used to have a good time together. Seeing his beauty, his character and the way he behaved, Candradhvaja understood that he had probably violated the harem, and that this was the reason why he should be killed. But wondering how he could destroy such beauty, he took him aside, told him the whole story, and showed him Mitraprabha's letter.

'Do as you feel,' Sujāta said.

'I shall not kill you,' the king answered. 'Do one thing. Remain hidden.'

And Candradhvaja got him to marry his sister Candrayaśā. How awful! She had a skin-disease. He lived with her. Sexual intercourse made the disease grow. Sujāta too slowly contracted it. Thanks to him, Candrayaśā too became a good Jaina laywoman. She was thinking, 'It's because of me that he also has been ruined,' and she felt disgust towards worldly life. She gave up eating, preparing herself for a pious death. Sujāta himself took care of her funeral.

Candrayaśā became a god; she made use of *avadhi*-knowledge. She saw the situation and came to Sujāta, bowed down to him and asked, 'What can I do?' He too felt disgust towards worldly life and thought, 'If I can see my parents, I shall leave worldly life.' The god magically created a rock above the city. The inhabitants came with incense in their hands, fell at the god's feet and politely asked about the incident. The god scared them, 'Sons of a slave, Sujāta, a true Jaina devotee, has been ill-treated by the minister in spite of his innocence. I shall make powder of you, and I shall release you only if you bring him here and please him.'

'Where is he?'

'In the garden,' the god said.

The king went there with the citizens and apologized. Sujatā took leave of the king and of his parents and left worldly life. His parents too did the same. All reached Emancipation.

As for the minister Dharmaghoṣa, he was sentenced to banishment. Later on, his qualities became known.

1. "As the eyes, so the character; as the nose, so the straightforwardness; as beauty, so wealth; as the character so the qualities."

Or:

2. "With half-dishonest and half-straight people men are half-dishonest and half-straight. With dishonest ones, they are dishonest. With straight ones, they are of straight behaviour, having seen how their hands and feet, their ears, their nose, their teeth and their lips are."

Later on, he also felt disgust towards worldly life, thinking that he indeed had been responsible for Sujāta's ruin because of his desire for pleasures. He departed. His wanderings led him to Rājagṛha. He left worldly life at the feet of an elder.

In the course of his religious life, Bahuśruta (viz. Dharmaghoṣa) reached Vārattapura. The ruler of this place was Abhagnasena. Vāratta was his minister. While he was wandering for alms, Bahuśruta went to Vāratta's house. A dish of milk-rice dressed with butter and honey was brought. A quarrel broke out, and a drop (of blood) fell in the dish. Bahuśruta did not want this dish on which something had fallen. Vāratta saw all that from a window. Then flies came down and landed on the rice. A pet-cuckoo wanted to catch the flies. A cat ran after the bird. A neighborhood dog ran after the cat. The house-dog too ran after him, thinking that the cat was his. Both started a fight. The dogs' masters too stood up. Scuffles broke out all round. Everybody went out. The guests joined forces and went out. It became a very big fight. Vāratta thought that this was the reason why the monk refused the food. This led him to good thoughts. He remembered his former births and became Enlightened. A deity brought to him the necessary equipment.

During the course of his religious life, the ascetic Vāratta reached Sumsumārapura where the ruler was Dhundhumāra. He had a very beautiful daughter called Aṅgāravatī who was a pious Jain laywoman. A non-Jain lady ascetic happened to come there and was defeated by Aṅgāravatī in a debate. She felt resentful about it, and thought, 'I shall make her fall in a family where there are many co-wives.' Thus she drew Aṅgāravatī's portrait on a board and went to king Pradyota in Ujjayinī. The king saw the portrait and put questions to the ascetic, who told him who it was. Then he sent a messenger to Aṅgāravatī's father's territory, but Dhundhumāra threw him out, saying, 'My daughter will be married for love and if politeness is shown.'

On his return the messenger exaggerated the matter to the king, who became angry and went out with all his army. He besieged Suṃsumārapura. Dhundhumāra stayed inside the city, because he had only a small army.

The ascetic Vāratta was standing in *kāyotsarga* in a *yakṣa*-temple located at a cross-road. The king Dhundhumāra was scared because of the power of his enemy. He asked his astrologer, who said, 'Wait until I examine the omens.' Some children who were playing took fright and came crying to Vāratta. 'Don't be scared,' he said. The astrologer came back and told the king, 'Victory will be yours.' Then at midday Dhundhumāra swooped down on his enemy when he was occupied with his meal. The king Pradyota, who had besieged the city, was captured. The gates of the city were locked.

'From which direction does the wind blow for you?,' Pradyota was asked.

'Do as you think right,' he said.

'How would the death of such an important ruler help?,' Dhundhumāra replied. Thus Aṅgāravatī was married to him with great pomp. The gates of the city were opened, and Pradyota stayed there.

(According to others, his tutelary deity told Dhundhumāra to keep a fast. The deity magically produced the children. The omen was obtained.)

One day Pradyota wandered around the city, and seeing that the king Dhundhumāra was not powerful, he asked Aṅgāravatī, 'How was I captured?' She explained what the monk Vāratta had said. Pradyota went to him saying, 'I bow down to a monk who has knowledge of omens.' The venerable Vāratta became fully aware: from the leaving of worldly life up to the children he had magically produced, everything came back to his memory.

Candrayaśā, Sujāta, Dharmaghoṣa and Vāratta, all reached the Goal through disgust for worldly life. (According to others, the succession starting with

Mṛgāvatī leaving worldly life up to Surambara should be narrated: this is also a possibility).[26]

18. Deceit* (paṇihī)*: about Sātavāhana's minister, and then about two non-Jain ascetics* (ĀvC *II 200,11-201,12).

a.[27] There was in Bhṛgukaccha the king Nahapāna whose power lay in his treasury. On the other hand, there was in Pratiṣṭhāna Sātavāhana whose power lay in his army. He attacked Nahapāna. As Nahapāna was very rich, he used to give a hundred, thousands, a hundred thousands, or millions to those who would bring back a hand or a head. So every day Nahapāna's men used to kill enemies. Sātavāhana's men also used to kill and bring back some, but their king did not give them anything. As Sātavāhana had no more soldiers, he retreated. The following year he came again, but then also he was defeated and went away. So time passed.

One day, his minister said to him, 'Accuse me of some crime, banish me, and imprison some men.' The king did exactly so. As for the minister, he left the place and went to Bhṛgukaccha, taking a load of sweet-smelling balls. He stayed in a secluded temple. The news spread in the neighboring kingdoms that Sātavāhana had thrown out his minister. In Bhṛgukaccha nobody knew him. If somebody asked him, 'Who are you?,' the minister said, 'I have been given the name of Lord Guggula.' If anybody recognized him, he gave the reason why he had been thrown out. They considered it was rather trivial.

Then Nahapāna came to know about all that. He sent some men to Guggula, but Guggula did not even want to hear about becoming Nahapāna's minister. The king himself came. He took Guggula back with him and appointed him. The minister, knowing that he was trusted said, 'Through good deeds one can get a kingdom. Let the path to another birth be prepared.' Nahapāna spent money on temples, stupas, ponds, and tanks, and thus all the money ran out. His former minister summoned Sātavāhana to come. Nahapāna again spent everything. He said to his minister, 'You are a resourceful man.'

'I shall manage,' Guggula said. 'Bring the ladies' ornaments.'

Again Sātavāhana went back to Pratiṣṭhāna. Then Nahapāna used up the ladies' ornaments. When they were all gone, Sātavāhana was summoned to come by his former minister. Nahapāna had nothing left which he could give. He ran away. The city was captured by Sātavāhana.

b. In Bhṛgukaccha there were the teacher Jinadeva and two non-Jain disputants, the brothers Bhadantamitra and Kuṇāla. They took the drum out in order to invite people to challenge them. While going to visit a Jain temple, Jinadeva came to know about it. He took up the challenge. The dispute took place in the royal court. The red-robed ascetics were defeated. Later on those two realized that without knowing the Scriptures of these Jains they would never be able to answer questions. So they deceitfully left worldly life at Jinadeva's feet. (See the account of Govinda for the full description).[28] Then they studied and understood the Scriptures. They really believed in them and became Jain monks.

19. Proper behaviour (**suvihi**)*: the two doctors.*

[See section A, story 1: above pp. 1-3].

20. Obstruction of karmic matter (**saṃvara**)***: about the nun Śrī*** (**ĀvC** ***II 202,2-7*****).**

Here is an example *a contrario* to illustrate obstruction of karman. In Rājagṛha Śreṇika put a question to Lord Mahāvīra: 'There is one celestial dancer who gave a show and then went away. Who is she?'

The Lord explained, 'In Vārāṇasī lived the old merchant Bhadrasena. His wife's name was Nandā. They had a daughter Śrī. She became an old maid and was never asked for in marriage. Lord Pārśva came for his general preaching in the park of Koṣṭaka. Śrī gave up worldly life. She was entrusted as a disciple to the nun Gopālī. She first led her religious life enthusiastically, but later on she became distressed: she used to wash her hands and feet all the time. (See the full description in the account of Draupadī).[29] When she was forbidden to do so, she got up, went elsewhere and settled in a separate house. She died without having made confession or repented and was born again on Mount Cullahim-avanta in a lotus-pond as a gods' courtesan called Śrī. She did not practice the obstruction of karman. One should behave exactly in the opposite way. (According to others: Śreṇika put the question because she had the appearance of a female-elephant and was trumpeting).

21. Refraining from personal faults (**attadosovasaṃhāra**)***: about the young Jinadeva*** (**ĀvC** ***II 202,8-13*****).**

In Dvāravatī lived the trader Arahanmitra and Anudharī, his wife. Both were true Jain devotees. Jinadeva was their son. He became sick and could not be cured. The doctors said, 'Eat meat.' He refused. All the relatives, his father and his mother, out of affection for their son, gave him permission. He did not want to, 'How could I break a vow which has been kept for so long? It is said:

1. Rather enter a blazing fire than break a vow practiced for a long time. Rather death, indeed, with perfectly pure conduct than the life of somebody who failed to observe good behaviour.'

Thus he refrained from personal faults. 'I am going to die,' he thought, and therefore abstained from all reprehensible action. Although he was beyond reproach, still he practiced abstention from food, etc. He left worldly life. As he had reached the stage of very pure thoughts, he became Omniscient, and was soon Emancipated.

22. Refraining from all sensual pleasures (**savvakāmavirattayā**)***: about a father and his daughter*** (**ĀvH** ***714b,5-715a,7*****).**

In the city of Ujjayinī, there was the king Devalāsuta, and his beloved wife, whose name was Locanā. One day, this king was lying on his bed, while the queen combed his hair. She noticed a grey hair and said, 'My lord, a messenger has come.' The king got up hurriedly, with fear and joy: 'Where is he?' So she explained, 'It's the messenger of religion.' Gently winding the hair around her finger, she pulled it out. It was placed on a golden tray wrapped in two fine pieces of cloth and circulated throughout the city. The king was restless, thinking, 'Our ancestors left worldly life before their hair had become grey, and I have not yet done so.' He then placed his son Padmaratha on the throne and left worldly life. His wife, too, did so. Out of affection for them, the male servant Sangaka and the female servant Manumatikā too left worldly life. All of them went to the hermitage for ascetics located on Mount Asita. After some time Sangaka and Manumatikā went back to worldly life.

The queen had not informed the king previously about her pregnancy. The embryo went on growing. The king was restless, thinking that he was now dishonoured, and he kept his wife hidden from the ascetics. The tender queen died during the delivery but gave birth to a girl. She was brought up drinking the milk of other lady ascetics. She was given the name Ardhasankāśā.

She became a young lady. She used to make her father rest on his way from the forest, and he fell in love with her young grace. He thought, 'Today or tomorrow I shall take her.' Once, as he started running with the intention of taking her, he fell on the wood pile of a hut. As he fell down he thought, 'Alas, such is the result of my action in this world! Who knows what it would be in the next world?' He became Enlightened, acquired the knowledge called *avadhi* and recited the lesson "One should indeed be averse to all desires."[30] Now free from attachments he entrusted his daughter to the nuns. As for him, he attained Perfection.

23. Renouncing the* m. (mūlaguṇapaccakkhāṇa)*: the Enlightenment of a barbarian king (*ĀvC *II 203,12-204,6).

In Sāketa there was the king Śatruñjaya. Jinadeva, a true Jain layman lived there. He went on a pilgrimage to Koṭivarṣa. The people of that place were barbarians. Cilāta was their king. Jinadeva offered him all types of precious stones, jewels and cloth-material. There, all these things were unobtainable.

'Wonderful! these beautiful jewels! Where do they come from?,' Cilāta asked. With the thought that maybe Cilāta could be Enlightened, Jinadeva explained that the jewels came from "another kingdom."

The king said, 'I want to go and see these jewels. But I am afraid of your king.'

'Don't be afraid,' Jinadeva replied. He then sent a message to his king, who answered, 'Let him come.' Cilāta was taken to Sāketa. It was Mahāvīra's general preaching. Śatruñjaya went there with his retinue. Crowds of people went with great pomp. Seeing all this, Cilāta asked Jinadeva, 'Where are these people going?'

'Here is the jewel-merchant,' was the reply.

'Let us go and see,' Cilāta said.

The pair of them went there. They saw the Master's rows of parasols, lion-thrones (The full description is to be supplied). Cilāta asked how the jewels might be obtained. The Master then described the material jewels and the spiritual ones.[31]

'Give me the spiritual ones,' Cilāta said.

The Master said that they were to be obtained by the monk's broom and the dust brush for the alms-bowl.[32]

Cilāta gave up worldly life.

24. Renouncing the* u. (uttaraguṇapaccakkhāṇa)*: about two monks (*ĀvC *II 204,7-12).

There was the city Vārāṇasī. Two monks were spending the rainy-season there: Dharmaghoṣa and Dharmayaśas. They were observing one month's fast. At the time of the fourth fast-breaking, after having done recitation during the first three hours, understanding during the second three hours, and after having remembered what they learnt, in the third three hours they went away, in order not to stay always in the same place. Overcome by autumnal heat, they were thirsty when they crossed the Ganges, but even mentally they did not long for water. They crossed over the river. The deity of the Ganges magically produced some cow-sheds: she showed full respect to the monks (The full description is to be supplied). Then she called to them, 'Come on, monks, take alms.' They were ready to accept. When they understood the form and shape of this, they refused the deity's offer, and ran away. Later, out of compassion, the deity magically produced a rainstorm. The earth became wet. Comforted by a cool wind, the monks reached a village. There they took suitable alms and broke their fast.

[25. Rejecting all possessions* (viussagga)*: the four Pratyekabuddhas (*ĀvC *II 204,13-208,14)]

[See the fully developed version of Devendra's Uttarādhyayana commentary edited by H. JAOCOBI, *Ausgewählte Erzählungen in Jaina Mahārāstrī*, Leipzig, 1886, pp. 34-66 and translated by J. J. MEYER, *Hindu Tales*, London, 1909.]

26. Not being careless* (appamāda)*: the story of Magadhasundarī, a courtesan (*ĀvC *11 209,1-8).

In Rājagṛha, the king was Jarāsandha. He had two very eminent courtesans, Magadhaśrī and Magadhasundarī. The former thought, 'If she were not there, the king would be mine alone, and also the fame.' So she started seeking weak points in her rival. One day when Magadhasundarī was to dance, she threw among the karṇikāra-flowers some golden needles smeared with poison so that they looked like saffron. Magadhasundarī's supervisor saw that the bees were not settling on the karṇikāra-flowers, but were attracted towards the mango-trees, from which she inferred that something was wrong with the flowers. She thought, 'If I say that worship made with these flowers would be impure, or that they are smeared with poison, it would be somewhat vulgar. So I shall use a device in order to stop Magadhasundarī.' And she went on to the stage. On other occasions she used to sing an auspicious composition, but that day she sang the following *gīti*:

1. 'Once the month of spring has come, once fragrance and joy are there, the bees leave the karṇikāras to settle upon the mango-blossoms.'

Magadhasundarī realized that this was not an ordinary stanza, and so understood that the karṇikāras had some defect. Trying to avoid them, she sang and danced gracefully, and was not tricked:

She avoided them, and, always careful, she danced and sang without mistake.

***27. Observing good conduct at every moment* (Lavālava)*: the perfectly careful novice Vijaya* (ĀvC *II 209,9-14*).**

This is vigilance: not to let oneself become careless even for a second or half a second.

In Bhṛgukaccha there was a teacher. He sent his pupil Vijaya to Ujjayinī on some matter. Vijaya started out. He was interrupted because of some work he had to do for sick monks. In the meantime he was stopped by pouring rain. Thinking that small herbs would sprout from the rains, he stayed in the village Naṭapiṭaka for the rainy-season in a Nāga-shrine. He thought, 'I am not staying with my teacher, but even here, I shall act as I have been taught to. So he put a *sthāpanācārya*-stand[33] in front of him. He used to measure the time, to observe the daily duties, the *kāyotsarga* and the *vandana*. He used to practice confession. In the middle of the day, also, after the *vandana*, he used spontaneously to make resolves about renouncing food. Then he used to report about the time, and would himself answer, 'Yes.'[34] (Like this, the entire corpus of rules for good monastic conduct should be described).

Thus he never failed. At every moment he was busy, 'What have I done? What is still to be done?'

***28. Obstruction of karmic matter through meditation* (jhāṇasaṃvarajoga)*: the enigmatic meditation of the monk Puṣyabhūti* (ĀvH *722a,5-723a,1*).**

In the town of Śimbavardhana, there was the king Muṇḍimbaka. There lived Puṣyabhūti, a very learned teacher. He pacified the king who became a Jain devotee. His disciple, Puṣyamitra, a very learned person, was for some reason depressed. One day, the teacher thought, 'I shall absorb myself in subtle meditation.' (It is similar to what is called *mahāpāna*[35], but when one gets absorbed in it, he controls his activities in such a way that he is unconscious). Since the monks who were at Puṣyabhūti's feet were only postulants, the teacher called Puṣyamitra, who came, and he told him about his plan. The disciple agreed. Then the teacher meditated in a secluded chamber where there was no disturbance, and Puṣyamitra did not allow access to the monks saying: "Pay your respects to the teacher from where you are. He is busy."

But one day, the monks started discussing with one another, 'What do you think would happen? Let us investigate.' One of them stood at the chamber-door and looked. He stayed there for a long time. The teacher did not move. Neither did he speak or stir in the least. There was also no sign of breathing in and out: his breathing was indeed so subtle! Then the monk went to tell the others what he had seen. They became angry, 'Brother, our teacher is dead, and you haven't even told us!"

'He is not dead,' Puṣyamitra said. 'He is meditating. Don't disturb him.' (According to others: Puṣyamitra did not tell the truth, because he was a Śaivite ascetic in disguise who in fact intended to propitiate the ghost of the dead, since he was a teacher endowed with all the auspicious marks).

'You can go and see tonight.' The monks started quarrelling with Puṣyamitra, but he stopped them. Then they went away, informed the king and made him come, 'Our teacher is dead, and this false ascetic does not allow his body to be taken away.' The king also looked and he too came to the conclusion that he was dead. He did not believe Puṣyamitra. A bier was arranged. When he came to know about this decision, the disciple thought that his teacher had probably died. The teacher had previously told Puṣyamitra that in case of a fire, or any other emergency, he should touch his toe. So he did. The teacher woke up: "Brother, why have you disturbed me?"

"Look at what your disciples have done!"

The teacher rebuked them.

Such is the type of meditation in which one should get absorbed.

***29. Forbearance of mortal pains* (udaa maraṇantie)*: the monk Dharmaruci* (**ĀvC** *II 211,1-9*).**

Even if there are pains which end in death, one should bear them. Here is an example.

In the city of Rohiṭaka, there was a group called Laliya. There lived Rohiṇī, an old courtesan. As she had no other means of livelihood, she used to cook food for the group, and so time passed.

One day, she took a bitter pumpkin, prepared it with lots of spices and cooked it. It was so spoilt that it could not be put in the mouth. 'The group is going to blame me,' she thought. So she quickly cooked another one. 'Let me give the bad one to monks wandering for alms so that it does not go to waste,' she thought. Then the monk Dharmaruci, who was at the end of one month's fast, came in. The pumpkin was given to him. He went back and confessed to his teacher about what he had received. The teacher took the dish. He perceived an acrid smell and investigated it. He realised that whoever ate the pumpkin would die and told Dharmaruci to throw it away outside.

The monk took the food and went to the forest with the idea of throwing it away at the foot of a dry tree. While he was removing the string binding his alms-bowl, his hand was smeared with some of the pumpkin. It came in contact with the food in one place. Because of the smell ants gathered. All that ate died. Dharmaruci thought, 'Let me finish this dish alone to avoid the murder of living beings.' So, alone in a pure place, he confessed and repented. He carefully examined his mouth-cloth, and, blameless as he was, ate that food. Very intense pains came. He endured them and was Emancipated.

***30. Renouncing attachments after careful consideration* (saṅgāṇam ca parinnā)*: the caravan-leader Jinadeva* (ĀvC *II 211,11-13*).**

In Campā there was the caravan-leader Jinadeva, a true Jain layman. After he had made a proclamation, he set out for Ahicchatrā. After sometime he reached a forest. The caravan was plundered by tribesmen. Our true Jain went on walking, got lost and entered the forest, and what then? In front of him was a fire; on the path were some tigers; on both sides was a cliff. He was afraid, realising that he was without any refuge; he spontaneously assumed the behaviour of a monk: he practiced equanimity, and stood in *kāyotsarga*. He was eaten by wild animals. He was Emancipated.

***31. Practice of atonements* (pāyacchittakaraṇa)*: the teacher Dhanagupta* (ĀvH *724a,6-8*).**

Somewhere, in a city, there is the teacher Dhanagupta. Although he does not possess Omniscience, he is said to know how to give atonements. He knows which one helps to purify and which one does not. He knows it through hints given by his pupils' gestures. The one who carries an atonement from him easily crosses over: he cleanses his transgression and gets a greater expulsion of karmic matter.[36]

***32. Devoted adherence to the precepts of Omniscient beings* (ārāhaṇā)*: the Emancipation of Lord Ṛṣabha's mother, Marudevī.* (ĀvC *II 212, 3-9*).**

Bharata was in Vinītā. It was the general preaching of Lord Ṛṣabha. (See the Kalpasūtra for the full description). Seeing Bharata's magnificence, Marudevī said to Bharata, 'Having given up such a magnificence as yours, your father is wandering alone without shelter.' Bharata said, 'What is my magnificence compared to my father's? If you don't believe me, let us go and see.' Bharata came out with all his forces, and Marudevī too. She sat alone on an elephant, and what then? She saw rows of parasols and a group of gods who were praising her son: the glitter of Bharata's clothes and ornaments faded away. Bharata said, 'Have you seen your son's magnificence? How could mine be compared to it?' She started to think with joy. She reached the eighth *guṇasthāna* called *apūrvakaraṇa*[37]. She did not remember her previous births since she had risen up from life in a vegetable body.[38] There itself, on the elephant's back, she reached Omniscience. She was Emancipated. The first human being to reach Emancipation in this descending era was Marudevī.

NOTES ON STORIES OF SECTION A

1. Apart from the 24 Tīrthaṃkaras Jaina mythology has other heroic categories who run parallel to them: the 12 Cakravartins, the 9 Baladevas, the 9 Vāsudevas, and sometimes

also the 9 Prativāsudevas. Kṛṣṇa is contemporary with the 22nd Jina, Nemi. The following episode is inserted in Nemi's legend, for instance in Hemacandra's *Triṣaṣṭiśālākapuruṣacarita* VIII 10.180-189: translation Helen M. JOHNSON. Baroda, 1960, vol. V p. 285-286.

2. One of the two doctors is slightly better than the other, yet both are imperfect; hence their respective rebirths.

3. This is how I render the recurring formula bhattaṃ paccakkhāmi which indicates that one prepares himself to fast unto death.

4. *īhāvūha*: the mental process through which one comes to connect his present and past existences.

5. The prophecy narrated by Nemi (told in the future) and the actual story (told in the past) overlap.

6. In Jain narrative literature the *avadhi*-knowledge ("visual intuition," N. TATIA, *Studies in Jaina Philosophy*. Varanasi, 1951, p. 63) is a characteristic of human beings reborn as gods who often resort to it to help their former acquaintances. See again p. 10, 70, 78.

7. The structure, motives and stanzas of this story have been dealt with at length by A. METTE, "The Tale of the elephant-driver in its Āvaśyaka version" in *Siddhantacharya Pandit Kailashchandraji Shastri Abhinandana Grantha*, Rewa, M.P., 1980, 549-559.

8. For (non Jaina) nuns as kind or wicked go-betweens see also below section C story 17.

9. Read *sā* instead of C ed. *so*.

10. For the positive effects of this formula in all sorts of dangerous circumstances see G. ROTH, "Notes on the *Pamca-Namokkāra-Parama-Mangala* in Jaina Literature" in *Adyar Library Bulletin*. Mahāvīra Jayanti Volume 38. 1974, 1-18.

11. *teṇa ya taṃ aṭṭhāvayaṃ laddhellayaṃ* not very clear to me. Perhaps Mt. Aṣṭāpada, the mythical mountain where the first Jina Ṛṣabha is supposed to have reached Nirvāṇa?

12. Throughout these translations this is my rendering of *samosaraṇa*.

13. = *Isibhāsiyāiṃ* No. 41.

14. A gift to a monk should be pure from four points of view: the substance, the place, the time, and the mental dispositions of the giver: se N. BALBIR, "The 'micro-genre' of *dāna*-stories in Jaina Literature" in *Idologica Taurinensia* 11. 1983. 145-161.

15. Read *bharitaṃ* instead of *bhaṇita*, C ed.

16. *sahassaṃ kappāsamolla*: not very clear. As a basis for my translation I may adduce the fact that the Arthaśāstra (2.23.2) mentions courtezans' mothers among persons who spin cotton for the king. See D. SCHLINGLOFF, "Cotton-Manufacture in Ancient India" in *Journal of the Economic and Social History of the Orient* 17. Part 1, 1974.81.

17. In Jaina narrative literature Abhaya is used as a model of cleverness, similar to Birbal in more recent times. See again below section B story 8a.

18. i.e. the one who had adopted Kṛtapuṇya and then thrown him out.

19. Similar phrase in section C story 23 (end).

20. Since it is connected with Kṛṣṇa's and Baladeva's former births this story also appear in Hemacandra's *Triṣaṣṭiśālākapuruṣacarita* VIII.5.1-23 (Johnson's translation vol. V, p. 153-154) and other Nemi's biographies; see also above n.1.

21. For conversion of tribal populations to Jainism see also section C story 23.

22. The negative particle, omitted in C ed., has to be supplied.

23. *hiṇḍati* C. ed. is obviously a mistake for *hiṇḍasi.*

24. See fig. 87 "Actors and pole-dancers" in Moti CHANDRA— U.P. SHAH, *New Documents of Jaina Painting*. Bombay, 1975.

25. See for instance Hemacandra's *Triṣaṣṭiśālākapuruṣacarita* trans. JOHNSON, Baroda, 1962, vol. VI, p.3.

NOTES ON STORIES IN SECTION B

1. This refers to the mode of argumentation known as *nikṣepa* on which see B. BHATT, *The Canonical Nikṣepa Studies in Jaina Dialectics*, Leiden, 1978 (Indologia Berolinensis 5).

2. This paragraph refers to the preliminary rituals to be performed before a construction (see *Aparājitapṛcchā*. Baroda, 1950, p. XIVff. and *Samarāṅganasūtradhāra*. Baroda, 1966, chapter 11) and is not found in *ĀvH.*

3. Parallel version in commentaries on *Uttarādhyayanasūtra* 4.10.

4. Cf. WH.R. RIVERS, "The Marriage of Cousins in India," *Journal of the Royal Asiatic Society* 1907.2.611-640, also about the part played by the maternal uncle in such marriages.

5. See an illustration of such a bamboo-pole for instance in *India Observed. India as viewed by British Artists 1760-1869*. Victoria and Albert Museum. 1982, No. 100.

6. Similar motif in story 8b of the the present section.

7. The same catchword *do kannāo* is used for stories, 5 and 6 and should be understood as *egā kannā* (No. 5) + *egā kannā* (No. 6). Parallel version to No. 5a in Jayasiṃhasūri's *Dharmopadeśamālāvivarana*. Bombay, 1949, p. 61.

8. And the Mango-trees are the best.

9. Parallel version in Jayasiṃhasūri's *Dharmopadeśamālāvivaraṇa*, p. 62.

10. A second quotation identical to O. BOHTLINGK, *Indische Sprüche* 5824 is adduced in *ĀvH.*

11. See no. 7 for the catchword. A story with a similar framework and partly different inserted riddles is found in the Uttaradhyāyana tradition in the saga of the Pratyekabuddha Naggai: see for instance J. CHARPENTIER. *Paccekabuddhageschichten*. Upsala, 1908, p. 134ff.; H. JACOBI, *Ausgewählte Erzählungen in Mahārāṣṭrī*, p. 49ff.

NOTES ON STORIES OF SECTION C

1. For the translation of the word *avalla*, I follow the Sanskrit chāyā available in *ĀvH* "*balīvarda.*"

2. Some words in this sentence are unclear.

3. See W. SCHUBRING, *Nāyādhammakahāo*. Das sechste Anga des Jaina-Siddhānta. Wiesbaden, 1978, p. 47: 15. Nandiphala.

4. This refers to the so-called *Jinakappika*, a very rigorous religious way of life suitable for spiritually advanced monks only, on which see for instance, C. CAILLAT, *Atonements in the ancient ritual of the Jaina monks*. Ahmedabad, 1975, p. 41.

5. See section A, note 14.

6. A very common Jaina ascetic posture especially well-known from the colossal image of Bāhubali in Śravaṇa Beḷgoḷa (Karnatak): one stands erect, does not move, and looks at the tip of his nose.

7. Thus this episode serves two didactic purposes. It has also to be supplied above in section A, story 10.

8. See Āgamic Index. Vol. 1 Prakrit Proper Names. Ahmedabad, 1970 s.v.

9. "A Canonical text not extant now": see *ibidem*.

10. See above note 4.

11. I.e. his nephew, see p. 58.

12. Avantisena is Maṇiprabha's elder brother and was born before their mother Dhāriṇī left worldy life.

13. I.e. Avantisena's wife, also named Dhāriṇī: see the very beginning of the story.

14. This refers to the Dhāriṇī of story No. 7 who became a nun.

15. = *Āv. niryukti* vs. 1290: three vaitālīya-padas and one cāruhāsinī-pada, as Prof. A. Mette (Münster) kindly suggests.

16. In the section which I translate here one only finds a cross-reference and must refer to the passage where the story has been first adduced, viz. as the seventh of the ten examples serving to illustrate the difficulty of getting human birth.

17. No satisfactory Sanskrit form is found for these slaves' names.

18. Translation based on the relevant passage in *ĀvH*, since *ĀvC* is not clear.

19. See *Nāyādhammakahāo* 16: SCHUBRING p. 52. The whole scene naturally reminds a reader of Draupadī's svayaṃvara in the Mahābhārata.

20. See n. 16.

21. Compare the sacrifice of a wheat-cock (*piṣṭakurkuṭa*) in M. BLOOMFIELD, *Life and Stories of the Jaina Saviour Pārśvanātha*. Baltimore, 1919, p. 196.

22. There are Tīrthaṃkaras, Cakravartins, Baladevas, Vāsudevas (and Prativāsudevas) in each region of the Jain cosmology: see, for instance, Helen JOHNSON's translation of the *Triṣaṣṭiśālākapuruṣacarita* vol. 1, p. 386ff.

23. For Nārada's childhood see for instance *Triṣaṣṭi* VIII. 5.28-42: trsl. vol. V p. 154-155. As a ṛṣi, Nārada is said to be the author of this sentence, the first one of the *Isibhāsiyāiṃ*.

24. This is an avatar of the *upasargas* the Jinas have to face in their religious lives. They can be mild or violent.

25. A sign of careful behaviour.

26. See E. LEUMANN, *Die Āvaśyaka-Erzählungen* Leipzig, 1897, p. 14ff. for the full story.

27. The rivalry between the Śātavāhana kings and the Śaka Kṣarahāta (represented by Nahapāna) is an historical fact: see Jyoti Prasad JAIN, *The Jaina Sources of the History*

of Ancient India. Delhi, 1964, p. 76, 92 and S.B. DEO *Indian Historical Quarterly* 30.3-4, 1954, p. 276ff. on the cleverness of Śātavāhana's minister.

28. For Govinda, the pattern of such stories, see *Nisīha-cuṇṇi* vol. III p. 260.

29. I read *hatthe pāde ya*, following *ĀvH*. Though the text refers to the account of Draupadī (= *Nāyādhammakahāo* 16), the whole story rather reminds one of the account of Sirī and other ladies whose lives are sketched in the *Pupphacūlāo* (10th Upāṅga of the Jain Canon). At first eager to follow religious life they later become disgusted, take care of their bodies in a way not allowed to nuns and refuse to change their behaviour.

30. This might be a quotation, but I could not trace it.

31. The *ratnatraya*, i.e. right faith, right knowledge and right conduct.

32. On *gocchaga* see S.B. DEO, *History of Jaina Monachism*. Poona, 1956, p. 614.

33. See J. JAIN—E. FISCHER, *Jaina Iconography*, Leiden, 1978, Part II, p. 10-11 and plate XVI. It acts here as a substitute for the teacher.

34. Measuring the time (*kālagrahaṇa*) in order to know when to perform or not perform religious acts is very important in Jainism and the topic is fully dealt with in the *Āv*.

35. A very subtle type of mediation where breathing becomes impossible to be perceived.

36. To give suitable atonements is one of the main functions of the ācārya: see C. CAILLAT, *Atonements* passim.

37. See P.S. JAINI. *The Jaina Path of Purification*. Delhi, 1979, chart p. 272-273.

38. Uncertain. I have not been able to trace any parallel to this feature of the story.

APPENDIX: The Stories of the Āvaśyaka Tradition

The literature that developed around the *Āvaśyaka sūtra* is so important and extensive that Ernst Leumann, a pioneer in the study of this field of Indology, was prompted to coin a special term for the *Āvaśyaka* and its commentaries. He called this entire corpus of material the "Āvaśyaka-Literatur," a term that is still current among students of Jainism.

In fact, the commentaries to the *Āvaśyaka* became so important that the actual *Āvaśyakasūtra* has been superseded by its oldest commentary, the versified *Āvaśyakaniryukti* in Prakrit which in its present form is comprised of about 2000 stanzas. Without its prose commentaries however, the *niryukti* could hardly be of any use; it really consists for the most part of lists of catchwords without any syntactical link between them and demands further explanatory material. Thus one has to read the *niryukti* simultaneously with its Prakrit *cūrṇi*, or commentary, which is ascribed to Jinadāsa(ca. 6th-7th cent.) and with the mixed Prakrit-Sanskrit *ṭīkās* by Haribhadra (8th cent.) and Malayagiri (11th-12th cent.; incomplete). These texts together form a coherent body of material. Another group of texts concentrates on a part of the *niryukti* and lays more emphasis on matters of philosophy and dogma. This trend is represented by Jinabhadra's *Viśeṣāvaśyakabhāṣya* and its prose commentaries.

All of these various methods of Jaina exegesis aim at helping the aspirant reach his spiritual goal by moral improvement, but they show considerable variation in the means they chose to carry out this task. Jain scriptural exegesis often resorts to highly formulaic and abstract schemes (such as the *nikṣepa*) which are designed to bring us as close as is possible to the true meaning of the fundamental words and notions in a text. On the other hand, as might be expected in the Indian context, Jain commentators also give to edifying stories a major role in elucidating important concepts, and it is here that the *Āvaśyaka* commentaries stand out. In fact they are the main source upon which many Śvetāmbara medieval narrative anthologies such as Jayasimha's *Dharmopadeśamālāvivaraṇa* (11th cent.), the *Ākhyanakamaṇikośa*, the *Mūlaśuddhiprakaraṇa*, the *Upadeśapada*, the *Upadeśamālā*, and the *Kathākośa* have drawn. Thus they are the starting point for any investigation into Jain narrative literature, its history and its remarkable vitality.

Stories are not distributed equally throughout the *Āvaśyaka* commentaries. They are concentrated into sections of various sizes organized around important terms. In my translations I have chosen to present three such sections (A:eleven stories; B:eight stories; C:thirty-two stories) which I consider as good representatives of the general process of storytelling in the *Āvaśyaka* commentaries. In sections A and B, which deal with the first and the fourth of the six necessary duties (*sāmāyika* and *pratikramaṇa*), the *niryukti* hands down two chains of catchwords: the first one lists technical terms and the second one offers a corresponding list of illustrations (*niryukti* 845-846, 1233, 1242). *Sāmāyika*, which has the restricted meaning of equanimity, here covers a very broad range of ideas (compassion, humble behaviour, etc.). It refers most generally to the acquisition of a state of mind which makes a person conceive of worldly life as negative and realize that he should leave it. As for *pratikramaṇa*, it is subjected to a specific exegetical device which consists in defining the meaning of a concept by giving "synonyms" (*egaṭṭha*; Sanskrit *ekārtha*) or rather, approximations. In section C, the biggest narrative section in the whole corpus, five verses list thirty-two catchwords which work as labels for different aspects of Jain conduct (*yogasaṃgraha*). Then comes for each story one stanza enumerating the proper names of characters and places or religious terms connected with that story (N1274-1320).

In several cases a reader may feel that the logical connection between a given term and the story meant to elucidate it is rather loose or unexpected (ex. C 23, C 24). The fact that the same story can be used two or three times, serving different didactic purposes, proves to some extent that the connection between story and the term it is meant to illustrate is not hard and fixed (ex. A 1 = C19; C9).

For all three sections, my translations are based on the texts of the full stories as they appear in the prose commentaries. Generally speaking, it can be said that the story handed down by the *cūrṇi* and by the *ṭīkās* is the same. Differences, where they occur, are mostly in the wording. In most cases, I have selected the *cūrṇi* version because it is considered to be older and was probably less affected by the process of Sanskritisation than the *ṭīkās* were. In a few cases, however, I have used Haribhadra's text. I have given the precise textual reference at the beginning of each translation. For the sake of convenience I have also provided the stories with titles and Sanskritised the Prakrit names. My Sanskrit renderings follow that given in the *Dictionary of Prakrit Proper Names*.

As can be seen, the stories represent different literary genres, though they are uniformly labelled as *dṛṣṭāntas* or *udāharaṇas* (examples) by the commentators. We thus read short anecdotes, the characters of which are anonymous, as well as parables, short stories, small novels, folk tales (A 2), humorous riddles, etiological tales given to account for a place-name (B 4), or even pseudo-historical accounts (C 18) and a Jaina avatar of the 1001 nights (B 6).

In my opinion at least two details prove that these *Āvaśyaka* stories represent an intermediate stage between an oral tradition which would give the narrator (a preaching monk) great freedom and a fixed written tradition which would imply a more rigidly unvarying text. In many cases, we are given a kind of narrative framework where episodes are quickly sketched in a somewhat abrupt manner and where descriptive elements have almost no place as such but are only referred to casually and meant to be supplied by the teller of the tale. This is conveyed by the technical term *vibhāsā* which I have always rendered as "the full description is to be supplied" (viz. from relevant Canonical sources, or by drawing from the narrator's imagination). On the other hand, phrases such as *anne bhaṇanti*, "others say," appear in the stories, referring to narrative variants and divergent opinions on some details of the stories; they imply a desire to fix the text and justify its authority. I have retained these phrases in the translations, using the formula "according to others," since they are characteristic of this stratum of narrative literature. They disappear for the most part in the later *Kathākośas*.

When compared with the later narratives of the *Kathākośas*, the *Āvaśyaka* stories seem much cruder. They are mainly concerned with the behaviour of the characters they show. Thus the narrative element prevails over description and even the religious background, though all-pervading, appears in a simple and discrete manner through a few recurrent terms or motifs (memory of former births, *kāyotsarga*, *pañcanamaskāra*, keeping of fasts, preaching of monks, criticism of meat-eating and sacrifice, *avadhi*-knowledge).

We are taken among merchants, acrobats, wrestlers, weavers, brahmins, monks and novices, kings and queens. We come across some customs of interest: marriage of cousins (B 4), marriage arranged during childhood without the children knowing about it (A 7), conflicts resulting from marriage between persons of different faiths (C 4). We learn about the technique of acrobats (A 11), about the training of wrestlers (C 1), about conflicts concerning deposits, a favorite topic for small anecdotes (B 6: sixth riddle), about traffic in ivory (C 2).

But social conservatism is the norm. We see how a king who wants to marry a poor painter's daughter buys her, how this girl must compensate for the social gap by telling stories (B 6: Jaina avatar of 1001 nights) and how she has to bear the envy of her co-wives. We learn how the difference in their social status plays a part in the different behaviour of a weaver's daughter and a brahmin's daughter who are close friends (B 5).

Editions used

ĀvC = *Āvaśyakacūrṇi*. 2 vols. (1-11). Ratlam, 1928-29. References are to the page and line of this edition. This uncritical edition is far from satisfactory. However in the present work notes concerning the wording have been limited to extreme cases of error (omission of negations...).

ĀvH = *Haribhadra's Āvasyakaṭīkā* (also containing the *niryukti*), Bombay, 1916-1917 (Agamodaya Samiti). References are to the page and line of this edition.

Bibliography of studies connected with the Āvaśyaka-commentaries

Ludwig ALSDORF, Jaina Exegetical Literature and the History of the Jaina Canon": *Mahāvīra and His Teachings*. Ed. A. N. UPADHYE et alia. Bombay, 1977: 1-8.

Ludwig ALSDORF, "Zwei neue Belege zur 'indischen Herkunft' von 1001 Nacht": *Kleine Schriften*. Wiesbaden, 1974: 518-558 [p. 545ff: text and translation of AvC 1 553ff].

Nalini BALBIR, "The monkey and the weaver-bird. Jaina versions of a pan-Indian Tale": *Journal of the American Oriental Society* 105.1.1985: 119-134 [Ed.trs] of *ĀvC* 1 345-346.

Nalini BALBIR, "The Perfect sūtra as defined by the Jainas": *Berliner Indologische Studien* 3.1987:3-21 [*ĀvN* 880-886].

Nalini BALBIR, "*Anadhyāya* as a Jaina topic": to be published in *Wiener Zeitschrift für die Kunde Südasiens* 1990 [AvN 1321-1417].

Klaus BRUHN, *Śīlāṅkas Cauppannamahāpurisacariya*. Ein Beitrag zur Kenntnis der Jaina-Universalgeschichte Hamburg, 1954 [esp. for problems connected with Ṛṣabha's and Mahāvīra's biographies as they are sketched in the Āvaśyaka-commentaries].

Klaus BRUHN, "Āvaśyaka Studies 1": *Studien zum Jainismus und Buddhismus*. Gedenkschrift für Ludwig Alsdorf. Wiesbaden, 1981: 11-49 [rich and suggestive methodological study].

Klaus BRUHN, "Repetition in Jaina Narrative Literature": *Indologica Taurinensia* 11.1983:27-75.

Jagdisch Chandra JAIN, *Prākrit Jain Kathā Sāhitya*. Ahmedabad, 1971 [Hindi paraphrase of some *Āv*. stories].

Ernst LEUMANN, "Die alten Berichte von den Schismen der Jaina": *Indische Studien* XVII.Leipzig, 1885:91-135 [*ĀvN* 778-784].

Ernst LEUMANN, *Die Āvaśyaka-Erzählungen*. Leipzig, 1897 [Critical edition of stories included in AvC 1 44-124 and connected commentaries. A presentation, translation and glossary are being prepared by Nalini BALBIR and Thomas OBERLIES].

Ernst LEUMANN, *Übersicht über die Āvaśyaka-Literatur*. Hamburg, 1934. [still the basic book for any study of this field of Jainism].

Adelheid METTE, "The tale of the elephant-driver in its Āvaśyaka-version": *Pandit Kailaschcandji Shastri Abhinandana Grantha*. Rewa.1980:549-559 [AvC 1 461-465:infra section A story 2].

Adelheid METTE, "The Tales of the *Namaskāra-vyākhyā* in the *Āvaśyaka-cūrni*. A survey": *Indologica Taurinensia* 11.1983: 129-144 [*ĀvC* 1 503-590].

Katrin VERCLAS, *Die Āvaśyaka-Erzählungen über die Upasargas des Mahāvīra im Vergleich mit den Versuchungen des Bodhisattva in der buddhisten Literatur*. Hamburg, 1976 [Dissertation; esp. stories in *ĀvC* 1 269-296].

Albrecht WEBER, "Über die heiligen Schriften der Jaina": *Indische Studien* SVII. Leipzig. 1885 [pp. 50-76 about *Āv. sūtra*, *ĀvN* and commentaries].

Theodor ZACHARIAE, *Kleine Schriften zur indischen Philologie, zur vergleichenden Literaturgeschichte, zur vergleichende Volkskunde*. Bonn und Leipzig, 1920.

The Tale of the Faithful Wife Rohiṇī

Translated by Dr. Prem Suman Jain

Introduction

Many short didactic stories were written in Prakrit. From time to time they were collected into anthologies that were known as *Kathākośas*, "Treasure Houses of Stories." The story of Rohiṇī occurs in the Prakrit verse commentary by Āmradevasūri to the *Ākhyānakamaṇikośa*, which was compiled around the twelfth century. There are many stories in Indian literature about virtuous women who preserve their chastity from all who would sully it. Such stories were particularly appreciated among the Jains, who told them both in the canon and in later texts. In the *Jñātādharmakathā* we read of how Malli talked six princes out of their lust for her by showing them the true nature of the body, using an image of herself that gave off a terrible smell to prove her point. In the story of Rājamati and Rathanemi in the *Uttarādhyayanasūtra*, 22, Rājamati uses the famous example of eating vomit as a comparison for resuming a life of pleasures after one has become a monk. Such inventive stories about the necessity to preserve womanly virtue continued to be told throughout the history of Jain story literature, with the story of Rohiṇī being especially popular. I have studied this story in my *Rohiṇīkathānak*, published in Udaipur in 1986. I take this opportunity to thank Dr. L.P. Mathur and Dr. Phyllis Granoff for reading my translation.

The Faithful Wife Rohiṇī

1. There lived in Pāṭaliputra a king named Nanda, who was radiant like the sun and a bee-like youth for the lotus-like hearts of beautiful damsels.
2. A merchant named Dhaṇāvaha, much honoured by the king and filled with good conduct as the moon is with nectar, also lived there.

3. Rohiṇī was the wife of that merchant, as the star Rohiṇī is the consort of the moon, which bears the mark of a deer on its surface; she was full of sparkling radiance, had a noble heart and restless eyes.
4. And a pair, a male cat and a mynah bird, that they had raised from infancy and were extremely dear to their hearts, lived in the residence of the merchant.
5. At one time anxiety arose in the mind of the merchant Dhanāvaha, and he thought that just as it is not proper (for anybody) to enjoy the wife of his father, similarly is it not proper for him to enjoy his father's wealth.
6. He thought, "Only those persons are the real ornaments of the world, with self-respecting virtues, passing their lives in a noble way, who bestow in charity to orphans the money that they have earned themselves.
7. Unlike itching that gets more and more with constant scratching, money spent never increases. Therefore, noble persons should strive hard to earn money."
8. Thinking like this, the merchant, who had a resolute mind bent on earning wealth, after collecting several saleable articles of trade, said this to his wife.
9. "O! Moon-faced Lady! I will have to go to other countries to earn my wealth. (Therefore) this residence should be carefully guarded by you.
10. And, O! Lady with a beautiful body! Take good care of this pair, the male cat and mynah bird, and talk to them nicely, three times every day.
11. And carefully preserve your womanly chastity, which is pure like the full moon and a natural ornament."
12. Then he put the residence and his wife specially under (the care of) the mynah bird and taking the male cat in his lap (he) caressed it with his hands.
13. The merchant, having honoured all of them, under auspicious stars, boarded the ship that was laden with saleable articles.
14. (That merchant,) by crossing the ocean, the master of the rivers and full of roaring waves, gradually reached the island of Siṅgāla, while here (in Pāṭaliputra) the king Nanda,
15. Mounted on an elephant named Jaya, fanned by two white whisks, obstructing the heat of the host of rays of the sun by his white canopy,
16. Ornamented with a necklace of thick pearls on his broad chest, more beautiful by the decorations on all parts of his body, the destroyer of the arrogance of his enemies,
17. Cutting jokes with his nearest friend named Ratikeli, who was sharp-witted when it came to narrating several tales from the treatise on Love,
18. Surrounded by a group of elephants full of black bees, greedy for the the scent of the fluid that flowed from the elephants' temples, and making

rhythmic sounds; surrounded too by a group of horses wearing bridals made of gold that made rhythmic sounds,

19. Followed by a group of kings, (King Nanda) moved out of the palace garden, sitting on a chariot with a group of small golden bells (ghunghru) that made rhythmic sounds.
20. And (the king) reached the area of the wall of the private residence of the merchant Dhanāvaha. In the balcony of that building was a damsel,
21. More beautiful in the full blossoming of youth, with her fair body like heated gold, similar to the bride of Kāmadeva (God of Love) but without him.
22. Moon-faced Rohiṇī was seen by the king Nanda. Instantly that king was shot by the cluster of arrows of the angry Kāmadeva.
23. After looking with a concentrated mind at her lotus-like face, that king began to act wildly, like an intoxicated elephant, right there on the spot.
24. Stopping before that Rohiṇī and craning his neck, time and time again king Nanda casts his eyes on her face.
25. That great lady, the truly chaste Rohiṇī, after seeing the king, with his not inconsiderable desire, viewing her with passionate eyes,
26. Went elsewhere with slow steps, descending from the balcony of the house. Not seeing her,
27. Burning with the flames of separation, the king with a sorrowful heart returned to his palace, giving out that he was suddenly unwell.
28. A pang of separation from her was kindled in the body of (the king) like a fire of dried cow dung. Due to pangs of suffering he (the king) does not enjoy anything, even for a moment.
29. Suffering from great passionate love-sickness, as if possessed by a mighty demon, that king (some times) like a mad man laughs, sings, weeps and circles here and there without any purpose.
30. Then the group of the citizens, ministers, divisional officers, feudal lords, and others felt great anxiety at seeing the king in such a condition.
31. Then the physicians, healers and astrologers were called by that group of citizens. And then the physician says, "The king is suffering from extreme delirium.
32. Therefore, take the king to an unairy place in the middle of a cell. Try to cover him after closing the doors.
33. Then O King! You drink the water of raw medicines and keep a fast in such a way that you may be free from this acute disease and become healthy in body again."
34. Then the different healers say,"The king has been eclipsed by evil stars, therefore he weeps, laughs and sees with a fierce vision.

35. Therefore having drawn on the ground an area of sacred space, and having written a sacred diagram ('yantra') which destroys evil spirits, worship it with flowers of oleander;
36. Having arranged betel nut, betel leaves, rice, kindling, earthen pots, etc., all of which are the constituents of worship, and invoking each group of the sixty-four goddesses, the Yoginīs,
37. Having made the king sit in the midst of the fragrance of the smoke of the flames and having uttered sacred mantras,
38. If then you rain blows on the king with fists full of mustard, urad (pulse) and rice, then there is no doubt that this unhappy king suffering from blows will be cured."
39. Then the astrologers say thus, "This disease would be cured by a ritual to bring calm. For it the worship of the heavenly bodies is auspicious and charity on the death anniversary of a relation is good."
40. At this time Ratikeli, dearest friend of the king, presented himself to bow down at the king's feet. Observing his condition, he salutes the king and says.
41. "O lord! You tell your sorrow to me. I will make efforts to remove that sorrow." Even after saying this, when the king does not say anything, then that Ratikeli
42. Knew from his cleverness that this king is sighing so deeply for his heart has been stolen by that woman named Rohiṇī.
43. Then he said, "O lord! Your heart has definitely been stolen by some lady. Therefore tell me (her name) so that I may bring her here soon."
44. Hearing this the king said, "How could you know it?" Then he said "O lord! from the strange glimpse in your eyes!
45. Words with hidden meanings, looking out of the corner of the eyes, deep hot sighs, these are found where gather people struck by love."
46. After hearing this the king says, "All these secrets will be told to a person close to my heart like you, because
47. Some things cannot be communicated even to mother, father, sister, brother and wife, but nothing is to be withheld from an affectionate friend.
48. The fact is that my heart is enchanted by Rohiṇī." Then Ratikeli asks whether her attitude of heart is known, "Is she infatuated or indifferent towards you?
49. Because it is said '(a lady inflicted with sexual desire) walks in that manner, yawns, speaks sweetly, twists her parts of the body, shakes her hair, has her body hair standing on end and bites her lips.
50. Snapping her fingers, showing her lotus-like navel in the same manner, and with her eyes full of pleasure derived from sexual urge she looks with a slow smile.

51. A lady suffering from the arrow of Kāmadeva presses her heavy breasts, loosens the knot of the cloth around her navel and kisses the faces of children.

52. She repeatedly utters the name of the person with whom she is in love and honours his friends; if she acts in this way, then that lady can be called passionately in love.

53. Where there is no waking in the night, no jealousy and no pain, no pride and no easy flattery, there is no love.

54. Young ladies having no passion breathe without yawning, pretend to be asleep, have headaches, and voices thick with exhaustion.' "

55. Then the king said, "I have not observed passionate desire in her (Rohiṇī)." Then it was said by Ratikeli, "Ladies do not exhibit their passions due to shyness.

56. And when this beautiful jewel (Rohiṇī) has been born in your country (kingdom), it is yours. Therefore you bring this jewel of a lady into your female apartments."

57. Then the lord of the earth (king) says, "I could do just that, but I feel ashamed before the citizens. Therefore think of another way."

58. Then Ratikeli says,"O lord! Become the guest of the lady, whose husband has gone to a far off country, and stay there in the night and enjoy pleasures with her."

59. "O friend! you have thought of a good way." In this manner, having praised Ratikeli, the king passed the rest of the day with difficulty by exchanging tales with his friend.

60. After that when there was thick darkness, wearing a long dark cloak so that he could not be seen, the king with Ratikeli,

61. Went out speedily, leaving his body guards and relatives behind, with a sword in hand which could destroy the enemy and which was ornamented with reddish colour like blood.

62. Then the king reached the door of the residence of Rohiṇī. He entered it (without Ratikeli) slowly, slowly, like a thief full of fear.

63. On seeing the king entering (the door), the male cat thought that he was a thief and began to cry in a loud voice.

64. When the mynah bird, becoming nervous on hearing the voice of the male cat, saw him, it realized that he was King Nanda and not a thief.

65. "There is something not proper in the king's coming here, for the king is nervous. He can't possibly be here to steal; therefore definitely he must be in search of love.

66. It is not proper for anyone to come alone at night to the house of a lonely woman, and surely it is even odder for the king to come like this. Then what has he come for? There is something not quite right here.

67. Should I make noise now too? or shall I wait and see what the king will do? If he tries to outrage the modesty of my mother (Rohiṇī) then I shall save her."

68. Then thinking like this, the mynah bird became still. After this, on seeing the king, Rohiṇī began to think like this.

69. "This King Nanda has definitely come to outrage my modesty. In what way now can I preserve my chastity?"

70. The king nervously sat on one portion of Rohiṇī's cot, just as she was thinking these things.

71. Then immediately Rohiṇī rose (from her cot) and sat on the floor. Then the king said these things to her in sweet words,

72. "O! Fawn-eyed lady! I, whose heart has been stolen by you, am always lost in thought of you. Or have you now come to rescue me from these burning fires of love?

73. But, cruel one! you have risen (from the cot) and sat on the floor. Such behaviour would be unseemly, even when some unimportant guest had come.

74. Is it not proper to honour the king, when he has come on his own, with affection in his heart, by offering him a seat and talking with him, at least?

75. Therefore, O beautiful one! Please sit on this cot and soothe me, with the cool water of your contact, for I am burning with the intense heat of Love."

76. After hearing this talk Rohiṇī says, "O king! For persons like you, who have been born in noble families, this type of behaviour is not proper.

77. O lord! you always give advice to other persons engaged in vices. But who is there to give advice to you when you (yourself) are indulging in vice?

78. If a gentleman king, who is expert in polity, forsakes (his) propriety of conduct, then who can blame common people for indulging in such actions? It has also been said,

79. 'Where a scholarly person leaves the path of noblemen and treads on the wrong path then it is useless to weep at the top of the voice, uttering 'ha ha' as if in a forest, with no one to hear.'

80. And another thing is that for all persons the king is like a father. Therefore never mind talking about this type of vicious action, it is not proper (for him)even to think about it.

81. O king! For women who are full of pus, impurity, fat, flesh and blood, why do you perform this improper act which is like a blemish on your noble family?

82. Even today the fame of Rāvaṇa is tarnished because of his kidnapping Sītā; (similarly) you might have momentary pleasure, but your fame would be tarnished in all the three worlds and your wisdom would be diminished.

83. And moreover, in youth, which is restlessly swift like the ripples of the water of a river, in the sweet love which is as fleeting as the water bubbles raised by a ship wrecked by the blows of the wind (and),

84. O king! In this swift life which is like the flashing of lightning in a fresh group of clouds, it is in no way proper for gentlemen like you to perform such an act.

85. O king! For the living beings severe results accrue for even small, improper acts performed under the control of passion.

86. Even after this if some improper task is performed in any way by a noble person, then the heart of that gentleman continues to burn. Therefore it has been said.

87. 'Improper tasks, performed without thinking by a noble person due to the intoxication of youth continue to give pain to the heart when he ripens into old age.'

88. Therefore, O king! You should abandon the idea of committing such an improper act in this purposeless world where results appear for a moment and are destroyed instantly."

89. When the tomcat, suspecting a thief, screeches again and again in a loud voice, then the mynah bird says these words,

90. "O tomcat! why do you scream? He is king Nanda and not a thief. Poison has been formed in nectar; the one who should have protected us now causes us harm."

91. After hearing the noble words of Rohiṇī and the verse of the mynah bird, the king with eyes full of tears of remorse thinks like this,

92. "See! They, who do not know the essential virtues, have virtues like this and I, who know the code of conduct (Śāstras) have such a sinful character.

93. It is regrettable that I, a person with improper conduct, a great sinner, came to perform an improper act at the house of this illustrious, pure and virtuous Rohiṇī!

94. This wretched Rohiṇī is commendable, who knows about the proper and improper actions of living beings but I, a person without virtuous results, am not noble."

95. Thinking like this, that king, rising suddenly, becoming immensely emotional and touching his head to the floor, touches the lotus-like feet of Rohiṇī.

96. And says, "O extremely virtuous one! I have been saved from remaining in the well of darkness of intense spiritual ignorance ('Moha') by your noble words.

97. Whatever evil words have been uttered by me in the madness of youth, kindly forgive by showing me kindness."

98. In this way, after asking for forgiveness and again touching her lotus-like feet with devotion, that king returned to his palace with his friend Ratikeli, (who had stayed outside Rohiṇī's house and was waiting for him).

99. Meditating in his heart on the sensible words of that Rohiṇī and enjoying the pleasure of sleep, the king woke up in the morning.

100. Then being extremely happy from the chastity and other virtues of Rohiṇī, the king, in order to bring to light the virtuous qualities of Rohiṇī, along with Ratikeli

101. Intrigues like this, "O, O, nobles, ministers! Some goddess appearing before me in the night said this,

102. 'O, O, king ! Hear, you will soon get rid of this disease by drinking the water over which a spell has been recited by the virtuous Rohiṇī.'"

103. They then spoke this way, "O lord! We know that Rohiṇī, she is famous in the community, decorated with the ornament of chastity, the wife of the merchant Dhaṇāvaha."

104. Then they all said, "You should send this old woman named Sundarī to fetch Rohiṇī here. Why should there be opposition to a work of welfare?" After this was said,

105. Sundarī along with her retinue was sent to the residence of Rohiṇī, and she, reaching the house of Rohiṇī, brought her with courtesy and affection.

106. That Rohiṇī, behind a veil of silken cloth, her lotus-like face slightly visible, looked like the glorious beauty of the heavens with the disk of the moon shimmering behind the redness of dusk.

107. The king rose to greet her, surprising somewhat his royal court full of ministers, nobles and warriors,

108. Seating her on a throne studded with diamonds, sapphires, emeralds, pearls and rubies, he praised her in front of the citizens.

109. "O! Crown of all the noble ladies! Residence of exquisite noble religion, deeds and pleasure! Best garden for the growing of the creeper of chastity, bright as a garland of pearls.

110. On account of the influence of the virtue of ladies like yourself, the sun rises for the day and the clouds rain down pure currents of water, like strings of dazzling pearls.

111. Your name has been recommended by the deity for curing my disease. Therefore O very chaste lady, give me water from your hand to drink."

112-113. Then it was done in that manner by Rohiṇī. Getting rid of the disease, the king became healthy in body. Then honoured and followed by the king, while eulogies to her were recited by the bards, her praises sung by the women of the city, and being worshipped by the old women of the city, that Rohiṇī reached her house.

114-115. King Nanda and the citizens all returned after making obeisence to her. And on the other hand, the husband of that Rohiṇī returned after crossing the fierce ocean, which is the lord of the rivers, with much wealth that he had earned. Then after hearing about the character of his wife he was filled with joy.

116. Then that merchant, in whose heart affection arose, enjoys fascinating pleasures with his wife. In the course of time a son was born to that Rohiṇī. He was named Dhanasāra.

117. Then after that, one day, struck by a strong desire for the religious life, that Rohiṇī begins to observe penance, having renounced the world under a nun.

118. Then, dying, she was born in the form of a 'deity' in a world of the gods. After being displaced from there, Rohiṇī, who was like a deity, in time will enjoy the pleasure of liberation, 'Mukti.'

The *Mūlaśuddhiprakaraṇa*: Three Stories

Translated by Phyllis Granoff

Introduction

The *Mūlaśuddhiprakaraṇa* is heir to the tradition of didactic story telling that begins with the *Āvaśyaka* commentaries. It has much in common with the *Ākhyānakamaṇikośa* that Dr. Jain has described in his introduction to the story of Rohiṇī. The *Mūlaśuddhiprakaraṇa* was written by the monk Pradyumna Sūri in the 11th century and the stories, in a medieval vernacular and including some Sanskrit, are contained in a commentary by the monk Devacandra Sūri written in 1089-1090 A.D. I have translated three stories on *dāna*, "giving," which are particularly rich in folk motifs and also have strong links to the tradition of the courtly romance in medieval Indian literature. An excellent general introduction to stories about giving in the Jain tradition is Nalini Balbir's *Dānāṣṭakakathā*, Paris, 1982. For comments on how I translated the stories the reader is referred to my appendix to Part II, chapter 2. I take this opportunity to thank Dr. Prem Suman Jain for his helpful comments on my translation of the story of Devadhara.

The Story of Devadhara, from the *Mūlaśuddhiprakaraṇa*, pp.160-169.

There is on our very own continent of Jambudvīpa, in the land of Bharata, in the territory of Kaliṅga, a city named Kancaṇapura, which surpasses the city of the Gods in its loveliness and all of its other wonderful qualities. There reigned King Bhāmaṇḍala, who with his great valour had conquered all of his enemies. He was greatly loved by all and he surpassed even Indra, the King of the Gods, with his handsomeness and other fine qualities. And his chief queen was Kittimai, who was as obedient to his every wish as is the shadow that follows a man.

Now in this same city dwelt the merchant Sundarī, chief amongst all of its wealthy inhabitants. His wife was Sundari. Now all of the children that were born to her died. Though she did everything that she could, not a single one lived. Greatly saddened, she then thought,

"Oh what good is my life, when I have not a single living child? My life is full of suffering; surely I must have accumulated not an ounce of merit, for not a single one of my children survives.

Surely I must have stolen great jewels from someone in a past life, and so my children die now, seemingly without cause.

Evil deeds that people so happily commit turn out to bear fruits like this, so terrible to endure."

And while she was pained by such sad thoughts, her beloved friend Piyamaī, the wife of the feudatory prince Sūrapāla, who was now away in his home territory, came to see her. She said, "My goodness! Why do you seem so dejected?" Sundarī said,

"'The secret that cannot be told even to a father, mother, sister or brother, not even to a husband or a son, can always be told to a friend.'

And so, my sister, I tell you. The cause of my distress is the death of my children." Piyamaī said,

"'You must have done some harm to some living creature in a past life. That is why, no doubt, my beloved friend, you must suffer like this in this life.'

But do not grieve. My dear husband has gone to his home territory, leaving me behind. I am pregnant. When my child is born I promise that I shall give it to you."

Sundarī said, "In that case then come and stay in my house. I too am pregnant. And if by some lucky quirk we should both deliver at the same time, then that would be ideal. But we must not tell this to anyone." And her friend agreed to it all and stayed there with her in her house. And the deeds that they had each done in their past lives determined things in such a way that they both gave birth at the same time. They exchanged the dead baby for the live one. Now a few days later Piyamaī died of childbed fever. And at the appropriate time Sundarī, summoning all the merchants and other people, named the baby Devadhara. He grew up and soon turned eight years old.

Now when he had mastered all the seventy-two arts, because of some bad deed he had committed in a previous life both his mother and his father died. His entire family line was wiped out and all of their considerable wealth was lost. He suddenly found himself alone, in the grip of dire poverty. With no other way open to him to support himself, he began to work as a servant in the home of the merchant Dhanasetthi. He was given his meals there as well. Because he was well brought up and because he was a pious Jain, he went to worship in the Jain temples every day. He worshipped the Jain images and he went to the monasteries and nunneries to bow down to the monks and nuns. And so time went on until one day on some occasion or another, Saṃpayā, the wife of the merchant, gave him particularly fine food to eat. Now at that very moment,

A pair of the most excellent Jain monks arrived there. They had abandoned all attachments; they had mortified their bodies with many strict ascetic practices; they had studied all the eleven Jain texts; they had conquered that most difficult of enemies, the God of Love;

They were protected by the three protectors, watchful of mind, speech and body; they practiced the five acts of attentiveness in everything that they did, in walking, in speaking, in eating, in receiving, in excreting, so as to avoid any harm to any living creature; they were possessed of moral courage, and they regarded everyone as equal, friend and enemy alike.

And when he saw them, Devadhara, his body rippling with joy, thought, "Oh! Today I have acquired the means to do good, something that is not easily acquired.

The recipient is pure, the gift is pure, and the mind of the giver is pure. All three are propitious, because of some good act that I have done in the past. I shall make my life fruitful by giving this food to these monks."

With this thought, he went and bowed his lotus-like head at the feet of the monks and proclaimed, "Blessed Ones! Show favour to me by accepting this gift."

And the monks realized the strong faith that motivated him and said, "You give us too little, layman!" And they held back their begging bowls.

And as the monks kept saying, "More, more," he became agitated and put all that he had into their bowls.

Thinking, "Today I have fulfilled all my desires," he sat down right there, placing his plate in front of him.

At that moment the merchant, who had gone inside to worship before he took his meals, saw Devadhara there. He said to his wife Saṃpayā, "Give something to Devadhara." She said, "I gave him all sorts of wonderful things, but he has given all he had to some monks." The merchant said, "He is lucky to have done something like that. Give him some more." She said, "I don't know what you are talking about." The merchant said, "Do not grumble and complain where you ought to rejoice and encourage a good deed. For by rejoicing in a pious deed a person can share in the merit it brings. For it is said,

'Both the person who himself does what is good and the one who rejoices in the good deeds that others do obtain a good result. Consider the story you know so well of the deer who rejoiced in the gift made by the carpenter to the monk Baladeva, and who died right then and there with the monk and the carpenter and achieved the same great result as they did, a long life in heaven.'

Let us both share in the fruit of his good deed by rejoicing in what he has done. Give him something else to eat right away." And with these words he went in to worship the Gods. Saṃpayā got busy and had not yet had the chance to serve Devadhara, when he finally got mad and began to think,

"How painful is poverty, which causes good men who should command respect and pull great weight, as a mountain stands mighty and firm, to be treated in this world as if they were of no more substance than the lightest blade of grass or cotton fluff.

What use is the life of those men who are pained by the burning fires of poverty and who must ever endure contempt and scorn from others who are scarcely their equal?

It is wealth alone of all the ends of man that in this world is paramount. For with it even men who are full of faults become greatly honored in this world.

Fortunate indeed are those who have put a lasting end to all humiliation ; those men are honored in the triple world, heaven, earth and the world below, who have become monks and are freed from all sin.

But I am truly wretched. I cannot become a monk and I must therefore endure this terrible pain of being humiliated."

While he was thinking in this way the merchant came out. And he saw him sitting there, still with an empty plate. The merchant said to him, "Get up, my child! Come and eat with me." And so Devadhara got up and he ate the very best of foods with the merchant. And the time passed for Devadhara, who would acquire the wealth of a great kingdom in this very life through the power of the gift that he had given to those monks; who was devoted to honoring the Jinas and the Jain monks and nuns, and who had yet to live out the fruit of the actions that he had done in a past life and which necessitated that he yet suffer some unhappiness in this life.

Now there also lived in that city a merchant named Rayaṇasāra. His wife was Mahalacchī. And as they enjoyed together the delights of love Mahalacchī became pregnant. Now when the child was just six months in the womb the merchant passed away. And when her time came, Mahalacchī gave birth to a daughter who surpassed even the women of the Gods in beauty and was endowed with every auspicious mark. But the king took away all of her husband's wealth, leaving only a meager amount for the support of the daughter, on the grounds that the merchant had no male offspring. When the time came Mahalacchī named the girl Rāyasirī. As she grew up, her mother used the money that the king had released for her use to have her educated in all of the arts.

In time, greatly pained by the death of her husband and the loss of her wealth and much troubled, Mahalacchī died. Rāyasirī was taken by her maternal aunt whose name was Lacchī. Lacchī went out to work in the homes of the wealthy so that she might support Rāyasirī. Now Rāyasirī was a pious Jain and she worshipped the Jina images every day and honored the Jain nuns and monks.

She also constantly upbraided herself because she was unable to practice such pious acts as giving to others.

"Alas, alas! What use is this life of mine which is totally worthless and which leads to no good result either in this world or in the next! It is no better than the useless breast that hangs from the neck of a goat.

In this life so bereft of merit am I that I am eating alive my very own aunt, who is like a mother to me, making her slave for me and do such harsh tasks.

And the next world also holds no fruit for me, since I am incapable of practicing the act of giving. Surely I have come into this world with great sins committed in another birth.

I cannot bear to eat without being able to give some food to some worthy person; my food eaten alone lacks all savour, but I have no wealth or goods that allow me to give."

And then one day her aunt received four choice sweetmeats as a gift for the work that she had done in the home of a wealthy merchant.

She said to Rāyasirī, "Sit down, my daughter, and eat. Today I brought you some fine cakes."

Now the young girl sat down and as she took the sweets, she glanced at the door. She was thinking, "Oh, if only someone would come, how fine that would be!

If I could only give these delicious things which my aunt has brought me today to some worthy person, I could fulfill all of my deepest desires and make my life one worth living."

And at that very moment fate decreed that some Jain nuns came there in search of alms. They were endowed with every virtue and had taken upon themselves that most difficult vow of chastity. Their bodies were thin from the ravages of their strict ascetic practices.

They cared the same for grass or pearls or jewels and their eyes and thoughts were concentrated only on the small space of ground before them.

And that young girl, her body rippling with joy at being given the chance to fulfill her deepest desire, her steps made unsure by her eagerness and haste,

Served those nuns with a gift of pure food in which the mind of the giver, the thing given, and the recipients were all pure and good. And as she did so, tears of joy flowed from her lotus-like eyes.

And by that gift in which the recipients were so pure and the mind of the giver so pure, she earned merit which ensured that she would have many enjoyments right in this very life. And that good deed was even further increased by the delight that she took in it, as she said to herself again and again, "Lucky am I! Lucky am I, for I have done such a righteous act." And her aunt too praised her, saying, "Lucky indeed is she, for though but a child she has done such a righteous act."

Now time passed and Lacchī found that she could no longer support the girl and so she gave her to the Jain nun Suvvaya, with these words, "Blessed One! I can no longer support this child. If it pleases you, then accept her for the Faith." The nun agreed. And so Lacchī left the child behind and went back home. When it came time to eat the nun said to the girl, "Daughter! Eat." She answered, "Blessed One! How can I, still a householder, eat this food that the nuns have brought with so much pain. For it is winter and they must be bitterly stung by the harsh cold winds as they go on their begging rounds." The nun said, "Daughter! When the right time comes I shall ordain you as a nun. Now you must eat." And so Rāyasirī ate. And when the nun saw how devoted Rāyasirī was to serving them, she asked the demi-goddess Kaṇṇapisāiyā, whom she commanded by means of a magic spell, "Is this girl worthy to be a nun or not?" The demi-goddess said, "Do not ordain her yet."

The nun, thinking that she would ask the demi-goddess again some time later, remained silent until the hot season had come upon them. Then one day Rāyasirī saw the nuns coming back from their begging rounds. They were roasted by the fierce rays of the sun; sweat was dripping from all over their bodies; they were suffering from hunger and thirst and they were burdened with their bowls of food and drink. And when she saw them Rāyasirī began to say, "Blessed One! I fear that I do our Faith great dishonour if I, still a householder, were to partake of the food and drink that these noble nuns have brought with such great pain. Please ordain me at once." The nun then said, "Be patient. For your propitious moment will come as soon as the rainy season starts, on the eleventh day of the bright fortnight of the month Phālguna." And only after she promised this did she then ask the demi-goddess. The demi-goddess told her, "She still has many fruits of her deeds to enjoy, which all entail that she should experience great pleasures."

The nun, thinking, "She will show great devotion to the images of the Jinas and the Jain monks and nuns," remained silent until the rainy season was upon them. The rains began to fall. Knowing that Rāyasirī had not had any change of heart, she then asked the demi-goddess once more, "What is the extent of her good deeds in the past that now entail that she must enjoy sensual pleasures?" The demi-goddess said, "She will be the chief queen of five hundred and five queens. And she will enjoy great sensual pleasures for five hundred years." Thinking, "One day the demi-goddess will give me permission to ordain her," the nun then did nothing.

Now one day Rāyasirī was seen by Devadhara who had come to the nunnery to pay his respects to the nuns. And he asked the nun, "Why have you not yet ordained this girl?" The nun answered, "She is not fit to be ordained." "In that case, then why do you feed and support someone who is a lay person?" She replied, "Because she will bring great honour to our Faith and do much to further its cause." He asked, "In what way?" She said, "I cannot tell you anymore." And so Devadhara made the vow to give up eating and die by starvation if the nun would not tell him all that she knew. And so the nun did tell him. And Devadhara thought to himself, "Oh! What wondrous things can happen from a person's own actions! This girl, born in a family of merchants, is to become such a magnificent, rich queen and have such royal splendour! Having enjoyed that royal splendour, I have no doubt that she will then suffer some terrible rebirth. I shall marry her so that she will neither obtain royal splendour nor be forced to suffer a bad rebirth." And with this in mind he said to the nun, "Blessed One! Why don't I marry her?" And she put her hands over both her ears, "Devotee! Why do you ask such a thing, as if you knew no better? We must not even speak of such things." Devadhara said, "Forgive me, I forgot myself. I meant no harm."

But then he went to see Lacchī. Very politely, he said, "Mother, give Rāyasirī to me." She said, "Son! I have already given her to the nuns." He told her, "But they will not ordain her as a nun." She asked, "And how do you know that?" He said, "They told me themselves." Lacchī said, "In that case, then, I shall ask them myself." He said, "Go ahead, but you must not then give her to anyone else." And so Lacchī asked the nun, "Is it true that you are not going to ordain Rāyasirī?" The nun said, "It is true." And then Lacchī thought, "Although he comes from a poor family Devadhara is a good young man. He is a believer in the Jain Faith and the son of a pious man. No wealthy man is going to take this girl from me, a simple servant who earns her keep by working in the homes of other people. And he does seem to want her very much." And with this in mind she gave Rāyasirī to Devadhara. And the deeds that they had done in the past determined that the day for their wedding was fixed as the eleventh day of the bright half of the month of Phālguna. But as the wedding preparations began Rāyasirī had her own thoughts.

"If I had not done some bad deed in the past which now obstructed my way, if I were not so without merit, then, today my relatives and other devoted Jains would be getting ready all my clothes so that, with my resolve firm, I might begin to undertake a life of difficult restraints." So she thought and was anxious and impatient as they began to ready her wardrobe.

And on the very day of the wedding, as they bathed her and anointed her body with fragrant substances, she thought, "Today they would be celebrating in honour of my going forth from the life of a householder to become a nun.

Surrounded by all of my relatives, adorned with beautiful ornaments, I would be standing now in the temple of the Jinas, as drums resound, marking the auspicious occasion."

And sitting in the temple devoted to the goddess, she thought, "Having circumambulated the images of the Jinas, I would then bow down to the Jinas with my teacher.

And in the presence of all the Jain community, my teachers would give my robes to me, and my dust-brush, and all the other things that a nun must carry."

And as they painted her hands with auspicious designs, she thought, "Ah, my soul! This is the moment when you, following the words of their teachers, should be taking your holy vows."

As she walked around the wedding pavilion she reflected, "And this would be the moment when I would circle round the entire gathering in reverence, while the community of the faithful sprinkled powder on me.

And then, having been honored by all present, I would listen in respect, deeply moved, to the religious instructions delivered by my teachers.

Alas, my soul, unfortunate soul! Why is that strong desire of yours to grasp firmly the treasure of restraining the senses thwarted by some obstructing past deed, now showing its might, as if by some terrible invisible goblin?"

And as she thought these things she was joined to Devadhara in marriage with all the proper ceremony. And Devadhara then told the merchant, "Father! Please give us some place to live." And so the merchant gave him a small grass hut within the boundaries of his compound. Devadhara then took Rāyasirī there. And she was totally devoted to her husband and deeply in love with him.

Now while Devadhara was enjoying the pleasures of love there with her, the merchant thought to himself, "This Devadhara is like a son to me; he is a noble man; a faithful Jain; he is courageous and high-minded and has so many fine qualities. I should allow him to carry out some trade. I shall see how clever he is. If he proves himself worthy, well then, I shall do what I see fit." And with this in mind he said to Devadhara, "Son! Take some goods from me and carry on some trade with vegetables and plants." And Devadhara did exactly as he was told. He earned his keep, at least, until the rainy season came upon them.

And then he said to his wife, "Get me some bricks from somewhere so I can cover over this veranda which is about to collapse. I don't want the roof to fall down on the children." And she did exactly as she was told. And as he was fixing the roof and removing some of the old crumbling bricks he discovered five hundred gold coins. Without showing them to his wife he hid them in a pot. And when he was done with his task he went alone to the market, and with one of the coins he bought her some clothes and jewelry. She said, "My beloved! How could you have afforded this?" He said, "I borrowed one hundred coins from some good man." She said, "In that case, then, I don't need any presents." He said, "Do not be afraid. My friend is a wealthy man and very kind. It was a trifling sum for him." And so she accepted the gifts. And he continued to carry on his business and in no time at all became lord of a thousand gold pieces.

Now one day Rāyasirī said to him, "Jains are not allowed to dig dirt in the rainy season. Bring me some kind of a shovel so that I can gather some earth." But he brought a heavy spade from the merchant's house. She said, "I can't dig with this." He told her, "When no one is around, just at dawn, I shall do the digging myself. You bring a sack and a basket so that I can fill the sack with earth. I too am embarrassed to be seen carrying dirt." And she did exactly as she was told. As soon as he struck the earth with the spade and broke ground he beheld a treasure of jewels worth hundreds of thousands of dollars. He said, "Beloved! Quick! Let's get away from this place." And when she asked, "But why?," he said, "My love, this will be the end of us!" She said, "This is not the end for us. This is not the God of Death. It is the Goddess of Fortune herself, come to us on account of the many wonderful great deeds that you have done in the past." He said, "But should the king come to know of it we will get into serious trouble, for all buried treasure belongs to the king." Now Rāyasirī thought , "Clearly he does not trust me," and so she said, "No one will hear of it from me. Go now, take what your own good fortune has brought you. Hurry, before someone comes." And so, breaking open with the spade the seal of the casket in which the jewels lay, he quickly stuffed the jewels and riches into his sack. He put the sack inside the basket and then carefully placed dirt on top of it. The two of them then went back home. They hid the treasure in a corner of their hut. But one day Rāyasirī told her husband, "These jewels are no better than stones.

Oh my best beloved! Wealth that is not used for making images of the Jinas, for making temples, for worshipping the images, bathing them and carrying out festivals, is no better than worthless stones.

Wealth that is not given to Jain monks and nuns for food, begging bowls, robes, beds, seats, housing, medicines and other basic needs, is no better than worthless stones.

Beloved! Wealth that is not used to give food, betel, seats and clothes to our fellow Jains, to me, is no better than clumps of earth.

My Lord! Wealth that is not used for its owner's personal delight, nor to help his friends, nor to aid those who are poor and in need, why that is no better than dust.

And so I ask you, why do we wrongly hang on to this wealth?" He said, "What else can we do under the circumstances?" She said, "Marry the merchant's daughter, Kamalasirī. And then everything will be as we wish. He hastily interjected, "But I don't need anyone but you." She said, "My Lord! You must consider what will lead to good results and what will lead to bad results and then do what will lead to a good end." He said, "Well, in that case, if you insist, then tell me, how shall I win her over?" Rāyasirī said, "You already know her. Now you must win her over with gifts of fruits and such. I shall do the same by giving her jewelry. For it is said,

'One should win the heart of a child with food and drink, of a young maiden with jewelry, of a whore with constant attendance, and of an old lady with abject servitude.'

Now she is both somewhat of a child and somewhat of a young maiden. And so she can be won over in this way." Devadhara then gave his consent, "You are surely right," he said, and from that day on he began to give Kamalasirī fruits and things every day. And she began to follow Devadhara around and followed him right back into his home. Rāyasirī then gave her some jewelry to wear every day. Now when she got back to her own home her mother asked her, "Who gave you these fruits? Who gave you this jewelry to wear?" She said, "Devadhara gave me the fruits and Rāyasirī put the jewelry on me." At this her mother asked her once more, "Who is Devadhara? Who is that woman?" She said, "Devadhara is the man who comes to our house everyday and the woman is his wife."

Now one day the mother saw her daughter following Devadhara all around and laughed at her. "My child! See how you stick to him, like glue! What, are you going to get yourself hitched to him for life?" Kamalasirī said, "But did you doubt that? If you give me to anyone else then I will kill myself." The mother quickly retorted, "Foolish girl! He already has a wife." Kamalasirī said, "She is like my elder sister. I don't want any other husband, not even the richest man in the world." Seeing that her daughter was madly in love with Devadhara, Saṃpayā told the merchant exactly what had happened. He said,

"My beloved! If our child is so insistent then let her marry him. For Devadhara is both handsome and virtuous. And I can help him to get rid of his poverty. But first I must win over his wife." And for her part Saṃpayā simply agreed with what her husband had said. And so the merchant instructed Devadhara, "My son! Let me see your wife." And Devadhara, humbly assenting, summoned Rāyasirī. She came out and fell at the feet of the merchant. The merchant took her on his lap, blessing her with the words, "May you never be a widow." And when he saw her beauty and her loveliness, which far surpassed the beauty and the loveliness of any other woman, the merchant Dhanna thought,

"Why would this man who shares the embrace of a woman of such beauty, a woman who is so devoted to him and so in love with him, want my daughter?

How could this Devadhara, who can always make love to this woman, who is like a flowing river of the divine nectar of womanly beauty, take pleasure in my daughter, pretty though she is?

And if this woman should turn against her, how could my daughter ever be happy? Ah, my daughter is foolish to desire this man for her husband.

But what can I do? I must first try to see what they really feel. Then I will do what I think is necessary." And with this in mind he said to Rāyasirī, "My child! My daughter Kamalasirī is deeply in love with your husband. If you have no objection then I shall give her to him." Rāyasirī said, "Father! I am delighted. Dear father, fulfill my little sister's wishes." The merchant said, "My daughter! In that case then I give Kamalasirī into your care. From now on you must look after her." Rāyasirī quickly said, "Father! I am honored." And then he turned to Devadhara, "My son! Take in marriage Kamalasirī, who loves you deeply." Devadhara humbly assented, "Father! As you command me so shall I do." And so the merchant made a wedding with all due pomp and splendour. He gave to Rāyasirī and Kamalasirī exactly the same jewelry. He set his son-in-law up in business and Devadhara earned much money. He used the wealth he had found earlier to build Jain temples and to perform other pious acts.

Now Kamalasirī had a friend named Paumasirī, who was the daughter of the king's minister Maisāgara. She had come to the wedding and when she saw Devadhara she immediately vowed before all her own girl friends,

"If that Devadhara by some act of fate can be brought to marry me, then and then alone will I enjoy worldly pleasures. Otherwise I renounce the world right here and now, in this very birth."

And when her friends heard that vow of hers they told her mother Piyaṅgasundarī at once. And she told the minister Maisāgara. He in turn summoned the merchant and respectfully gave Paumasirī to Devadhara. Devadhara married her with great ceremony. And the minister gave to all three women exactly the same jewelry.

From then on the minister often brought Devadhara to the king to pay his respects. The king showed him great honour and offered him the finest seats to sit upon. And one day, while the king was himself being charmed by Devadhara's good looks and his many virtues, the queen Kittimai, realizing that Devadhara was a good match for their own daughter Devasirī, dressed Devasirī up in all her finery and her jewels and sent her to bow down to the feet of her father. The king lifted her onto his lap. And as he looked her over it suddenly came to him that she had reached the age for marriage. And no sooner had he turned his thoughts to finding a suitable husband for her, than he noticed how Devasirī was looking again and again at Devadhara out of the corner of her eyes, with a glance that revealed that she had fallen in love with him, her bright pupils darting back and forth. At this the king thought, "Oh! She seems indeed to be smitten with this fellow. And he is both handsome and virtuous. Let her enjoy the pleasures of wedded bliss with him." He then said to Maisāgara, "I give our very own Devasirī to your son-in-law. As the ocean is filled with jewels, so is she filled with virtues." The minister replied, "I am honored." And so the king made a splendid wedding, sparing no expense. He gave to all four women exactly the same jewelry. And he gave to Devadhara the large territory that bordered the domains of his vassal Narakesari, and which was the most important of all the territories. And Devadhara lived indeed like a God, enjoying the pleasures of love with Rāyasirī and his other four wives, ensconced in a seven-storied palace that was filled with all sorts of costly things that the king had given him.

Now King Narakesari came to hear that the territory bordering his own had been given by the king to his own son-in-law, a mere merchant. And so, burning with such rage that the very flames of anger seemed to leap from his mouth as he spoke, he told his own servants, "See with what contempt the king Bhāmaṇḍala treats us! He has given the task of protecting our flanks to a veritable barbarian. Let us raid his territory and teach the king a lesson so that he will never do anything like that again." And as soon as he spoke they raided

Devadhara's territory and sent word to King Bhāmaṇḍala that they had done so. And no sooner did he get the news, than furious with this insult delivered him, the king caused the drums to beat to announce the departure of his own army. And so the king's army set out,

Swift as the wind, swift as the mind, gold ornaments flashing like bursts of lightning, rut dripping like rain from their temples, the elephants went forward like new-formed rain clouds.

Filling the world with their neighing, kicking up heaps of dust as their sharp hooves dug into the earth, making terrifying noises from their mouths, gums drawn back, the horses went forward.

Having proved their prowess many a time by slaying their proud and wicked enemies, sauntering, shouting, the foot soldiers went forward.

The very heavens seemed rent asunder with the trumpeting of the elephants, the clanking of the chariots, the neighing of the horses, the shouts of the warriors and the beats of all the war drums.

And when he heard this terrible noise, like the roar of the turbulent mighty ocean, Devadhara asked his chamberlain,

"Are the very heavens being rent asunder? Has the earth split open? Are the mountains tumbling down? Or is this the very end of the world? Tell me sir, what is this noise?"

And the chamberlain, who knew exactly what was going on, told him in great detail about everything that had happened. At once Devadhara spoke up. And as he spoke his lips quivered in anger at the insult he had been dealt; his forehead was marked by three fierce lines of a frown, and his hand reached again and again for his sword. "Hurry, make ready my elephant so that I may follow my father-in-law into battle." And his men did exactly as he commanded. Devadhara mounted his war elephant and rode to the king. He was freshly bathed and his body had been anointed with fragrant substances; he was adorned with garlands of white flowers and wearing his most costly clothes; his crown was surrounded by lotuses with fine long stalks; and he carried with him his sharp sword that was like the tongue of the God of Death. When the king saw him coming he thought to himself, "Lucky am I to have such a fine son-in-law. Or perhaps it is the good fortune of Devasirī that she has found such a fine husband." And as he was thinking this, Devadhara threw himself at his feet and proclaimed, "King! Lions do not attack jackals, forgetting about maddened elephants that are their more worthy foes. And so I beg you, command me so that I may pacify this disobedient vassal Narakesari. Besides, it was because he thought of me as a mere merchant that he dared to attack my territory. And so, O King, it seems only fitting that it is I who should go there." The king, his body rippling with joy, said to him, "My son! Do not ask that of me. Truly I shall not feel satisfied if I do not go out against Narakesari myself." And Devadhara, realizing how the king felt, was silent. But a few moments later he asked again for permission to proceed, "O King! Command me!" The king replied, "Ask for what you wish." He said, "In that case I wish to proceed in the vanguard against Narakesari." The king said, "My son, I do not like what you ask. I cannot bear the thought of being without you even for a short time and we are yet hundreds of miles away from Narakesari." Devadhara told him, "Each day I shall come back by some swift conveyance and bow down to the king's feet." And when he realized that Devadhara was not to be dissuaded the king gave him permission to go. Devadhara left at once and soon reached the border of Narakesari's territory.

His enemy, having learnt form spies that he had arrived, bellowed, "Seize that barbarian who does not know how powerful I am! "And as soon as he had uttered these words his army stood armed and ready. And it was a mighty army indeed that went forth from Narakesari's domains. And when they saw it coming Devadhara's soldiers armed themselves at once. And there ensued a terrible battle.

Here men's heads lay cut off by sharp swords; there the headless corpses of warriors, jerking violently, put on a dancing show;

Here lay pearls fallen from the temples of elephants that had been torn open with sharp lances; there heaps of chariots that had been smashed to smithereens with strong maces lay clanking against each other;

Here she-goblins danced, drunk on blood; there jackals howled like ghouls, feeding on human entrails and flesh;

Here the sky was covered with streams of sharp arrows shot from taut bow-strings; there sparks shot out as weapons clashed and clanged together;

Here horses, elephants, and chariots roamed aimlessly, no longer carrying riders; there hosts of gods showered flowers, pleased by the warriors' brave acts;

Here ghosts laughed and hooted, each more terrible in form than the next; there terrifying demons brandished sharp cutting tools in their busy hands;

And as this terrible battle raged Devadhara, the prince, mounted on his elephant, shouted, "Lead my elephant towards Narakesari's elephant."

And taking up the command, the skillful elephant driver led Devadhara's elephant so close to Narakesari's mount that the two beasts could touch each other with their tusks.

And then Devadhara jumped onto the back of Narakesari's elephant and taunted him, "Here I am, king, your barbarian! Stand tall now!

Take hold of your weapon now! You will see what prowess even a merchant's son can have!" And the king, thinking that such a lowly foe was beneath him, yet had no choice and took hold of his magnificent sword.

And each blow that the impatient king levelled Devadhara skillfully warded off. And he seized the king and he was filled with pride at his own act.

And Devadhara's ministers sent word with a swift messenger to king Bhāmaṇḍala to inform him that Devadhara had met the enemy army. And he quickly rode out with his best soldiers. The prince Devadhara handed Narakesari over to him. Filled with joy the king embraced the prince and then released Narakesari from his bonds. He honored him as was his due and then told him, "You should continue to rule your own lands as a servant of this prince." And Narakesari, giving to the prince his own daughter Mittasirī, too full of pride to serve under the prince, abandoned his kingdom and became a monk under the guidance of a good teacher. The king and the prince Devadhara crowned Narakesari's son as king and then went back to their own city.

The king, realizing that the moment had come, then said to all his sons, "My sons! If you agree then I will crown your brother-in-law as king." They all said, "Do so. Whatever you wish is also our desire." And so he informed all his ministers and chief councilors and on an auspicious moment the prince Devadhara was made king of both kingdoms, his own and the kingdom of Bhāmaṇḍala. And King Bhāmaṇḍala became a Jain monk and looked after the matter of his own spiritual welfare.

Now Narakesari's loyal retainers gave to King Devadhara their own daughters, two hundred and fifty of them, and many precious gifts. And his other vassal kings did the same. And so he came to have five hundred and five queens and he made Rāyasirī the chief queen amongst them all. She enjoyed great wealth and splendour. And Devadhara the king became a great king, lord over a vast territory, his commands honored by all.

And one day, recalling their previous poverty, the king and the queen began to carry out pious acts to further the Jain Faith. They had Jain temples built; they had Jain images consecrated; they had the images bathed, anointed and properly worshipped; they sponsored great religious festivals; they proclaimed that no one in their kingdom should ever take the life of any creature; they had the chariots belonging to the temples led around the city with the sacred images in them; they gave to the poor and miserable, gifts of compassion; they did honour to fellow Jains; they gave great gifts to the Jain nuns and monks, gifts of food and other necessities; they had books copied and properly worshipped; they listened to the words of the Jinas; they themselves observed the required daily duties of pious Jains; they fasted on the fast days; what more need I say? They spent their time doing just about everything conceivable that would further the cause of the Jain Faith.

Now one day there came the Blessed Jasabhaddasūri, who was so wise he was almost omniscient. The king and his queen went to pay their respects to the monk. They bowed down to him, full of true devotion. They sat down on the ground, making sure that there were no living creatures there that they would crush. The Blessed one began his discourse:

"Wealth is by nature fickle; this miserable body is ever subject to the ravages of old age and sickness. Love is like a dream. And so I say put your efforts into the practice of religion.

And in their best of teachings the Jinas have likened the difference between the life of a householder and the life of a monk to the difference between a mountain of gold and a mustard seed.

The happiness that monks know, having renounced all pleasures of the senses, and being free from pain caused by others, cannot be experienced even by the emperor of the entire world.

This religious practice which so many monks follow is like a thunder bolt to cleave the rock that is the accumulated effects of all of a person's past deeds, evil, heavy, accumulated over many a lifetime.

Someone who has been a monk even for just one day is honored by kings and queens alike. Behold the power of the religious life, O king!

A soul having been a monk even for a day, intently devoted to the monastic life, may not get absolute release, it is true, but for sure he becomes a god in heaven.

Practicing austerities brings even greater merit than building the most magnificent of temples, with thousands of pillars, all of gold, silver and gemstones.

And so, O king, abandon the householder's life, which is the abode of all suffering. Follow the course that monks follow, the one that destroys the cycle of rebirths."

And when he heard these words the king Devadhara indeed felt a desire to renounce the world. He said, "Blessed One! As soon as I crown Rāyasirī's son Gunahara as king I shall accept the course that you describe. But I have one small request. Tell me, why did I and my queen have to suffer the loss of our parents when we were just children? Why were we oppressed by such terrible poverty?" The Blessed One said, "Listen, great king.

Just one birth ago you were born to a good family in the village of Nandivaddhaṇa. Your name was Kulavaddhaṇa. And your queen was then also your wife; her name was Santimaī. By nature both of you had few faults, were little given to anger and other evil passions, and were devoted to giving to others. Now one day two Jain monks in the course of their wanderings chanced to come to your house. Seeing them you said to your wife, 'Beloved! Just look at these monks. They never give anything to anyone and have abandoned their duties to take care of their immediate family, their friends and their other relatives. What use are any of the religious austerities they do anyway, since they ignore their own people?' Santimaī said, 'My lord! What you say is absolutely true. There can be no doubt that what you say is just so.' That is the deed that you both did that led later to your own loss of your relatives."

Now there was also in that village a rich Jain temple. A certain wealthy Jain layman, Jinadeva by name, was in charge of looking after the properties of the temple. Now one day you lost a quarrel with Jinadeva, which prompted the angry Santimaī to say, "Lord! That temple servant is blinded with all that wealth that belongs to the temple as sure as if he was drunk with wine. And so he disregards everyone and everything. As far as I am concerned, we'd all be better off if all the wealth belonging to the temple just disappeared. "And you said, "Beloved! That would suit me just fine." And with those bad thoughts you both insured that you would suffer poverty. And you died without repenting your bad deeds and were reborn as you now are."

When they heard this account they both remembered their former births. And they said, "Your account is absolutely true. We remember everything now with the power to recollect our past lives. But what deed did we do then that enabled us to acquire this kingdom?" The Blessed One said, "That you gave food with reverence to Jain monks and nuns in this birth of yours resulted in your enjoying the kingdom, right in this very same life. As the sacred texts say,

'Some deeds done in this birth give their fruit in this very same birth; some deeds done in this birth give their fruit in a future rebirth. Some deeds done in a different birth give their fruit in this birth; some deeds done in a different birth give their fruit in a different birth.'

And so you must always endeavour to do good deeds." The king and his wife, agreeing, went back to their palace. Installing the prince on the throne, with great splendour the king and the queen renounced this world. They fulfilled the rest of their ordained days by living a pure life, and fasting to death they attained rebirth as gods. When they fall from heaven they will be reborn in the land of Mahāvideha where they will achieve final liberation.

The Story of Devadiṇṇa, from the *Mūlaśuddhiprakaraṇa*, pp. 169-179.

There is on our very own continent of Jambudvīpa, in the land of Bharata, a city named Tihuyaṇapura, "The City of the Triple World," which was indeed an ornament to the Triple World of Heaven, Earth and the Nether World. There reigned King Tihuyaṇasehara, "The Best in the Triple World," who was a veritable sun to chase away the deep darkness of his stalwart enemies. And foremost amongst the women in his harem was Tihuyaṇā, his queen. And from her womb came forth the prince Tihuṇahadatta, "Gift to the Triple World."

Now in this very city there also lived a merchant named Sumaī, "The Clever," who was the leader of all the eighteen minor and major guilds of merchants, who had fathomed the meaning of that best of all religious doctrines, the Jain doctrine, which teaches such things as the distinction between living beings and insentient matter. And this merchant was greatly honored by the king. And he had a wife named Candappahā, "Moonlight," who by her beauty surpassed all of the heavenly damsels. And she and the queen Tihuyaṇā were devoted friends. One day the prince Tihuyaṇādatta, along with his retinue, went to see Candappahā, whom he called "auntie." She bathed him tenderly, massaged him with fragrant ointments, adorned him with jewels and then sat him on her lap. She placed her lips to his head and breathed in gently, and as she did this she thought,

"How fortunate is my friend and what good deeds she must have once done! Her life is fulfilled, she has accomplished her goal in having such a wonderful son!

Many are the women who have fulfilled themselves in this world, bantering softly to their handsome children, the fruit of their very own wombs. And sitting there on their laps, the children coo back to them, showering them with playful words of love.

But I am the most miserable of women, for I do not have even one child."

And as this thought ran through her mind she let out a deep sigh and sent the prince back to his own home.

Now when the prince got home the queen asked, "Who put all these jewels on the prince?" His servants told her, "Your friend. But you must quickly sprinkle the prince with salt and say the right prayers so that no harm will come to him, for she let out a deep sigh right over the prince." The queen said, "Don't talk such nonsense. Her sigh will be like a blessing for the prince." At this the servants fell silent. And the queen thought, "Now why did she let out a sigh when she saw the prince? Oh, I know. She has no child, poor thing. Now what kind of friend would I be if I did not give her my own child and fulfill her deepest wish?" And as she was pouring over this thought the king entered. He asked, "Queen, how is it that you seem to be disturbed by something?" And so she told him everything that had happened. He said, "If that is the case, then do not be distressed. I shall find some means by which your friend will get a child." The queen said, "My Lord, your favour is great."

The next day the king told the merchant, "You have no son. You must propitiate my clan deity, the Goddess Tihuyaṇādevi, in order to gain a child. She has great powers and when worshipped grants whatever she is asked." The merchant then said, "King! What good is it if my son is then taken away as a result of some bad deed that I have committed in a previous life?" The king replied, "Never mind, even if that is so you must do as I insist." Considering in his mind that this was tantamount to an order from the king, the merchant went back home. He told Candappahā what had happened. She said, "My lord! If you do that you will insult the true faith, for we are Jains." Sumaī said, "Beloved! If I do it as an order of the king, then there can be no insult to my faith." And so the very next day the merchant, taking with him all the things that he needed to worship the goddess, went to the temple of Tihuyaṇādevi along with his wife. There they had the image of the Goddess bathed, anointed and worshipped, and when that was done the merchant addressed the Goddess, "O Blessed One! The king said that I should ask you for a son. So, give me a son." At this the Goddess thought, "He surely does not seem very enthusiastic about all this! But for the sake of my own reputation I cannot afford not to show myself to him." With this the Goddess said, "Sir! You will have a son." He said, "How do I know?" And thinking, "I shall cause that unenthusiastic fellow a bit of trouble," the Goddess said again, "When your child enters your wife's womb she will see this dream: she will go to a Jain temple to worship and she will behold the temple falling." The merchant, thinking, "Some harm is about to be befall the Jain faith," was indeed troubled in mind as he went home that day.

Then one day his wife did see that dream that the Goddess had foretold. When she woke up she said to her husband, "Lord, I saw that dream, but it was a little different. When I had taken all the things for my worship and was entering the Jain temple I did see it falling, and as I feared that it would fall right on top of me I kept my eyes fixed upward as I worshipped the Jina. But then once I got outside the temple I could see that it was exactly as it had always been, only where there had been but one flag there were now five splendid flags. And I was filled with joy as I woke up. Tell me, what do you think?" He said, "Beloved! This dream indicates that at first there will be some difficulty, but that in the end everything will turn out just fine. And so I think that you will have a son. For a time he will suffer misfortune, but afterwards he will acquire great wealth." And she too agreed that such was to be the case and she wore the necessary amulets. All her desires fulfilled, when her time came she gave birth to a son who was handsome, his every limb just perfect. And the merchant was given this great news by her maidservant named Suhankarā, "The Bringer of Joy." He gave the maid-servant a handsome gift and made a great party in honour of his son's birth. And there,

"The drums beat with a great thundering sound. Courtesans danced, wealth was distributed to all, with no one left out, and the leading citizens came to offer their congratulations.

All manner of rites and rituals were carried out to perfection and the relatives were all feted and honored. Prisoners were freed from their chains and the most excellent Jain monks were offered the proper alms.

The Jain images were worshipped, all the relatives were respectfully treated. In truth, how can I describe this party? Why, even the king and his harem showed up!"

And so the party was held. And when the baby was twelve days old they named him Devadiṇṇa, "Gift of the Gods." He grew up and when he turned eight they handed him over to a teacher to learn the many arts. And he did grasp all of the arts.

Now one day when he did not have any lessons, he sat down where someone was discoursing on religion. And at that very moment the subject of the discourse was the duty of giving. Here is what was said:

"By a gift you can bring people under your control. With a gift even hostility can be brought to nought. Even an enemy becomes a friend with a gift. A gift destroys all of a person's troubles.

By giving a man becomes an emperor. By giving a man becomes king of the gods. By giving a man attains great glory. In time giving leads a person to great peace."

And when he heard these words he thought, "This person says that the act of giving alone is capable of warding off all harm in this world and granting peace and happiness. I should put all my efforts there." And so he gave food and other necessities to the hungry. And as he got older he began to take things from the storehouse and give them to beggars and supplicants. He worshipped the Jina images, and with great faith in his heart he gave food, clothing and begging bowls to the Jain monks and nuns. He did honour to his fellow Jains. Now one day the keeper of the storehouse, Taṇhābhibhūya, "Overcome by Greed," seeing that so much wealth was disappearing from the stores, told the merchant, "Master! Devadiṇṇa is overcome by the vice of excessive giving and is destroying a vast amount of wealth." The merchant said, "Do not stop him. Let him give what he wants. Just be sure to replace what he takes out." The other one replied, "How shall I know how much he takes?" The merchant said, "First do your measuring, then get ready what he needs and let him give it." And he did just this. As for Devadiṇṇa, he gave away everything and anything that came into his mind. And so time passed.

Now it happened that Taṇhābhibhūya had an exceptionally pretty daughter named Bālā, "Child," from his wife Muddhā, "Charming." Because she was so clever people called her Bālapaṇḍiyā, "Child-genius." One day while she was roaming Devadiṇṇa happened to see her. And as soon as he saw her he thought,

"Surely this maiden was made by God with a beauty that is not to be touched. For I have never known such loveliness in any woman that I have embraced.

I think that the creator must have taken all the loveliness from every woman to make her body. In no other way is her beauty to be explained!

Wherever this young maiden goes, herself unmoved, the young men are all astir with passion.

What else can I say? Maybe she, radiant with a fiery beauty, was even made by the God of Love himself out of his own power, like a magic herb to conquer all men.

He alone is fortunate, he alone is happy, he alone fulfills his life who kisses her beautiful face, as a bee drinks the nectar of a lotus.

What good is the life of a man who does not toss to and fro amongst her broad breasts, like a snake struck by a stick, wriggling and writhing all the while.

What else can I say? Lucky is the man who like a swan nestles in her, for she is like a divine river whose waters are the honeyed pleasures of love."

And being thus struck with desire for her he thought, "How can I get her to be mine? I know. I shall win her father over with gifts and things. For it is said,

'Whomever you wish to seize, seize first with a lure. And then greedy for more, he will do whatever you wish, good deed or bad.'

If I do not get her then I will leave this place. I must be clever and somehow make this known to her and to her father."

And so the next day he gave Taṇhābhibhūya a fine necklace. He said, "Master! What is the meaning of giving me this necklace?" The young man answered with a riddle that involved a play on the word for necklace. In one sense he merely said, "I am giving it to you; you are my servant and must accept it. Now take it and do with it what you wish." But Devadiṇṇa really had another meaning in mind; for as he gave it to Taṇhābhibhūya he announced his intention to give himself up to the girl as a thief might do to a guard, and he proclaimed that his fate was in her hands. But Taṇhābhibhūya did not understand that meaning. Still he did aṣ he was told and took the necklace. He gave it to Bālāpaṇdiyā. She asked, "Father, where did you get this necklace?" He said, "Devadiṇṇa gave it to me." Now she too had been in the throes of great passion ever since she had seen the young man. She had also noticed his intentions, and so to find out exactly what lay behind all of this she asked, "Father! And did he say anything at all to you?" He repeated exactly what Devadiṇṇa had said. At once she understood its true meaning and so she recited this verse, playing upon a like set of double meanings:

"The thief is not sent away from the palace for his act of thievery, and the necklace does not go far from the treasury, occasioning a loss of wealth. Indeed I bear this necklace on my breasts and so shall he rest there too, ever so contentedly."

The word "treasury" here can also mean "the surrounding walls of the castle." The word "necklace" means the "young man." "Not taken far" means "not cast aside, not sent away in exile," because he has stolen the wealth. Rather she will bear the "necklace," or the "young man," in her heart, and he can live there happily. This was what she really meant to imply as an answer to his words.

The father, who did not understand any of this, said nothing. She thought, "My goal can be accomplished if I am clever enough," and so she said one day to her mother, "Mother! Give me to Devadiṇṇa." Her mother said, "My child, you are always so smart. Why do you say something so foolish, as if you did not know a thing? Your father is his servant. How can you marry him? Choose someone of your own station." She said "Mother! At least try. Otherwise I swear that I shall take to my bed." And she did just so. Now Muddhā saw how deeply in love she was and so she told Candappahā what had happened. And she in turn told her husband. He said, "It is true that her father is our common servant. But I too have heard from our son's friends that he is also deeply in love with her. Let me see what our son feels and then I shall do what is right." And so the merchant just happened to recite this verse within earshot of his son, "A person should never abandon his father and friends. He should never trust his wife nor take her money and he should never lust after one of his servant maids."

Immediately realizing his father's intentions, the young man spoke up, "Father! If a weak wall is about to fall, is it better if it falls inward or towards the outside?" The merchant said, "If it falls towards the inside then none of the bricks will be destroyed. And so I suppose that is to be preferred." The young man said, "If that is the case, then why did you say what you did?" The merchant, having understood his son's feelings, made him a wedding with all due pomp and splendour. And while the happy couple were shamelessly enjoying the delights of sex and falling deeper and deeper in love with each other, one day it so happened that Bālapaṇḍiyā went out for something. And a woman, seeing her, remarked to her own companion,

"My friend! Surely this woman is the foremost of lucky women who have accumulated merit through many past lives, for she has been taken as a bride into a house that is so rich and wealthy."

The other one said,

"Oh, my friend! Don't speak so fast. To me that woman is blessed who, marrying a man whose wealth is gone, brings him great wealth and fortune."

Now when she heard these words Bālapaṇḍiyā thought, "Truly she has spoken words which require some thought. And when you think about them they do indeed seem to be true. I must send my own husband somewhere to earn money, while I remain at home devoted to pious acts, so that he many increase his great wealth." And with this thought she went home. There she saw her husband, sunk as it were, in an ocean of worry.

And when she saw him like that she asked, "My Lord! Why do you seem to be so distressed? "He said, "Beloved! I have good reason to be distressed. Today, dressed up in all my finery, surrounded by all my friends, I was seen by two men. One of them said,

'Here is one who always seems to enjoy great wealth. And he is forever giving away things, as an elephant drips juice from its temples when in rut.'

At that the second one said,

'Sir! Why do you praise him? All he does is enjoy what his father acquired, like a son enjoying his own mother!

He who can do all that this one does with wealth that he has acquired through the strength of his own arms is the one I would consider to be valiant. Anyone else is a coward.'

And so, beloved, as long as I do not go abroad and acquire wealth with the strength of my own two arms, I shall find no peace of mind."

At this she was filled with joy and she said, "My Lord! What a fine idea! For,

'He alone is fortunate, he alone is wise, he alone is learned, who wins fame through the wealth that he has acquired by the strength of his own two arms.'

My Lord! May your every wish be fulfilled. Do as you desire." And he thought, "No wife would ever say such a thing when her husband expressed a desire to go abroad. For,

'All the joys of life are gone for a woman when her husband is abroad; women enjoy the pleasures of life when their beloveds are at their beck and call.'

But she says all of this with a straight face. For sure she must have a lover. What do I care, for at least she has not tried to stop me." Determined to go, he went to his father and informed him,

"Father! Grant me leave to go. I wish to journey abroad in order to acquire wealth. I shall do many brave and valiant deeds."

His father said,

"My child! We already have so much wealth in our family that is at your disposal for whatever you wish, for giving away, for enjoying and even for frittering away if that is what you choose.

Use that wealth and stay here, free from care, for I could not bear to endure being separated from you."

Devadiṇṇa said,

"What decent man would not shudder at the thought of living off the money that his ancestors had earned?

And so I beg of you, out of your love for me, to grant me leave so that I may justly earn my fame with the wealth that I have acquired through the strength of my own two arms."

When they realized that his decision to go was so firm, his mother and father both gave him their blessings and dismissed him from their presence. When all the preparations were finally underway for his departure, his parents feared that their daughter-in-law might prevent her husband from going, and so they said to her, "Your husband seems eager to make a journey abroad." She said, "Father! And what can be unusual in my noble husband's resolve? For he has been born to parents like you two and is merely following in the footsteps of his honored ancestors who have gone before him. For it is said,

'These creatures leave their place of birth: lions, noble men, and elephants. And these creatures die where they were born: crows, cowardly men and deer.'"

When they heard these words they had the same reaction as had their son and so they remained silent. Now when the young man was ready, the merchant assigned eighty-four traders to accompany him, giving them each goods for trade. On an auspicious day, then, the young man appeared, mounted on an elephant. He distributed great wealth to those assembled and stood ready in a special pavilion erected to bless his departure. And Bālapaṇḍiyā, too, was mounted on a magnificent elephant. She was dressed in her most splendid finery and her lotus-like face was aglow with happiness. She went forward to bow down to her husband. An instant later she announced, "My Lord! Command me as you wish!" And the young man, in keeping with established custom, offered her a flavored betel leaf with some flowers. As she put the betel into her mouth she proclaimed, "My master! May I enjoy many a betel leaf that you yourself place between my lips!" And with these words she bound her hair into a tight braid, and her heart overflowing with joy, she returned to her own rooms. And as they observed her behaviour, all the townspeople were struck with doubt as they returned to the city.

And the young man, too, had his thoughts. "Strange indeed are the ways of women! No one can ever know what they are really thinking." Turning this over in his mind, he proceeded on his journey. In time he reached the harbour named Gambhiraya, "Deep," as is its description here with its many embedded and hidden meanings, puns and word plays. For there he saw the ocean and the ocean was like a magnificent elephant, like a grand palace, like a great jewel, like an excellent ascetic and like a lord of men. And what was their similarity? It was that they could all be described by just one adjective, if you are careful enough to turn the adjective this way and that. And when you do you see that the adjective means many things: the ocean was teeming with large sea creatures, while the elephant drips with ichor when in rut, the palace is abustle with pleasures, the jewel is ever desired, the ascetic is without passion and the king is forever proud. Again, it was like a cremation ground and like the Saṃkhyā school of philosophy, for they each can be described by the same adjective, read anew each time. The sea was filled with many types of shells; the cremation ground holds great terrors; and the Saṃhkyā school is made up of many great men who adhere to its tenets. In the same way it was like an excellent chariot, the sea having birds with the word "wheel" in their name, and the chariot having real wheels. It was like a temple which has a platform on which the image stands, in having a firm floor which is called by the same name. It was like an army marked by forbearance, in having many fish named by the same word that can indeed mean "forbearance." It seemed to rise up to greet him with its great waves that reached upward; it seemed to want to embrace him with its arms made up of garlands of waves. The ocean seemed to call out to him with the thunderous roar that the creatures in its depths made as they were churned hither and thither. And it seemed to smile and laugh with the white froth of its waves which were like the dazzling teeth in a person's mouth when he smiles and laughs. It even seemed to chatter away at him with the clatter made by the birds there. He prayed to the ocean and then began to examine the boats that were there. And from them he chose to rent one particular boat that was like the teachings of the Jinas. It was unblemished and possessed of all the best qualities. It was covered with fine cloths that could be called by the same term used to designate the robes of the Jain monks. It had an excellent sail of white cloth, while the Jain doctrine has excellent monks who wear white garments. It was to be the cause of great success for him, as the Jain doctrine leads to the highest goal for men. Like the Jain doctrine, too, it rewarded those who trusted in it, and was capable of saving and bringing to shore those who were drowning, and it was protected by Gods of great strength. He loaded all of his goods onto this boat.

He gathered grains, water and sticks and performed a ceremony to worship his teachers and the Gods. He gave away great wealth and then with his followers he got onto the boat. The boat was dragged to the shore; all the things necessary for carrying out religious rituals were brought there; flags were hoisted, the anchors were raised, the sails were hoisted, the helmsman and the first mates, the second mates and deckhands were stationed at their posts, and the boat pushed off from the harbour. And as the wind was favorable in just a few days they traveled over thousands of miles of ocean.

In the meantime, Bālapaṇḍiyā gave up bathing, anointing her body with fragrant ointments and wearing her jewels. She devoted herself to observing religious fasts, and for the most part she stayed in a nunnery with Jain nuns, praying and dedicating herself to the faith. Finally she won over everyone who saw her, and the nuns, her mother and father, her mother-in-law and father-in-law, in short everyone said to her, "Child! Your body is so delicate. Do not perform such strenuous asceticism." She said,

"Elders! Do not be troubled. I shall carry out these penances for only six months. After that I shall fast to death if my husband has not come back, all his wishes fulfilled. I swear to this today, right before all of you."

They said, "Daughter! Your husband has gone far, far away. He cannot come back here in just six months. You must not make a vow like this." She said, "But I have made it already. Do not say another word about it." And because they realized that she was firm in her resolve, they all kept silent.

One night, when the cold season had already begun to make itself felt, she was meditating without any cloak in a section of the nunnery that was exposed to the elements. There came by chance the demi-god Raisehara, "Best Lover of All," who was a complete non-believer. And he saw her. His mind was overcome by her great beauty and he made himself visible to her and said,

"O Young Lady! Take me as your lover. For I am charmed by your fair qualities. O my beauty! Know that I am Raisehara, the God.

But though I am a God I am your most humble servant from this day forward, my love! So give yourself to me. You will not find one like me so easily again, nor will you always have such a body.

For this body is formed by chance when the five physical elements come together. There is no such thing as morality, no such thing as the next world, and no such thing as spiritual liberation."

And when she did not answer him as he was going on in this way, that wicked one began to try to enjoy her by force. And when he could not break down her resistance, for she had great power from her religious practices, then his mood changed and he became angry. He thought, "I shall kill the husband of this useless woman to whom she is so faithful, so that she will die of grief at his death, burnt up by the raging fires of her pain." Now he knew through his supernatural knowledge that Devadiṇṇa was in the middle of the ocean and he sped there and delighted, jumped onto his boat. Taking on a terrifying form, he shouted, "Hey you! Pray to your favorite God. For I shall sink this boat of yours right here in the middle of the ocean." Devadiṇṇa said, "What have I done wrong that you should act this way?" The God replied, "This is the fault of that wicked wife of yours." "Surely what I suspected before has come to pass, for even a God says such a thing about my wife." With this thought, the young man again spoke up, "If she has been false in her heart then, God, why do you not chastise her directly?" He said, "I cannot do anything to her because of the great power of her religious austerities."

With this the young man realized, "This is some terribly wicked being who has no religious belief. He failed to tempt my beloved wife from the true path of virtue and from her true faith. And so he has come here in anger. And he might well do what he says to us." And as he was about to recite to himself simple words of praise to the holy men of the Jain faith, that demi-god cast the boat into the sea and then returned whence he had come. All of the merchants were saved over the course of time by clinging to pieces of wood from the broken ship and they reached various islands.

Devadiṇṇa also got hold of a plank. And as he was intently reciting words of praise to the Jinas and those who had sought and found liberation in the Jain faith, he was carried safely ashore. And in accordance with what his past deeds had determined for him in this life, he was seen there by the superintending deity of the salt ocean, Suṭṭhia, "Well-established ," who recognized him as a fellow Jain and delighted said to him, "Sir! I am the ocean. I am pleased by the faith you had in the words of praise to the Jinas. Go, my friend, to the demi-god Maṇoraha, "Wishes," who dwells in the midst of a jungle near the city Rayaṇapura, "Jewel City," which is five hundred miles from here. If I tell him to do it he will give you whatever you ask." Devadiṇṇa said, "Blessed One! How can I travel such a long distance?" At this Suṭṭhia gave him a fruit that was filled with a magic nectar and said to him, "Eat the seeds of this fruit as you go. Because of their magic power you will feel no hunger, no thirst, and you will not be tired. You will reach there in no time at all."

Devadiṇṇa replied, "As you command." And with these words he set out. And indeed he did reach that jungle in just a few days. He saw the abode of the demi-god Maṇoraha, made of all sorts of jewels, redolent with the deep fragrances that came from burning incense sticks of aloe and camphor and other aromatic woods. The temple was presided over by a large jewelled image of the demi-god and in it the demi-god's followers had carried out ceremonies in his worship. No sooner had he entered the temple than the demi-god Maṇoraha appeared to him in person and said, "Sir, have you been sent here by the ocean?" And when he replied, "That is so ," the demi-god said, "In that case go at once to the city Rayaṇapura, not far from here. The king there is named Sakka, just like the King of the Gods. Whatever you desire in your heart he will give to you four-fold."

And so he went and he saw that absolutely everyone there was absorbed in enjoying all the pleasures of all of the senses; no one did a stitch of work, not trade, not farming, not clerical work, not soldiering. They all seemed to be doing nothing but playing. And looking at so many things that amazed him he reached the royal palace itself. There he saw the king, like Indra, the King of the Gods, enjoying himself with every imaginable pleasure, and giving to people four times what they had wanted. He asked one man,

"No one in this city does anything to make money, not trade nor any of the other usual occupations, and yet where do they get all the money they clearly enjoy without the least little effort?"

He said to him, "Have you come up from the nether world or fallen from the heavens? Or have you come from across the ocean that you ask such a question?"

Devadiṇṇa said, "Do not be angry, for it is true that I have come from across the ocean and have been shipwrecked here. Please tell me exactly what goes on in this place."

The man told him, "In that case, listen. This king of ours goes every day to the nearby jungle and there by his great courage he pleases the powerful demi-god Maṇoraha. The demi-god, satisfied, grants him a very great boon. Through the power of that boon the king gives to every person four times what he desires."

When he heard this Devadiṇṇa thought, "In that case why should I bother humbling myself before the king? I shall win over the demi-god himself. But I must see what the king does to please the demi-god." He then went to the temple of the demi-god and concealing himself behind a tree, he hid there until after the first watch of the night, when the king appeared all alone, with only his own sword to guard him. The king worshipped the demi-god and proclaimed,

"O, O, great demi-god! You who are possessed of such great power and unthinkable magnanimity ! You who rescue all living creatures who display their faith in you through acts of courage! Appear now in person to me!"

And with these words King Sakka threw himself into a fire pit from which terrifying flames leapt.

The demi-god lifted him up with his lance and sprinkled him with water from his water pot. The king was as good as new. The demi-god said, "Great Being! Choose a boon." He said, "In that case may I be able to give every man four times what he wishes through your powers." "So be it." When the demi-god had replied, the king bowed down to him and then went back to his palace.

On the very next day it was Devadiṇṇa who spoke in this way to the demi-god and who jumped into the burning fire pit. In the very same way the demi-god came to grant him a boon. Devadinna said, "Keep it in trust for me," and with that he jumped into the fire pit yet a second time. The demi-god gave him a second boon. This repeated itself yet a third time. The fourth time, as he was about to jump into the fire pit, the demi-god grabbed him by the arm and said, "Sir! Indra has given me this lance which has three prongs. Through the power of this lance I can grant three boons and no more. Now ask for what you want." Devadinna said, "In that case, then, for my first boon give me the power that you give to the king every time he asks for a boon, but let me have that power for the rest of my life. As the second boon I ask that as long as I am alive you do not give that power to anyone else. I shall hold the third in reserve." The demi-god agreed to this and Devadinna stayed there in his temple, concealed from the sight of anyone else.

The king soon arrived at the temple, but the demi-god barred him from entering. The king asked, "Why do you keep me out?" The demi-god said, "I have already given three boons to some great being." At that the king returned to his palace, greatly troubled in mind. He lay down on his bed. The king spent the entire night tossing and turning in his bed like a fish thrown up onto hot sand, like a snake struck by a stick, like a deer caught in a trap. When morning came Devadinna went to see the king. He saw that everyone in the palace was overcome by grief. He asked someone, "Why is it that everyone in the palace seems to be overcome with grief?" He was told, "Sir! For some reason our king has declared that today he will immolate himself. That is why everyone in the palace is overcome with grief." Devadinna said, "In that case, take heart. I shall see that nothing bad happens and everything returns to normal." With these words of comfort he went directly into the presence of the king. He said, "King! Why do you act like some common person?"

The king said, "Sir! What is it to you?" He said, "King! I have a reason for my question. Please, just answer me, my lord!" Realizing that Devadinna would not give up, the lord of men said, "Sir! I am addicted to giving away my wealth. All this time I have been able to fulfill my desire to give through the power of a demi-god. But today I am without his favour and I cannot give like I used to. Anyway, what use is my life without the favour of that demi-god? That is why I am so upset and have decided to kill myself." He said, "If that is all, then, through my magic power which will last as long as I live you can continue to give away great wealth. You do not need to propitiate the demi-god from now on." The king was amazed by all of this, but he eagerly agreed to do as Devadinna suggested.

Devadinna then went back to the jungle. There, as he was getting out of a lake where he had been bathing, some middle-aged woman called out to him, "O noble one! Where have you come from and what are you doing here?" He said, "I have come from across the ocean. The presiding god of the sea, Sutthia, was pleased with me and sent me to the demi-god Manoraha." At this the woman was just delighted. She said, "In that case, come sit here under this tree so that I can tell you a secret." He did just as she said. She too then sat there and began to tell him her tale.

"There is a wonderful mountain named Veyaḍḍha, with so many high peaks that reach up to touch the top of heaven's vault. It is home to all of the Vijjāharas, who have supernatural powers, and is adorned with many Jain temples made entirely of precious stones. There is a city on that mountain called Gayaṇavallaha. It is protected by King Candasehara, who is the crest-jewel of all the kings of the Vijjāharas. He has five chief queens, all foremost in his harem, and their names are Sirikantā, Kaṇagamālā, Vijjumālā, Mehamālā, and Sutārā. And they each have a daughter who is skilled in all the arts and who surpasses in beauty the women of the Gods. Their names are Kaṇagappahā, Tārappahā, Candappahā, Sūrappahā, and Telukkadevī. Their father Candasehara consulted an astrologer about them. "Who will be their husband?" The astrologer said,

"Your younger brother Sūrasehara on his death became the demi-god Maṇoraha. He still bears you great affection. If your daughters stay with him they will surely get the right husband for themselves." And so their father gave the girls to Maṇoraha to take care of. Maṇoraha hid them all in an underground structure near his temple and he gave them all such a fiery complexion that no ordinary man could look at them. Each girl he made more blindingly bright than her sister, with Telukkadevī the brightest. If you want you could ask for the girls. I am their former nursemaid named Vegavaī, and won over by your good qualities and handsome looks I have told you all of this."

Devadiṇṇa then said, "I shall do as you command." With that he went back to see the demi-god. He told him, "Blessed One! For my third boon that I left in trust with you give me those maidens who are here in their underground chambers." The demi-god at once thought, "Now surely those girls have been struck with desire for this man and have shown themselves to him. How else could he even know that they exist?" He said to Devadiṇṇa, "There are girls here, but they are so fiery bright that no one can look at them." He said, "That doesn't matter. Just give them to me." At that the demi-god showed him four of the girls, all except Telukkadevī. And as soon as they got near Devadiṇṇa the fiery brilliance that the demi-god had given them disappeared. Then he asked, "Why did you not show me the fifth girl?" The demi-god said, "She is three times brighter than even these girls and you would never be able to look at her." Devadiṇṇa said, "Never mind. Just show her to me." With that there appeared a girl who was as hard to look upon as the orb of the sun. But she too at once assumed her normal appearance when she got close to Devadiṇṇa. All of them as soon as they saw him fell deeply in love with him. The demi-god was amazed at this and thought to himself, "Surely they belong to him." He said, "Children! Do you want this man for your husband?" They said, "Father, it would be a great honour for us." Manohara told them, "He already has a wife who is the abode of so many good qualities. And even as your husband he will still always be devoted to her." They all said, "And what could be wrong with his being devoted to his senior wife?" At that the demi-god gave him the girls. He summoned King Candasehara and with much pomp and splendour they celebrated their wedding. The demi-god gave great wealth to all the girls. Then Telukkadevī said, "Father! Will you not also give something for our elder co-wife who is like our sister?" At this the demi-god gave her a jewelled signet ring. She said, "What kind of a gift is this?" He said, "My daughter! This is a magic jewel that grants all wishes." Delighted, she accepted the ring. Candasehara took his leave of the demi-god and went home. And the girls through their magic powers made a magic castle for them all to live in. Devadiṇṇa stayed there with them enjoying pleasure after pleasure.

Then one day, wondering what her elder co-wife was doing, Telukkadevī used her supernatural knowledge and saw that Bālapaṇḍiyā was intent on beginning her fast to death. For the six months period had lapsed and her husband had not yet returned. Clothed in the stained robes of a nun, she was sitting deep in meditation. Realizing, "Surely this noble lady will fast to death tomorrow morning if her husband has not returned," Telukkadevī went to the demi-god. She told him exactly what was happening. He too believed that what she said was going to happen and he said, "My child! Go quickly, for the night is almost up. And he sent with her his servant, the demi-god named Dharaṇīdhara. And that one made a magic chariot which he filled with jewels, precious stones, pearls, coral, gold and other valuables. They put Devadiṇṇa in the chariot, fast asleep. Then the girls and their servants got in. Dharaṇīdhara held the chariot on the tip of his finger and hurtled it upwards. It sped onward with great speed and Devadiṇṇa was suddenly awakened by the jingling of the bells that hung along its sides. He asked Telukkadevī, "What is going on?" And she told him everything.

As they watched the earth speed by them with its cities, towns and villages, in the twinkling of an instant they arrived at their destination. They saw Bālapaṇḍiyā in meditation at the nunnery. And when she saw her, Telukkadevī threw a garment of fine silk over her. Distracted, Bālapaṇḍiyā quickly uttered a few words of praise to the Jinas and came out of her meditation. She looked up to see what was happening. When she saw the chariot she was frightened and went inside. She asked the other nuns, "What is happening?" They told her, "It must be that some God has come here, drawn by the power of your austerities." And no sooner had they said this than the chariot came down from the sky and stopped right there in front of them.

The sun came up. They all got out of the chariot, and having uttered the traditional words renouncing mundane concerns, they entered the holy precincts. They bowed down to the nuns. Bālapaṇḍiyā, seeing her husband, in a flurry rose to greet him. She fell at his feet. When they heard that Devadiṇṇa was back, the king and all the townspeople, his father and all his relatives, came to see him. He sent Dharaṇīdhara back, and taking all the valuables from the chariot, with great pomp and splendour Devadiṇṇa returned home. A huge celebration was held in his honour.

Now his friends began to ask Devadiṇṇa what had happened to the other merchants who had gone with him. When she saw that Devadiṇṇa did not answer, Telukkadevī, with her magic powers realized what was on his mind and she thought, "Nothing should spoil a happy moment like this." That was why she said, "My noble lord has come swiftly on this magic chariot. The others all tarried a bit, doing various services for the local ruler and receiving in turn much honour. They will surely arrive soon." Devadiṇṇa was delighted and thought, "How clever my beloved is with words."

But when people began to ask about the other merchants every day, then Devadiṇṇa remembered the demi-god. And through the power of the magic wish-granting jewel that the demi-god had given for Bālapaṇḍiyā, at that very instant the demi-god came to him. He asked, "For what reason have you summoned me?" Devadiṇṇa said, "Because I cannot make what your daughter said come true." The demi-god said, "If that is all then I shall do everything that is necessary. I'll be right back." Devadiṇṇa said, "Please." And the demi-god did do all that he had promised. Devadiṇṇa then spent many happy years like this, all of his wishes fulfilled by the power of the magic wishing jewel that he had gotten as a result of his acts of giving away wealth, acts that bore their fruit right here in this world. He was devoted to worshipping the Jinas and the Jain monks; he gave away wealth to the poor and the unfortunate; he fulfilled every wish that he had ever had, and he enjoyed to the fullest every conceivable pleasure of the five senses. He had many sons who were worthy of him.

Now one day in the course of his monastic tour the Jain monk Sīlasāgara came there. Devadiṇṇa and his wives went out to greet the monk and they bowed down to him with their hearts filled with faith. Receiving his blessings, they all sat down on a clean spot of ground from which all living creatures had been gently removed. The monk began to give a discourse on the Jain faith. He began, "When a man has been fortunate to have been born as a human being and in a country where the true religion is taught, then he should spend his efforts in religious pursuits. Listen,

All you noble souls! It is not such an easy thing to have been born as a human being and in the right country. Most good people know this.

Now you have all attained such a birth on account of the good deeds that you must have done in a past life. Now you should put your mind to that religion which has been taught by the Omniscient One.

And that religion is said to be two-fold in practice, for the monks and for the lay believers. You should put all your effort into religion, for it has been said by the wise:

There will always be unending misfortunes; there will always be the cycle of passion and other bad feelings; there will always be the origin of karma and there will always be the cycle of births;

There will always be miseries and there will always be false and vain hopes; there will always be men pitifully complaining to other men;

There will always be poverty, there will always be disease, there will always be this terrible ocean of transmigratory existence with its many sufferings,

Just as long as this true religion spoken by the Jinas is not encountered by people. But as soon as people, even by chance, encounter this teaching, then

Shaking off all sin they will reach the highest place which is filled with unending happiness and is devoid of all suffering."

At this there arose in Devadiṇṇa a desire to practice religion and he said, "I shall make arrangements for my family and then I shall obey your command by becoming a monk."

The teacher said, "Do not wait." "I shall be back." With these words he returned home. He appointed his eldest son Dhaṇavaī, "The Rich," as head of the family. And as festivities were celebrated in the Jain temples, as hosts of monks and nuns were given pure alms, as fellow Jains were honored and feted, as wealth was distributed to the poor and the needy, what more can I say, as everything that was supposed to happen was carried out to perfection, Devadiṇṇa and his wives were ordained by the teacher. He gave them this instruction:

"Hear this! There are people who drink the drink of immortality, the nectar of the Gods. They are the people who have become monks and nuns and are filled with a happiness that nothing can sully.

And now you all have taken this Blessed Ordination. You have obtained what there is to be obtained in this ocean of births.

But I warn you that as long as you live you must be careful and exert yourselves, for it is said,

'Those without good fortune, those lowest of men, do not master the religious life. But those who do are the best among men.'"

And when Devadiṇṇa said, "We desire further instruction," the teacher handed the women over to the nun Sīlamaṇi. They all took upon themselves two sets of vows. They lived a perfect life as ascetics for many years. At the end of their appointed life span they all fasted to death and became gods in the twelfth heaven. When they fall from there they will be reborn in Mahāvideha where they will achieve their ultimate liberation.

And so I say,

"The fact that although he had fallen into distress, the lord of the ocean Suṭṭhia was pleased with him, and the fact that he was able to return to his parents, all of this is the result of his giving away wealth.

The fact that he obtained those women to enjoy sensual pleasures with, women who had conquered the women of the Gods with their charm and their beauty, all of this is the result of his giving away wealth.

The fact that he got so many gorgeous silk clothes, fine, beautiful, of every different colour, all of this is the result of his giving away wealth.

The fact that he got so many glowing jewels, wishing jewels, cats-eyes, diamonds and more, all of this is the result of his giving away wealth.

The fact that he got heap upon heap of valuables, jewels, pearls, coral, gold and other such things, all of this is the result of his giving away wealth.

The fact that he enjoyed so many pleasures that delighted his ears, his sense of smell, his taste, touch and eyes; the fact that he got unparalleled glory, all of this is the result of his giving away wealth.

Considering all of these fruits that come about in this very life from the act of giving away wealth, give all you can with all your might!"

The Story of the Merchant Abhinava, from the *Mūlaśuddhiprakaraṇa*, pp.179-180.

There is on our very own continent of Jambudvīpa, in the very center of the area known as Southern Bharata, an ancient city named Vesālī, which was exceedingly famous. There once reigned King Ceḍaa, who like some mythical beast that slays the proud lion of the jungle, had slain his proud and mighty enemies. He was lord over eighteen vassal kings. And there dwelt in that city two merchants. One was named Juṇṇaseṭṭhī, "The Old Merchant," and the other was called Ahinavaseṭṭhī, "The Young Merchant." The first was as poor as poor can be, while the other was as rich as rich can be.

Now one day the lord of the triple world, the lord of heaven, earth and the nether world, the Jina Mahāvīra came into that city in the course of his monastic wanderings. This was in the time before he had reached his state of perfect enlightenment. And one night the rains began. Mahāvīra took refuge in some shelter there and assumed a posture of meditation that he would keep for the four months of the rainy season.

The old merchant saw him there and his heart was filled with feelings of awe and reverence. Waves of joy flowed over his whole body and he proclaimed, "Today truly my whole life's purpose is fulfilled. Today my life indeed seems worth living. For today I can bow down to the feet of the Blessed One, which are like pure water to cleanse the dirt of sin." And with feelings like this every day he went to bow down to the feet of the Blessed One. He would stay a few moments each day, with his hands joined together and held over his head in a gesture of reverence, and worship the Blessed One. And he thought, "Now I come here every day and it seems that the Blessed One never moves from this place. He is ever engaged in meditating, his body unmoving, as he observes the fast for four months of the rainy season. If only the Blessed One would break his fast at my house when the time comes, then truly I would consider myself to be the most fortunate man in the world."

And while he occupied himself with pious thoughts like these, in no time at all the four months of the rainy season passed and there came the day for the Blessed One to break his fast. Bowing down to the Blessed One the old merchant said, "Friend to all the world! Lord of Ascetics! Blessed One, bless me today by breaking your fast at my house." And with these words he returned home. There he made everything ready and he waited expectantly looking at the door. He kept thinking to himself all the while, "The Blessed One is coming, the Blessed One is coming, and I shall fulfill my every desire by giving him food to break his fast. If the Lord of the Jinas comes to my house, then I shall have crossed this ocean of rebirths, whose waves are our sufferings, and in whose depths lurk countless misfortunes like so many sharks."

And as his desire for the highest bliss grew and grew and waves of joy coursed through his body while he waited there, the Jina passed him by and went into the house of the young merchant. And the young merchant, recalling the teaching that a gift given to the proper recipient leads to fruits right in that very same lifetime, fed the Blessed One. And at the very moment that he did so the five marvelous signs appeared on account of the power of that gift that was given to such a worthy person as Mahāvīra. A rain of jewels fell from the sky, while the Gods waved the ends of their robes in congratulations. The Gods beat their heavenly drums and a fragrant perfumed rain fell from the sky. Heavenly voices could be heard, praising the gift.

Now when the old merchant heard the sound of the heavenly drums beating he wondered what had happened. Someone then told him, "The Blessed One has been given food to break his fast." His earlier religious resolve was thus broken. In the meantime the Blessed One continued on his wanderings, leaving that city.

Now it chanced that the Jina Pārśvanātha came there. All of the townspeople reverently rushed out to greet the Jina. And that Blessed One discoursed on the Jain religion, which is like a boat for fortunate souls, ferrying them across the ocean of rebirths.

"Listen, all of you fortunate souls who are destined to achieve final release! The Jain faith alone is your refuge in this cycle of rebirths. All of the rest is mere delusion.

All material prosperity, every worldly joy comes from this religion if it is well practiced. Indeed it leads even to heaven and final release.

And its duties are said by the Jinas to be four-fold, giving to others, observing a moral life, practicing austerities, and engaging in right meditation. And so you should practice these things, particularly giving, so that you may obtain the bliss of true peace."

Now at that time, all the townspeople, who had been amazed by the great merit that the young merchant obviously had, seeing their chance, humbly asked the Blessed One:

"Blessed One! Right now, here in this city, who is the person who has the most merit?" And at that the Blessed One pronounced the old merchant to have the greatest merit.

The people all quickly replied, "Blessed One! But he was not the one to give the Jina food to break his fast. The other one did, and the five divine signs appeared in his house."

But the Blessed One told them, "If the old merchant had not heard that the Jina had already been given food to break his fast, for sure he would have obtained omniscience just one second later. Now it is true that the young merchant experienced the divine signs in his house, and it is true that he achieved merit that will give rise to its fruit right here in this very lifetime, but he did not acquire any merit that will carry over into a future rebirth, for he lacked the proper mental attitude for that when he gave his gift."

And when they heard that answer all the townspeople felt great respect for the old merchant. Having bowed down to the Blessed One they all went back to their own homes.

The Story of King Yaśodhara

Translated by Friedhelm Hardy

Introduction[1]

The tribulations of King Yaśodhara, spread out over seven rebirths, make fascinating and at the same time terrifying reading. A seemingly minor offense against Jaina ethics is punished on a scale that appears totally out of proportion. Yet more than mere punishment is involved, for parallel to the gruesome external tortures endured by the king and his mother runs a process of inner purification. The overt intention of the story is to demonstrate the consequences of *hiṃsā*, a sacrificial killing of living beings for the sake of some personal benefit. The price that will have to be paid for this turns the culprit into a victim of similar acts of *hiṃsā*. Into the rich texture of this story are woven other themes. We can recognize an attack on the Hindu veneration of goddesses, for they are predominantly associated with blood sacrifice. But behind this can also be detected another intention: to reveal the intrinsic connection of *hiṃsā* with *kāma*, of violence with sexual passion. Thus it is not an accident that Yaśodhara is motivated to commit his act of *hiṃsā* after a traumatic erotic experience; that time and again in his subsequent lives sex and violence go hand in hand; and that (as versions other than the present one make clear)[2] his final purification is brought about by the desire for sexual prowess of another king. It is a tale painted in lurid colours and not meant for the squeamish, but at the same time we can see in it clues to the existence of a highly sophisticated Jaina psychological theory. Yaśodhara's story can be regarded as one of the great cultural constructs of Jainism. It is uniquely Jaina. Traces of it may have entered into the *Arabian Nights*,[3] but in India it was Jaina authors alone who wrote about it. Versions are found in practically all the languages that were used by the Jains: Prakrit, Sanskrit, Apabhraṃśa, Tamil, Kannada, Gujarati, Hindi.[4] We know of more than two dozen authors who wrote about Yaśodhara,[5] spanning a period of a thousand years. It was in the *Yaśastilaka* that the story found its most sophisticated expression. Since the message is conveyed by the story as a whole, I have chosen to translate a much briefer version of the tale which dispenses with all ornamentations and elaborations. It is found as number 73 in Hariṣeṇa's collection of tales (written in Sanskrit) known as the *Bṛhatkathākośa.*[6]

Hariṣeṇa wrote his work in Kathiawar in 931 A.D. and that makes him the earliest known and extant author of the story of Yaśodhara in the form which became standard for later writers. The rationale of Hariṣeṇa's collection is not brought out in the text itself, but can be unravelled from another work, the *Kahakosu*[7] which Śrīcandra composed during the second half of the 11th century A.D. in Apabhraṃśa and which can be regarded almost as a free translation of the *Bṛhatkathākośa*. Now Śrīcandra makes it clear that the stories are meant to spell out in concrete detail matters alluded to in the *Mūlārāhanā* (or more popularly, *Bhagavatī Ārādhanā*), a Prakrit text on ethics.[8] Unlike Hariṣeṇa, he actually quotes a number of verses from this work. Rather predictably, the heading under which the story of Yaśodhara is presented is *hiṃsā.*[9]

What follows is a complete and fairly literal translation of Hariṣeṇa's version.[10] To my knowledge only one other version has ever been rendered into English.[11]

Translation[12]

There was in the great country of Avantī the city of Ujjayinī. Its king was Kīrtyogha, and Candramatī was his lovely wife. Yaśodhara was born to them, after they had been longing for a son (for quite a while). He was handsome, well-mannered, and no-one surpassed him (in any of his fine qualities). Amṛtamatī became his chief queen: like the petals of the blue lotus were her eyes, beauty radiated from all her limbs, and she was dear to his heart. A son, prince Yaśomati, was born to them; he was brave, polite, well-mannered, and a delight to both their families.(1-4)

One day Kīrtyogha looked into a clear mirror and saw his first grey hair. This made him (think of death and) further rebirths, and terrified thereby he relinquished the pleasures of this world. To his son Yaśodhara he handed over the splendours of kingship, and took from Abhinandana initiation into the Digambara order.(5f)

Yaśodhara ruled gloriously over Ujjayinī. All his vassals paid heed to his command, bowing their heads before him in submission. His days were filled with great happiness; he enjoyed to the full the pleasures of making love to his chief queen Amṛtamatī.(7f)

But then one day Yaśodhara caught sight of his beloved queen having sex with a hunchback[13] in the middle of the night. All matters of sexuality ceased to interest him. (He reflected:) "As an excuse that can explain my (now) becoming a monk, while remaining in my palace, I will have to tell my mother something about a made-up dream."[14] (So he told her:) "Listen, mother! Last night, during the final watch, I had the following clear dream: I was falling at great speed from my seven-storeyed palace, and then crashed on to the ground which was covered with broken bits of stone. Yet soon I got up and men who were standing on the palace and had to do with magic and deceit applauded me with false eulogies. I became filled with a strong aversion to the affairs of the senses, put prince Yaśomati in charge of the kingdom, and took to the asceticism of the lord of Jinas."(9-14)

When Candramatī heard this, she replied: "The dream you have had, my son, is not auspicious. Firm in mind you must now perform those rites which ward off the influence of evil. Make an offering to our family goddess with animals you have killed with your own hands. Then, my son, when you have done everything required for this ritual of pacification, you will soon forget about becoming initiated into the order!"[15] (15ff)

Yaśodhara followed the advice of his mother and did as she had suggested, in his desire for her well-being, (but only to the extent that) he killed a cock made of flour at the feet of the goddess, in the company of his mother Candramatī. At that moment,[16] the chief queen (Amṛtamatī) murdered both (her husband Yaśodhara) together with (her mother-in-law) by putting poison into a sweet dish. Such was the (karmic) consequences of performing that evil act (of sacrificing the cock).(18ff)

There was a lofty mountain in the southern part of the Himalayas. A great variety of trees made it very attractive, but it was dangerous with its lions and tigers. There Yaśodhara was reborn as a peacock, out of a pea-hen's womb. His mother was killed in a snare by some man; he was then taken from that man by yet another man who raised him. This man wished to make a present to King Yaśomati, and he offered him the peacock. Since the king felt delight at the sight of the bird, he accepted the gift. Thus he came to stay (once again) in (his own) royal palace, roaming about freely.(21-24)

She who had been called Candramatī in her previous life and had been Yaśodhara's mother, was reborn in the country of Karahāṭa as a fine-looking (male) dog. He was then taken away from there to the town of Ujjayinī by someone who wanted to make a gift to King Yaśomati. When the latter saw the dog, he was delighted and accepted him, handing him over with care to a man who became his master.[17] In this way, as a result of the strong bond that had united them in their previous life, the two animals, peacock and dog, became favourite pets of the king (here) on earth.(25-28)

(One day) the peacock was perched on the roof of the palace, and he spotted a window. As soon as he gazed, mesmerized, at its centre that was illuminated by a jewel-lamp, he suddenly remembered his former life. When the bird then looked through the window into the harem, he discovered the chief queen (his former wife Amṛtamatī) sitting on the lap of the hunchback mentioned above, and the couple were engaged in making love. When the peacock saw this, in a rage he flew at them and tried to tear their hearts out with his claws. They hit back at him with their jewellery and ornaments, but as they were exhausted from their love-making, he managed to get out of the palace in a panic. Since the bird had been wounded badly by their strokes, he could merely crawl and he got to King Yaśomati at a moment when he was engrossed in a game of dice. When the dog saw the peacock approaching, whose whole body was trembling, he went for him and killed him on the spot. (This disturbance annoyed) the king who hit the dog over the head with his dice board. The dog collapsed on the ground, did not stir, and was dead. When the king realized that both his pets had died, he uttered from his troubled heart a lament that would have touched even an ascetic. He mourned over them for a long time, and then had them cremated, using for the purpose pieces of sandal wood. Their ashes were taken to the Ganges and scattered over her water, and then the king freely handed out gifts of gold, coins, jewels, cows, clothes and so on, so that their rebirth should take place in heaven and be a happy one. (29-39)

There was a mountain Suvela in the southern region of the country, impenetrable with jungles that were infested by lions and many other kinds of wild beasts. He who had been a peacock in his previous life was reborn (there) as a mighty mongoose,[18] (the offspring) of a blind female and a lame male animal. He was left lying in a ditch after his birth, and because he could not get even a little bit of milk from his mother whose teats had completely dried up, he became crazed with hunger, as a consequence of his bad *karma*. But by eating snakes he managed to survive. (And it happened that) she, who had been the cruel queen Candramatī and had found her second death as a dog, was reborn in that same hole in the ground as a cobra. Just when this snake was about to devour some frogs, her tail was firmly caught by the mongoose. But the cobra managed to attack the mongoose from behind, furiously biting him with her fangs. While both were thus busy trying to devour each other with great fury, a hyena pounced on the mongoose and killed it. Then it tore the cobra to shreds with its teeth and killed it.[19] (40-48)

He who had been the mongoose that was killed by the hyena was reborn as a *rohita* fish in a pool of the river Siprā (which runs through Ujjayinī). The cobra too was reborn in the same place, as a terrifying crocodile that (grew) so large that it looked like the noose of the god of death.(49f)

One day the fish was gliding through the clear water of the pool, when suddenly that horrific crocodile caught him by his tail. But by then the king's troupe of entertainers, hunchbacks, dwarfs, and so on, had arrived there to enjoy a swim and had got into the clear water. A fine old midget woman, frolicking about in the water in their company, (slipped and just at that moment happened to) fall on that fish. The crocodile let go of the fish, but in a rage it attacked the dwarf woman and sunk its teeth into her leg. The moment this happened to her, she screamed out loudly — which put a sudden end to the games of the troupe of women who fled. Their bodies shaking with fear, they reported the whole incident to the king. "Your majesty! Just now your favourite midget woman has been caught by a terrible crocodile in a pool of the Siprā river!" When the king heard this, his eyes became red with fury. He ordered all the fishermen — his voice reverberating in the sky: "Hey fishermen! Immediately catch in your nets all the fish!" No sooner had he stopped speaking than all the fishermen took their nets and merrily ran to the river pool. The fish, which had been released by the crocodile, escaped from the pool in panic — for destiny meant him to live happily (for a while at least). Biting their lips with anger, all the fishermen cast out their strong nets (once again) into the pool. They caught the crocodile and pleased with their catch took it straight to king Yaśomati, before whom they released it. Seeing it lying before him, he said: "Take this vicious, murderous beast to the place of slaughter. Tie it up with strong fetters and torture it to death. But make sure you keep it alive as long as possible, to prolong its agony!" They followed his instructions, and thus the crocodile died an excruciating death.(51-66)

Some time later, the fishermen returned to the pool and cast their nets. (As they were pulling them in,) the *rohita* fish was caught and dragged on to the shore. Still alive, he was taken by the fishermen to the king as a present. When Yaśomati saw him, he was pleased and sent the fish to his mother, the former chief queen Amṛtamatī (with the following instruction:) "Please give the meat of this fish, along with a curry sauce, immediately to the Brahmin priests as a meal in honour of my father and so on!" When the fish heard these instructions, instantly he remembered his former lives. As he helplessly stared at the queen, his tail portion was cut off by her order and taken into the kitchen — for the benefit of (the soul of) the king's father (himself)! Then Yaśomati added: "Choose another portion, mother! which will be a treat for you and me at dinner tonight." She heated some ghee in a frying pan, put the remaining part of the fish into it, and he died instantly — the result of his *karma*. (67-74) After its execution, the crocodile was reborn as a she-goat in a hamlet of untouchables. The soul of the *rohita* fish entered into her womb and, once born, turned into a hefty billy-goat. When he had reached maturity, he mounted his own mother. Just when he was shedding his seed into her, he was killed by another billy-goat: the latter's horns gored him, tore him open, and he died, his mind clouded, having succeeded in impregnating his mother with his own soul. (75ff)

One day king Yaśomati went out (hunting) and by the power of *karma* he saw the pregnant she-goat standing in front of him[20] and shot at her with an arrow. The poor female was struck and fell lifeless on the ground. Then by the order of the king untouchables[21] cut open her abdomen and made a fine kid fall out of her belly to the ground. When the king saw the young animal, a thrill of delight shot through his limbs and he handed him over to his goatherd. In due course the kid reached maturity and spent his days copulating with his 'cousin' she-goats and so on. (78-82)

One day king Yaśomati had a particular wish, due to the power of his evil *karma*[22] and he promised twenty buffaloes to his family goddess, should she fulfil it. By sheer coincidence[23] the wish of him, whose mind was cruel due to his abundant evil *karma* and who was now piling up more of it, came true. Overjoyed at seeing his wish fulfilled, the king sacrificed to his family goddess Kātyāyanī those buffaloes, his heart filled with devotion. Their meat was taken into the kitchen where it was left (for some time), heaped up in large piles, covered with flies and looking like flowers of the silk-cotton tree. After a little while, the cook spoke to the king: "Your majesty! The crows and dogs have eaten most of the meat, but some of it is still left. Were a billy-goat to sniff at it, it would cease to be polluted (and you could still eat from it. But naturally,) it is up to you alone on earth, great king! to decide what must be done." This suggestion of the cook aroused the king's appetite and pleased with it, he replied: "Good man! In your desire to do me a favour you have spoken well. Right now I shall act upon your words which are respected among gods and brahmins." Thus at the cook's suggestion, the king had the billy-goat quickly fetched. Standing there in the kitchen among the meat, the goat remembered his previous lives. Then (the king's mother) Amṛtamatī spoke to the cook: "Today I don't feel at all like having buffalo meat. Bring me now a piece of meat from some animal instead, which will please my heart." When Yaśomati, who loved his mother and was devoted to her, heard this, he ordered the cook: "Now prepare a piece of meat of that billy-goat and bring it here, so that my mother will be happy." At these words of the king the wicked cook quickly sliced off a chunk of flesh from the back of the billy-goat. He prepared it in great haste and together with various side-dishes he rushed with it to the queen mother. Then he was ordered by the king: "Take the (remaining meat) to the brahmins, (prepared) in the way they like it, for the benefit of my father's soul and that of my grand-mother!" (The billy-goat reflected:) "Even that (meat of the fish) which by the king's orders (had been given) previously to the brahmins — not even a bit of it has till now come to me, although I am standing right next to him.[24] Here I am (instead), my back-side cut off, suffering from hunger and thirst, tortured from unbearable pain, and my whole body trembling with fear!" (83-100)

She who had (first) been Candramatī and (eventually had become) the she-goat shot dead by the king, was reborn as a (male) buffalo of mighty bulk in the country called Kaliṅga. From there he came, carrying cauldrons in the company of other hefty buffaloes, to holy Ujjayinī which was splendid with its row of banners. When his load had been taken off, he bathed his body, that the sun's heat had burnt, in the water of the Siprā river to recover from his exhaustion. Just then the favourite horse of the king (had entered the river) and was gored by the buffalo with his horns and killed. The king received the news about this incident from his servants. He was caught by rage and had the buffalo immediately brought to his palace. He had the animal bound, so that he could not stir, with iron fetters on his four feet. The he had a blazing fire lit all around him. In front of him was placed a cauldron filled with hot water into which had been thrown Asa Foetida, salt, cloves, areca-nuts, nutmeg and many other spices. (When, desperately thirsty, he had drunk) that hot water, his innards began to burn and soon he passed all his dung through his 'hind door'.[25] Also the previously mentioned billy-goat, whose hind part had been cut off, was placed next to the buffalo.[26] While both animals were thus rapidly roasting over the fire, once again their souls left them (but,) as if scared, only very slowly. (101-110)

In the outskirts of holy Ujjayinī stood a hamlet of (untouchable) *mātaṅgas*. It was 'decorated' with bones, manure, dogs and other kinds of filth. There the two of them, mother and son, were reborn inside a hen as a pair of chickens, with bodies generated by their evil *karma*. (An outcaste called) Caṇḍakarmā saw the two birds, took them and carried them to king Yaśomati as a gift. Seeing the pair of chickens, the king was very pleased — for which son would not be pleased seeing his father! Then the king handed the birds back to Caṇḍakarmā, who was one of the watchmen of the city and who took them to his hut. (111-115)

One day Yaśomati, full of high spirits, went out with the women of his harem into the park, to frolic in its groves. Caṇḍakarmā followed them to a fine grove, with the two chickens which he was keeping inside an iron cage. There he saw a lofty, charming palace that was radiant with many colours and looked like a turban.[27] In a colourful tent that stood near the eastern gate of that palace, that was radiant with jewels and resembled an autumn cloud, he let the fine pair of chickens, — who were gentle and attached to each other in mutual affection, one looking as pretty as the other, and who were making soft noises — out of their cage.[27] (116-120)

Then Caṇḍakarmā saw an ascetic standing by the side of a tree: his arms were hanging down, his gaze was fixed on to the tip of his nose; he was full of compassion and a treasure-house of asceticism; he had his abode at the foot of the tree that is freedom from grief, resembled an embodied form of the god of righteousness and was in full control of the wild gang of the senses. Spotting that *yogī*, Caṇḍakarmā of impure mind and cruel thoughts paid him mock respect. He reflected: "How could that sage violate — like a cruel snake that puts terror into people — the king's palace?" While the wicked man was thus reflecting, the yoga of the wise sage reached its culmination. When Caṇḍakarmā of brutal mind saw this, he spoke to the perfectly controlled sage who had destroyed all links with the passions. "Tell me, sage, why you — a king famous among people and honoured by your subjects — choose to undertake meditation?" (121-127)

"Listen carefully," replied the sage, "I shall tell you about it. When I was passing through the cycle of transmigration that lacks any inner substance, when I was taking on and then discarding innumerable bodies, I began to reflect on the grand, faultless question: how can I put an end to all the suffering which has been befalling me, being conceived (time and again) in so many different wombs?" (128ff)

When Caṇḍakarmā heard this, he asked: "O sage! How can it be that the body is one thing and the soul another?" The sage, who knew the content of all the sacred scriptures,[29] had destroyed all reasons for scepticism, and saw with eyes that were his *avadhi* knowledge[20], uttered this truth: "You, you, beloved of the gods! Surely this is not an issue about which you could have any doubts. You must realize that the body and the soul are different things." But Caṇḍakarmā replied: "No, a body and a soul do not exist separately (from each other). Instead, all the beings that live in the forest of earthly existence that has wombs for trees, have a soul and a body that are the same. And here is the proof. (Some time ago) I cast a robber into a big cauldron and covered it with lac to make it completely air-tight. Naturally he died because of this, but: I did not notice any soul escaping. Thereby I learnt, my lord! the true state of things: on earth the soul comes into being (and thus it is not eternal) just as the body." (131-138)

When the *yogī* heard this argument, he replied: "Were one to throw a man together with a conch into a vessel of the kind you mentioned, the man could merrily blow the conch inside and people would hear its sound; yet it could not be detected how it comes out. And just as the exit of the conch's sound from the cauldron cannot be seen, the escape of the soul from the body cannot be seen, however many people may be watching. For this reason you must accept my words that the soul is different from the body." (139-142)

But Caṇḍakarmā replied to the sage's argument: "Your words do not hold true, as the following illustration will show. Once I weighed a thief on a balance, and quite clearly his weight remained the same, when he was alive and when I had killed him. For this reason you must accept my proposition that a (living) body is the same as a corpse plus life." (143ff)

"Then listen," replied the sage, "to this charming allegory of mine. A cowherd fills a leather bag with air and weighs it, but the balance fails to register a difference (from the weight of the empty bag). He empties it again, but whether empty or filled (with air), the balance keeps on showing the same weight. In the same manner a man will show the same weight, whether he is alive or dead (viz. with or without a soul). For this reason accept my words that body and soul are different." (146-150)

"I cut up," answered the watchman, "a certain robber's body. I cut it into smaller and smaller pieces, but whether looking inside or outside, I failed to detect anywhere in his body a soul. As no soul-chunk could be detected in any of the pieces of his body, soul and body must be the same." (151ff)

But the sage replied to Caṇḍakarmā: "Listen to this clear illustration which I shall give you. Should a man cut up a fire-stick into finer and finer bits of word, and investigate it over and over again, he still would not discover the fire, you cruel man! However small he may make the pieces and how carefully he may look, he will not detect the fire inside the fire-stick. Now just as a man on this earth, however wide he may open his eyes, cannot see the fire which he knows to be present inside the fire-stick, people cannot see the soul particle, because it lacks (physical characteristics by which it could) manifest itself to the eyes, although it is present in every part of the body. For this reason have faith in my words that the body is one thing and the soul is another."[31] (154-159) Now Caṇḍakarmā had to reply: "I am at a loss for an answer. What can I do? Have pity on me!" The mind of the sage melted from compassion and he said to him: "Practice *dharma*, you great being! which is the friend of all embodied beings!" Then Caṇḍakarmā requested him: "Please tell me now clearly, my lord! about the consequences of *dharma* and its opposite." (160ff)

"A married life full of pleasures, piles of money, a long life, an untainted reputation, power and health — these come about due to *dharma*. *Adharma* on the other hand gives rise to poverty, ugliness, a miserable married life, lack of friends, untimely death and stupidity." Excited by devotion, Caṇḍakarmā asked further, after this brief summary of the results of *dharma* and *adharma*: "Briefly instruct me in what I should do as a householder, O you savior from the ocean of rebirth!" The sage replied: "Once you have gained the true faith, perform the smaller vows." (Caṇḍakarmā requested the sage:) "Lord, tell me briefly about the smaller vows which are the cause of rebirth in heaven and of final liberation and which bring about happiness and riches." The five smaller vows and the secondary and practice vows, avoidance of honey and of the five types of figs, not eating at night, the fivefold veneration, true faith, and the obeisance to the teacher — in all these[32] the ascetic instructed Caṇḍakarmā. (163-170)

Then the latter replied to the sage: "I accept all this, true faith and those vows, but I cannot accept this one vow, viz. not to harm any living being. The *dharma* appropriate for me, because of the tradition of my family, is to kill living creatures." (171f)

When the sage heard these words which hold true on the face of this earth, he replied to that brave man, whom devotion had made excited: "If you do not abandon the *dharma* customary in your caste, consisting in killing living beings, you will pile up very rapidly evil *karma*. (Look! This is what happened to) that pair of chickens who did not discard the *dharma* of their family tradition. They had to endure a series of deaths which were all accompanied by very great pain. Similarly you, my friend, will have to suffer a series of rebirths and deaths full of pain, if you adhere to the *dharma* of your caste." At these words the watchman was struck with wonder; eagerly he once again addressed the ascetic: "How did these two birds come to suffer a series of deaths for not abandoning, in a previous life, their family *dharma*?" (173-178)

"Concentrate and listen, replied the sage, to what I am going to tell you! This cock here is the (reborn) king Yaśodhara who in a previous life was the father of our king Yaśomati. And this hen was in a previous existence Candramatī, the crude mother of the same king Yaśodhara. Not being prepared to relinquish (totally) their customary *dharma*, they slaughtered a cock made of flour as sacrifice to the goddess to whom they were devoted. Due to the maturation of that evil deed they have become this pair of chickens whose minds are now at peace, being intent on listening to my discourse on the true religion. (Earlier) they had been a peacock and a dog, then a serpent and a mongoose, a fish and a crocodile, male and female goats, buffalo and goat, (before they became these two chickens.)" (179-184).

When Caṇḍakarmā had heard all this, his body began to tremble with fear and he was struck by panic. He said to the ascetic: "In thought, word and deed I am now renouncing my family *dharma*, O sage! I accept now the excellent religion of the Jinas. Through them I have become a lay follower and have taken upon myself the smaller vows along with true faith, etc. with devotion." (185ff)

The two chickens had listened to the entire exposition of the true religion which had wafted from the sage's mouth-lotus. The narration of their own previous existences filled them with boundless grief. They accepted the religion of the Jinas and, overcome by devotion to them, they joyfully uttered a gentle crow. (At that moment) king Yaśomati, who was inside the tent, heard the crowing[33] and he spoke to his queen Kusumāvalī: "Look, look, my beloved one! my slender one! how skilled I am in the art of archery! Right now (without even seeing them) I shall shoot that pair of chickens with my arrows!" With these words the king pulled an arrow out of his quiver, placed it on the string of his bow, pulled it right up to his ear and succeeded in killing both birds with one powerful shot. (188-193)

After their death they were conceived as twins in the womb of that same queen Kusumāvalī.[34] (This rebirth once again as human beings was) due to their meditation[35] and to their enthusiastic devotion to the Jinas. They emerged from Kusumāvalī's womb as a prince and a princess who, in the course of time, became experts in all the fine arts. (194)

One day an ascetic called Sudatta had during his wanderings arrived in the park outside Ujjayinī, surrounded by many followers. Meanwhile the king, impelled by the great mass of his evil *karma*, had set out with his retinue from Ujjayinī (to go hunting). When he saw the ascetic Sudatta seated under a tree, (he got furious at this bad omen for the hunt and) let his hounds loose to kill him. But every single one of those five hundred hounds circumambulated the monk three times and merrily returned to his master. When the king saw all his hounds act in this manner, his eyes became red with rage and, waving his sword in his hand, he rushed towards the sage. But a merchant called Kalyāṇamitra who belonged to the true faith led the king towards the sage. As he looked at him, his mind became delighted and he reflected: "How could I, wicked that I am, think of committing the murder of a sage! I must make amends for this. Yes, I shall cut off my own head and hand it over to that pure one, to do penance for my evil intentions." With this idea in his (now) purified mind, without further ado the king went before the ascetic, along with his friend. But the sage restrained the king: "No, king! it would not be right to commit such an act!" Yaśomati got embarrassed and felt ashamed that the sage, who had achieved enlightenment, should be able to read his thoughts. He prostrated himself before him and paid him his respect. His mind was struck by a loss of interest in worldly matters and he spoke to the sage: "I am a wretch — please forgive this evil act of mine (viz. trying to kill you)." At that the ascetic replied "Get up, get up, O king! beloved of the gods, illustrious one! We who desire final liberation must bear with all people, so why waste any further words? Particularly you (the king) need not do so." Then the king asked him: "Bhagavān! Tell me now clearly what I had thought!" The sage who saw with the eyes of his *avadhi* knowledge[30] replied: "Concentrate and listen to what I shall tell you." This must surely be on earth the ritual act of expiating my (wanting to) kill a sage: cutting off my head I shall offer it before his feet. "Thus you thought, and extremely inappropriate it was! For the learned regard suicide as the cause of (painful) rebirths." (196-213)

Then the pure-minded Kalyāṇamitra spoke to the king whose heart was filled with both grief and joy: "Brave king! Illustrious one! Why should you be surprised that this sage should have known *one* thought of yours? Actually he knows the past, future and present. If you have any doubt at all, ask him anything you like." The king (once again) showed his respect to the ascetic and with devotion addressed him: "My grand-parents, my mother and my father — where did they all go after their deaths? How have they been reborn, and what pleasures and pains are they experiencing? Now tell be this briefly, taking pity on me!" (214-219)

The master-ascetic narrated this to the curious king: "Your Majesty! When your grand-father Kīrtyogha saw the first grey hair on his head, he took initiation into the order of the Digambaras. He performed the five-night mortification and died through *samādhi.*[35] Now he abides in the realm beyond *Brahmā* and enjoys divine happiness. Your mother Amṛtamatī, my son! who was the chief queen, killed her husband (viz. your father, and your grand-mother) with poison and went down (after her death as a leper)[36] into the sixth hell. There she is now abiding, having to endure gruesome tortures and unbearable pain, and the cruel woman is cursing herself for staying alive there. Furthermore, your father, king Yaśodhara, and his mother, your grand-mother Candramatī, together killed in front of the goddess Kātyāyanī a cock made of flour.[37] That evil deed brought about their mutual destruction, for they were reborn time and again in various animal bodies. They were reborn as two chickens, who kept the smaller vows and were meticulous about the five obeisances, but you killed them once again. They were conceived in Kusumāvalī's womb and were born as these two here, the prince and princess, whose bodies are adorned by their (skill in the arts) and who are living in your palace: your son Abhayaruci and your daughter Abhayamati." Listening to this series of rebirths, King Yaśomati became utterly amazed and developed complete loss of interest in all worldly matters. After listening to a sermon on the truth, he along with his friend (the merchant) and the ladies of his harem, took the vows of an ascetic in front of that sage. (220-232)

At the same time, when the prince and the princess heard of their previous existences, their minds too were struck by a total indifference to the affairs of the world and they themselves remembered their past lives. The thought of taking initiation put their minds at rest and devoutly they approached the sage Sudatta. Three times they walked around him in clockwise fashion and, devoutly prostrating themselves before him, requested him: "Please give us the Jaina initiation, O sage!" The latter was impressed by their courage, but replied: "Both of your minds are still immature and your bodies are not yet fully developed, so that you are not ready to endure the hardships that will follow after taking the Jaina vow. But it would be appropriate if you accepted the rules laid down for novices. Then I shall grant you in due course the full Digambara *dharma*." So at the advice of the sage, Abhayaruci who was immersed in devotion to the Jinas, accepted devoutly the *dharma* of novices, and Abhayamati did likewise in the presence of the nun Kṣāntikā who knew all the scriptures.[29] (233-240)

Now there was the fine town of Rājapura in the Yaudheya country. Māridatta was its king and he was an ardent devotee of its goddess. This horrific family deity of his abided in the southern part of the town: her mind was cruel and she was known by the name of Caṇḍamāri. The citizens led by Māridatta, their minds filled with devotion, used to perform all the rites of her worship by killing living beings with their own hands. Were they not to perform these sacrifices for her, this family goddess would have killed them all instantly. (241-244)

(On one such occasion,) Māridatta went to the temple of the goddess; he was accompanied by a variety of people and by his entire harem. At the same time, the master-sage Sudatta along with his congregation arrived in the cremation ground near the park of the town. People were taking pairs of living beings of many varieties, like peacocks, chickens and so on, to the feet of the goddess. Then the courtiers addressed the king: "Protector of the earth! It would be best, if a fine pair of human beings, who are endowed with all positive characteristics, were to be sacrificed." Heeding their advice, the king ordered his henchmen: "Quickly fetch a fine pair of human beings!" They obeyed his command, respecting it like the gift of a god,[38] and merrily rushed out to their task. (245-250)

By that time the two novices (Abhayaruci and Abhayamati) had respectfully taken leave of the sage and were on their way into the town to beg for alms. The king's henchmen spotted them, as they came slowly walking towards them.

They said to each other: "Men! These two are worthy (victims) for the goddess, to be slain by the king." When the two novices heard these appalling words, they gave each other courage and stopped there waiting, all fear cast off. The henchmen caught hold of the two perfectly built novices and took them before the king Māridatta. The novices saw him standing by the side of the goddess, with a terrific sword in his hand. While still at a distance, they both called out these greetings while looking at his awe-inspiring appearance: "Victory! Like the elephants of the quarters (you support the earth)! King of golden glory, free from stains, radiant with your fame that resembles the white jasmine! Victory to you for a long time, for all eternity!" When the king heard these thunder-like shouts of victory, (it took him a moment to) see that they belonged to a male and female person (and not a cloud). When he then saw the pair of novices in front of him, he asked: "Which is (your) mighty lineage that is adorned by (your) exceedingly handsome forms? Why did you take to asceticism which is so difficult to endure? All this you must tell me, splendid ones!" (251-261)

At these words of Māridatta, which were spoken lovingly, Abhayaruci narrated in detail, in the middle of the large gathering in which people, children, old folks and babies were crowding together, the whole sequence of events involving Yaśodhara and so on which was connected with himself and which caused people's amazement.[39] He told it in such a manner that (all the people,) all the king's men and Caṇḍamāri herself gave up the killing of living beings and gained tranquility in their minds. So when the goddess had listened to the whole story, she discarded her own terrific appearance and changed into a pleasant shape. Then she circumambulated the novice devoutly three times and poured from the golden pitcher she was holding in her hand a libation over his feet while clutching them. Looking most charming and filled with affection for him, her mind overflowing with love, she spoke in front of all the people to the novice: "My master! Show your benevolence and your great mercy to me: just now initiate me into the asceticism which puts an end to the ocean of transmigration!" But Abhayaruci replied to the goddess who devoutly was holding her hands folded against her forehead: "Rise, rise, dear lady! Initiation has been restricted to human beings. Gods, animals and denizens of the hells are excluded from it." Once again the goddess prostrated herself and requested: "In that case instruct me in the meritorious acts that I, a miserable being, can do." (262-271)

"True faith and worship of the Jinas are meritorious acts suitable for gods. Beautiful lady! Worship of the Jinas is not included in the *dharma* appropriate for the denizens of the hells. But true faith, the culmination of the threefold world, is found among them, and it is also found among the animals, for the wise declare that animals happily imitate the *dharma* of human beings." (272ff)

When Caṇḍamāri heard this, she accepted with devotion the true faith and the worship of the Jinas, and she learnt how to perform it properly. Then she addressed the king and the crowd of the citizens; "From now onwards, O king! let there never occur another animal sacrifice for my sake. Let all the citizens become peaceful (towards other beings). Otherwise, if in spite of this prohibition someone should kill a living being, I will kill all the people of the town!" Then the goddess bowed to Māridatta, his citizens and the novice and freely went away. When the heavenly sages heard of this miracle, they beat their drums in honor of Abhayaruci, and they resounded gently. The delighted gods shouted: "Well done!" and in great commotion, full of joy, showered garlands of flowers down upon him. (275-281)

King Māridatta had listened to the sermon on the religion propagated by the Jinas, which is the gospel for all beings and wholesome and which the novice had expounded; he had heard about the gruesome sufferings which arose form killing the cock (made of flour); he witnessed the conversion of the goddess. So he spoke to Abhayaruci: "Novice! My lord! Initiate me into the asceticism that destroys rebirth and that will allow me, by your grace, to achieve my own salvation." But he replied: "Rise up, my king! I am not entitled to give you initiation. But there is my wise and pure teacher — his fame pervades all the quarters — who is entitled to do so." (282-286)

Māridatta, pure of heart, became very enthusiastic when he heard this. He pondered: "All the people, along with my vassals, come to my feet in submission. Thus all-powerful, I have nevertheless resorted to the feet of the goddess. She in turn has taken refuge at the feet of a novice. Yet even he who is such (a powerful person) has his superior teacher. Oh! The greatness of these ascetics and of their mortifications, by which they become worthy of worship even by the gods and demons!" Thus he stood there, facing the novice, his mind purified through the contact with the Jaina religion. (287-291)

Meanwhile Sudatta had found out about the great miracle worked by the brave couple of novices by means of his divine knowledge, and also about how the goddess had been restrained and how she had been converted, and about wise Māridatta's determination to become an ascetic. So the steadfast sage, who was filled with affection for *dharma* and who was like an embodiment of *dharma* itself, went there. Māridatta along with all his relations and subjects prostrated himself respectfully before the master-ascetic and requested initiation into the order, while mighty gods applauded him. (When this wish of his had been fulfilled,) he handed over the kingship to his son and in turn handed over his son to all his subjects. Along with his court priest, chief minister, vassals and ladies of the harem he became an ascetic. The two novices who had become completely detached from all worldly pleasures were allowed to terminate their preliminary status and were given the full initiation by their teacher. They performed, for as long as they stayed alive, the fourfold *pādopagamana* ceremony (of ritual suicide)[40]: they refrained from all food and remained engrossed in the *dharma* and meditation. In no time they died through *samādhi*[35] and were reborn as gods in the Svayamprabha heaven. Of those who witnessed this extraordinary event, some became sages, others lay followers, and yet others acquired a station between these two (viz. as novices). The master-sage Sudatta reached the highest abode of the gods, after venerating according to the rules the whole of the fourfold *ārādhanā*.[41] Māridatta too and all the others whom pure faith had purified reached stations appropriate to their destiny, after venerating the *ārādhanā*. (292-304)

For he who carelessly effects the killing of *one* living being will wander aimlessly on earth through many a rebirth.(305)

Thus (ends) the story of Yaśodhara and Candramatī, which includes their progress over seven subsequent rebirths, (after they) slaughtered a cock made of flour for the goddess Kātyāyanī.

Notes

1. I am in the process of putting together an anthology of about fifty Jaina stories (all taken from sources in Apabhraṃśa and including extracts from Puṣpadanta) which deal with the theme of sexual passion and the typically Jaina philosophical and psychological reflections on it. Some of this material is discussed or alluded to in my forthcoming *Power, Love and Wisdom — themes in the religious culture of India*, London (Unwin Hyman), 1990.

2. The *vidyādharas* symbolize in the Indian imagination irresistible sexual attraction and prowess. Esoteric religious rites are believed to allow human beings access to these superhuman powers; the sacrifice of human beings to the goddess Caṇḍamāri is one such ritual. Thus we read in Somadeva's *Yaśastilaka* (part I, p. 44): "The king (viz. Māridatta) had formerly heard from his family priest called Vīrabhairava that he could gain, by means of a sacrifice of all (species of) living beings, in front of the goddess Caṇḍamāri in his own royal palace, and by means of personally killing a pair of human beings endowed with all auspicious marks, the attainment of the sword called 'vanquishing the world of the *vidyādharas*,' and since his mind was eager to look into the eyes of *vidyādhara* girls, ... he ordered his soldiers..." Similarly Puṣpandanta in his *Jasahara-cariü* (I, 7, 4.5.7.12.15) brings out the connection between the human sacrifice and the hope to obtain *vidyādhara* powers by means of a pun. On the one hand the king desires to be able to 'fly through the sky' (*kheyaratta*), but on the other hand this puns with 'to become a *vidyādhara*.' Indeed in line 12 we hear that this power will make the *vidyādharas* serve him. The entire episode is still absent in the *Samarāiccakahā*; in Māṇikyasūri (Hertel p. 82) the purpose of the human sacrifice is the protection of the kingdom, and in Vādirājasūri (Hertel p. 91) the motivation is very similar to the one found in the present version by Hariṣeṇa: unless worshipped, the goddess would cause havoc.

Who would expound such teaching about human sacrifice as the means of gaining the powers of the *vidyādharas*? I translated above as 'family priest' *kulācārya* (parallel to *kula-devatā*, 'family goddess'). The commentator is certainly wrong when he identifies the priest with 'a disciple of the loathsome Cārvāka.' (On actual 'materialistic' teaching see vs. 131-160 of the following translation, with note 31). At least in two versions, the identification of the source of this gruesome teaching is quite clear. In Māṇikyasūri (Hertel p. 82) we hear of 'verworfene Kaulas' whom Hertel (p. 81 note 2) identifies with the Śāktas. Puṣpadanta (*Jasaharacariü* I, 6, 2) describes a weird mendicant Bhairavānanda who had appeared in Māridatta's town and gave 'initiation into the Kaula religion' (*Kula-magga-dikkha*). This points us towards the nebulous realm of 'Tantrism,' the eroticism and sexual practices of which are well known. For bibliographic references see notes 4 and 11.

3. I am thinking here of the introduction to the work which tells about the two kings' traumatic discoveries of their wives' unfaithfulness with black slaves. (See e.g. vol. 1, pp. 20-23, of E. Littmann's *Die Erzählungen aus den tausendundein Nächten*, Insel Verlag, Wiesbaden, 1953.)

4. By far the oldest version is found in Prakrit in Haribhadra's *Samarāiccakahā* (edited by H. Jacobi, vol. I: text and introduction, Calcutta, 1926, pp. 237,17 — 285,16, = *Bibliotheca Indica*, Work No. 169) which was written during the middle of the 8th century A.D. From 931 A.D. we have Hariṣeṇa's Sanskrit version which is translated here. Then come, also in Sanskrit, Somadeva's *Yaśastilaka* of 959 A.D. (edited originally, in two parts by Kedāranātha Śarmā and Vāsudeva Śarmā Paṇśīkar, with the commentary *Candrikā* by Śrutadevasūri, Bombay 1901-1903, = *Kāvyamālā* 70; new edition by Śivadatta Paṇḍit 1916), and still from the 10th century A.D. Vādirājasūri's *Yaśodhara-carita* (edited (Tanjore, 1912). Puṣpadanta composed in Apabhraṃśa his *Jasaharanacarü* c. 975 A.D. (edited P.L. Vaidya, *Jasaharacariu of Puṣpadanta*, Karanja, 1931 (Ambādās Chaware Digambara Jain Granthamālā, or Karanja Jain Series, vol. I.) Of c. 975-1050 A.D. is the anonymous Tamil version *Yacōtarakāviyam* (edited by T. Venkatarama Iyengar, Madras 1908; see also e.g. K.V. Zvelebil, *Tamil literature*, Wiesbaden, 1974, p. 140).

Apparently not yet printed are versions in further languages: in Kannada Janna wrote one c. 1209 A.D. (and there are hints that an earlier version existed); in Gujarati a variety of works span a period between 1463 and 1619 A.D.; and in Hindi we have by Lakhmidas a version of 1724 A.D. (For further details see P. L. Vaidya, op. cit., pp. 27f.—Ibid., pp. 24ff, manuscripts of later Sanskrit versions are mentioned.)

I have discovered a South Indian manuscript with a collection of Jaina stories in Tamil, which appears to include a (prose) version of the story of Yaśodhara. I hope to publish this material in the near future.

5. A list of 29 authors is provided by P.L. Vaidya (op. cit., pp. 24-8). The works of the majority of these are only found in manuscripts.

6. Hariṣeṇa's *Bṛhatkathākośa*, edited A.N. Upadhye, Bombay, 1943 (Bhāratīya Vidyā Bhavan, Siṅghī Jaina Granthamālā, vol. 17). Our story is numbered 73, consists of 305 *ślokas*, and can be found on pp. 169-178 of the Sanskrit text.

7. *Kahakosu* by Muni Śrīcandra, Apabhraṃśa text edited by H.L. Jain, Ahmedabad, 1969 (Prakrit Text Society Series no. 13). It was written in Saurāṣṭra.

8. Generally *ārādhanā* refers to the cultivation by the monk of mental attitudes like detachment and indifference, particularly at the time of dying. A host of works dealing with the relevant material was produced, and most of these carry '*ārādhanā*' in their title (see Upadhye's introduction, pp. 47-50). The oldest of these (perhaps of the 4th or 5th century A.D.) is the *Bhagavatī Ārādhanā* attributed to Śivārya or Śivakoṭi. It was used in ascetic circles to prepare a dying monk for his death (vs. 303f of the translation may well be referring to this custom), by reading out certain portions of it. A commentarial literature developed, but the Sanskrit authors (like Āśādhara) did not narrate the stories

that were alluded to in the text. Instead, separate *kathākośas* were produced, which specialized in telling those stories, and Hariṣeṇa's work is one of them. But Āśādhara himself refers to Prakrit commentaries on the *Ārādhanā* where such stories were told, and therefore it seems likely that Hariṣeṇa wrote on the basis of this Prakrit material. (For details see Upadhye pp. 57f.)

9. *Kahakosu, sandhi* 30 (p. 306) begins with a quotation of *Bhagavatī Ārādhanā* verse 802:

māredi egam avi jo jīvaṃ so bahusu jamma-koḍīsu /

avaso mārijjanto maradi vidhānehī bahuehī //

'He who kills a single living being, will in many millions of rebirths die by being killed in many different ways, unable to defend himself.'

(Compare with this the concluding verse, 305, in Hariṣeṇa.) Then follows a brief Sanskrit commentary on the verse, which concludes:

atrārthe Yaśodharākhyānaṃ kathyate /

suprasiddhatvān na likhitam /

'For the sake of (illustrating this) the story of Yaśodhara is told here. (But) since it is so well known, it has not been (re)written (in Apabhraṃśa).' The 'here' very likely refers to Hariṣeṇa's story 73.

The previous *sandhi* 29 has already two stories dealing with the theme of *hiṃsā* and *ahiṃsā*, just as the first story actually told in *sandhi* 30 (*kaḍavakas* 1-7) has the same topic. This section is surrounded by stories about 'the true faith' (*saṃyaktva*) in *sandhis* 24 (from *kaḍavaka* 4) to 28 (end) and about the value of telling the truth in *sandhis* 30 (from *kaḍavaka* 8) to 31 (end). For a brief survey of the contents of the *Bhagavatī Ārādhanā* itself see Upadhye pp. 50 f.

10. Hariṣeṇa's style is both tedious and difficult. He has a tendency to overload the latter part of many of his *ślokas* with stereotyped attributes; thus not every time for instance an ascetic is called 'pure-minded' has this been translated. Every direct speech is followed with a stereotyped 'having heard these words of ...' and I have frequently used briefer means of translating such basically oral features. The difficulties lie in the fact that Hariṣeṇa is often extremely brief and elliptic, assuming an independent knowledge of the story. Thus a generous scattering of square brackets was unavoidable. My 'he' or 'she' with a particular animal may not always correspond to English usage, but it is meant to assist in maintaining an awareness of the fact that, according to Jaina beliefs, these creatures are capable of memory, understanding and even minimal religion (see vs. 99f and 270-274 on this.) — I would like to thank Gyan Pandey for some useful stylistic suggestions.

11. H. Jacobi (op. cit., pp. 1X=1XV) provides a summary of the story as told in Haribhadra's *Samarāiccakahā*. M. Bloomfield (*The life and stories of the Jaina savior Pārçvanātha*, Baltimore, The John Hopkins Press, 1919, pp. 195-8) briefly summarizes the story as found in Pradyumnācārya's *Samarādityasaṃkṣepa* (correct p. 196, line 2 accordingly), IV, 260ff. This work is itself a summary in Sanskrit of Haribhadra's *Samarāiccakahā*. — J. Hertel (*Jinakīrti's "Geschichte von Pāla und Gopāla,"* Leipzig, B.G. Teubner, 1917 = Berichte über die Verhandlungen der Königl. Sächsischen Gesellschaft der Wissenschaften zu Leipzig, Philologisch-historische Klasse, 69. Band, 4. Heft) summarizes two Sanskrit versions, both called *Yaśodharacarita*, by Vādirājasūri

(pp. 91-8) and Māṇikyasūri (pp. 81-91). — Somadeva's *Yaśastilaka* has been discussed in detail by K. K. Handiqui, *Yaśastilaka-campū and Indian culture*, Sholapur, 1949 (Jīvarāja Jaina Granthamālā). A very brief summary is found in A.B. Keith, *A History of Sanskrit literature*, London, 1928 (and many reprints), pp. 333-6. — P.L. Vaidya (*Jasaharacariü of Puṣpadanta*, pp. 28-31) summarizes Puṣpandata's version. — Finally, the anonymous Tamil verse version, *Yacōtarakāviyam*, is summarized by M.S. Purnalingam Pillai in his *Tamil literature*, 1929, pp. 145ff. The edition of Vādirāja's version edited by Dr. K. Krishnamoorthy, Dharwar, 1963, also contains an English translation.

12. The text edited by Upadhye has remained imperfect, in spite of the great efforts made by the editor, in his footnotes, notes, glossary (pp. 102-110) and Corrigenda (p.400), to improve on the state of the manuscripts. I have indicated the more important changes I have made to Upadhye's text in the footnotes. Here are some minor points: v. 1 *-ogha* (for *-augha*, in line with vs. 5 and 221); v. 22 *yūna eke* (for *yūnāikena*); v. 67 *jāla* (for *jala*); v. 174 *Yuṣmat* (for *asmat*, Upadhye p. 386); v. 175 *yathedam* (for *-ai-*); v. 262 *-aṃ aśeṣa-* (for *śeṣa-*); v. 277 *jāyatām* (for *jaya-*).

13. I read in v. 9: *kubjakenāinām bhuñjānām*. — Other versions add further unpleasant or even disgusting characteristics. Thus the *Samarāiccakahā* (pp. 240f) suggests a sadistic streak in the lover and later authors developed this theme extensively. Or Puṣpadanta (*Jasaharacariü*, II, 6, 10) mentions that his body looked as black as 'a tree-trunk burnt in a forest fire,' a feature which the *Arabian Nights* (see note 3 above) draws attention to.

14. Hariṣeṇa's account makes little sense, but unfortunately the other versions all go their own separate ways in dealing with the dream. Generally the point of what Yaśodhara tells appears to be that he must become an ascetic, in order to avoid disaster to himself and the kingdom. In Puṣpandanta (*Jasaharacariü*, II, 13, 13-22) we hear not only that he fell down from the palace, but also about the apparition of a terrifying warrior who threatens him with disaster, if he does not become a monk. Māṇikyasūri, according to Hertel (p. 84) tells us 'he dreamt that he was sitting on his throne on the seventh floor of his palace, that his mother pushed him off it and made him roll down to the ground floor — herself rolling down after him — ...that he then got up again, as a shaven Śvetāmbara monk, and climbed back to the seventh floor.' Vādirāja (Hertel p. 93), on the other hand, has Yaśodhara recite a punning verse about the light (viz. Amṛtamatī) abandoning the moon (viz. himself) and uniting with the darkness (viz. the black hunchback), which his mother fails to understand.

15. In v. 17 I read: *svalpaṃ dīkṣaṇam*, lit. 'initiation will have no value to you.'

16. *Tat-kṣaṇāt* in v. 20 can be explained as follows. A *modaka*, 'sweet sidh,' is (certainly in Mahārāṣtra today, where it is ubiquitous during the Gaṇeśa festival) a round ball of sweetmeat, made of flour, lots of sugar and spices. Thus it could have been the *prasāda* from the rites performed for Kātyāyanī. However, other versions of the story let Amṛtamatī mix the poison directly into the ingredients used for making the 'flour cock.' For all we know, the cock-shaped offering was actually a *modaka* (naturally to be eaten after the sacrifice). — The psychology behind the murder should become clear from v. 298; were the king to become an ascetic, his queen would be expected to become a nun, something she obviously was not keen on.

17. In v. 27 we could construct: *sva-pateḥ gṛhītaḥ puruṣasya ca samarpitaḥ*, 'he took him from his (former) master (viz. the *kenacit* of v. 26) and handed him over to a man.' But in v. 81, in a similar situation, a goat is handed over to the king's goatherd and perhaps we ought to read *śva-pateḥ*, 'handed him over to a man who was his dog-keeper,' as Upadhye p. 386 suggests.

18. The critical word (in v. 41 etc.) is *jāhaka*. The conventional dictionary meaning is 'hedgehog, porcupine' (see also Vādirāja, Hertel, p. 94, 'Stachelschwein'; Tamil (III, 17ff) has paṉṟi, 'pig,' but the editor (p. xxxiv) renders it *mu̱ḻḻam paṉṟi*, viz. 'porcupine'). Upadhye tentatively suggests in his glossary (p. 105) 'chameleon.' But given Indian folklore, the most natural enemy of the cobra is the mongoose. Indeed we hear in Māṇikyasūri (Hertel p. 86) of 'Ichneumon,' and *sub nakula* Monier-Williams lists Viverra Ichneumon. Now Puṣpadanta (*Jasaharacariü*, II, 36, 6) mentions *pasavi* and *pasaviya* (for which Hariṣeṇa, v. 41, has *paśavī* and *paśava*, explained by Upadhye (p. 106) 'a kind of animal' probably on the basis of the *Pāiasaddamahaṇṇavo* (*sub pasaya*), '*mṛg-viśeṣ*') which Vaidya (Index p. 141) explains '"*nakula*" *ity arthe deśī*.' In the light of this, I have chosen 'mongoose' in the translation.

19. I have left the final part of v. 48 untranslated. It reads: *vairaṃ dyuphaṇena hi khādyate*. If we change the last word into *svādyate* (for which it is, according to Monier-Williams, a frequent v.l.), we would obtain 'for enmity is relished between/by...' But I cannot make sense of *dyuphaṇa*, for which Upadhye (p. 106) has a mysterious **dviphaṇa*, 'double-hooded (serpent?).'

20. I read in v. 78 *sva-puraḥ-sthita* (for *-pura-sthe-*). — Other versions explain this vicious act by stating that the king had been unsuccessful during his hunt and let out his frustration in this way. We might connect the *pāparddhyā* with this idea: 'because of very bad luck, (he had no success).'

21. This according to Upadhye (p. 106); *narādhama* would literally be 'lowest among men.'

22. I read in v. 82 (*pāparddhyā varam* (for *-oddhi-varam*) as in v. 78.

23. *Kāka-tālīya-yogena* in v. 84. This refers (see Monier-Williams) to two events happening at the same time, but without being connected causally. (The crow sits down on a palm-branch, when the over-ripe coconut happens to drop down.) The point is that the goddess (however 'real' she may be), would not have the power to fulfill anybody's wish.

24. A very elliptic verse; the translation is tentative. It looks like an elaborate paraphrase, which lost its poignancy. For Māṇikyasūri (Hertel p. 87) makes the goat say '*ete me*' which not only means 'that (food given to the brahmins in honour of me) belongs to me, to me,' but also imitates the animal's sounds.

25. On this gruesome scene of v. 106b-108 we have to consult Puṣpadanta (*Jasahara-cariü*, III, 12, 13b-17) who describes it as follows. 'Under its belly, a fire was set alight, and while he was roasting in the flames of that lively fire and stuck out his tongue and roared miserably, water with the three "biting" flavours, viz. acrid, (spicy-)hot and bitter, was brought and placed before him. When he had drunk it, all dried up from thirst that he was, his inside was hit by the foul drink and whatever impurities were inside his stomach came out by the "hind door".' Thus it is clear that, more originally, a purgative was intended which was forced into the animal by making it thirsty. Hariṣeṇa either misunderstands this, or alludes to a different practice by means of which the roasted

animal gets internally flavoured. — Anyway, the locatives of *nire* etc. (in 108) should be changed into instrumentals.

26. In this v. 109, I cannot make sense of either *dhṛta-paścima-bhāgakaḥ* (and translate instead, from v. 100, *chinna-*) or *jvālābhāsita-sarvāśo* is this meant as an adverbial clause, 'while all the quarters were illuminated by the flames,' or should we read *-aṅgo*, 'all his limbs shining with the flames,' or **bhāsmita-*, 'all his hopes burned to ashes by the fire'?

27. A weird expression, regardless of whether we read *cīra-paṭṭa-sama* with the text or change it to *cīna-*; the attribute would be more appropriate for the tent (see next note).

28. Hariṣeṇa is clearly confused about the precise location of the various characters. In v. 190 (where the main narrative continues) he locates king Yaśomati inside the tent and the two chickens outside at a distance. This makes better sense, since the ascetic, whose discourse the birds hear, would not be standing close to the king who is dallying with his queen.

29. In v. 132 (also v. 240), *ekādaśāṅga-dhārī*, lit. 'having memorized the eleven Aṅgas.' The works called Aṅgas constitute the second major group of Jaina canonical scriptures. Knowledge of the first, called Pūrvas, was apparently lost after 300 B.C. after some of their contents had been integrated into the twelfth Aṅga (*Diṭṭhivāya*). But even this twelfth Aṅga became extinct. Thus 'eleven Aṅgas' denotes the first and foremost available section of the Jaina canon. However, the Digambaras maintain that even the Aṅgas had become extinct by the second century A.D. But since we do not know in which period Hariṣeṇa, who is a Digambara, envisaged the events narrated in our story to have taken place, we need not search for a contradiction here. (At least according to the interpretation of the editor of the Tamil *Yacōtarakāviyam* (p. iii), Yaśodhara's father was the famous king Aśoka of the 3rd century B.C. It is true that the Tamil text reads Acōkan (II, 1.11 etc.), but this is merely a rendering of Sanskrit Yaśas+ogha, corresponding to our Kīrtyogha. For information on the Aṅgas see Padmanabha S. Jaini, *The Jaina Path of Purification*, reprinted Delhi, 1979, pp. 47-55.

30. In v. 132 *avadhi-jñāna*, also in v. 211 *avadhi-locana*. This is the third among the five types of knowledge distinguished by Jaina authors. Innate to gods and denizens of the hells, it can be obtained by human beings through meditational practices. Knowledge here transcends the senses and can, which is essential in our story, grasp past events without having witnessed them. See Jaini, op. cit., pp. 121f.

31. This long passage, v. 131-159, appears somewhat out of place in Hariṣeṇa's otherwise very concise narrative. Indeed it is absent in the earlier version found in the *Samarāiccakahā*. However, an almost identical passage is found in the same text, but as part of the main narrative and not of the emboxed Yaśodhara story, viz. pp. 164, 18 — 179, 19 (with the three arguments about the nature of the soul found pp. 172, 13 — 174, 19). There it is a *nāhiyavādi*, viz. *nāstika-vādin*, 'materialist,' called Piṅgakesa who claims that the soul does not possess autonomous, independent existence from the body. I cannot tell whether it was Hariṣeṇa himself who chose to insert that discussion into the present story, or whether he found it like this in his source. But given the detail with which he writes about the discussion, one might be tempted to regard it as Hariṣeṇa's own innovative addition to the story of Yaśodhara. — The passage as found in the *Samarāiccakahā* is itself much older, for we find another version in a canonical scripture, the second Upāṅga *Rāyapaseṇaijja*. Moreover, it appears that also the Buddhists adopted

the arguments found there, in their *Dīghanikāya* 23 (Pāyasisuttantan). See on these passages E. Frauwallner, *Geschichte der indischen Philosphie*, vol. II, Salsburg, 1956, pp. 297-300 (with note 381), and on the Lokāyata system attributed to Cārvāka, ibid. pp. 302-309. By claiming that the soul and the body are not different, ideas are alluded to which are associated with the Lokāyata: consciousness (and life) are seen there merely as products of the body (as alcohol is the product of the fruits, sugar, etc.).

Particularly vs. 135 and 145 are not clear. In the former verse, there is first the problem that normally the Lokāyata rejects the concept of transmigration. Secondly, my translation of *dehināṃ sa jīvas tac chairīrakam* as 'body and soul that are the same' is tentative. In v. 145b, the text is definitely corrupt (*yathāhaṃ savajjīvo 'sti tadevacca śarīrakam*). Upadhye first emends *śavajīvo 'sti tadevaṃ ca*, from which I have derived my translation, although the details of the construction remain obscure to me. Then he suggests (p. 386) *yathā sa eva jīvo 'sti tad eva ca (śarīrakam)* (from v. 153b), 'how the soul is, so is the body.'

32. The three sets of vows are the *aṇu-vratas* ('smaller vows'), *guṇa-vratas* and the *śikṣā-vratas*. Details on these can easily be found in Jaini, op. cit., pp. 170-181; Frauwallner, op. cit., vol. I, pp. 256f; R. Williams, *Jaina yoga : a survey of the medieval śrāvakācāras*, London, 1963. In Williams, op. cit., p. 53, the five types of *udumbara* (Hariṣeṇa's text, v. 169, has a Prakritic *pañc' umbara*), 'figs,' are listed with their Latin names. On the rationale behind this prohibition, and that against eating honey, see Jaini, op. cit., pp. 167ff. The fivefold veneration (*pañca-namaskāram*, v. 170) salutes five types of holy beings, *arhats*, *siddhas*, etc. For the full Prakrit text, with translation, of this prayer see Jaini, op. cit., pp. 162f. 'True faith' translates here and elsewhere *samyaktva* or *saṃyag-darśana*, which includes that first flash of insight when the Jaina teaching begins to make sense (for details see Jaini, op. cit., pp. 141-151).

33. See note 28 above.

34. Vs. 194f show a remarkable Freudian slip, by reading *puṣpāvatī*, 'menstruating'; v. 229 reveals the secret: Puṣpāvalī, which is no more than a synonym of Kusumāvalī.

35. V. 195 *samādhānāt*, and similarly *samādhinā* in vs. 222 and 301. The state of mind in which a person finds himself at the time of dying is considered by Jaina authors as an important feature determining the kind of the next rebirth. The two expressions refer to dying while fully conscious and concentrating on the truths of the Jaina religion. (See Jaini, op. cit., pp. 227f and Upadhye, op. cit., p. 57.) The alternative is referred to in our v. 77, *mūḍha-manas*, 'with clouded mind,' where the goat (unlike his subsequent rebirth) had learnt nothing and thus does not move upwards on the scale of life.

36. Although Amṛtamatī's crime was infinitely greater than Yaśodhara's, our story ignores her fate almost entirely. In Māṇikyasūri (Hertel p. 87) we hear that when Yaśomati organizes a feast in honour of his dead father (corresponding to our v. 98) which is witnessed by the goat, all of Yaśodhara's wives participate, except for his chief queen (our Amṛtamatī). She has contracted leprosy from eating the piece of *rohita* fish (see our vs.73f), a misfortune attributed by her co-wives to her murdering Yaśodhara. The goat then sees her, ugly and deformed by her disease. — The same situation is found in Vādirāja (Hertel p. 95). The goat hears from the servants in the kitchen that Amṛtamatī's body exudes a foul smell and is covered in boils. This is attributed by them partly to her eating meat, partly to her sleeping with the hunchback, and partly to her having

murdered her husband. When he sees her, he concludes that she must have contracted leprosy from the hunchback (who also in other versions is said to have been a leper).

37. I have left out in v. 226 *bhavataḥ paṭṭa-bandhaṃ ca* which is out of place here.

38. *Śeṣā* in v. 250 literally refers to an offering made to a deity, which is taken back, after the deity has 'left' it, viz. hallowed it (compare note 16).

39. I change the text of v. 263a into *ātma-sambandhaṃ loka-vismaya-kāraṇam.*

40. The name (in v. 300) of this mode of committing religious suicide is a wrongly Sanskritized Prakrit *pāovagamana*, which ought to be *prāyopagamana*. It is one of the three modes mentioned in the *Ācārāṅga-sūtra* (I, 7, 8, translated by H. Jacobi, *Sacred Books of the East*, vol. 22, pp. 74-78.) However, it could be argued that it is used here in a non-technical sense, as a synonym for the less obscure *sallekhanā*. For details see Jaini, op. cit., pp. 227-233, where (p. 229) four situations of it are mentioned. A less likely explanation of the 'fourfold' could be the classification found in the *Uttarādhyāyana-sūtra* (30, 12f, translated H. Jacobi, *Sacred books of the East*, vol. 45, p. 176.) The *Bhagavatī Ārādhanā* discusses *pāovagamana* in vs. 2062-2077.

41. This may well be a reference to the ceremony conducted at the time of dying, involving the concentrated listening to the *Bhagavatī Ārādhanā* (see note 8). 'Fourfold' is explained (Upadhye p. 47) as involving 'faith, knowledge, conduct and penance.'

Part II

Of Peoples and Places: Stories from the Biography Collections and a Pilgrimage Text

Jain Biographies: Selections from the *Prabandhakośa, Kharataragacchabṛhadgurvāvali, Vṛddhācāryaprabandhāvali, and the Ākhyānakamaṇikośa*

Translated by Phyllis Granoff

Introduction

Telling the deeds of famous monks and kings, wealthy lay patrons and exemplary devotees, was an important part of medieval Jain literature. Stories of people who were important to the tradition were told in Sanskrit and in the medieval vernaculars; in addition monks wrote elaborate poems and prose compositions telling of the deeds of the Jinas, both in their most recent life and in their many past lives. Some of the stories that were told of famous monks were preserved in the didactic story collections which owe so much to the *Āvaśyaka* literature. Others seem to have circulated at pilgrimage centers and were told both in special biography collections and in texts that collect stories about pilgrimage sites. The special biography collections were compiled by monks often for the benefit of a wealthy and powerful lay patron. Most of them date from the 13th-14th century, and many of them even include stories about famous poets and kings who were not specifically connected with Jainism. Still other stories formed part of the sectarian histories that were written by particular groups of monks. These histories detail the transmission of the teachings from monastic leader to monastic leader and are called *gurvāvalis*.

The various stories of monks and important patrons of the faith that these sources preserve are as varied as surely the people they honour must have been. I have translated a selection of stories from a number of different texts. The *Prabandhakośa* of Rājaśekharasūri was written in 1349 A.D. The Sanskrit

Kharataragacchabṛhadgurvāvali was written in two parts and probably belongs to the early part of the 14th century. The *Vṛddhācāryaprabandhāvali*, in Prakrit, belongs to the same period and recounts the deeds of the same monks as the *Kharataragacchabṛhadgurvāvali*, but as the translation of the accounts of Jineśvarasūri shows, it preserves a different tradition. The *Ākhyānakamaṇikośa*, which is a didactic story collection and not properly speaking a collection of biographies, preserves its stories largely in its Prakrit commentary which dates to 1134 A.D. I have commented on how I did the translations in a brief note that can be found after Chapter 2.

Bhadrabāhu and Varāha, from the *Prabandhakośa*, pp.2-4.

In the South, in the city Pratiṣṭhāna, lived two young Brahmin boys called Bhadrabāhu and Varāha, both without a penny to their names and with no one to look after them, and both gifted with much native intelligence. Now the Jain monk Yaśobhadra, who was one of those rare individuals to possess knowledge of the fourteen ancient scriptures, chanced to come to that city. Bhadrabāhu and Varāha heard him preach. This is what he said,

"Pleasures, in all their many forms, are treacherous and impermanent, and from them arises this cycle of births. O see here now, all you people, why do you look for what is eternal and true in all of this? Your doings are in vain!

Make your mind pure and calm, free from the snares of all your desires, and concentrate it in meditation on that highest abode of eternal bliss, if you trust in my words."

As soon as they heard these words, they were awakened to the truth, and when they got home they took counsel with each other, "Why do we lead our lives in vain? To begin with we have no money to get pleasures for ourselves; we should instead practice religion."

"Listen, O mind of mine, let him lust after the taste of worldly pleasures, before whom walk bards, singing praises; let him hanker after sensual delights, who walks in step with gifted poets from Southern lands, bantering with them in well-honed verses, and who hears behind him all the while the enticing jangling of the bracelets of the young women who wave ceremonial fans over him in honour. But if a man lacks all this, well then, O mind, he should direct you at once into the stillness of meditation on the Supreme Truth."

Thinking this both the brothers became monks.

Bhadrabāhu became a famous monk, a leader in the monastic community, conversant with the fourteen ancient scriptures and possessed of the thirty-six qualities of a holy man. He was celebrated as the author of commentaries to these ten texts, the *Daśavaikālika*, *Uttarādhyayana*, *Daśāśrutaskandha*, *Kalpa*, *Vyavahāra*, *Āvaśyaka*, *Sūryaprajñapti*, *Sūtrakṛta*, *Ācārāṅga*, and the *Ṛṣibhāṣita*. He also wrote a text which was entitled the *Saṃhitā* of Bhadrabāhu. Now at that time there also lived the Jain monk Ārya Sambhūtivijaya, who was also one of those rare individuals gifted with knowledge of the fourteen ancient scriptures. It came time for the Glorious monk Yaśobhadra to sojourn in Heaven. Bhadrabāhu and this Sambhūtivijaya, cherishing great affection for each other, wandered separately around the land of India. They were like two suns that make bloom the lotuses that are the fortunate souls who are ready to accept the true doctrine.

Now Varāha was also a learned man. But he stood high atop the mountain of terrible pride and he kept asking his brother Bhadrabāhu to install him as a leader of the group of monks. Bhadrabāhu told him, "Brother, true it is that you are learned and that you carry out all your duties with care, but you are stained by pride. I cannot give someone who suffers from pride the office of a leading monk." Though these words were true they did not appeal to Varāha, for it is said that the words of a teacher, even when they are crystal clear like pure spring water, sting the ears of a disciple who is not fit for receiving the true doctrine. And so it came to pass that Varāha abandoned his monastic vows. He returned to his earlier false beliefs and began to dress and behave as a Brahmin once more.

He boasted that he had written a new text known as the *Saṃhitā* of Varāha, which in fact was based on the knowledge that he had acquired during the time he had been a Jain monk. But he told everyone, "I have been studying the position of the planets and heavenly bodies ever since I was a child. And I have always been totally absorbed in this pursuit. Once, just outside the city of Pratiṣṭhāna I happened to draw an astrological calculation on a rock. When evening came I left my calculations there and went home to sleep. In my dreams I suddenly remembered that I had not erased my scribblings. And so I went back there to erase what I had written. There on the rock on which I had written my astrological calculations sat a lion. No matter, with one hand I stroked his belly and with the other I erased the notes I had made. At that the lion turned into the Sun God right before my very eyes. He spoke to me, 'Son, I am pleased with your firmness of determination and your devotion to the science of astrology. I am the Sun; ask of me some boon.' I, for my part, then replied, 'O master! If you are pleased with me, then let me ride in your chariot awhile and show me all the heavenly bodies in their courses.' And so it came to be that I was permitted to roam the heavens with the Sun in his very own chariot. And partaking of the nectar of immortality that he magically transferred into my body, I felt no pang from hunger or thirst or any other unsatisfied bodily need. And when I had accomplished my task, I bade farewell to the Sun and I returned to this world to roam around and serve the earthly realm with my knowledge. That is why I am called 'Varāha of the Sun,' Varāhamihira."

He did not hesitate to spread all sorts of tales like this. And because there was just the slightest grain of possibility in all of his stories he came to be greatly honored in the world. In the city of Pratiṣṭhānapura he won over the King

Śatrujit with his many talents. And the king made him his own court priest. So it is that they say,

"A man's fine qualities lead him to a position of respect, not any fiddle-faddle about his birth and family; we treasure a flower grown in the woods, but throw away in disgust the dirt that comes from our very own bodies."

Now he began to abuse the Śvetāmbaras, saying, "What do those old crows know about anything? Like naughty school children confined to their rooms they mutter and mumble to themselves, buzzing like flies, wasting all their time. Oh well, let them do what they want. Why should I care anyway what they do?" The lay disciples who heard his taunts were pained by his words; why, their heads throbbed as they heard them. They gathered together and said, "What use is it to be alive if we must just stand by and hear our teachers being abused? What can we do? The king honors this Varāhamihira, considering him to be a man of many talents, and people do say, 'He who is honored by kings is honored by the world.' There is nothing we can do about that. But we can summon Bhadrabāhu, at least." And this is exactly what they did. The Glorious Bhadrabāhu arrived there. The lay disciples welcomed him with a great celebration in his honour, and with such pomp and ceremony as to excite the envy of anyone watching. They lodged their teacher in comfortable quarters. The members of the king's court were daily treated to a feast of lectures delivered by Bhadrabāhu. Varāha was not a little chagrined by Bhadrabāhu's arrival; nonetheless there was nothing he could do against him.

In the meantime a son was born to Varāhamihira. Delighted at the birth, he spent a vast sum of money entertaining his friends and making donations to the poor. And for all of this he was even more greatly honored in the community. He proclaimed before the king and all the courtiers in the royal assembly hall, "My son will live a hundred years." And at his house he gave party after party in celebration of the birth. One day Varāha publicly declared, "Now see here. Even though he is my very own brother Bhadrabāhu did not come to the party I gave in honour of the birth of my son. Henceforth he shall be an outcaste amongst us, never to be invited to any of our family festivities." When they heard these words, the lay disciples told Bhadrabāhu, "This is the kind of thing he is going around saying. You must go to his house one day. It is not right that the enmity between you should grow any more." The Glorious Bhadrabāhu instructed them, "Why do you make me undertake not just one but two difficult tasks? This child that has been born to Varāhamihira will be killed by a cat in the middle of the night when he is just seven days old. And when he dies I shall have to go anyway to express my condolences." At this the lay disciples said, "But that Brahmin proclaimed before the king himself that the child has a life span of one hundred years. And now you say otherwise. What are we to believe?" The Glorious Bhadrabāhu told them, "Truth depends on corroboration. For that is something that cannot happen if what a man says is untrue." The lay disciples were silent.

It was seven days after the birth. And on that very day, when the night was only two-watches deep, the wet-nurse sat down with the baby to let it nurse. A heavy iron door bolt fell from the top of the door lintel as someone opened the door to come into the room. And it struck the baby on the head. The child was dead. There was much wailing and crying then in Varāha's house. A crowd gathered. And Bhadrabāhu told his lay disciples, "It is a monk's sacred duty to relieve people of their grief. I must go there at once." The teacher then went there, accompanied by hundreds of his lay disciples. Varāha, though dazed and wounded by grief, was properly respectful to him and rose to greet him. And he said to him, "Teacher! Your prediction has come true. The only thing that was not exactly right was that you said a cat would kill him, but the door bolt has killed him instead." Bhadrabāhu said, "There is a line drawing of a cat on the tip of that iron door bolt. I did not speak untruthfully." They brought the door bolt and examined it; it was exactly as Bhadrabāhu had said.

Varāha then said, "I am not as pained by the death of my son as I am by the fact that the prediction, which I made before the king, that my child would have a life-span of a hundred years has turned out to be false. I curse those books of mine which I trusted so when I boasted of my great knowledge. They are all a bunch of liars. I'll wash their filthy mouths with soap and water." And with these words he had the servants fill cauldrons with water. As soon as he was about to carry out his threat and wash the books with water, Bhadrabāhu grabbed him by the arms and stopped him. "Why should you be angry at the books when the fault was yours alone? It was your own failure to understand them that led you to make false conclusions. These books do in fact record what the Omniscient One said, only it is not so easy to find someone who understands them correctly. I can show you the very places where you went astray; it is you yourself whom you should be cursing. You know yourself what people often say,

'The favour of the king, youth, riches, good-looks, high birth, valour in battle, learning, all these things make a man drunk even though they are not wine.'

And how can a drunkard have the subtle understanding that is necessary to comprehend a difficult treatise? You must not destroy these books."

With these words Varāha was restrained from his rash act; non-plussed at the turn of events, he did nothing more. At that point a lay disciple, who had been quite upset by Varāha's denunciation of the Jain doctrine, stepped forward and said, "Wretched little worms you are, who glow in the deep darkness of night.

Now the world is aglow with the brilliance of the mid-day sun. Even the moon does not dare to show its light. Wretched little glow worm, look what's happened to you now!"

And with these words he beat a hasty retreat. Varāha was exceedingly pained. By this time the king himself had arrived on the scene. The king told him, "Do not grieve. O wise man, this is the way of the world." At that a minister of the king, who was a Jain devotee, spoke up, "The new teacher is also here, the one who predicted that the boy would live only seven days. He is indeed great, for his words have proved to be true." Someone then pointed out Bhadrabāhu to the king, saying, "This is the one." With those words the Brahmin was made even more miserable; he alone could have described his own mental torment. The king departed; Bhadrabāhu too departed, and finally the crowd dispersed. The king accepted the Jain doctrine and became a lay disciple.

Varāha in his humiliation became a Vaiṣṇava monk and endured all sorts of penances out of ignorance. On his death he became a demi-god who was hostile to the Jain faith. With all his hatred, though, he was not able to trouble any of the monks, for it is true what they say, "Austerities are like a suit of armour made of the hardest diamond; they permit a sage to repel the attacks of others just as armour repels swarms of arrows deftly shot at it." And so Varāhamihira began instead to torment the lay disciples. He caused disease to occur in every house. Distressed and suffering, the lay devotees approached Bhadrabāhu, "O Blessed One! That even while you are here with us we are so tormented by diseases is proof of the saying, 'Even when he is mounted on an elephant, a man may still be gnawed at by mice." The teacher answered them, "Do not be afraid. You remember that Varāhamihira. Now he seeks to harm you all because of the hatred he nourished for you when he was alive. I can protect you even from the hand of the Wielder of the Thunderbolt, Indra, the King of the Gods, should he wish to strike you down." And then, taking from the ancient scriptures such hymns as the hymn which begins with the words, "Lord Pārśva who removes obstacles," he wove a hymn of praise which contained five verses and he recited it before everyone. All of their troubles instantly ceased. Even today those who desire to be rescued from some difficulty recite this hymn. It is like a wonderful wishing jewel with unimaginable powers. It is said that after Bhadrabāhu his student the Glorious Sthūlabhadra also possessed knowledge of the fourteen ancient scriptures and defeated many rivals in debate.

Āryanandila, from the *Prabandhakośa*, pp. 5-7.

In the city Padminīkhaṇḍa was a king named Padmaprabha. His wife was named Padmāvatī. In that very city also dwelt the merchant Padmadatta. His wife was named Padmayaśā. They had a son, who was named Padma. The travelling merchant Varadatta pledged his own daughter, who was named Vairoṭyā, to this son of theirs in marriage. And he married her in due time.

One day Varadatta, the father of Vairoṭyā, was on his way to foreign lands with all of his family, when they all perished in a forest fire. Vairoṭyā, though she served her mother-in-law faithfully and humbly, met with only contempt from the older woman who knew that she had lost her father. For what they say is true:

"That women seem beautiful and possessed of hidden wealth, that women seem strong and spirited and enjoy their husband's favour, that women wield authority in their home, for sure all of this is nothing but the result of the status and power of their fathers, who are always there behind the scenes."

But though she was exceedingly pained by her mother-in-law's words, which burned like a raging fire as it consumes dry chaff, she cursed her own bad luck and never uttered a word against her mother-in-law. And she thought to herself,

"Everyone reaps the fruit of his own past actions. Another person is just the incidental cause of our misery or happiness, which we alone bring about through our very own deeds."

One day Vairoṭyā had a dream in which the Snake King announced her impending pregnancy to her and she conceived a child. She began to crave sweet milk pudding. It was then that the Jain monk Āryanandila happened to stop in a nearby public garden; like Āryarakṣitasvāmin before him, he possessed knowledge of thirteen of the fourteen ancient texts. Now that mother-in-law proclaimed, "This woman will give birth to a daughter; she will never produce a son." The chaste and faithful Vairoṭyā, pained by the harsh words of her mother-in-law, which pierced her ears like a sharp sword, went to pay her respects to the Jain monk. She bowed down to the monk. She told him about her dreadful relationship with her mother-in-law. The monk said, "This is the fault of some previous deed that you have done in another life. Do not let your anger grow. Do not let it grow, because it is the cause of rebirth and continued suffering. O daughter! In this birth, anger gives rise to such things as bodily harm, constant fighting and even undying hatred; and in the next world, it results in the most terrible suffering that comes from rebirth in hell and similar terrible misfortunes. I promise you, you will give birth to a son. I know that, since you have become pregnant, you long to eat sweet milk pudding. I promise you that somehow your craving will be fulfilled."

Delighted by these words of the monk, she went back home. And she thought to herself, "What they say is true:

'No matter how long we wander this earth, which is girded by the four vast oceans, we will never meet a person of truly noble nature to whom we can tell the long-kept secrets of our many miseries or even joys, and thereby for a minute, or even for a half a minute, feel suddenly at rest and peace.'

But I have met such a person today in meeting this monk."

One day, Padmayaśā, for her part, on the full moon night of the first month of spring, performed a ritual fast and was about to break her fast with appropriate ceremony. On that day it was the custom to give to the monks an ample portion of sweet milk pudding and to show particular generosity to all the lay members of the Jain faith. She did all of that. But because she hated her daughter-in-law, she gave her only coarse fare of cheap grain. Now the daughter-in-law secretly took some of the sweet milk pudding that was left over in a large cauldron and hastily poured it into a small pot, which she concealed under her clothes as she went out to the lake to fetch water. She set the pot down under a tree and went to wash her hands and feet.

Now it so happened that at this very moment in time there was a snake named Aliñjara, who lived in the underworld, and whose wife was also pregnant and longing to eat sweet milk pudding. She had come out from the nether regions and was now roaming the earth in search of some sweet milk pudding. That was how she came to see the pudding in the pot under that tree. And she ate it all. The snake lady then set out for her home by the very same path that she had taken to come up from the underworld. When Vairoṭyā had finished washing up and got back to the tree, right away she saw that there was no sweet milk pudding left in the pot any more. But even so she did not get angry and she did not utter a single nasty word. Instead she spoke these words of blessing,

"May you find fulfillment of your wishes, whoever you are, who ate this pudding."

Now Aliñjara's wife, concealed from view by the tree, heard her words of blessing. She returned home and told her husband what had happened. Vairoṭyā went home too. That night, the wife of the snake Aliñjara appeared to a neighbor of Vairoṭyā's in a dream and said, "Fair lady! I am the wife of the snake Aliñjara. Vairoṭyā is my daughter. She is pregnant and longs to eat sweet milk pudding. You must fulfill her wish. And so I instruct you that you should say these words to her, 'Your father is gone. But I shall take care of you as your own father would have done. I shall cool the burning pain that you feel from the fire of your mother-in-law's wrath.'"

The next morning Vairoṭyā's neighbor treated her to a meal of sweet milk pudding. Her pregnancy longing fulfilled, she gave birth to a son. As for the snake lady, she gave birth to a hundred sons. When the day came for Vairoṭyā's son's naming ceremony, the snake Aliñjara made a huge party for her. He had all the snakes in the underworld build a magnificent and beautifully appointed mansion on the spot where her father's house had stood. All the snakes gathered, with their troops and their elephants, their horses and their finest chariots. They filled her house with riches. And Aliñjara's wife, who now considered Vairoṭyā to be her adopted daughter, went there too, along with her husband and her many sons, and showered her with the most beautiful gifts of the finest clothes, silks, gold, and bracelets and necklaces all studded with precious gems. And Vairoṭyā began to visit Aliñjara's wife frequently after that. Vairoṭyā was treated with great respect by Aliñjara's wife and shown much honour. Her mother-in-law, seeing that Vairoṭyā's father's house now had returned, as it were, to its former wealth and splendour, began to treat Vairoṭyā with great deference, for it is true what they say, "People show respect to someone whom others already honour."

The snake lady sent her very own young sons to protect Vairoṭyā and watch after her. She put all those snakes into a pot. Now one day a servant girl chanced to put that pot on top of a metal pan that had just been heated on the stove. At once Vairoṭyā took it off. She sprinkled the snakes with water and revived them. But one baby snake had lost the tip of his tail. As she saw him slither and slip, having trouble without his tiny tail, she affectionately called out, "Long live my clown of a tailless one, who'll show us all a trick or two before he's done." And the snakes, who were bewitched by Vairoṭyā's charming son and loved him very much, all became like members of her own family and they gave her fine costly garments, gem stones and gold. And having made such a fine celebration for her son's naming day, eventually they all went back to their own homes. Vairoṭyā came to be the object of everyone's respect because of all the wonderful things the snakes did for her.

One day the snake Aliñjara noticed that one of his sons had lost his tail and he became furious. "What wicked person has damaged my son's tail?" And when he knew through his supernatural powers that it was Vairoṭyā who was responsible for the loss of his son's tail, then, despite all the kind feelings he had cherished for her up until that moment, he became enraged at her now. And in his anger he went to her home in order to do her some harm in return. Aliñjara hid himself in her house. Now Vairoṭyā had come to have the habit that whenever she entered a dark room, she would call out a little blessing to that snake that she had inadvertently injured, in order to ward of any evil that might lurk there. She would say, "Long live my little clown of a tailless one," as she had called him that day. Now when he heard Vairoṭyā call out these words, the snake king was pleased with her and gave her a pair of anklets. And he showed his favour to her with these words, "My daughter, from this day on you must come regularly to us in the underworld and the snakes will come to you." And Vairoṭyā, through the power of this boon from the snake, did indeed come and go between the earth and underworld as she pleased. She called her son "Nāgadatta," "Gift of the Snakes."

At that time the Glorious monk Āryanandila told Padmadatta, Vairoṭyā's father-in-law, "You must tell Vairoṭyā, 'Go to the domain of the snakes and say to the snakes, You must help everyone in our world. You must never bite anyone.' Her father-in-law related these words of the monk to her and she told them to the snakes. She went down there and she told them in a loud and clear voice, "Long live Aliñjara's wife. Long live Aliñjara. They restored my father to me even though he was dead by restoring the prestige of his house. They were my refuge when I had no refuge. Hear, hear, all you young snakes. The Great monk Āryanandila commands, 'Do not trouble our world. Help every one of us.'" Vairoṭyā then went back home. The monk composed a new hymn called "Praise to Vairoṭyā." Whoever recites this "Praise to Vairoṭyā" need not fear any harm from snakes.

Vairoṭyā brought all the snakes to the monk, who had become her teacher. He instructed them in the Jain faith. They all became calm and pure in mind. Vairoṭyā's son, who was called Nāgadatta, became a rich and prosperous man. Padmadatta became a Jain monk and his beloved wife became a Jain nun. He practiced austerities and went to heaven. And for her part Padmayaśā became his divine wife, according to his wishes, for he had achieved the power to bring into being anything that he desired. And Vairoṭyā died while meditating on the king of snakes and was reborn as the wife of the snake Dharaṇendra, a protector of the Jain faith. In that rebirth she kept the name Vairoṭyā.

The Glorious Jīvadeva, from the *Prabandhakośa*, pp.7-9.

There is in Gujarat a prosperous town named Vāyaṭa, which was founded by the God Vāyu, God of the Wind. In that town there lived a wealthy merchant named Dharmadeva. His wife was called Śīlavatī; she was like the Goddess of Domestic Prosperity and Bliss incarnate. They had two sons, Mahīdhara and Mahīpāla. Mahīpāla only wanted to amuse himself; he never studied any of the traditional skills. Scolded by his father, he left home in anger and went abroad. The merchant Dharmadeva passed on to the other world. And Mahīdhara also left the world; he became a Jain monk under the tutelage of the Glorious Jindatta, who belonged to the lineage of monks known as the Vāyaṭa Gaccha. He became a leader of the monastic community and his name as a monk was Rasillasūri.

Now it happened that Mahīpāla, too, became a monk; in the East, in the city Rājagṛha, he became a Digambara Jain monk and he was honored for his learning and known as a great teacher. His name as a monk was Suvarṇakīrti. His teacher Śrutakīrti gave him two magic spells, the one enabling him to summon the protecting Goddess Cakreśvarī, and the other enabling him to enter into someone else's dead body and reanimate it. When Dharmadeva went to heaven, Śīlavatī was deeply saddened, for what they say is true:

"Like a river without the ocean, like the night without the moon, like a lotus pond without the sun to make it bloom, so is a good woman without her husband."

She learned from someone who had come from Rājagṛha that her son, who was now called Suvarṇakīrti, was there, and she went there to see him. She found Suvarṇakīrti. Both son and mother felt great affection for each other. One day she told Suvarṇakīrti, "Your father has gone to heaven. You are now a monk here. But your brother, Mahīdhara, has also achieved fame as a monk; he occupies a position of great respect in the Śvetāmbara Jain community and is known as the monk Rasilla. He is active in Vāyaṭa. You two should get together, settle your differences and espouse the same faith."

She brought Suvarṇakīrti back to Vāyaṭa and the two brothers were reunited. Suvarṇakīrti's mother told him, "Son, become a Śvetāmbara. "Suvarṇakīrti replied, "Let Rasilla follow in my footsteps and become a Digambara monk." When things had come to this impasse, the mother prepared two dishes for them to eat. Now one of the dishes she made had been specially prepared for them and it was rich and delicious. The other was nothing special; it was just taken from the usual cooking that she had done for everyone else in the household. She summoned the Digambara first. He ate the first dish, the specially prepared rich food, to his heart's content. He didn't even so much as cast a glance at the ordinary food in the second dish. Two students of Rasilla then arrived. They both took the ordinary fare, desirous of burning off the effects of the bad deeds they had done in the past through the correct observance of their monastic vows. After everyone had eaten, the mother said to the Digambara, "Son, these Śvetāmbaras are pure. You don't seem bothered by any rule that says that a Jain monk cannot accept food that has been specially prepared for him. These Śvetāmbaras on the other hand firmly declare,

'The monk who accepts food that has been specially prepared for him and does not refuse such delicacies, indeed hankers after them, must be considered as outside the pale of the true Jain community. Such a monk fails in his duties.' And these Śvetāmbaras steadfastly practice what they preach. For this reason, you should join their group if you truly are seeking final release from the bonds of this world."

Suvarṇakīrti, brought to his senses by these words of his mother, became a Śvetāmbara monk. His name as a monk was Jīvadevasūri, and it was a name that soon became known all over the world. He wandered from place to place, accompanied by five hundred monks. And this Glorious Monk, a leader among monks, destroyed forever the disease of false belief for those noble souls whose time had come for them to accept the true faith, showering on them the magic healing elixir of his preaching of the true doctrine.

One day a strange ascetic showed up at one of his lectures. In fact he was trying to master a certain magic spell that would enable him to conquer all the three worlds, heaven, earth and the nether world. To that end he was in search of a man who possessed the thirty-two marks of greatness. Now at that time in history there were only three such men alive. One was King Vikramāditya; the second was the Glorious Monk Jīva, and the third was the ascetic himself. There was no one else on earth who was so great as to bear the entire thirty-two marks of greatness on his person. Now he could not kill the king, but he needed to eat his one daily meal by begging for it with the skull of such a great man as his begging bowl for a full six months in order to accomplish the magic spell. That was why he had come to the Jain monk to try to work black magic on him so that he could murder him and get his skull. But because the monk had an even more powerful spell, a Jain spell, although his monastic robe turned black and rotted, his body was untouched by the ascetic's magic. Then the ascetic paralyzed the tongue of the monk who was standing next to the Great Jīvasūri and whose duty it was to recite the sacred texts. The Great Jīvasūri in turn paralyzed the ascetic's speech in retaliation. Then that one wrote on the ground with a piece of chalk,

"Everyone does a good deed to the person who has done him a service. There's nothing to that. But rare indeed is the man who helps out someone who came to do him harm.

I came here to work black magic on you. You figured that out and have taken away my powers of speech. Show mercy on me. Release me from your grip. Take pity on me."

Anyway, this was the gist of what he wrote there. And so, out of compassion, the noble monk released him; the ascetic left Vāyaṭa and took up residence in a monastery just outside the town. The monk called together all the members of his own monastic group and told them, "That wicked ascetic is staying in a monastery over there. Take care that no monk or nun goes near the place, no matter what." They all accepted this prohibition without any dissent. But then two nuns, simple souls, got curious and they went to that very place that had been forbidden them. The ascetic saw them there and brought them under his control with some magic powder so that they never left his side. The Jain monk, Jīvadevasūri, remaining right there in his own lodgings, made a grass effigy. When he cut off the hand of the effigy, the ascetic's hand fell off. The ascetic released the two nuns. They were restored to their normal selves after they washed their heads, removing the last vestiges of the ascetic's magic spells.

Now one day in Ujjain, King Vikramāditya decided to start a new era which bore his name. In commemoration of that great event he sent the minister Nimba to Gujarat as part of his larger plan to free all his territories of poverty and make every place in his realm rich and prosperous. That Nimba built a temple to The Glorious Mahāvīra in Vāyaṭa. The Glorious Jīvadevasūri performed the consecration ceremony for the image in this temple.

At exactly that time there was in Vāyata a merchant named Lalla who was a devout follower of the false faith. He began right then and there to carry out a costly and lavish Vedic sacrifice. All the Brahmins gathered. Oppressed by the smoke from the sacred fire, a snake fell out of a nearby tree and landed on the edge of the fire pit. The cruel Brahmins picked up that poor creature and hurled it right into the fire. Seeing that, Lalla was suddenly disgusted with the Brahmins. He said, "Look how cruel they are; they actually enjoy taking the lives of living beings. I do not need to make men such as these my teachers in matters of religion." And with those words, he dismissed all the Brahmins and returned to his own home. He looked everywhere for a religious teacher. One day at mid-day a pair of monks who were the disciples of the Glorious Jīvadevasūri came to his house for alms. He was pleased with their demeanour and the way they took only pure food. He asked the two monks, "Who is your teacher?" They told him it was the Glorious Jīvadevasūri. Lalla went to see him. He formally became a lay devotee, accepting the twelve rules of conduct for a lay disciple. One day Lalla told him, "I had set aside a lakh of gold as a donation on the occasion of the festival to the Sun God. I have spent half of that sum. Please take the other half." The teacher did not accept the money, for he was without any greed or desire for worldly wealth. Lalla was even more pleased with his new teacher than before. The teacher instructed him, "You must bring to me the gift that you will receive tonight while you are in the middle of washing your feet." Obedient to his teacher's words Lalla went home.

That evening someone brought him a gift of two bulls. Lalla brought them to his teacher. The teacher told him, "Let these bulls go on their own. Build a temple on the spot where they stop." Again, obeying his teacher's words, Lalla released the bulls. The two bulls then went as far as the village Pippalana and then just stopped somewhere there. At that very place Lalla began to construct a temple. When it was finished, a strange Śaiva ascetic arrived on the scene. He declared, "There is a flaw in this temple." The people asked, "What is the flaw?" He said, "There is a woman who will haunt it." Lalla had heard all of this and he went back and told his teacher what was happening. The teacher said, "You must rid the spot of that offending ghost and then rebuild the temple. Lalla! Do not worry about where the money will come from. The Goddesses whose task it is to look after the temple will provide all the money that you will need." They began to dismantle the temple. They heard a voice, "Do not take down this temple." They told the teacher Jīvadevasūri about the voice. He withdrew into meditation. The superintending Goddess appeared. She said, "I am the daughter of the king of Kanyakubja. My name is Mahaṇīka. A long time ago, when I was living in Gujarat, Muslim armies invaded. I fled, but the soldiers pursued me, and in my terror I jumped into a well. I died and became a demi-god. I will not permit you to clear the ground by digging up the bones of my body. Make me the superintending Goddess of your temple and I shall make your temple rich and prosperous. "

The teacher agreed to do as she said. On a spot of land that she showed them they built a small shrine to her. And on that very spot they found all the money they needed, so much that they could not even begin to count it. Lalla became the happiest man in the world; no one could have vied with him for that distinction; the Jain community was also pleased. Angry at Lalla, the Brahmins placed a dying cow in the Jain temple. It died there. The lay disciples told the teacher about this. Through his magic powers the teacher moved the dead cow and put it in the temple of the Brahmins. As they say, "Plot against another and it happens to you." Desperate, with no other recourse, the Brahmins sought to appease the Glorious Jīvadevasūri, crying out, "O Jīvadevasūri, rescue us." The Glorious Jīvadevasūri scolded them and then told them, "If you all worship in my temple like faithful Jain lay believers and show my successors respect, if you donate a sacred thread made of gold on the occasion of the installation of my successor in my position, and if you promise that you will carry his sedan chair on your own shoulders, then and then only will I remove this cow from your temple." And they were so desperate that they promised all that he asked. They even fixed the agreement between them in writing, with seals and all.

Then the teacher, with his magic, removed the cow from the Brahmin temple. All the four castes were pleased at this.

Later when he knew that it was his time to die, the Jain monk, fearing that ascetic who had sought his skull to accomplish his evil magic, instructed the lay disciples to break his skull. He was afraid that if the ascetic succeeded in his designs he would trouble the Jain community. They did exactly as he asked. The ascetic, deprived of any hope for success, cried for a long time.

Āryakhapaṭācārya, from the *Prabandhakośa*, pp. 9-11.

In some lineage of monks there appeared the Glorious Āryakhapaṭācārya, who possessed very many marvelous supernatural powers and was like a sovereign lord among the host of other teachers known in his faith. He had a student who was also his nephew and whose name was Bhuvana. Now one day the great Jain monk came to Bhṛgupura. There one Balamitra, a devout follower of the Buddhists, was king. Now the Buddhists were extremely haughty; for one, they were gifted in the science of logic and argumentation, and for another, they had just secured for themselves such an impressive patron; as the saying goes, "To begin with a she-monkey is wild by nature, and one that has been bitten by a scorpion knows no limits at all." They threw bundles of grass into the Śvetāmbara holy places, as if to say, "You are all no better than dumb beasts." Āryakhapaṭācārya was not in the least perturbed by their displays of contempt, because he was a great man. For it is said,

"Noble men do not get angry at the lowly creatures who harass them; after all what can tiny minnows fluttering here and there do to the mighty ocean, Lord of the Waves?"

But Bhuvana was good and mad. Accompanied by a crowd of a hundred lay disciples he sought an audience with the king. With the permission of the master and of the Jain community at large, he shouted loudly before the king,

"Let those scoundrels beat the drum to challenge all and sundry to debate; let them praise themselves and show contempt for their betters as long as I do not stand before them, with my many arguments all in readiness, to scorch them and burn them to nothingness like the soaring flames of a fire that has been constantly fed with dripping ghee."

King Balamitra said, "O holy man! How dare you speak this way?" Bhuvana said, "Your teachers, who brag that they are the world's greatest logicians, like dogs that bark on their own doorstep but cower once off the porch, have been abusing the Śvetāmbaras. And so I have come to your court to challenge them to a debate. Let them test their mettle against me just one time. Let everyone come and make a day of it, listening to our debate."

And so the king summoned them. He organized a debate in the presence of the full royal assembly of ministers and wise men. The Buddhists, like jackals silenced by the blows of a lion's paws, were silenced at once by the blows of sage Bhuvana's logic. The king and all the bystanders proclaimed victory to the doctrine of the Śvetāmbaras. In all the Jain temples there was great rejoicing, but the Buddhists were like clusters of lotuses whose beauty had been destroyed by a sudden frost.

When he learnt of this humiliation of the Buddhists, the great logician named Vṛddhakara came from Guḍaśāstrapura to Bhṛgupura. He told the king, "Arrange a debate between me and the Śvetāmbaras." The king, who was overwhelmed by Bhuvana's brilliance, tried to dissuade him, but he was adamant. And he, who had never before been defeated in debate, was defeated by Bhuvana, as if to prove true the proverb, "The King of Death never has his fill of eating human beings." Bhuvana, having secured victory, proclaimed to all the witnesses in the royal assembly,

"What a chisel is to stone, what the sun is to darkness and the moon to a host of Śephali blossoms; what fire is to a moth and a thunder bolt is to a mountain; what a hurricane wind is to a cloud and an ax to a tree; what a lion is to an elephant, that am I to any man who seeks to argue philosophy."

The members of the royal assembly were all greatly impressed and they shouted out, "Victory to the doctrine of the Śvetāmbaras!"

Vṛddhakara, in the meantime, burning from this public humiliation, which had struck him as suddenly as a bolt of lightning, fasted to death and was reborn in Guḍaśāstrapura as a demi-god. Because of the hatred he had for them in his previous birth he sought out the Jains and tormented them by making them sick, by terrifying them and by robbing them of their wealth, for a start. The local Jain community sent word to Āryakhapaṭācārya, telling him of their travail, and so he went to Guḍaśāstrapura. He entered the temple of the demi-god and straightaway placed his shoes on the ears of the demi-god. He then put his feet on the chest of the demi-god. A crowd gathered. The local king appeared on the scene. Now when the king showed up, the teacher covered himself completely with his white monk's robe and lay there quietly. No matter where the king pulled back the robe, he was treated to the lofty sight of the teacher's bare buttocks. Furious at this, the king ordered his men to beat Āryakhapaṭācārya. Those blows fell instead on the limbs of the king's wives in his harem, limbs tenderer than the soft inside of a Śirīṣa flower. A hue and cry arose from the women in the harem, "O Lord! Save us! Save us! Some invisible demon is beating us. We're dying! We're dying!" The king's mind was filled with wonder at the supernatural powers of the Jain monk and he threw himself at the monk's feet, and these are some of the words he uttered, "Show mercy on me! I beg of you. Allow me and mine to live. You are a compassionate soul, I know." As for the demi-god, he got up from his seat and went over to the monk and submissively began to massage the monk's feet for him. He said, "I am but a worthless worm. It is not right that you should send a well-equipped army against me." More and more people gathered. Āryakhapaṭācārya told the demi-god, "Hey! Wretch! So you want to make trouble for my followers? Well then, make all the trouble you want. That is, if you can!" The demi-god said, "There is a saying, 'When a monkey is there to guard the spoils how can mere birds snatch them away?' I am your loyal servant. Do not hurt me. From now on I shall protect your followers as if they were my own brothers."

The king and all the others who were present there enjoyed the spectacle and were suitably amazed by what was happening; they all became devoted followers of the monk. Now when the monk left the temple, the demi-god, who after all was nothing but a stone, went out after him. Two other stones, two stone pots, and some minor demi-gods also followed him. When he got to the city gate the Lord of Monks bade them take their leave and they all returned to their own places, except for the stone pots, which the monk stationed firmly at the city gate as a reminder to everyone of what had happened. The king received religious instruction and immediately became a lay disciple. He went back to his own palace. Everyone in the city, of every caste and station, praised that Lord of Monks, calling him the "Dancing Master of the Dancing Girl, Spreading the Faith."

At this juncture two monks arrived from Bhṛgupura. They told the master, "O Blessed One! One of the apprentice monks read the notebook that you hid when you left Bhṛgupura to come here. And in the process of reading your secret book he obtained a magic charm that allows him to transport objects through the air. With that charm he caused the food that was cooked in the homes of wealthy merchants to fly through the air to him and he was feasting on it like a king. The community of monks found out about this and told him to stop but he did not listen, because he is a slave to his lust for food. Finally the community of monks kicked him out. Furious, he has gone and joined the Buddhists. He has practically become their leader. He directs the begging bowls of the Buddhists from their monastery to the homes of the householders and then brings them back to the monastery through the air, filled with food. Everyone can see this marvel, and whoever sees it wants to become a Buddhist. Please, do whatever you think should be done." Āryakhapaṭācārya thought for a moment and making up his mind as to what he should do, he went to Bhṛgupura. He remained incognito once he got there. The begging bowls of the Buddhists, filled with food, were flying here and there. He broke them in mid-air by means of a stone that he magically caused to appear. From the broken bowls sweet meats and candies pounded down on the heads of all the innocent bystanders. The wretched student, figuring that his teacher must have come, beat a hasty retreat. The Jain monk along with his followers went to the Buddhist monastery. The stone Buddha image rose to greet them. It praised him with words like these, "Victory! Victory to the Crest Jewel of all Great Sages!" Once more the Doctrine of the Lord of Jinas shone brilliantly. Āryakhapaṭa then went elsewhere to continue his duties as a monk.

At the same time as all of this was taking place, King Dāhaḍa in the city of Pātaliputra, who was a devout follower of the Brahmins, summoned all the Jain monks and ordered them, "You must bow down to the Brahmins." The Jains told him, "O King! Your order is unjust. For they are householders and we are monks; it is we who are worthy to receive honour from them." Dāhaḍa said, "If you do not bow down to them, then I shall cut off your heads." The Jain monks asked for a respite of seven days. The king granted their request. It just so happened that at that very moment a disciple of Āryakhapaṭa, the teacher named Mahendra, arrived there from Bhṛgupura. The Jain monks told him of their troubles. He reassured them. The next morning Mahendra took with him two tree branches, one red and one white, and went to see Dāhaḍa. This was the morning of the eighth day. The king said, "Call the Śvetāmbara monks so that they may bow down to the Brahmins." They were summoned; they stood before him, in a neat row, straight and tall. Mahendra waved the red stick and said to the king, "Shall we bow down to the Brahmins starting from this end of the row, or from that end of the row?" And at the very moment that he uttered these words the heads of the Brahmins fell off like so many ripe palm fruits and rolled on the ground. Seeing this the king was struck with terror and he began to try to win over Mahendra with honeyed words. He said, "I shall never again show disrespect to these monks." At this Mahendra recited the following verse:

"Who would touch the thick and luxurious mane of the roaring lion with his bare hand? Who would scratch his very own eyes with the sharp blade of his sword? Who would try to steal the jewel that the King of Cobras wears in his hooded crown? That is what the person who would dare treat with contempt the worthy monks of the Śvetāmbara persuasion indeed does try to do."

The king, even more terrified now of the power of the Doctrine, threw himself at Mahendra's feet. At that Mahendra waved his white stick in both directions. The heads of the Brahmins were back on their shoulders. The king and all the Brahmins came to accept the true doctrine. In this way the cause of the Jain Faith was greatly furthered. Even Bhuvana then left the Buddhists and returned to his own teacher. The teacher forgave him. The teacher then showed him much respect. After this Bhuvana became good, humble, pious and learned. Āryakhapaṭa installed Bhuvana as his own successor and leader of the community of monks and fasting to death he went to Heaven.

Harṣakavi, from the *Prabandhakośa*, pp.54-58.

In the East, in the city of Vārāṇasī, Govindacandra was king. He had plucked the blossoms of virginity from seven hundred and fifty young maidens in his harem, enjoying as it were their new fragrant pollen and freshly coursing sap. His son was Jayantacandra. The father, giving the kingdom to the son, devoted himself to religious austerities and conquered the next world. Jayantacandra conquered this earth that measured a full seven hundred leagues. His son was Meghacandra, who with his loud and imposing voice that was like the roar of a lion could have destroyed even a pride of lions, to say nothing of what he could have done to a herd of elephants in rut, blinded by their condition. And because when the king was marching with his army, his soldiers were not satisfied with any water other than that of the holy Ganges and Yamunā, the king secured both those rivers. And they became his walking canes as he marched through the lands; and so people called him the "Lame King." And the River Gomatī, like an obedient servant that puts armour on the horses to prepare them for battle, overran the lands of his foes as if on a military rout and caused them to tremble in fear, leaving the king with no need to lift a finger.

That king had many learned men at his court. One of them was a Brahman named Hīra. He had a son, an Emperor Among All The Wise Men, Śrī Harṣa. At the time when these events happened he was still a boy. Śrī Hira was beaten in debate by one of the scholars in the king's court, in front of the king, and he was silenced in shame. He was so humiliated that he felt as if he had slipped in a pool of mire from which he could never climb out. He bore undying hatred for the man who had defeated him. On his death bed he said to Harṣa, "Son! I was cruelly defeated by that man, a court poet, in the very presence of the king. That is the source of all my grief. If you are truly my son then you will defeat him in debate in the court of the king." Śrī Harṣa said, "I promise you I shall."

Hīra went to heaven. And Śrī Harṣa, entrusting the responsibility of supporting his family to some relatives, went to foreign lands, and studying under many different teachers soon became master of all the sciences, a brilliant scholar of logic, poetics, music, mathematics, astronomy, gemology, spells and grammar, among other subjects, and capable of commanding much learning at will. For one year he practiced a spell called the "Wishing Gem Spell," which his teacher had given him, there on the banks of the Ganges, without wavering for single moment. The Goddess Tripurā appeared to him in person. She granted him a number of boons including the ability to command her as he pleased.

From that time on he began to wander from the court of one king to the court of another. He would offer a host of arguments, but they were all phrased in such an unusual way that no one present could understand them. This time, oppressed by the fact that he had too much wisdom that was beyond the range of the understanding of ordinary mortals, he summoned the Goddess of Learning to him once more and said to her, "Mother! This time my excessive learning has turned out to be a disadvantage for me. Make me capable of being understood by others." At this the Goddess said, "If that is what you want, then, at midnight smear yogurt on your wet head and then go to sleep. You will be made somewhat dull-witted by the phlegm that is produced in this way." He did exactly as she said. Now people could understand what he said. He composed more than a hundred works including the *Khaṇḍana*.

Having accomplished what he set out to accomplish, he returned to Kāśī. He stayed just outside the city. He informed Jayantacandra, "I have completed my studies and am back now." The king, who was ever partial to the virtuous, along with the court scholar, who had once defeated Hīra, and an entourage made up of members of the four castes went to the outskirts of the city. He greeted Śrī

Harṣa with respect. Śrī Harṣa responded by greeting the members of the king's entourage as was fitting, but he praised the king with these words:

"Young women everywhere! Do not cast lustful eyes on this king, just because he is the son of one Govinda, as the God Love was the son of another Govinda, and do not be drawn by his handsome good looks. For if the God of Love makes women into weapons in his conquest of the world, this one too plays tricks with the sexes, turning men into women by depriving them of their manly courage."

And he explained the complicated puns in the verse in a loud voice. The courtiers and the king were all pleased. But when he saw among them the court scholar who was his father's sworn enemy, then with brow furrowed in anger, he said,

"Whether it is poetry that I am composing, soft and delicate, or philosophy, with tightly pulled knots and twists, the Goddess of Learning dances at my side. Whether they lie on a bed covered with the softest quilt or on the earth strewn with grass, if the man should please them then women take their pleasure just the same."

Hearing these words the scholar said, "My Lord! Lord of all Philosophers and Scholars, Master of the Goddess of Learning! There is no one who is your equal, no one who surpasses you! For true it is that they say,

'There are many ferocious creatures in the jungle, who boast of courage and strength; but we single out for praise only the lion, who in his might is greatest of all. For at the sound of his haughty roar herds of boar give up their rambles, elephants maddened in rut stand humbled, wild hunters cease their quarrels and buffalo leave behind their sport."

When he heard these words Śrī Harṣa seemed almost mollified. The king said, "You have risen to the occasion." He was addressing these words to the enemy of Śrī Hīra. The Lord of the Earth commanded the two men to embrace each other. He led Śrī Harṣa to his palace with great fanfare, welcomed him with appropriate ceremony and then sent him home. He gave him a lakh of gold pieces.

One day, relaxed and without a care in the world, the king happily said to Śrī Harṣa, "O Lord of Poets! O King of Philosophers! Write some jewel of a work." And so he came to write the great poem *Naiṣadha*, which was filled with the most subtle poetic flavor and laden with rich hidden and concealed meaning. He showed it to the king, who said, "This is absolutely magnificent. Now you must go to Kashmir. Show it to the learned men there and place it in the hands of the Goddess of Learning. For the Goddess of Learning is present in the temple there in real physical form. She throws away, like so much rubbish, a bad book that is placed in her hand, while she accepts a great work, shaking her head in approval, and uttering the words, 'Well-done!' Flowers fall from on high."

Śrī Harṣa, taking with him all sorts of things for the journey that he had obtained through the generosity of the king, went to Kashmir. He placed his book in the hand of the Goddess Sarasvatī. She threw it far away. Śrī Harṣa said, "Are you now so old that you have lost your wits and so throw away my work as if it were any ordinary work?" Bhāratī said, "Hey! Revealer of other people's dark secrets! Do you not remember how in the eleventh chapter in verse sixty-four you said,

'The Goddess, who sanctifies by her presence the left side of the four-armed God Viṣṇu, spoke once more to the dignified and beautiful young woman, saying, 'Show favour on all good qualities by taking the hand of this man, who bears an unsheathed sword in his palm.''

And by telling the world that I am the wife of Viṣṇu, have you not sullied forever my reputation as a virgin? That is why I threw your book away. For what they say is true:

'A suppliant, a deceiver, an illness, death and someone who reveals another person's weaknesses, these five would bring distress even to the mind of a saint.'"

Hearing these words of the Goddess of Speech, Śrī Harṣa said, "Then why did you take Nārāyaṇa for your husband in one of his incarnations? Even the *purāṇas* know you as the wife of Viṣṇu. Why should you be angry if I have told the truth? And has anger ever freed a person from scandal?" At those words she picked up the book herself and held it tightly in her hand. And the book was highly praised by the scholars who were members of the king's court there.

Śrī Harṣa told all the local scholars, "Show my book to your king, Mādhavadeva, and send a letter to King Jayantacandra saying, 'The work has passed the divine test.'" But even though he told them this and they knew that the book had been acclaimed by the Goddess Bhāratī, they did not send any such letter; nor did they show the book to their king. Śrī Harṣa waited there for several months. He exhausted all his funds and the supplies that he had brought with him for the journey. He sold the livestock he had with him. He dismissed all but a few of his servants. One night in secret he recited a sacred formula to Śiva in a small temple that was right on the edge of a river bank. Two saucy servant girls from two different households were down at the river and were fighting over which one of them had the right to draw water first. They bashed each others' skulls in with their water pots. They each then brought their complaint to the court of the king to be settled. The king searched for a witness to their quarrel. He asked them, "Was there anyone who saw your fight?" They said, "There was a Brahmin there, intent on his sacred devotions." The king's men went out to look for him.

Śrī Harṣa was brought to the king and asked which of those two women was right and which was wrong. Śrī Harṣa said in Sanskrit, "I am a foreigner. I do not know what these two said to each other in their own language. All I know is what sounds they made." The king said, "Tell us." And he told them everything they said, in the exact order in which they said it, word after word, hundreds of words. The king was amazed. "What wisdom you have! What a memory!," he cried. And he decided for himself which of the servant girls was right and to the best of his abilities he chastened the one and rewarded the other and sent them on their way.

Then he spoke to Śrī Harṣa, "Who are you, O Crest Jewel Among the Wise?" Śrī Harṣa told him his whole story. "O King! I have endured much misery in your city on account of the wickedness of the learned men here." The king, who knew well their relative merits, summoned all the local scholars and said to them, "You disgust me, you fools! Do you mean to say you feel no affection for a jewel such as this man? True it is, what they say:

'It is better to jump into a blazing fire than to show even the slightest jealousy towards a person who has special qualities.

Best of all is that state which is beyond all qualities, for even noble men can be downcast in the presence of someone of special qualities; just as it is better to see blossoms in their natural state, for flowers will wilt once strung in a garland.'

Therefore I say that you are all a bunch of scoundrels. Go now, and each of you invite this great man to your homes and show him due honour." At this Śrī Harṣa said,

"What woman can steal the heart of a lad the way she can a young man who is ripe for love? If my words, like the drink of immortality, stir the hearts of the wise, what need I taste the flattery of men who lack the very sense to appreciate me?"

And all those scholars were deeply shamed. They invited Śrī Harṣa into their homes, did him great honour, won him over, and then had him honored by the king, after which, those wise men sent Śrī Harṣa back to Kāśī.

He met Jayantacandra. He told him all that had befallen him. The king was pleased. The poem *Naiṣadha* became very popular.

While all of this was going on, Jayantacandra's chief minister named Padmākara went to the Glorious city of Aṇahilapattana. There on the banks of a river he saw a swarm of bees alighting on a cloth that a washerman was washing, as if it were a Ketaki flower. Surprised, he said to the washerman, "Show me the woman to whom this garment belongs." The minister had decided that she must be a special kind of woman. That night the washerman took him with him when he went to return the garment and showed him its owner, a woman named Sūhavadevi, who was the widow of a weaver and still in the full prime of her youth. He sought permission to take her from the King Kumārapāla, and this granted, he took her back to Kāśī with him, stopping along the way to make a pilgrimage to the holy temple at Somanātha. He gave that lovely woman to Jayantacandra for his pleasure. She was known as Sūhavadevi, and because she was so proud and so clever people also came to call her "Kalābhāratī," "the Goddess of Wisdom for all the Arts." And they called Śrī Harṣa "Narabhāratī," "the Goddess of Wisdom in Masculine Form." Now she was so given to jealousy that she could not bear to hear him called by this title.

One day she summoned Śrī Harṣa with great deference. She said, "Who are you?" He said, "I am the Omniscient One, Knower of all the Arts." The queen said, "In that case make me a pair of shoes." If you ask what her intention was, it was this. Should he say, "I do not know how," because he is a Brahmin and Brahmins cannot touch leather, well then he would have shown that there is something he does not know. Śrī Harṣa thus said yes to her. He went home. The next morning, red-eyed from all the work he had done to turn out slippers from tree bark, he summoned his mistress, remaining at a respectful distance from her. He then had her put the slippers on, following exactly the custom of shoe-makers, saying these words, "Anoint me, I am your shoe-maker." And telling the king of her wickedness, wearied and distressed, he abandoned the world to become a monk on the banks of the Ganges.

And that Sūhavadevi, the real master of the realm, gave birth to a son. He in turn gradually became a young man. He was determined but given to wicked ways. And that king had a minister named Vidyādhara. He was known as a second Yudhiṣṭhira on account of the fact that he fed eight thousand and eight hundred Brahmins through the power of a touchstone which was famous for turning all base metals into gold, and which he had received as a boon from the God Vināyaka, The Wish- Granting Jewel. He also had a mind as sharp as the pointed tip of a blade of grass. The king asked him, "To which of the princes shall I give my kingdom?" He said, "Give it to Meghacandra, who is of a distinguished lineage, and not to the son of your concubine." But Sūhavadevi worked her magic on the king and he was about to give the kingdom to her son. Thus there arose ill feeling between the king and his minister.

Somehow the minister was able to persuade the king to ignore the queen Sūhavadevi's words and give the kingdom to Meghacandra. The queen was furious. Because she had abundant wealth at her disposal and because she was always free to come and go as she pleased, she was able to send some of her trusted and loyal servants to the Muslim overlord of Takṣaśilā and to convince him by giving him lakhs and crores of gold at every step of the way to come down and destroy Kāśī. He came. But Vidyādhara came to know of her plans through his spies. He told the king. The king, totally deluded by all her sorcery, said, "She is my beloved wife; she would never rise against her husband like that." But the minister said, "Lord! The Sakha king has already reached this point that I show you here on the map in his journey." He was sent away by the king and went home. He thought to himself,

"First of all the king is deluded and the queen is very strong. She has followers everywhere and will stop at nothing. If I can die before my master, then I shall count myself among the lucky."

Early in the morning the minister left his own home. As he was going along the road he came upon an oil cake and wanted to eat it. As he went ahead a bit he noticed a cracked cake made of lentils and suddenly felt like eating it. Aware from these two wicked acts that his days of good fortune were numbered, he went to the king and announced to him, "My Lord! I shall plunge into the Ganges and drown myself, if you so command me. The king said, "If you die then at last I can live in peace. You will stop giving me a headache with all your useless prattle." The minister was despondent. For he thought of what they say,

"When a man does not heed words said for his own benefit; when he acts unjustly; when he displays hatred towards those who love him and shows disrespect towards his elders and betters, these are surely the fore-signs of his death."

He knew that the king's death was near. Taking leave of the king he returned home, and giving all his possessions to the Brahmins, disgusted with worldly existence, he walked into the water of the Ganges and said to his family priest, "Accept my gift." The Brahmin held out his hand. He gave to him his touchstone. The Brahmin said, "What kind of a gift is this? You give me a stone?" Furious, he threw it into the water. The Goddess of the River Ganges took the stone herself. The minister sank into the water and died. The king had no one to help him. The Sultan came. The city was filled with headless corpses; they lay strewn one atop the other. The king went out to meet him in battle. From his own retinue rose up eight thousand four hundred cries, but the king heard not a one of them. He took his leave of those who stood by him. They said to him, "Nothing can be heard over the sound of the bows of the unbelievers." The king lost heart. No one ever knew if he was slain, fled or died. The city was overrun by the Muslims.

Madanakīrti, from the *Prabandhakośa*, pp. 64-66.

In Ujjayin dwelt the Digambara Viśālakīrti. He had a disciple named Madanakīrti. Now this Madanakīrti, having defeated all his rivals in debate in the three directions, the East, West, and North, and having obtained the honorific title, "Crest Jewel among all the Philosophers," had come back to Ujjayin, which was graced by the presence of his teacher, and there he had humbly submitted himself to Viśālakīrti. Madanakīrti had become famous everywhere, and everywhere people talked of him. He boasted to his teacher and his teacher was amused. Then after a few days Madanakīrti said to his teacher, "O Blessed One! I want to defeat in debate the philosophers in the South. Please, let me go to the South." The teacher said, "My child! Do not go to the South. For that is the land of pleasures. No monk could go there and not be shaken from his vows, no matter how great an ascetic he might be." Madanakīrti was puffed up with pride in his own learning and so he ignored these words of his teacher. And he set out with a host of disciples, carrying with him a net, spade and ladder, to seek out any possible rivals in the seas, on earth and in heaven. After he had first crushed all the philosophers in Mahārāshtra, Madanakīrti finally arrived in Karṇāṭak.

There in the city Vijayapura he sought an audience with the king. Formally ushered into the royal assembly hall by the door-keeper, Madanakīrti saw the King Kuntibhoja seated amongst all his courtiers. Now this king was himself learned in the Three Vedas and he was eager for the company of other learned men. Madanakīrti praised the king with these verses:

"Lord, how can we tell which one is the snake Śeṣa or which are the stars? How can we know which is the milk ocean and which is the moon; which is a jasmine blossom and which is a lump of camphor; what is a hail stone and what is mother of pearl? How can we find the Himalaya mountains, when everywhere is made shining white by your fame, which shimmers like so many drops of molten mercury, heated to the boiling point by the blazing flames of your military prowess, which leap and sputter from your valiant and prideful strong arms!"

"Your fame, O Kaikaṭa, Kuntibhoja, plunges deep into the heavenly river, the Ganges; encircling the Guardians of the Quarters and looking like a blazing ball of light, it traverses the seven oceans, and as if to proclaim to all and sundry that it belongs like a faithful wife to you and you alone, it touches the world of Viṣṇu on high, and reaches below into the netherworld to stroke the many crests of the snake Śeṣa who supports the universe."

The king was charmed with his words. The Digambara was given lodgings near the royal palace. The king commanded him, "Write a book that tells of the deeds of my forebearers." Madanakīrti said to the king, "My Lord, I can compose five hundred verses in a day, but I cannot write them down that fast. Give me a scribe to assist me." The king said, "My daughter, whose name is Madanamañjarī, will sit behind a curtain hidden from your sight and write down your verses for you."

The Digambara began to compose the work. The princess wrote down five hundred verses each day. And so passed a few days.

One day the princess heard Madanakīrti's voice, which was sweet like the voice of a warbler in springtime, and she thought, "He must be as handsome as his voice is beautiful. But how can I see him from behind this curtain? I must think of something. I know, I shall have the cooks put too much salt into his food." Now Madanakīrti also wanted to see the princess, who was so learned and who also had such a sweet voice. When he found his food too salty, the Digambara said, "How this makes me shiver!" The princess replied, "A cold wind blows no good!" And with their coquettish banter back and forth and their clever puns and jibes, both pushed back first the curtain of respectful distance demanded by convention that had kept them apart, and then, the real curtain of cloth that divided them from each other. They beheld each other's divine beauty. At once the Digambara said,

"In vain does the lotus creeper spend its life, if it has never beheld the orb of the moon with its delicious cooling beams."

And the princess, for her part, replied,

"And the moon, too, rises in vain, if it does not awaken the lotus creeper with its touch."

And as the saying goes, "The many arrows of love strike fast and furious once lovers have enjoyed the first pleasurable glimpse of each other"; so these two gave up their virginity for passionate love-making.

People began to talk. The book was not progressing very fast. One evening the king took a look at the work. "Why did you do so little today?" All the Digambara had written there were two or three verses of quite poor quality indeed. And then he said to the king, "Lord! Long ago I made the solemn promise that I would never recite my work and have it written down by someone who was not learned. Now your daughter did not understand this section very well. And so it took some time. That is why the book is not progressing so fast." The king thought to himself,

"This sounds like a sorry excuse to me. I shall have to take a good look and see just what those two are doing together."

One day, as soon as the sun came up, the king went alone in disguise to the room where they were wont to work and hid behind one of the wall-partitions. At that very moment the Digambara said these words to the princess, words that a lover would say to his angry mistress:

"O you, with your lovely eyebrows! Since you became angry with me, I have stopped eating; I cannot bear even to mention a word about women and I have not touched my fine perfumes and vials of fragrant incense. O angry one, be angry no more. I throw myself at your feet. Have mercy on me now. Without you, my beloved, the world is a cold and joyless place for me!"

When he heard this poem, the king was sure that the two were behaving wantonly and he crept silently from that room. The Lord of the Earth returned to his assembly hall. Furious, he summoned the Digambara to him at once. When the Digambara got there, the king said to him, "O scholar! What is this new verse I heard you recite, the one that starts off, 'O lovely one! Since you became angry with me, I have stopped eating?'" The Digambara reflected, "The king has definitely seen me. I have been caught red-handed. Never mind. I still must answer him in some way or another." And he thought of all sorts of things and, finally, he said to the king, "My Lord! For the last two days my eye has been hurting me terribly. I was addressing my eye with this verse, trying somehow to make it stop tormenting me." And with those as opening words, that Digambara, undaunted, went on and on like this, explaining away his extraordinary behaviour. The king was secretly delighted by Madanakīrti's clever speech, but he was still furious over his unpardonable offense. And so raising one eyebrow in an expression of his fury, he called to his servants, "Tie this fellow up! And kill him for his criminal acts." Madanakīrti was bound by the king's men.

Having heard what had happened, the princess grabbed a knife and rushed into the assembly hall with thirty-two of her friends who were similarly armed. She stood right before the king and said,

"If you release my beloved, then all will be fine. If you do not release him, then you will be guilty of thirty-four murders. One will be the murder of the Digambara and the others will be the murder of these thirty-three young women." At that point the king's ministers advised him,

"My Lord, you yourself brought these two together. And the presence of a woman for a young man is the springtime shower that makes the tree of love blossom in all its fullness. Who is to blame for what has happened? For what they say is true:

'The glances of women, even in a painting, rob the minds of those who see them; what chance does a man have before the throbbing glances of a live woman, with all her amorous games?'

Show mercy and release the Digambara. And give your daughter to him." He listened to their words, released the Digambara and made his daughter the Digambara's wife. And the Digambara was given a share of the kingdom. He gave over to his father-in-law whatever riches he acquired in conquest. Abandoning his religious vows, he enjoyed worldly pleasures.

From Ujjayin, his teacher Viśālakīrti heard all these things that had happened to Madanakīrti. And he thought, "How mighty is the power of wealth, youth, and the company of bad friends; for through these things even a man like Madanakīrti, faithful to his monastic vows, learned, a fine philosopher, and adept in spiritual exercises, has stumbled onto a false road that can lead only to the most terrible rebirths in the next life. Alas, alas!

'The mind is beset by some strange distortion, rife with all the many delusions that arise upon the destruction of right discrimination; unknowable, never even experienced before in any other birth, this strange process at once is like ice to the warmth of wisdom within and causes terrible burning pain.'"

Thinking such things, he sent four of his most skilled disciples in order to bring Madanakīrti back to his senses. When they got there they said to him,

"'O wise one! Turn away from the momentary pleasure of the company of a woman, a pleasure that will soon vanish. Seek the company of the damsels Compassion, Wisdom, and Friendliness. For in hell no firm breasts adorned with pearl necklaces will save you, nor any woman's thighs with jangling girdle bring you solace.' Your teacher recalls you to your senses with words like these. Accept his instruction. Do not be deluded."

Shameless, Madanakīrti wrote down some verses for his teacher on a piece of paper and told them to deliver them. They went back there. The teacher read the verses:

"Logic can be twisted to prove anything you want. The scriptures are all different. There is no teacher whose words can be accepted as the absolute truth. They say that the real truth is hidden in a secret place. The true path is that one followed by every man."

"Seeing my beloved is the only divine sight I need. You may call your philosophy divine sight, but who needs it, when even the man with lust and sin can feel such bliss from the sight of the woman he loves."

"The man who has passionately and forcibly kissed his angry mistress, while she was biting her tender sprout-like lips in rage and furiously shaking her fingers at him, while her eyebrows danced up and down as she shouted, 'Let go of me, you good-for-nothing! Let go of me!,' and her eyes were clouded from the steam of her own breaths that escaped, despite everything, from the passion of the moment, such a man has truly tasted the nectar of immortality. Seeking this divine drink, the Gods were silly, indeed, to have gone to such fuss to churn the ocean."

When he read these verses and others similar to them, the teacher was silent. As for Madanakīrti, he had a very good time for himself indeed.

Mallavādin, from the *Prabandhakośa*, pp. 21-24.

"Having bowed down humbly to Glorious Indrabhūti, I now begin the tale of the deeds of Glorious Mallavādin, Lord of Monks, Crest Jewel Amongst Those Who Furthered the Cause of the Faith."

There is in the Kingdom of Gujarat a large and prosperous city called Kheṭa. There dwelt the Brahmin named Devāditya who knew all the Vedas and had penetrated their secrets. His daughter, who was named Subhagā, had been widowed as a child. She obtained a magic spell to summon the Sun God from some holy man to whom she was devoted. And the Sun God, called to her by the power of that spell, made love to her. Not long after she enjoyed his touch she found herself pregnant. Although it is certainly true that a woman cannot be made pregnant by a God who bears a body that has been supernaturally created for temporary purposes, there was nothing untoward in this case, for the God had a real physical body from which the woman received his semen.

Her father, seeing that her cheeks had taken on a particular pallor and that her body had become weak, asked her, "My child, how could you have been so shameless and disgraceful?" She answered him, "Father, I did not act out of rash impulse or lust. I had no choice at all in the matter; I summoned the Sun God to my side with the power of my magic spell and this is what he left me with, a precious trust to guard and watch over."

But even though this was what his daughter told him, Devāditya was despondent over her wicked deed, and he sent his daughter away to the city of Vallabhī with only a servant to accompany her.

When her time came she gave birth to a son, who was radiantly beautiful, and to a daughter. And she dwelt there for a long time, living off the money that her father had provided for her. And those two children gradually grew up, splendid both of them like the newly risen sun. When eight years had flown by, like the twinkling of an eye, they were both entrusted to the care of a teacher who was to instruct them. Now it happened that the school children chanced to quarrel with the boy, and they taunted him, saying that he had no father. The child was grieved by their remark and he asked his own mother, "Mother, is it really true that I have no father, just as everyone says?" The mother snapped back, "How should I know? Now stop pestering me with your questions."

Even more grieved at this, the child, possessed of great manliness and courage, determined to put an end to his own life, if not by poison then by some other means. The Sun God appeared to him in person and said, "Child, I am your father. I promise you that I shall take away the life of anyone who insults you." And with those words he gave a small pebble to the child, instructing him, "Whosoever does you any harm you shall strike with this pebble. And he shall die instantly, I swear to you."

Armed with this weapon, a tiny pebble, the child, who was already strong, became even stronger; he killed each and every school mate who teased or taunted him in any way. But the king of the city of Vallabhī heard about the murder of the school children, and furious, he ordered the citizens to bring the boy before him. He said to him, "Hey! Heartless and cruel boy! Why do you kill these young children?" The boy replied, "I can kill not only these children, but kings as well." And as he spoke these words he struck the king with his pebble. He became himself the mighty ruler in the empire that had once belonged to the king who thus met his end.

Known as "Śilāditya," "The One Who Was Given a Stone by the Sun God," he was like the sun in the kingdom of Saurāshtra. And he received a divine chariot from the Sun God that was capable of crushing the realms of all his enemies.

He gave his own sister in marriage to the king of Bhṛgukṣetra. She gave birth to a son, of divine radiance, possessed of all the marvelous signs of a great man. And Śilāditya restored the Jain temples on Mount Śatruñjaya, joining the ranks of such famous lay men as King Śreṇika.

Now one day some Buddhists, puffed up with pride for their skills in the science of logic and debate, came to that city and said to Śilāditya, "There are so many Śvetāmbaras here in your realm. Let us decide-- if they can defeat us in debate, then they shall live here in peace, but if we defeat them, then they must go elsewhere." And as fate would have it, the Śvetāmbaras were all defeated in debate by those Buddhists, and they all sought refuge in other lands, waiting for the right moment to reclaim their lost position. King Śilāditya became a great devotee of the Buddhists and showed them much honour, and they worshipped the image of Ṛṣabhanātha at Śatruñjaya, considering it to be an image of their Buddha.

In the meantime Śilāditya's sister had lost all interest in the world after the death of her husband and had become a Jain nun under the guidance of Susthitācārya. She also had her eight year old son ordained as a monk and had him taught some of the rules that govern the correct behaviour of a monk. Now one day the child, who was easily roused to anger, asked his mother, "Why is our community so small? Was it always small like this?" And with tears in her eyes she told him, "How shall I answer you, when I am so much to blame? At one time the Glorious community of Śvetāmbara Jains prospered in every city in the realm. But, because for a long time there has been no great monk to further the cause of the Faith, our enemies have won over King Śilāditya, your own uncle and my brother. The holy place Śatruñjaya, which is celebrated as the cause of final release, without the Śvetāmbaras to guard it, has been overrun by the Buddhists, as if by a host of goblins and ghosts. The Śvetāmbaras, all living now outside this realm, somehow bide their time, unable to carry on their duties, bereft of their former pride and strength. "

When he heard this, the child became furious at the Buddhist aggressors and he made this vow in a voice as loud as a thundering rain cloud at the opening of the monsoon season, "If I do not uproot those Buddhists, like so many trees clinging to the river's bank, then may I be tainted with the heinous sin of killing the Omniscient One." And with those words the child took leave of his mother, and raging like the fire at the end of the universe, he went to Mount Malla and practiced the most extreme and severe austerities. He broke his fast with food that he begged from a nearby village. In a few days the Protecting Goddess of the Faith came to know of his austerities, and she spoke to him from the sky. "What are sweet?," she asked. And the child, his eyes fixed upon the heavens, answered her from his own recent experience, "The coarsest of grains." Six months later she asked him again from the sky, "With what?" And that child-sage, for his part, replied, "With fine ghee and brown sugar." She knew then, from the remarkable strength of memory that he displayed, that he was worthy, and so the Protecting Goddess appeared to him in person and said, "Son! May you destroy those who do not share your Faith. Noble One! Take this text of logic, the *Nayacakra*. Words will never fail you; they will be the infallible charm that destroys the snake of wicked arguments that your opponents advance."

The child-sage set that book down on the ground; on such an occasion it is not hard to make a careless mistake, particularly when a person is so young and under the sway of youthful fancies. Enraged, the Protecting Goddess told him, "Because you have shown such disrespect to the Faith, I shall never appear to you in person again, although I shall always be by your side."

Mallavādin, having obtained that book, was even more radiant and resplendent than before, just as Arjuna, the son of Pāṇḍu, was after he had obtained the magic weapon from Siva. He returned to the port of Vallabhī, the jewel of the kingdom of Surāshtra, and, blazing fiercely like the sun at the end of the world, he spoke to Śilāditya, "The world has been devoured by the Buddhists to no good end. Here I am to fight them, ever vigilant, Mallavādin, your very own nephew, daughter of your sister." In the presence of King Śilāditya, that chief of debaters debated with the eloquent Buddhist master, with mighty and terrible arguments, loud and forcefully delivered. And when Mallavādin, invincible and terrible to encounter, backed by the might of the *Nayacakra*, fired volley after volley of clever inferences for six long months, that Lord of the Buddhists knew in his heart that all was lost.

On the last night of that debate, which had gone on now six months, as day began to break, the Buddhist took one of his own logic texts from his library and began to read a little. His mind was so injured by blows of worry that he could not make out a thing he read; that Buddhist thought, "On the morn, I shall be completely defeated, shorn of any vestige of glory and respect. That spark of a Śvetāmbara indeed has a different kind of flare, a powerful fire that I have never seen before. The Buddhists, who have enjoyed power and prestige in the empire, will surely be expelled from the kingdom. How true it is, what they say, 'Lucky are those who do not see their country destroyed, their family ruined, their wife in another's hands, and their beloved friends in dire straits.'"

And at that moment his heart broke from the pressure of all his sufferings. The next morning when the king's men came to fetch him, his poor disciples would not open the door at first, saying, "Our teacher is not well today. He won't be able to come to the king's assembly hall." When they went back to the assembly hall and Malla heard their report, he was delighted. He said to Śilāditya, "That Lord of the Buddhists has died of grief." Śilāditya went to the Buddhist's lodgings in person and he saw him, dead like that. He expelled all the Buddhists from his kingdom, for no one cares much for the man who has fallen from grace. He made the master Mallavādin, who was the Lord of the Goddess of Speech, his teacher, and the king then recalled from abroad all the Śvetāmbara sages. The king returned to the control of the Śvetāmbaras the Lord of the Jinas, who has broken out of the cage of worldly existence, and organized a pilgrimage to the holy place of Śatruñjaya.

Now some time later there was a merchant in that city who was named Raṅka. A wandering ascetic entrusted a vial of magic elixir to him to keep for him while he was on a pilgrimage. When he saw that base metal turned to gold at the touch of a drop of the elixir, the merchant moved his shop elsewhere and by cheating the wandering ascetic Raṅka became a very rich man. His daughter and the daughter of the king became close friends. One day the king's daughter noticed a bracelet on Raṅka's daughter's arm. It was gold and studded with divine jewels. She asked her for the bracelet. When Raṅka would not give it up, the king himself demanded that Raṅka hand the bracelet over to the princess. And just because of this one act, which made him so jealous of the king's power, Raṅka led an army of barbarians into the kingdom. The city Vallabhī was destroyed and everything was wrecked. Śilāditya was brought to ruin by that merchant with all his great wealth. All the Śāka soldiers, who had been tempted with money and brought there by the merchant and thrown into battle, eventually succumbed to thirst; the terrible havoc that they wrought was finally stilled.

Five hundred and seventy three years into the Vikrama era occurred this sack of Vallabhī. The wise men, who could see into the future, deserted the city before it even fell. The images in the Jain temples flew through the sky to settle in other lands. For in cases such as this, images, guided by their superintending deities, can indeed move. And the great sage Mallavādin, who had foreseen what would happen, along with his followers went to the city Pañcāsara. He became the leader of the community in those holy places that were under the control of the monks of the Nagendra gaccha. His group wielded authority even in the holy place, the Glorious Stambhana.

"O Good Men, who are destined for release! Hear this account of the deeds of Glorious Mallavādin, pure and uplifting in that it tells of the spread of the glory of the Jain Faith, and do you yourselves further enhance the cause of the Faith with such wonderful gifts as you may possess, like poetic talent and fine speech!"

Mallavādin, (*Ākhyānakamaṇikośa*, pages 172-174).

In the city of Bharuyaccha, which was like the ocean with its store of rich gems, like a vast and spreading forest with lush undergrowth in its seemingly endless extent, and like the very abode of the Gods with flowering coral trees in all its splendour and prosperity, there lived a Jain sage, Jiṇāṇanda by name. And there lived in this city a Buddhist monk, too, who was called Buddhāṇanda. The two of them engaged in a debate in the presence of the king. They had agreed as the condition of their debate that the loser must leave the city with his followers. And as soon as they set these terms, they began straightaway to debate with each other. Now fate would have it that the Lord of the Jain Monks was defeated by the Buddhist, and with the entire Jain community he left that city and went to the town of Vallabhī. The sister of that Jain monk, Dullahadevī, was ordained as a Jain nun and with her three sons were made monks. Their names were Ajiyajasa, Jakkha and Malla, and they were all pure and sincere. All three of them soon mastered all the Jain scriptures, particularly Malla, with the exception of the entire *Nayacakka*, *The Wheel of Reasoning*, which belonged to a class of the sacred texts that had in part been lost in antiquity and whose few remaining works were carefully protected. The text consisted of twelve sections that were like the spokes of a wheel and it had been rescued from the lost ancient works. Whoever studied the text was supposed to worship the Jina at the beginning and end of each stanza; not to do so meant certain disaster for the entire Jain community, whether the text was being expounded to a group or simply read by a single monk.

The Jain monk gave this nun his box containing the sacred texts and one day, when he had to go elsewhere, he said to Malla, "You must not try to read this book, the *Nayacakka*." With these words he departed. Now it so happened that the nun also went out to do something or other. Malla, curious to know what was in that book, took it out and opened it. He took the first page in his hand and began to read aloud its first verse in a sweet voice, a verse that stood as proof for the entire teachings of the Jain faith. He read, "All teachings other than the Jain teachings are false like so many meaningless words, because they are devoid of the correct analysis of the physical and mental world in terms of the many possible viewpoints of understanding. And this statement should be understood as showing the absence of the quality under discussion, truthfulness, in that which does not possess the characteristic of employing the correct analysis of the world." As he was pondering intently the meaning of this cryptic verse, the Presiding Goddess of the Faith, knowing that he had not performed the proper rituals of worship before reading the text, snatched away the entire book, including this first page. And when Malla could not find the book he became downcast.

The nun returned and asked him, "What troubles you so?" He told her how he had lost the book and she in turn told the entire community what had happened. When they heard the story all of the Jains became extremely pained. Malla thought, "I must not live here as long as I cannot get that book back. And I must subsist only on the coarsest of foods, in fact on coarse grains alone." The others told him, "You will become ill if you eat only coarse grains. You must also take something richer." Accepting this command of the other Jains, he went and took refuge in a mountain cave, subsisting only on coarse grains with molasses and ghee. The other most excellent monks brought to him in the cave the necessary foods with which he could break his periodic ritual fasts. After some time, to test his wit, the Presiding Goddess of the Faith spoke to him late one night, asking, "What are sweet?" He immediately answered, "The coarsest of grains." At the end of six months she asked him again, "With what?" The novice Malla replied, "With molasses and ghee." The Goddess, delighted with his obvious intelligence, told him, "Malla! Ask of me anything that you desire. For I am pleased with you." So the novice Malla said, "Give me the book, the *Nayacakka*." The Goddess told him, "You will yourself be able to write that book from the first verse that you read."

And so it came to pass that through the grace of the Goddess he did indeed compose the *Nayacakka*. And he was welcomed back into the city of Vallabhī by the entire Jain community with much pomp and splendour.

By that time his teacher had returned from his monastic tour and he came to know all that had transpired. Realizing that Ajiyajasa, Jakkha, and Malla were all endowed with excellent qualities, he installed them all in positions of the highest leadership among the monks. And they all became like lions to the elephants who were their rivals in debate. Now one day the Glorious Malla chanced to recall how the Jain monks had been defeated in debate by the Buddhist Buddhānanda, and how they had been forced to leave Bhṛguyaccha with the entire Jain community. Learning more from his teacher about the humiliation of the Jain community and their ignominious defeat, Malla, the Lord of Monks, hastened to Bhṛgukaccha. Having made exactly the same wager as had been made earlier between the Buddhists and Jains, he began to debate against the Buddhists in the court of the king, in the presence of many learned witnesses. The Buddhist gave Malla the chance to speak first in the debate, saying, "I have already defeated the teacher of this child, who was in fact a great debater, and secondly I surely need not fear one so young and inexperienced."

And Malla, praying to the Presiding Goddess of the Faith, began to state his position. He took six full days to present his arguments, which included all the varying viewpoints under which reality is examined in the Jain texts. When he was done he said, "Repeat everything that I have said and show this assembly exactly where I have gone wrong." That night the Buddhist monk Buddhadāsa, back in his lodgings, lit his oil lamp and took in his hand a new piece of white chalk. But when he went to write down what Malla had said on the white wall of his cell, try as he might, it all got mixed up in his mind and he could not remember Malla's words correctly. He felt a sudden stab of pain in his heart and he thought, "What shall I say tomorrow in the king's court?" And his fear was so great that he dropped dead right then and there.

When the monk did not show up the next day and the wise men had all gathered, the king sent his men to fetch him. When they got there they saw the monk sitting in front of the wall, his eyes fixed vacantly on the ceiling, chalk in his hand, without a breath of life. They returned to the king and told him what they had seen. The king thought from what they had told him that the monk had surely died of fear. In any event, he had lost the debate. The king conferred victory upon Malla, the Debater, and the Jain community was given a great boost. The king proceeded to exile all the followers of the Buddhist monk, but was stopped by the compassionate Malla. The Jain monk Jinānanda was brought back to the city by the king, who went in person to meet him and welcome him with great ceremony. The Glorious Monk Malla for many years to come performed great deeds in service of the Faith and destroyed many rivals in debate. Having brought to many worthy souls the true teachings, which were so sweet to hear, the Glorious Malla, the Debater, then died and went to heaven.

Jineśvarasūri, from the *Kharataragacchabṛhadgurvāvali*, pp. 1-6.

In the country Abhohara lived the master Jinacandra, who belonged to the faction that held that Jain monks ought to dwell in special monastic establishments built exclusively for their use. He had jurisdiction over eighty-four temples. He had one particular student who was named Vardhamāna. Now while this student was trying to master the Jain doctrine, he encountered the eighty-four problems that lead to misapprehension of the doctrine and a display of disrespect for the faith. As he was overcoming each of these problems, it occurred to him, "If only I can protect myself in these trying moments, then all will be well." He told his problems to his teacher, who was guiding him in his spiritual practices. The teacher realized, "He is not happy here," and he granted him special honour. Despite this Vardhamāna could not reconcile himself to the practice of Jain monks dwelling in special monasteries. And so with the permission of his teacher he left there, and accompanied by a few fellow-monks he wandered from place to place, including in his tour such cities as Delhi, or Dalī, as it is also called.

At that time it chanced that in that very city of Delhi there lived the most excellent monk, the master Udyotanasūri. He learned from him the true meaning of the Jain scriptures and made the decision to serve him faithfully and obey his words. Not long after this took place, Vardhamānasūri thought to himself, "I wonder which God it could be who presides over the magic formula that my teacher has taught me?" In order to find out the answer to this question he undertook three fasts. At the end of the third fast the Snake King Dharaṇendra appeared to him. He told him, "I am the superintending deity of your magic formula." And then he explained to him the wonderful results that were guaranteed from reciting each individual word in the formula. This was how Vardhamāna mastered the magic formula and gained, in addition, the ability to call up its presiding deity when he wished. And at this very same moment Vardhamānasūri and his followers all became possessed of this special ability to summon the minor protecting deities.

At this juncture, the scholarly Jineśvara, who led his own small group of disciples, announced to Vardhamāna, "O Blessed One! What is the use of knowing the Jain doctrine if we do not go somewhere and reveal it to others? I understand that the country of Gujarat is vast and that it is has been overrun by those who believe that Jain monks should dwell in special monasteries. Clearly we must go there."

Vardhamāna replied, "What you say is correct, but let us first examine the signs and portents, so that all will be well with us on our journey and in our undertaking." This done, he set off with a sizable retinue of learned men, seventeen of them in fact. In time they reached Palli. Vardhamānasūri and the scholarly Jineśvara, one day on their rounds, tending to their bodily needs, happened to meet a Śaiva ascetic named Somadhvaja. They began to chat pleasantly, and Vardhamāna, perceiving praiseworthy qualities in Somadhvaja, exchanged this light banter of questions and answers, each answer supplying a letter of the ascetic's name, "Somadhvaja." Here is how it went:

"Who is it that destroys misery and suffering? "Sa," which is a name for the Goddess of Fortune. And what is the word that at once is the name for the Gods

Viṣṇu, Brahmā and Śiva? It is the word "om." What kind of tiredness must travellers carefully resist? Tiredness that comes from their journey, "adhvaja." And there you have it, "Somadhvaja." But let us go on, for we can do this last part in yet another way. Now, what gives beauty to the abodes of the Gods? Flags, which are spelled "dhvaja," and that gives you the one who is known to all for his gentleness and his wisdom, "Somadhvaja."

The ascetic was delighted. He became an ardent devotee of the Jain monk.

After this encounter, Vardhamāna proceeded on his way with the very same group of learned men with whom he had begun his journey. In time he reached Aṇahilapattana. They stopped at an open pavilion that was a public resting place for travellers. At that time there was no enclosed shelter to the place; there was also no Jain lay devotee in the city who respected the true teachers and thus whom they might ask to house them. As they sat there they all were affected by the intense heat of the sun. And so the scholarly Jineśvara said, "O Blessed One. You will surely not accomplish anything by sitting in this place." "My best student, then tell me what we should do." "If you allow me, I shall go to that lofty mansion that you can see just off a little ways in the distance." "Go then." And so, bowing respectfully to the lotus-feet of his teacher, he set off in the direction of the mansion.

Now the mansion belonged to the personal priest of the King Durlabha. And when he got there that priest was in the process of having a massage. He stood before him and recited this benedictory verse:

"O King Among the Brahmins! May the Gods Brahmā, Viṣṇu, and Śiva, who give joy to those who revere them, and who have many wonderful qualities and work many wondrous deeds, riding on their respective mounts, the goose, snake and bull, grant you everlasting prosperity."

The priest was pleased and thought that whoever he was, the monk was surely a clever fellow, for embedded in the adjective used to describe the mounts of the Gods was yet another divine epithet. Now the monk could hear some students reciting their portions of the Veda from somewhere inside the house and he called out, "Do not chant like that." "How then should we chant?" "This way." At this the priest said, "Outcastes have no right to recite, study or teach the Vedas." Then the scholarly monk said, "I am a Caturvedi Brahmin, a Brahmin who is learned in all four of the Vedas, in deed as well as in name." The teacher was pleased with his remark. "Where have you come from?" "From Delhi." "Where are you staying?" "At the tax barrier, the gate to the city. We cannot find a place to stay, for the city is overrun by our enemies. My teacher and some more disciples are also there; we are eighteen monks in all." "My house is large; there are four separate pavilions here with separate entrances. Gather together your group and all of your things and take one of the buildings to use as you please. When the proper time comes for you to beg your food, then take one of my men along with you on your rounds. Go to the homes of the Brahmins; you will have no trouble getting alms."

Then in the city of Aṇahilapattana the news quickly spread, "A group of Jain monks has come and they hold to the view that monks ought not to live in special monastic establishments, but should reside temporarily in the homes of lay devotees." The monks in the big Jain monasteries heard the news. And they knew that the arrival of these monks did not bode well for their own faction. There is a well-known proverb to the effect that an illness must be crushed while it is still mild. Now these monks who lived in monasteries taught the sons of the wealthy and powerful in the city. And so they bribed these students of theirs with tasty delicacies and sweet candies and ordered them, "You must spread this rumour wherever you go, 'These people who have come from abroad are really the King Durlabha's enemies who have merely disguised themselves as monks.'"

And the rumour spread like wild fire among all the people in the city. And as it spread here and there it also came to be bandied about in the court of the king. The king asked, "If it is true that such vile creatures have entered our city, then tell me, who has dared to give them lodging?" Someone answered him, "My Lord, your own priest and teacher has quartered them in his home." The king then commanded, "Bring my priest here." The priest was brought there and the king asked him, "If the strangers are really as people say, then why have you given them lodging in your home?" He replied, "Who accuses them in this way? I make this wager. Here is my sack of coins. If the strangers are in any way at fault, then let those who would accuse them take my purse." But there was no one who accepted the challenge. Then the priest said before the king, "My Lord! Anyone who sees them can know at once that those men who are staying at my home are the very embodiment of righteousness. They could never commit any foul deed."

When they realized what was happening in the king's assembly, then the false monks, Sūrācārya and the others, thought, "We shall defeat the newcomers in debate and see to it that they are driven out of here." And so it was that they then said to the priest, "We are eager to discuss philosophical issues with those monks who are staying in your home." He told them, "I shall ask them and give you their reply." The priest then went home and said to them, "O Blessed Ones! Your rivals desire to discuss philosophy with Your Honors." They replied, "That is fine with us. But you need not fear anything on our account. You must go back and say this to them, 'If you wish to debate with the newcomers, they agree on the condition that the debate be held in the presence of the King Durlabha.'" Now the false monks thought to themselves, "The king's ministers and courtiers are all firmly in our pockets. We need not fear any harm from them. Let us have our debate in the presence of the king."

A proclamation was released informing the populace that the debate would take place on a certain day and in a certain temple. In private, the priest told the king, "My Lord! The local monks wish to debate with the monks who have newly arrived. Such a debate is best when held in the presence of a just and fair king. I beg of you, Your Majesty, to grace the debate with your august person." The king replied, "Right you are. I shall do as you say."

And so on the appointed day in the stated temple, the Glorious Sūrācārya and his followers, numbering a total of eighty-four monks, assembled. Each monk sat on the seat that was commensurate with his particular status. The king was summoned there, along with his most important ministers and courtiers. He too took a seat. The king said, "My priest! Call those monks whose side you have taken." He went to them and informed Vardhamānasūri, "All the Lords Among the Monks and their followers have gathered and taken their seats. King Durlabharāja awaits your presence in the temple; he has already shown the other monks honour by offering them betel to chew." When he heard these words of the priest, the Glorious Vardhamānasūri, meditating upon the great former leaders of his group, the Glorious Sudharmasvāmin, Jambusvāmin, and the others, left his lodgings under auspicious signs, accompanied by a few learned monks, including the scholarly Jineśvara. He reached the temple and sat down at the place indicated for him by the king and on a seat that Jineśvara proffered. Jineśvara himself sat down at his teacher's feet, on a seat that the teacher indicated was appropriate for him. And when the king began to offer them all betel to chew, in the presence of that entire assembly, the teacher proclaimed, "O King! It is not proper for holy men to take betel. As it is said,

'For those who observe the rules of celibacy and women whose husbands have died, eating betel, O Brahmins, is not different from eating beef.'"

With this, those who were particularly astute in that company realized the greatness of the teacher. The teacher then said, "The scholarly Jineśvara will debate today. Everything he says you may consider to be my own views." All those present replied, "So be it." The leader of the group, Sūrācārya, then spoke up, "Those monks who lodge with lay followers are outside the accepted religious groups, which are six in number. Most people understand by these six groups the Buddhists, the Jains, the Śaivas and so on." And to prove his point he grabbed a book of philosophy which had only recently been written. At this point in the debate, calling upon the dictum, "Present practices continue past customs," the Glorious Jineśvara said, "O August King Durlabha! In your realm do you carry on affairs of state in keeping with the rules laid down and followed by your ancestors, or do you pursue some new-fangled course that somebody or other has thought up for you?" The king answered, "In our land I rule according to the ways of my ancestors and in no other way." At this the Glorious Jineśvara said, "O Great King! We have come from afar. We did not bring with us the books that our forbearers wrote and that we consider to be authoritative. O King! Have someone bring from the monastery of these monks the ancient texts, written by our forbearers, so that we may determine what is the right path and what is the false path."

The king then said to Jineśvara's rivals, "He is correct. I shall send my men. Give the order for your people to hand over the books to my men." Now they knew full well that Jineśvara's side was going to win; that was why they did not say a word, either way. The king sent his men, saying, "Go quickly and fetch the bundle of authoritative texts." They brought the bundle at once. And as soon as the bundle was carried into the assembly it came unwrapped. By the grace of God, the *Daśavaikālika* was exposed. This text had been written in times of old by a monk who was conversant with the fourteen scriptures. And from that text the first verse that they saw was this one,

'A monk should live in a dwelling that has not been made exclusively for his own use, that has a place for him to ease his bodily needs, and that is not frequented by women, eunuchs and beasts' (*Daśavaikālika*, 8.51).

Jineśvara explained that the meaning of the verse was that monks should live in an ordinary dwelling that has these characteristics and not in a special monastery or temple. The king thought to himself that this seemed correct. The courtiers realized, "Our teachers have been put to shame." And so these officers of the court, from the chief minister on down, one by one, all proclaimed in the presence of the king, "The newcomers are our teachers." In this way each of the king's officers accepted one of the newcomers as his teacher. Each one thought, "The king honors me; for my sake he will honour my teacher. The king is just." When things had proceeded this far, the Glorious Jineśvara said, "Great King! The Chief Minister has this monk for his teacher; the lesser minister has chosen yet a different monk as his teacher, and so it is down through the ranks of your officers. Tell me, My Lord, in your kingdom, to whom does the orphan whom no one claims belong?" "To me," said the king. "In that case all the other monks now belong to someone. I am like the orphan, I belong to no one." And so the king made Jineśvara his personal teacher. And the king said, "Everyone has offered his teacher a jewel-studded throne to sit upon. How can it be that only my teacher sits on a plain, low seat? Do you mean to say I have no jewel-studded throne to offer my teacher?" At this Jineśvara replied, "Great King! It is not proper for holy men to sit on thrones. For it has been said,

'If a monk adorns his body he will surely break his vows, O Best of Kings! And he will be a laughing stock among the people. He will get attached to such things and too much accustomed to comfort. It is not right for someone who desires release to make use of thrones and such things.'"

And he went on and explained this traditional verse. The king then said, "Where will you stay?" He replied, "Great King! How shall we find a place to stay, when our enemies are so strong?" Without even taking a minute to think the king gave them a place to dwell. He said, "There is a vacant house in Karadihatti; its owner has died without issue. You may stay there. But how will you eat?" And Jineśvara explained to the king that, for the same reason, it was difficult for him and his fellow monks to obtain alms. "How many are you altogether?" "O Great King! We are eighteen." "You need no more than what it takes to feed a single elephant!" At this Jineśvara said, "Great King! It is not permitted for a monk to accept food from a king. Our scriptures prohibit this."

"In that case you will take one of my soldiers with you on your rounds; you will meet no opposition in that way and you will easily obtain alms."

Thus, having engaged their rivals in debate and bested them, they entered their lodgings, accompanied by the king and by the king's soldiers. This was the first time that the practice of Jain monks' dwelling in ordinary lodgings and not special temples was established in Gujarat.

The day after the debate, realizing that two of their schemes had already failed, the monks who were hostile to Jineśvara and his group got together and formulated yet another plan. The king was known to be devoted to his Chief Queen; he did whatever she told him to do. Now all the officers of the court, as if to celebrate their new choice of teachers, filled bowls with various fruits, including grapes, mangoes and bananas, and took fine cloth and jewels as presents to the queen. They set all these gifts before her, like so many offerings to the Lord Who is Without Passion, the Jina himself. The queen was pleased with this attention and willing to do their bidding. At that very moment it so happened that the king had some business with the queen. He sent a man, who was a native of Delhi, to her with a message, saying, "Tell the queen that this is what I need." The man, saying, "I shall tell the queen what you say," hastened away. He told the queen what the king required. When he saw all the court officers there and all of the gifts that they had brought, he thought, "Clearly this is another plot to get rid of the teachers who have come from my homeland. I must say something to the king that will help them." He went back to the king.

"My Lord! I have told the queen what you require. But Sire, I have seen the most curious thing there. The queen looks like the Jina himself; they have placed lavish offerings before her just like the offerings people place in front of the Jina in the temple." The king thought, "Those monks are still after my teacher, the newcomer who spoke so wisely and whom I have accepted as my preceptor." Then the king turned to that man and said, "Go back to the queen at once and tell her this. Say, 'The king commands you. If you take even a single fruit from those gifts that are before you, then I am not your beloved and you are not mine.'" And when she heard those words the queen was frightened and she said, "Sirs! Each of you take back what he has brought. I do not need your gifts." And so this stratagem too was foiled.

They then hit upon a fourth plot. "If the king insists on honoring those foreign monks, then let us abandon all the temples and go elsewhere ourselves." Someone told the king of their scheme. The king said, "If they do not like it here, then let them go elsewhere!" He hired some Brahmin boys to perform the ceremonies in the temples; they agreed to carry out the rituals in the Jain temples because they knew well, as do all people, that all of the Gods are to be worshipped without distinction. But those Jain monks who had abandoned their temples could not find anywhere else to stay and so they began trickling back, one by one, offering some lame excuse or another for their return. As might be guessed, eventually they all came back and resumed living in their monasteries.

The Glorious Vardhamānasūri, for his part, was greatly honored by the king, and with his followers he travelled freely in the king's realm. No one dared to say a word against him. On an auspicious day, he installed the Glorious Jineśvara in his position as leader of the community of monks. He made Jineśvarasūri's brother, Buddhasāgara, second in rank in the group. Their sister, Kalyāṇamati, was made head of the nuns. After that the Glorious Jineśvara, in the course of his wanderings, gathered around him a number of disciples, including Jinacandra, Abhayadeva, Dhaneśvara, Haribhadra, Prasannacandra, Dharmadeva, Sahadeva and Sumati. In time Varddhamanasūri, following the time honored practice of his faith, fasted to death on the holy mountain Arbuda and was reborn as a god.

Later on the Glorious Jineśvarasūri, recognizing that both Jinacandra and Abhayadeva were virtuous and worthy, honored both these monks, who eventually became known as foremost in the monastic community. He honored two other monks, Dhanesvara and Jinabhadra, by name, and placed Haribhadra just below them in the hierarchy as Master. Dharmadeva, Sumati and Vimala were given the rank of instructor. Dharmadeva had the brothers Harisimha and Sarvadevagaṇi as disciples, as well as the scholar Somacandra. Sahadevagaṇi had Aśokacandra as his disciple. Everyone was extremely fond of him, in fact. The Glorious Jinacandrāsuri singled him out and took particular pains to teach him and eventually installed him in the high position of Head Master. He in turn took Harisimha as his successor. There were other monks to receive high honors; Prasannacandra and Devabhadra were their names. Devabhadra was the disciple of the teacher Sumati. Four of these monks, including Prasannacandra, studied logic under Abhayadevasūri. Thus it is said,

"Even today they are like pillars commemorating his ever-spreading fame, the Glorious Prasannendusūri, the Glorious Varddhamanasūri, the King of Ascetics, Haribhadra, and the saint Devacandra, who are like vast oceans of learning; their words are clever and well-chosen, from their long study of proper argumentation and logic, and they are devoted to the faith."

The Glorious Jineśvarasūri came once to Āśāpallī. There were many clever people who attended the lectures he gave there. This is where he composed his romance, *Lilāvatīkathā*, which is rich in meaning and can be read on so many levels. Then in Dindiya village he wrote his *Kathānakakośa* to use in one of his lectures. First he had asked the head of the local group of monks for a book to use in his talks; this group belonged to that faction that held it proper for Jain holy men to dwell in monasteries. The local monk would not lend him a book. And so, in the last two watches of every night, he composed part of the *Kathānakakośa*, which he then used the next morning in his lecture. In this way he wrote the whole of the text during the rainy season.

Now it happened that the nun, Marudevigaṇi, resolved upon a fast. She fasted for forty days. The Glorious Jineśvarasūri was amazed by her resolve and filled with awe, he asked, "Please tell me where you are reborn." She said, "I shall do that." Now there was a lay devotee who could not decide if a true Leader of the Faith had been born, and he went to the holy mountain Śatruñjaya, and in order to find out whether there was any such great man alive he began to undertake a series of fasts. It also happened that the demi-god Brahmaśānti went to the country Mahāvideha in order to worship the Jina. The God that had formerly been the nun Marudevi gave him this message.

"The nun who was called Marudevi and who led a small group of nuns in your community went to the first heaven and became a God with great supernatural powers.

She has a life span of two divine aeons. Tell this to that Lord of Monks, the Glorious Jineśvarasūri.

This has been told by one who came to Takka in order to worship the Jina. Exert yourself for the faith. Forget everything else!"

But the demi-god did not go and directly repeat these verses to Jineśvara. He told the lay man who was engaged in his fasts, "There are some letters written on the edge of your garment, *ma,sa,ta,sa,ta,ca,* Go to the city Pattan; the Master who can understand their significance, and who, by washing the garment with his own hands, can make the rest of the letters that go with them appear is the true Leader of the Faith." The layman went everywhere the monks stay; he showed the letters to every monk he encountered, but no one could understand their significance. Finally he came to the lodgings of the Glorious Jineśvarasūri. He showed him the letters. He thought about them for a moment and then he washed the garment. The three verses appeared. The layman knew, "He is the true Leader of the Faith." With deep reverence he accepted him as his teacher. The Glorious Jineśvarasūri kept on performing acts like this in service of his Faith and then went to Heaven.

Jineśvarasūri, from the *Vṛddhācāryaprabandhāvali*, p.90.

Now on one occasion, in the course of his monastic wanderings, the Glorious Varddhamānasūri happened to come to Sīdhapura where the river Sarasvatī always flows. There were many Brahmins who bathed in that river. Amongst them was a certain Brahmin named Jagga from the Pukkharaṇa gotra, learned in all the sciences. One day after his bath this Jagga chanced to meet the Jain monk who had gone out to relieve himself. He began to make fun of the doctrine of the Jains, saying, "These Śvetāmbaras are like the lowest of the low in the Hindu caste system, for they are not permitted to study the Vedas and they are impure." At this the teacher replied, "Sir, Jagga, the Brahmin! Tell me, what good has it done you just to clean your body on the outside? I say, your body did not get purified in the least, for you carry on your head an unclean and polluting corpse." They decided to debate the issue, and Jagga offered this as the wager, "If there is a corpse on my head, then I shall be your student. But if there is not, then you must be my disciple." The teacher said, "So be it." Then that angry Brahmin unwrapped his turban. A dead fish fell out of it. He had lost the wager. He became the master's disciple. He was ordained as a monk and received instruction and became thoroughly knowledgeable in the Jain doctrine. He was given the name Jineśvarasūri. After some time Vaddhamānasūri voluntarily stopped eating and went to the world of the Gods. Then Jineśvarasūri, the leader of the community of monks, travelling from place to place, arrived in the city Aṇahillapura. There he saw many rich monks, members of the group called the Culasīgaccha, who were monks in appearance only, and who lived in richly appointed temples and controlled wealthy monastic establishments. And when he saw them behaving like that, in order to further the true Jain Faith, he had a debate with them in the court of the Glorious King Durlabharāja. In the year 1024 he defeated those arrogant teachers. The king, who was pleased with him, gave him the honorific title, "Kharatara," "Fierce One." From that time on the group became known as the Kharataragaccha.

The Origins of a God and Goddess, from a medieval pilgrimage text, the *Vividhatīrthakalpa* of Jinaprabhasūri, 1333 A.D.

Translated by Phyllis Granoff

Introduction

The *Vividhatīrthakalpa* is a collection of stories told of many of the holy places of medieval Jainism. The collection was made by a monk who travelled from place to place. He based his accounts on what he heard from other monks and local people, and occasionally on written sources as well. The text is written in both Sanskrit and Prakrit and occasionally shows striking resemblances to the medieval biography collections, selections of which were translated in Part II, chapter 1. The two stories I have translated here tell about the origins of a minor protecting god and goddess. They belong to a recognizable group of stories told of the origins of clan deities, usually goddesses, among the Svetambara Jains of Gujarat and Rajasthan. In the clan goddess stories a woman, often wronged, commits suicide and returns as the clan goddess. Such stories circulated in vernacular clan histories and were also occasionally incorporated into the collections of biographies of famous monks. I have written about some of these stories in an article to appear in *East and West.* John Cort has given further information about the text and its author and the institution of pilgrimage in medieval Jainism in the introduction and appendices to his translations that follow as chapter 6.

The Story of the Goddess Ambikā, *Vividhatīrthakalpa*, number 61, pp. 107-108.

Bowing down to the holy mountain of Ujjayanta and to the Jina Nemināthā, I write the story of Kohaṇḍidevī as I have heard it from the elders.

There is in the territory of Surāṣṭra a city named Koḍīnagara, bustling with rich people who have plenty of gold and money. In that city dwelt a wealthy Brahmin named Soma, who was punctual in his performance of his religious duties and was knowledgeable in the Vedic scriptures. His wife Aṃbinī wore costly ornaments on her person, but her greatest treasure was her purity of conduct. As this couple enjoyed the pleasures that life can bring they produced two sons. The first was named Siddha and the second was called Buddha. Now it happened that the time had come to perform a ceremony on behalf of the family ancestors and the Brahmin Soma invited many Brahmins for a ritual meal to take place on the day of the memorial service. Some of the Brahmins were engaged in reciting the Vedas; some made offerings to the ancestors; others performed sacrifices and made oblations into the sacred fires. Aṃbinī prepared many foods for the occasion; she made cakes of rice and lentils; she made spiced delicacies with the finest condiments and even sweet milk pudding.

And then, when her mother-in-law went to take her bath, at that very moment a Jain monk came to their home looking for alms so that he might break his fast that had lasted one month. As soon as she saw him, Aṃbinī was filled with joy; as she rose to serve him she felt her body tingling with excitement. Her heart filled with devotion, she offered the Jain monk the first serving of the foods that she had prepared.

As soon as the monk accepted these alms, the mother-in-law reappeared on the scene, back in the kitchen after her bath. She could see that some of the food was gone. Furious, she kept asking her daughter-in-law what had happened. Aṃbinī told her exactly what had taken place, and her mother-in-law began to scream at her and abuse her. "You slut! Now what have you done! You haven't even worshipped our family deity, you haven't yet served the Brahmins, you haven't put out the offerings for the ancestors. How dare you give the first food to some Jain monk!" And the mother-in-law told the Brahmin Soma what his wife had done. He was enraged and he threw her out of the house, fearing that she would bring ill luck upon them all.

Despondent at this humiliation, Aṃbinī took Siddha by the hand and carrying Buddha on her hip she left the city. As she walked on, the children became oppressed by thirst and begged her for water. Her eyes filled with tears, but then, lo and behold, a dried up lake that lay in their path became filled with water by the power of her pure conduct. She gave them both cool water to drink. Then the children grew hungry and begged her for something to eat. A mango tree on the road at once burst into fruit. She gave them ripe mangoes to eat. The children felt satisfied.

Now hear what happened while she was sitting down to rest in the shade of that mango. When she was still at home she had fed the children and she had then taken the leaves that they had eaten from and thrown them away outside. A guiding Goddess of the Jain Faith took pity on her and was moved by the great power of her purity and turned all those leaves into gold platters and dishes. And the drops of children's saliva that had fallen from the leaves onto the ground were turned into costly pearls. Even the food that she had given to the Jain monk was magically restored to the pot from which she had taken it. Her mother-in-law saw this miracle and told the Brahmin Soma. And she also told him, "Son, your wife will bring us good fortune and is a faithful and pure wife. You must bring her back, for she will be the support of this family." Thus it was that the Brahmin Soma, obeying his mother's command, and burning with the painful fires of remorse, went to bring his wife back home. But when she saw that best of Brahmins coming after her Aṃbinī was terrified. She looked this way and that in search of rescue. And then she saw an old well right in front of her eyes. Her mind fixed on the best of Jinas, her heart rejoicing in the gift that she had made to the monk, she threw herself into the well. Giving up her life with her mind filled with lofty thoughts she was reborn as the powerful Goddess Aṃbinī in the sphere of the Gods known as Kohaṇḍa, just four leagues from the heaven Sohamma. She is also known as Kohaṇḍi after the heavenly sphere in which she was reborn. For his part, the Brahmin Soma, seeing that most faithful of wives jump into the well, threw himself in the well after her. He, too, died and became a god in the very same heavenly sphere. By the power of his magic he transformed himself into a lion and became her mount. Others say that Aṃbinī jumped off the summit of Mt. Revaya and that the Brahmin Soma followed her and died in the same way. They relate all the other details of the story in exactly the same way.

This Blessed Goddess holds the following attributes in her four arms: in her right arms she holds a sprout of mangoes and a noose and in her left arms she holds a child and an elephant goad. The colour of her skin is the soft and gentle glow of liquid gold. She lives on the peak of Mt.Revaya as the protecting Goddess of the Jina Neminãha. Adorned with every kind of ornament on every part of her body, sporting a crown, earrings, a pearl necklace, jewelled bracelets and anklets, she grants all the wishes of faithful Jains and prevents any harm from coming to Jain believers. She shows to those who are devoted to Jainism all kinds of spells and magic diagrams and displays before them many a wondrous power. Through her power no evil spirit, ghost, goblin or witch can work its magic on a devotee and the faithful grow rich, become kings, and have fine wives and sons.

The Story of the *Yakṣa* Kapardin, *Vividhatīrthakalpa*, number 30, p. 56.

Offering a prayer to the image of the Jina Ṛsabhanātha consecrated on the summit of Mt. Śatruñjaya, I now relate the story of the *demi-god* Kapardin who is his devoted servant.

There is in the land Vālakka a city named Palittāṇaya. There dwelt a village headman by name Kavaḍḍi. His thoughts were ever given over to wicked deeds; he drank liquor, ate meat, killed living creatures, lied, thieved and committed adultery. He had a wife named Anahī who was of like mind and with her he indulged himself in sensual delights. So it was that he passed his time. Now one day when he was lolling about on his terrace it just so happened that two Jain monks came to his house. He lowered his eyes in respect to them and with his hands folded in humble greeting, he asked them, "O Blessed Ones! Tell me, why have you come here to my house? I have plenty of milk, yogurt, ghee and butter milk; we have all sorts of rich delicacies to eat here. Please, tell me what it is that you need." The holy men replied, "We have not come to you looking for alms. Our teacher has arrived here with many of his disciples in the course of his pilgrimage to Mt. Śatruñjaya. But the rains have come upon us and it is no longer fit for monks to travel. And so we have come to you to ask for a place to stay for our teacher and his disciples." The village headman replied at once, "Consider your request met. I shall give you a place to stay. Tell your teacher to come and to remain here as long as he wishes. There is only one thing— you must tell him never to talk to me about religion; I prefer sin myself." The monks answered, "So be it."

The teacher came to the village and spent the four months of the rainy season there. He was always occupied with his study of the Jain scriptures and he constantly mortified his body with fasting. Eventually the rainy season was over and the teacher asked the village headman for permission to seek alms to break his fast of the rainy season. The village headman was pleased with the monk for having kept his promise not to bother him with matters of religion, and granted him leave to gather alms anywhere in his territory, up to the very borders of the land under his control. The monk, having been given this permission to wander freely up to the very borders of the headman's territory, then spoke to the headman, "O Headman! You have shown us many kindnesses, allowing us to spend the rainy retreat here and now with this great boon. Now I shall instruct you in my religion and thus repay this debt."

The headman at once spoke up, "Don't tell me anything about fasting or restraining my senses. That's not for me. Teach me some magic spell, if you must." And so, out of great compassion, the teacher instructed the headman in the use of the marvelous formula that praises the Jain worthies; he taught him how it could be used to cause water to appear, to make fire burn and to stop moving creatures in their tracks. The teacher then added, "Every day you must face Mt.Śatruñjaya and recite this formula." The village headman agreed to do as the monk said and bowed down to him in respect. He then returned home. The monk continued on his wanderings.

In time the headman came to occupy himself more and more with reciting the sacred words and observing various religious practices. Now one day he had a fight with his wife and she chased him out of the house. He started to climb Mt.Śatruñjaya. He sat down in the shade of a tree and was about to lift his wine cup to take a drink when he saw a vulture above him carrying a snake in its mouth; he saw, too, how a drop of the snake's poison fell into his cup. And when he saw all of this his mind was filled with disgust for the pleasures of the world. He put his wine cup down, and no longer interested in this world, he undertook a voluntary fast to death. At the moment that he left this life his thoughts were pure; his mind was fixed on the lotus feet of the first Jina and on the sacred words that the Jain monk had given him. Because of the great power of that holy mountain and the power of the sacred words that he had been given by the monk he was reborn as the *demi-god* Kavaḍḍin. With his supernatural knowledge he was able to remember his previous existence and he worshipped the first Jina with all his heart. Now that wife of his, hearing what had happened to him, went to where he had died and rebuking herself she too undertook a voluntary fast to death and passed away. She was reborn as a magnificent elephant and became his mount. Kapardin holds in his four arms a noose, an elephant goad, a purse of money and a citron fruit.

On another occasion Kapardin looked around the earth with his supernatural knowledge and, finding his teacher from his previous existence, he appeared before him and prostrated himself at his feet. Having greeted his teacher with devotion, he humbly folded his hands in supplication and announced to him, "O Blessed One! By your grace I have obtained these powers. Please instruct me. What may I do for you?" The teacher said, "You must always stay in this holy place, Śatruñjaya; you must worship the first Jina each morning, noon and night; you must ward off all harm that might befall the faithful." The demi-god knelt down again at the feet of the teacher and promised to obey his command. This king of the demi-gods then went back to the summit of Mt. Śatruñjaya. He did exactly as the teacher instructed him.

Jinaprabhasūri has written this story of the demi-god Kavaḍḍi and the story of the Goddess Ambādevī that goes with it in accordance with what he heard the elders tell him.

A Note on the Translations

When I decided to translate a selection of Jain stories I had in mind a non-specialist audience. This led me to make certain choices. For all of the stories, instead of using footnotes, I have included right in the body of the story explanatory information about technical terms in Jainism where I felt such information could be given briefly and might be useful. So, for example, if a didactic story made passing reference to the "five divine signs" or the "three restraints" I spelled out there exactly what these terms meant.

Each text presented its own challenges. I decided to try to retain as much of the double-entendre and word plays as I could from the original. Instead of explaining word play in footnotes, though, I explained double meanings in the translations themselves, for example in the description of the ocean in the story of Devadhara. I also attempted to gloss riddles for the reader right in the text rather than in appended footnotes. Occasionally I went so far as to create dialogue when I could not render the original into English and keep the double meanings; my attempt was to provide a comparable English passage. Thus I tried to create a dialogue similar to the one Madanakīrti and the princess exchange in the biography of the Digambara monk Madanakīrti. The princess has too much salt put into the monk's food; he exclaims "how salty," but the word can also mean "what great feminine charm." I also resorted to supplying sentences for single terms when I felt a term in the original was too rich in meaning to be translated simply by a single English word. As such a case I might cite my translation of the term *bāṇḍa* in the story of Āryanandila from the *Prabandhakośa.* The snake has just had its tail cut off and is slithering around pathetically. Vairoṭhyā affectionately calls him *bāṇḍa*, which I take as the same as the Gujarati *bāṇḍa*, meaning "tailless." But the word also means something like a jester or a buffoon. It seems to me that it is in all these meanings that Vairoṭhyā uses the term. The snake is *bāṇḍa*, deprived of an essential part; it is slithering around and performing antics like a jester or buffoon, and it is the naughty one, in the way a specially loved young child is. I tried to convey some of this in my translation, but I needed a sentence or two in which to do it.

There were other times when after considerable thought I settled on a style of translation that is close to the original, but might need some getting used to for an English reader. I did this in an effort to convey something of the particular flavor of a story. Anyone who reads the story of Devadiṇṇa, for example, is sure to notice the number of times the word "and" appears at the beginning of a sentence. The original connects almost every sentence with an "and"; to me it seemed to use "and" so frequently that I felt that these "ands" constituted almost a mark of the author's style. Each time I would remove them in the service of greater English readability, I felt that I had lost something of the flavor of the original and eventually decided to retain most of them and leave a reader to decide whether the net result was a loss or a gain. In short, these translations represent a compromise in an effort to make these delightful stories accessible to an English audience. I hope that in the main I have been faithful to the spirit of the texts and yet provided translations that the general reader will enjoy.

In conjunction with a research project on religious biographies in Asia carried out under the auspices of the Social Science and Humanities Research Council of Canada and headed by Dr. Koichi Shinohara at McMaster University, I have written about some of the biographies that I translate here. Readers are referred to the volume edited by Dr.Shinohara and me entitled, *Monks and Magicians: Religious Biographies in Asia*, Oakville: Ontario, 1988, particularly for some indication of the bibliography available on this aspect of Jain narrative literature. I have two articles in that volume on the biographies of Nāgārjuna and Āryakhapaṭa and Mallavādin, primarily devoted to a study of the sources of these biographies and their possible paths of transmission. I also have some information on some of the Kharatara biographies in several articles that I have done recently. One on biographies and Jain clan histories will soon be published in *East and West*; another, on Siddhasena is to appear in the *Journal of Indian Philosophy.* I have also used material from the Kharatara biographies for a study of the role of written texts in medieval India in a paper that will be published in the forthcoming festschrift for the veteran Jain scholar J. Deleu, whose work on the *prabandhas* was an invaluable aid to me. Finally I have translated and studied other portions of the *Vivdhatīrthakalpa* in an article on Jain attitudes towards Muslim iconoclasm which will appear in *East and West*.

I have used the edition of the *Ākhyānakamaṇikośa* published by the Prakrit Text Society in 1962 and the edition of the *Mūlaśuddhiprakaraṇa* edited and published by Amritlal Mohanlal Bhojak in the Prakrit Text Society Series No. 15, Ahmedabad, 1971. All the other texts have been published by the Singhi Jain Series. There is a Gujarati translation of the *Prabandhakośa* done by Hiralal Rasikdas Kapadia in 1914 and published from the Forbes Gujarati Sahitya Sabha. Kapadia is one of the foremost scholars of Jainism, and I benefitted greatly from having his translation available to me. The *Kharataragacchabṛhadgurvāvali* was translated into Hindi by Mahopādhyāya Vinayasāgara, with an introduction by Agarchand Nahta in the *Kharataragaccha kā Bṛhaditihāsa*, Ajmer: Dada Jinadattasūri Aṣṭamaśatābdi Mahotsava Svāgatakāriṇī Samiti, 1959. I have also benefitted greatly from consulting it in places where I was unsure of the use of a particular term.

Hemacandra's Pariśiṣṭaparva
The story of Cāṇakya

Translated by Rosalind Lefeber

Introduction

Hemacandra's Pariśiṣṭaparva tells in verse the lives of the early Jain teachers; so at first glance it seems odd that it should include a story-cycle about Cāṇakya. This Brahman counsellor of the first Mauryan king, Candragupta, was probably not a Jain, though the king himself may have been. Moreover, Cāṇakya is legendary not as a model of morality but as a shrewd and ruthless strategist to whom are ascribed the pragmatic doctrines of the Arthaśāstra.

But Hemacandra made use of popular stories from many sources, and in this case, Cāṇakya has been given a pious Jain beginning and a pious Jain death, with unexpected twists. Though all the episodes are held together by the thread of Cāṇakya's political career, these stories are in the folk-tale tradition. They are less about religion or politics than about quick wit and personal survival, the same themes celebrated in collections like the Pañcatantra or Aesop's Fables. The listener or reader understands that he is not meant to emulate the expedient behaviour of the protagonist, but only to enjoy his exploits and perhaps to be wary of cunning adversaries in real life.

Hemacandra's Pariśiṣṭaparva

The story of Cāṇakya

Sarga 8, verses 194-469; Sarga 9, verses 1-13

Sarga Eight

194. In the Golla region, in a village called Caṇaka, there was once a Brahman named Caṇin, whose wife was Caṇeśvarī.

195. Caṇin was known from his birth on as a Jain layman and learned Jain monks used to stay in his house.

196. Now one day Caṇin had a son who was born with a full set of teeth. As soon as he was born, Caṇin presented him respectfully to those holy men.

197. Told by Caṇin that the baby was born with teeth, the learned monks said: "This boy will be a king."

198. Caṇin thought that the violence required by kingship would doom his son to hell, so without regard for the pain he was causing, he had the baby's teeth knocked out.

199. He reported this to the monks, but they replied: "Because his teeth have been knocked out, he will instead become the power behind the throne."

200. To this son of his, Caṇin gave the name Cāṇakya, and in time Cāṇakya became a Jain layman thoroughly versed in all branches of learning.

201. He was always rich in happiness because he served the Jain ascetics, and later he obtained one of the daughters of a well-born Brahman as his bride.

202. Now one day Cāṇakya's wife returned to her maternal home where there was to be a great wedding celebration for her brother.

203. Her sisters arrived for that great celebration wearing fine clothing and ornaments, for they had rich husbands.

204-205.

They all came in painted carriages, all were surrounded by maid-servants, all had parasols and other signs of high rank, all wore garlands on their heads, all were annointed with the finest fragrant ointments, and all had betel-leaves in their hands. In fact, they were all like miraculous embodiments of the goddess of wealth.

206-208.

As for Cāṇakya's wife, day and night she wore the same clothing, her only ornament a modest, plain necklace. Her bodice was old and she wore an old shawl dyed orange with safflower. Her mouth showed no sign of betel-leaf, her only unguent was the dust on her body, and her ear-rings were made of tin. Her hands were rough with the work she always did, and her hair was soiled. Her sisters, who had married wealthy men, made fun of her.

209. All the other people assembled for the wedding laughed at her as well. She felt so ashamed that she hid in a corner and then left the wedding.

210. Her face dark with despair, she reached Cāṇakya's house and sat with her tears washing away the kohl from her eyes and spotting the ground around her.

211. When Cāṇakya saw her face as faded as a water-lily in the morning, he was grieved by her pain and spoke these gentle words:

212. "My dear, why are you so distressed? Have you been insulted in some way by me or by a neighbour or in your father's house?"

213. But she was so tormented by her disgrace that she was unable to speak. Nevertheless, her husband persisted and so she finally explained.

214. When Cāṇakya learned the reason for his wife's suffering, he tried to find some infallible means of procuring money and he thought:

215. "In the city of Pāṭalīputra is king Nanda, who bestows exceptional gifts on Brahmans. I shall go there for that purpose."

216. Having made this decision, he went there and entered the king's dwelling where he sat down in the first of the seats that were placed in front.

217. But that first seat taken by Cāṇakya was always graced by Nanda himself, for it was his throne.

218. Now when Nanda and his son entered, the latter remarked: "This Brahman has trampled on the king's shadow by sitting there."

219. So one of the king's maid-servants suggested to Cāṇakya in a conciliatory way: "O Brahman! Please sit here on this second seat."

220. "My water-jar can rest there," said he, and put his water- jar on it. But he did not give up the first seat.

221. And as he was repeatedly asked to get up, he occupied in the same way a third seat with his staff, a fourth with his rosary and a fifth with his sacred thread.

222-23.

Finally the maid-servant declared: "Well! This impudent fellow won't give up the first seat, and what's even more outrageous, he's taken over the other seats as well. What's to be done with this impudent, crazy Brahman?" So with her foot she pushed him to make him get up.

224. At once Cāṇakya became furious, like a snake jabbed with a stick. With everyone looking on, he made this vow:

225. "I shall uproot Nanda, together with his treasure and his attendants, his friends and his sons, his troops and his chariots, just as a mighty wind uproots a tree."

226. Angry as a blazing fire, his face red as heated copper, Caṇin's son left the city at once, scowling fiercely.

227. Cāṇakya, foremost of the wise, then recalled the prophecy of the wisemen that he himself would become the power behind the throne.

228. And because he had been insulted, he wandered over the earth looking for some man worthy of kingship. For proud men never forget an insult.

229. One day this Brahman son of Caṇeśvarī came to the place where the breeders of king Nanda's peacocks lived.

230. Dressed in his wandering mendicant's clothing, Caṇin's son entered the village to beg a little food.

231. Now the chief peacock-breeder's daughter was pregnant and had a morbid craving to drink the moon (candra).

232. Her parents reported her morbid craving to Cāṇakya, and asked how it could be satisfied, to which he replied:

233. "I will satisfy her craving to drink the moon, but only if you give me her son as soon as he is born."

234. The mother and father were afraid that if her craving were not satisfied, she might lose the child anyway, so they agreed to his request.

235. Then Cāṇakya had a grass shed constructed with a hole in the roof, and had a man, who was to remain hidden (gupta), climb on top with a cover for the opening.

236. Beneath the opening he placed a bowl of water in which at midnight during that autumn month the full moon was reflected.

237. When he showed the reflected full moon to the pregnant woman and told her to drink, she began to do so, her face beaming with joy.

238. And as she drank, the hidden man with the cover gradually closed the opening in the roof of the grass shed.

239. In this way her craving was satisfied, and in due time she gave birth to a son, who was given the name Candragupta by his parents.

240. Like the moon for whom he was named, Candragupta grew bigger day by day, brightening the lotus-beds of the peacock- breeder's family.

241. As for Cāṇakya, he traveled about, determined to acquire gold, and began to seek out people skilled in alchemy.

242. Meanwhile Candragupta played each day with the other boys, continually bestowing on them villages and other gifts, as if he were a king.

243. He climbed on the backs of the other boys, treating them like elephants or steeds. There are usually early indications like these of future royal dignity.

244. In due course Cāṇakya in his wanderings returned and was greatly astonished to see this child behaving as he did.

245. So in order to test him, Cāṇakya said to him: "O king! Bestow something on me, too!"

246. Candragupta replied: "If it pleases you, O Brahman, take these village cattle. Who will dare object if I give them to you?"

247. Smiling, Cāṇakya asked: "How can I take these cows? I am very much afraid of the cows' owners, who will surely kill me."

248. "Don't be afraid!" answered Candragupta. "By all means, take the cattle I offer you. The earth is there to be enjoyed by heroes."

249. Cāṇakya said to himself: "Well, well, this boy is certainly worldly-wise," and he asked the other boys nearby who he was.

250. The children explained: "He's the son of a wandering mendicant. When he was already in the womb, his mother promised him to a mendicant."

251. Then Cāṇakya recognized him as the boy he had arranged to take for himself, so he said to him: "I am the one to whom you belong. Come with me and I will give you a kingdom."

252. Eager to be king, Candragupta took hold of his hand; and Cāṇakya ran off with him at once, just like a thief.

253. Cāṇakya was determined to destroy Nanda utterly, so with the wealth he had acquired by alchemy, he assembled an army complete with foot-soldiers.

254. Then with all his assault troops, those forces complete with foot-soldiers, he attacked Pāṭalīputra from all sides.

255. But the king made a sortie, and since Cāṇakya's troops were relatively weak, Nanda was able to crush all of them as easily as a flock of goats.

256. So Cāṇakya fled with Candragupta, for he knew what was right for that moment. One should save one's life by escaping, if need be; for where there's life, there's hope.

257. But a king does not tolerate those who covet his kingdom, so Nanda ordered his best horsemen to pursue Candragupta.

258. Meanwhile, Nanda himself, proud of his victory, returned to his city where the citizens held a celebration befitting their wealth.

259. Not far away, one of the pursuing horsemen on his swift steed had nearly caught up with Candragupta.

260. Seeing that rider approaching from afar, quick-witted Cāṇakya gave the following orders to Candragupta:

261. "Dive into this pond adorned with lotus-beds as if you were a water bird, and don't come out until I call you."

262. So Candragupta at once plunged into the deep water as calmly as if he knew the magic art of making water turn solid.

263. As for himself, Cāṇakya sat motionless on the bank of the pond and made believe he was a meditating yogin, indifferent to the world.

264. Then Nanda's horseman arrived with the speed of the wind, his horse's hooves pounding on the ground like drum-sticks on a drum.

265. And he questioned Cāṇakya, saying: "Venerable father! Tell me quickly, did you see just now a very young man?"

266. Canin's son, pretending to be afraid of breaking his meditation, gave an irritable grunt and pointed towards the pond.

267. The horseman meant to plunge into the water and catch Candragupta, so he began to remove his armour, as a dancing girl might remove her skirt.

268. But cruel Cāṇakya seized the horseman's own cruel sword and cut off his head as if to offer it to the goddess of the waters.

269. Then Cāṇakya called: "Come here, my child, come here!" And out of the pond came Candragupta, as the moon once rose from the ocean.

270. After lifting Candragupta onto the soldier's horse, Cāṇakya asked him: "What did you think when I pointed you out to the horseman?"

271. Candragupta replied: "Venerable master, what I thought then was that it is surely not I but my master who knows what is best."

272. And Cāṇakya thought: "He will always be submissive and obey me, just as a well-trained elephant obeys his driver."

273. Now as these two proceeded on their way, behind them there came, like some prodigious messenger of the God of Death, another of Nanda's horsemen on a steed swift as the wind.

274. Upon seeing him rushing towards them, Cāṇakya again ordered Candragupta to plunge at once like a swan into a near-by pond.

275. There was a washerman on the shore, and Cāṇakya said to him: "The king is furious with all those of your trade, so if you do not wish to die, be gone!"

276-77.

Now the washerman saw at a distance the rider with his sword upraised, and concluded that all this was true. So to save his life he ran away, leaving behind the clothes he had been washing in the pond. Then Caṇin's son himself began to launder those clothes.

278. And when the horseman arrived and made inquiries, the son of Caṇin, his wits as sharp as the tips of kuśa grass, killed him just as he had killed the other soldier.

279. Now Cāṇakya and Candragupta left that place, and as they went on their way, Candragupta's belly grew thin and he was tormented with hunger.

280. Leaving Candragupta outside, Cāṇakya went towards a village to get food, for where there is no village, there is no food.

281. He saw coming from the village a learned Brahman who had just eaten. He was walking very slowly and stroking his bulging belly.

282. So Cāṇakya asked him: "Do people here start up their cooking pots for Brahmans?" Said the Brahman: "Yes, indeed. They started one up for me just now."

283. Again Cāṇakya questioned him: "Learned Brahman, what did you eat?" "Rice mixed with curds," he replied, "with tasty yoghurt."

284. Now Cāṇakya reflected: "It might take time for me to walk around inside the village in search of food. And meanwhile, what might become of Candragupta without me?

285. "Nanda's horsemen, whose valor is irresistible, may arrive. And if Candragupta is all alone, they will seize him as dogs seize a boar.

286. "And if the boy Candragupta is seized by Nanda's troopers, then my hopes for kingship will fade like a dream.

287. "So that his life may be preserved one way or another, I'll give him the food I take from the stomach of this Brahman."

288. Thereupon Cāṇakya at once slit open the Brahman's belly as a cook might split a pumpkin.

289. And in a moment Cāṇakya himself took the food from the Brahman's stomach as if from a pot, and he fed it to Candragupta.

290. Then moving on with Candragupta, Cāṇakya came in the evening to a village, as a partridge comes to its nest.

291. As Cāṇakya entered the village to beg for food, he happened upon the house of poor old woman.

292-93.

She was serving a dish of hot gruel to her children. One of them was exceedingly hungry and stuck his hand in it, and then began to cry because his fingers were burned. The old woman said to the boy: "You fool! You're just like Cāṇakya: you don't know a thing."

294. When Cāṇakya heard what the old woman said, he entered her house and questioned her: "Why are you using Cāṇakya as a bad example for this child?"

295. The old woman replied: "Stupid Cāṇakya made himself vulnerable by besieging Nanda's capital city without first conquering the outlying regions.

296. "In the same way this boy burned his fingers on the hot food by sticking his hand right in the middle of it, instead of eating a little at a time from the edges."

297. Cāṇakya said to himself: "My, my! She may be only a woman, but she certainly is wise." So he went off to live in Himavatkūṭa.

298. There Candragupta's teacher made friends with Parvataka, the king, because he wanted his assistance.

299. One day Cāṇakya said to him: "Together, let us drive king Nanda from his throne, seize his kingdom and share it like brothers."

300. Parvataka agreed to his suggestion and became Cāṇakya's ally, like a lion ready to fight.

301. Then Cāṇakya, Candragupta and Parvataka set about conquering the outlying regions of Nanda's kingdom.

302. But there was one city they besieged that could not be taken by assault. So Cāṇakya went there in mendicant's clothing as if to beg for food.

303. And as Cāṇakya walked around inside the city dressed as a wandering mendicant, he discovered the statues of all of the Seven Mothers, the eternal goddesses.

304. Cāṇakya said to himself: "All these goddesses must be guardians. Surely it is their power that keeps the city from being taken."

305. Just as Cāṇakya was wondering how to get rid of the Mothers, the citizens, who were suffering from the siege of the city, came and asked him:

306. "Holy one, when will the siege of our city be lifted? Tell us, please, for men like you usually know everything."

307. Candragupta's teacher answered: "Listen, you townspeople! How can the siege be lifted while these Mothers are here?"

308. At once the citizens removed the whole circle of Mothers; for there's nothing that a person in distress won't do, especially under the influence of a cheat.

309. Then at a signal from Cāṇakya, Candragupta and Parvataka withdrew, to the great joy of the townspeople.

310. But those two soon returned, as irresistible as the ocean's tide; and since they were unexpected, they were able to enter the city and destroy their enemies.

311. After they had taken that city, those two great chariot warriors, guided by Cāṇakya as if by a charioteer, went on to conquer the rest of Nanda's country.

312. Finally, armed with Cāṇakya's wisdom, that valiant pair besieged the city of Pāṭalīputra from every side with unlimited forces.

313. And because Nanda's religious merit was exhausted, he found himself with army, treasury, skill and prowess all exhausted; for good fortune lasts only as long as religious merit.

314. On the verge of losing his life, Nanda begged from Cāṇakya permission to leave safely. Is there anyone to whom life is not the dearest possession?

315. Then Cāṇakya announced to him: "Sir, you may leave, but with only one wagon. On it you should load as much as you can of whatever you value most.

316. "And don't be afraid. No one will attack you if you leave with just one wagon. Rest assured that you will not be killed: you'll be as safe as if you were a Brahman."

317. So king Nanda loaded onto the wagon two wives, his only daughter, and as many valuables as possible and then left the city.

318. But once on the wagon, Nanda's daughter saw Candragupta coming along and immediately fell in love with him, staring at him with the unblinking eyes of a goddess.

319. With her beaming moon-like face and sidelong glances, Nanda's daughter seemed to promise Candragupta all the pleasures of love.

320. Nanda said to her: "My dear child, feel free to choose your own husband, for such a free choice is usually recommended for daughters of the warrior-caste.

321. "Farewell and may you live long. Get down from the wagon and leave me. May the pain your marriage causes me leave with you."

322. When she heard this, she quickly got down from the wagon and began to climb up onto Candragupta's splendid chariot.

323. But as she was climbing up, nine spokes of Candragupta's chariot-wheel were broken like sugar-cane stalks crushed in a mill.

324. Candragupta said to himself: "Who is this unlucky woman climbing onto my chariot?," and thinking that she might destroy his chariot, he tried to stop her.

325. But Cāṇakya said: "Candragupta, don't stop her! This is a favourable omen, make no mistake about it.

326. "What this omen means, my child, is that for nine generations your descendants will enjoy continually increasing prosperity."

327. Then when Candragupta and Parvataka took over Nanda's palace, they set about dividing up Nanda's immense wealth.

328. Now among his possessions there was one maiden who was guarded as if all his treasures were somehow united in her, for king Nanda had fed her from birth with poison.

329. And Parvataka felt such love for her that he enshrined her in his heart as if she were to be meditated on like some deity.

330. So Candragupta's teacher gave her to Parvataka alone, and the marriage ceremony was performed at once.

331. But while Parvataka was holding her hand in the marriage ceremony, the heat of the sacrificial fire made her perspire, and the poison passed from her to him.

332. Parvataka felt pain as the transferred poison began to work, and then all his limbs became weak. He cried out to Candragupta:

333. "I feel as if I had drunk poison, and I can barely speak. Help me, my child, or I will surely die at once!"

334. But as Candragupta was repeatedly calling for doctors and sorcerers, Cāṇakya quickly whispered in his ear:

335. "If an illness goes away on its own, there's no need for medicine. If this plague Parvataka goes away without your intervention, just let him go. Keep quiet and wait, for you'll be well off without him.

336. "He who does not kill an ally who takes away half his kingdom will himself be killed. So if this one whom you must kill anyway dies by himself, you are indeed lucky."

337. Admonishing Candragupta Maurya and signaling to him with frowns and scowls, Cāṇakya, foremost of wisemen, stopped him from getting help.

338. Then the king of Himavatkūṭa went to his death, and in this way Candragupta gained sovereignty over two kingdoms.

339. And so, one hundred fifty-five years after the death and liberation of glorious Mahāvīra, Candragupta became king.

340. Now in Candragupta's kingdom, certain men who were still followers of Nanda stayed in the rugged countryside and lived as robbers.

341. So Cāṇakya went off in search of some man capable of protecting the city, and he came upon a man of low caste.

342. This man was just then engaged in setting fire to a termite nest. When Cāṇakya asked him what he was doing, he replied:

343. "I'm busy killing off these evil termites that hurt my children. Evil creatures don't deserve any better."

344. Cāṇakya thought to himself: "For a low caste man, he shows remarkable intelligence and energy"; and then he returned to Candragupta.

345. Caṇin's son, a skillful teacher, had Candragupta send for the low caste man and put him in charge of the city.

346. Once in charge, he first reassured Nanda's thieving supporters with gifts of food and the like, and then killed them. So Cāṇakya's plan was, as usual, effective.

347. Now a long time before, the Mauryan's teacher had once failed to obtain alms in a particular village, so he summoned the householders residing there.

348. Still angry with them, Caṇin's son with malicious intent gave them the following order: "Make a bamboo mango fence."

349. So acting on Cāṇakya's instructions, the village householders cut down the bamboos and made a fence for the mango trees.

350. The Mauryan's teacher pretended to be angry and said: "You fools! What I told you to do was make a fence for the bamboos out of the mango trees!"

351. In this way, Cāṇakya contrived to put the householders at fault, and in his wrath he had the village burned, complete with its children and old people.

352. One day, concerned that Candragupta's treasury was empty, Cāṇakya filled a bowl with gold coins and announced to the public:

353. "Play at dice with me. Whoever beats me will win this bowl full of gold coins. That is my stake.

354. "But anyone I beat will give me just one gold coin. Men, this offer is as firm as if it were carved in stone."

355. Then Candragupta's teacher began to gamble with people day and night, and since the dice were loaded, he beat them all.

356. But that way of acquiring wealth was slow and produced very little, so to try a different scheme he sent for all the townsmen.

357. First he fed them and then he gave them excellent wine to drink. And during the drinking bout, he had noisy dance music played.

358. Now Cāṇakya was skillful about ways of acquiring wealth, so laughing, dancing and singing, he pretended to be drunk, and he recited:

359. "I've got two garments dyed red, the triple staff of a mendicant, a golden water-pot and a submissive king, so sound the lute!"

360. And then, when the musicians had played the lute music, a drunken townsman, waving his arms, declared:

361. "Ha! Every step an elephant takes on a journey of a thousand leagues I could honour with a thousand gold pieces -- and I could do it every day."

362-63.

As before, after the lute was sounded, another man announced: "If you sow a bushel of sesame seeds and they all sprout and produce lots of sesame seeds, that's how many thousands of gold pieces there are in my house. Nobody could count them all."

364-65.

As before, after the lute was sounded, someone else declared: "With the butter produced in a single day from my cows I could build a dam to stop the flow of the rushing mountain streams swollen with water during the rainy season."

366-67.

As before, after the lute was sounded, another said: "With the hair from the manes growing on my new colts of fine breed born on a single day, I could wrap up the whole city of Pāṭalīputra as a spider might wrap a tree with a web."

368-69.

As before, after the lute was sounded, someone else spoke: "In my house there is a single rice plant that, each time it is cut, generates grains of rice. Another plant, called donkey-rice, reproduces itself again and again whenever it is split. Such is this pair of gems, you people!"

370-71.

As before, after the lute was sounded, another man, excited by drunkenness, said: "I am free of debt, and in my house there are valuables to be counted in the thousands. I smell nice because I'm smeared with excellent sandal paste. My wives are always obedient. Nobody is as well-off as I am."

372. As before, the lute was sounded. In this way, Caṇin's son, that ocean of intelligence and learning, discovered the riches of all the rich men.

373-75.

Then gold pieces equal to the number of footsteps of an elephant going just one league; as many thousands of gold pieces as the number of sesame seeds produced by a single plant; each month the clarified butter produced in a single day from the fresh butter of the cows' milk; the colts of fine breed born on a single day; and as much rice as would fill the store-rooms -- all this had to be given by the wealthy to Cāṇakya, for he had learned all their secrets.

376. With this wealth, the son of Caṇin made the Mauryan very powerful; for a minister who is an ocean of wisdom can be a veritable wishing-well for kings.

377. Now during a time of terrible hardship lasting twelve years, a holy teacher named Susthita was dwelling in Candragupta's city.

378. Because the shortage of food made it impossible to survive, he sent his own school of followers to another country while he remained behind.

379. But two of the young monks turned around and went back to him. And when their teacher asked why they had returned, they declared:

380. "We are simply unable to bear separation from our venerable teacher. Therefore, if we can just be at your side, it will be fine with us if we live or die."

381. The teacher said: "What you have done here is not good. You two fools will sink in a bottomless ocean of imperfections."

382. Yet after their teacher had said this, he gave them permission to stay; so they remained there serving him, like two bees at his lotus-like feet.

383. Due to the severity of the famine, these two obtained very little by begging; and since they ate only after feeding their teacher, they began to waste away.

384. These young monks, never satiated, perishing with hunger, at last took counsel together in secret:

385. "Once we heard our teacher speaking to ascetics who had completed their studies, telling them about the divine, magic eye-ointment that makes people invisible.

386. "Therefore, let us make use of this magic spell to fill our bellies. For once our bellies are full, we will be able to serve our venerable teacher free of care."

387. So that very day those two made themselves invisible and went at mealtime to Candragupta's palace.

388. Since no one could see them, those young monks ate as much as they wished from Candragupta's own plate, as if they had been relatives as dear to him as his own life.

389. And as those two fed themselves day after day, the king got up from his meal with an empty belly, like an ascetic practicing austerities.

390. Since his food was being stolen by those two, king Candragupta gradually grew thinner, like the moon during the dark fortnight of the month.

391. Nevertheless, he told no one that he was never satiated, even though hunger tormented him as if he were a rutting elephant.

392. Then one day in private the Mauryan's wise teacher questioned the Mauryan: "My child, why are you wasting away day by day, as if you had consumption?"

393. The Mauryan replied: "It's not that they don't serve me enough food, but it's as if some ghost is snatching it away from me.

394. "Everyone near me believes that I am eating plenty of food, yet I don't consume even half of my meal. I really don't understand it at all."

395. Cāṇakya said: "How can you still be so foolish that you have tortured yourself all this time, as if you were some ascetic who didn't know the true doctrine?

396. "Well, at least now you have spoken up properly. Before long I will catch your food-thief."

397. With these words, he spread a powder even finer than barley-meal on the ground in the place where Candragupta took his meals.

398. And when the king had sat down to eat, those two young monks also came to eat, leaving footprints on the powdered ground.

399. After the monarch had eaten and risen, Caṇin's son saw the traces of their feet and said to himself:

400. "Surely the person who is taking food from the king's dish with such ease is a human who walks on the ground, but he must have a magic ointment that makes him invisible."

401. So on the following day right at mealtime, Cāṇakya created in the dining hall a smoke so thick that you could cut it with a knife.

402. And when, as before, those two came and ate from the king's dish, the penetrating cloud of smoke made their eyes water.

403. All of the eye-ointment that made them invisible was immediately washed off by their streaming tears and carried away like so much mud.

404. Once the ointment was gone from their eyes, they could be seen eating from the dish by the king's attendants, who all frowned angrily.

405. Yet from fear of Cāṇakya, nobody said anything to shame those two, and Cāṇakya himself was afraid of showing disrespect for the monks, so he said:

406. "Worthy fathers, you are gods in the form of ascetics. Please be gracious to us and go back to your own abode."

407. When those two had gone, the king said in despair: "I have been polluted by eating food left on the plate by those two."

408. But Cāṇakya replied: "Don't misinterpret an advantage as an offense. You have acquired merit by sharing your food with sages.

409. "Fortunate is he who gives food to a wandering ascetic! Will you not be spoken of even more highly now that you have shared your plate with guests who were sages?"

410. Cāṇakya instructed the Mauryan with these words, but he also went to the worthy teacher and reproached him for the unseemly behaviour of the young monks.

411. The holy teacher retorted: "What fault is it of these two young monks if people like you, the laymen of the religious community, care only for filling your own bellies?"

412. Then Cāṇakya apologized for his own misdeeds and bowing to that holy teacher, he replied: "You are right. I have been thoughtless and you have instructed me.

413. "From now on, whatever benefits holy men -- food, drink, and other means of subsistence -- will be made available in my house."

414. Cāṇakya took this vow and remained firm in his decision from then on, fulfilling his responsibilities as a householder.

415. It happened that Candragupta was devoted to the false ideas of the heretics, so Cāṇakya, who loved him like a father, set about educating him:

416. "These wicked ones lack self-control and are by their very nature lecherous. They are not fit even to talk to, let alone revere.

417. "They are like trees on which the birds of passion roost. Any gift to these ungrateful, evil men produces no benefit, like rain showered on salty soil.

418. "If you rely on them, they will make you sink in the ocean of worldly existence as if you had boarded a boat made of iron. Therefore you must not put your faith in them."

419. The Mauryan replied: "Master, your words have complete authority for me. All the same, please prove to me that these men lack self-control."

420. So Cāṇakya had a proclamation made throughout the city to this effect: "The king wishes to hear the doctrines of all heretics."

421. After they had all been summoned, the highly intelligent minister seated them in a secluded spot that was close to the women's quarters of the palace.

422. But earlier, Cāṇakya had sprinkled on the ground near the women's quarters a dust so fine that it was invisible.

423. After he had brought the heretics in to be seated, they realized they were in a secluded spot and walked over towards the women's quarters.

424. And since by their very nature they lusted after women, they could not control themselves and began looking at the king's women through the openings in the window lattice.

425. These wicked men kept staring at the king's wives while they waited for the king. But as soon as he arrived, they returned to their seats.

426. They expounded their doctrine to Candragupta and then departed, all the while wishing to come back again to look at the women in the harem.

427. Now when they had gone, Cāṇakya said to Candragupta: "Look, my child, at the signs of the heretics' lust for women.

428. "For until your arrival, these men couldn't control their senses and were peeking through the window-openings into your harem.

429. "Look at this set of footprints clearly visible beneath the window-openings and you will be convinced."

430. And when the king had been convinced, his teacher summoned for the following day the Jain sages who were also to expound their doctrine.

431. These holy men sat down at once on the seats and awaited the king's arrival with the obligatory recitation of sacred texts to themselves.

432. And then, when they had expounded their doctrine, they left to go home, looking only at the ground because they adhered to the careful behaviour required of Jain religious mendicants.

433. Cāṇakya then inspected the dust beneath the window-openings and showed Candragupta that it was undisturbed.

434. He said: "These sages did not come over here as the heretics did. Otherwise, wouldn't we see footprints here?"

435. So the king was then confident that the Jain holy men were truly venerable, and he turned away from the heretics, as a yogin turns away from sense objects.

436. And so, more than once, Cāṇakya showed the efficacy of his wisdom, and proved to be an arbour on which flourished the vines of the Mauryan's prosperity. One day he reflected:

437. "Little by little I must accustom Candragupta to eating poisoned food, so that it will become the same as an elixir of life for him. Then no poisoner can prevail over him."

438. So each day the Mauryan was fed more and more poison in his food by his teacher, who was like the wise teacher of the gods.

439. Now one day the pregnant queen Durdhara, out of her great affection for Candragupta, started to share his food with him.

440. When Cāṇakya saw her eating the poisoned food, he rushed up at once and cried out: "What have you done?" for he was afraid the baby would be lost.

441. At the mere taste of the poisoned food, the queen died, but Cāṇakya determined that the child should not die as well.

442. So he quickly cut open the belly of the dead woman and removed the baby from it as one might take a pearl from an oyster-shell.

443. And since a drop (bindu) of the poison had already reached the head of that infant, Cāṇakya named him Bindusāra, the "strength of the drop."

444. Now when Bindusāra had reached the age most pleasing to the God of Love, Candragupta achieved death in meditation and went to heaven.

445. Then Cāṇakya, wise and competent, appointed Bindusāra to the kingship. And the new king became the executor of Cāṇakya's commands, for his success depended on his chief minister.

446. Now Canin's son had earlier instructed the Mauryan to name as one of his ministers a clever man named Subandhu.

447. But this man was envious of Cāṇakya and wanted to become an independent minister. So in order to ruin him, he spoke to Bindusāra secretly:

448. "My lord, although I am not the final authority here, I shall tell you something that will be helpful in the end; for that is what well-born people do.

449. "Do not trust treacherous Cāṇakya, for it is a fact that this wicked man cut open your mother's belly."

450. Right away Bindusāra summoned the nurses and questioned them. And because they too said that it was so, he became very angry with Cāṇakya.

451. Cāṇakya noticed that the king was angry, and said to himself: "That ingrate Subandhu has turned the king against me.

452. "I myself made him a minister, and now to repay me he is using slander against me.

453. "Well, my death is near at hand, and I am through worrying about the kingship. But even so, I will think of some way to avenge the wrong done to me.

454. "My devilish intellect will devour him so that he will never taste the pleasure of kingly rule. I'll do him some injury that really suits the circumstances."

455. And since he had dreadful ingenuity, he used magic mantras to give special powers to fragrant substances of the finest kind. These he placed in a box, along with a piece of birch-bark on which he inscribed certain words.

456. Coating the box with lac, he placed it in a chest, which he then locked with a hundred locks.

457. He placed the chest inside his house as if it contained all his treasures, and then he distributed his riches to the poor, to orphans and to other deserving people.

458. Afterwards, he seated himself on top of a heap of dry cow- dung outside the city, where he began fasting to death, intent on destroying his karma.

459. Meanwhile, Bindusāra learned from the mouth of his own nurse the whole story of how his mother died. He was filled with remorse and went to where Cāṇakya was.

460. And Candragupta's son begged his pardon, saying: "Please conduct the affairs of state for me again. I will be obedient to your commands."

461. But the Mauryan's teacher declared: "Enough of this begging, O king! I am indifferent even to my own life, so what use are you to me now?"

462. Bindusāra realized that Cāṇakya was as fixed in his vow as the ocean within its shores, so he returned to his palace.

463. But barely had Bindusāra reached home than he began to rage at Subandhu. Subandhu trembled as if he were freezing and said to him:

464. "Your majesty, I accused Cāṇakya falsely because I didn't know the whole story. Please be merciful and let me go at once to ask his forgiveness."

465. With these words, Subandhu went and asked forgiveness. But this was just deceit, for what he was thinking was: "He must never return to the city."

466. So with a wicked ulterior motive, he told the king that he wanted to show proper honour to Cāṇakya because he had wronged him.

467. Subandhu received the king's permission and went to show honour to Caṇin's son, who was fasting to death.

468. And Subandhu arranged this ceremony of honour so that its beauty concealed calamity, for unseen by anyone, he dropped a glowing ember of incense onto the cow-dung.

469. Fanned by the wind, the ember quickly set the dung-heap ablaze, and the Mauryan's holy teacher, motionless in spite of the fire, burned like a

stick of wood. And when he was dead, he was transformed into a goddess.

Sarga Nine

1. The next day Subandhu asked Bindusāra's permission to live in Cāṇakya's house, for he assumed there were riches there which he wanted to obtain.
2. With the king's permission, Subandhu went into the dwelling and found the chest locked with a hundred locks.
3. And he thought: "Cāṇakya's entire fortune must be here. Otherwise he would not have secured this with a hundred locks."
4. So Subandhu broke the locks on the chest as one might break the fetters of a prisoner released from jail.
5. When he saw that there was a box inside, he said to himself: "This must surely be a jewel case, since it is so well- protected."
6. So he broke open the box as if it had been a coconut, and found inside those fragrant substances that surpassed the finest perfumes.
7. Subandhu inhaled the sweet-smelling perfumes like a bee seeking nectar, shaking his head with growing amazement.
8. Just then he saw the birch-bark with writing on it, and thinking it must be a list of Cāṇakya's valuables, he read it out loud:
9. "Whoever smells these fragrances and then does not lead the life of a Jain monk will at once become a guest of the God of Death."
10. When he read these words, he was plunged into despair, for he knew that no magic spell of Cāṇakya's would ever prove ineffective.
11. Still, Subandhu wanted to test what was written on the birch-bark, so he made someone smell the perfumes and then eat luxurious food.
12. The man died at once, whereupon Subandhu immediately began to lead the life of a wandering monk, not letting himself even think about enjoying sense objects.
13. But he was not destined for salvation and could not free himself from his desires; and so foolish Subandhu wandered over the earth, dancing like a puppet on a string, still tugged by his attachment to life.

Note on the Translation

Hemacandra's verses here are disarmingly simple and swift- moving, but by no means artless: puns and similes abound, and there are a fair number of long compounds. And since the stories were no doubt familiar ones, the language is often so concise as to be elliptical. The translation does not do justice to the style; instead, similes, idioms and allusions are expanded or even altered without brackets in the hope that the stories may be readily understood by the non-specialist reader.

Hemacandra's Pariśiṣṭaparva: The story of Cāṇakya

The Sanskrit is heavily influenced by the vernacular, and some of the vocabulary is rather obscure even when the general sense is not. I am indebted to Phyllis Granoff for many helpful suggestions, but the following lexical problems remain: v. 282, lagati; v. 359, jhumbarī; v. 360, kolika ; and v. 369, gardabhikāśālī.

The Story of Bharata and Bāhubali

Translated by Ralph Strohl

Introduction

The passage that follows comprises chapters 34-36 of the *Ādipurāṇa* of Jinasena, an early- to mid-ninth century A.D. Sanskrit account of the life of Ṛṣabha, the first *Tīrthaṃkara* of this age, and his children, Bharata and Bāhubali. These chapters recount the story of Bharata's quest for dominion over his numerous brothers (of whom Bāhubali is the youngest), his ignominious defeat by Bāhubali, and Bāhubali's renunciation of the world he has just won in favor of the Jaina mendicant's life.

The *Ādipurāṇa* is an important text in the Digambara tradition. It is unusual in that it is written in formal Sanskrit, for the Digambaras preferred the various vernaculars for story telling. It also contains the earliest formal recounting of the Bharata-Bāhubali saga extant. Within the next hundred and fifty years a cult of worship would develop around Bāhubali and the retelling of his story would continue well into the seventeenth century. The *Ādipurāṇa*'s importance lies, further, in the significance of the overall issues that the text raises. To some extent the text is a response to the great Hindu epic, the *Mahābhārata*. This seems clear in the manner in which Jinasena addresses themes of *karma* and action, *dharma*, and even sacrifice and worship in the context of battle. The issue for Jinasena is, "Where and how is the truly meaningful battle fought?" and nowhere is this issue more poignantly handled than in story of Bharata and Bāhubali.

The Story of Bharata and Bāhubali, from the *Ādipurāṇa*
Chapter 34

Descending Mt. Kailāsa, as the King of the Gods descends the Lord of the Mountains, the emperor, holder of the discus weapon, set off on his march toward Ayodhyā city.

On the march to his capital city, Emperor Bharata, followed by his forces, resembled the ocean; he was as irresistible as the rushing waters of the Ganges River at flood tide. Only after several days' march did the emperor's forces reach Ayodhyā, the elegant houses of which had gaily decorated archways. The city was resplendent at her Lord's arrival, sprinkled with sandal paste as if she had been anointed by an unguent.

When the time to enter the city was at hand, the discus weapon lay down by the encamped emperor, and did not approach the city gates.

The city gleamed with a saffron color, tinted by the rays emanating from the discus encamped at its gate, and resembled the setting sun. Now, certainly, King Bharata was considered the greatest among emperors, and the city, before which the shimmering discus stood, seemed to be swearing to that fact, touching the flames of the discus as if in a divine trial by fire.

Then some of the gods who were guarding the discus, the emperor's great jewel, suddenly noticed that it was stopped, and they were amazed. Some of those gods rose up angrily, saying, "What?! What is this?!" and reeled about like firebrands, their hands clutching the hilts of their swords. Others, in their perplexity, asked, "Is there a reflected form of the sun suspended from the sky? Why is a mock sun brought into being? The discus weapon's deviant behavior, like that of an inauspicious planet, suggests that untimely demise of an opposing army."

Because the discus wavered indecisively, some men of discernment began to wonder whether or not there yet remained an unconquered opponent. When the Commanders-in-Chief of the army acquainted Bharata with this situation, he was greatly perplexed, and he reflected, "Why on earth does the discus, which heretofore has been purposeful in its conduct, now falter, while I stand here with no rival to countermand my orders? Certainly this must be investigated!"

The steadfast emperor summoned his royal chaplain and spoke to him in a very firm voice. The beautifully-adorned goddess of speech, Sarasvatī, whose meaning is always apparent, proceeded from the lotus-like mouth of Bharata, as a lady messenger from the Goddess of Victory:

"The discus has trod the entire earth, stuck fear into its enemies, and humbled the sun's splendor. Why has it not approached the gates of Our city? When its conduct had been unfaltering in the conquest of the four cardinal directions within the bounds of the eastern, southern and western oceans, and in the two well-known caves of Mt. Vijayārddha, on what account does the discus now falter in the courtyard of Our palace? There must be an opponent who desires to conquer Us. Is there someone among Our vassals who is as yet not conciliated and hates us still? Or could it be that a kinsman of evil intent despises us? Is there, perhaps, some rogue who hates Us without cause and does not welcome Us? Generally speaking, the minds of evil persons waver, even among the great. Minds of great men are not envious of others' prosperity. The minds of the petty, on the other hand, are. Perhaps there is someone in Our own family who is drunken with foolish pride and is, therefore, disrespectful, and so the discus now waits to cut off his pride. Certainly, such a person is not to be overlooked. Even an insignificant opponent must be destroyed quickly, for an overlooked enemy causes suffering like a small grain of sand in one's eye. And even a very tiny thorn must be extracted by force, for such a thorn in one's foot can cause agonizing pain if it is not removed. Indeed, this exalted, celestial discus is the greatest of an emperor's jewels. Therefore, its hesitating is not without cause. So this behavior that it manifests is not sufficiently understood, honorable Sir. Surely such evident agitation on its part is for no inconsequential reason. Therefore, O wise Sir, that reason is to be pondered until you've understood its nature. Ill-defined actions do not meet with success, either in this world or the next. Such a knowledge of affairs rests in you, in your supernatural vision. What else is the dispelling of darkness than the arising of the sun?"

Here Bharata, having communicated the needful to this man who knew the celestial realms, ceased his measured speech, for the mighty usually speak little. Then the chaplain replied with pleasing speech ornamented by words of depth and clarity, intended to enlighten the Lord of the Bhāratas:

"Your speech manifests sweetness, splendor, well-chosen words, all of which convey meaning. Is there anything else that is good that is lacking in Your speech? We know only the śāstras, the law-books, and are unlearned in the performance of deeds. Who, apart from Yourself, knows how to apply these law books to the affairs of state? You are the first king, the royal sage. Knowledge of statesmanship is made manifest for the first time in You. How may we not feel bashful, knowing that fact and yet attempting to act? Nonetheless, the extraordinary regard in which you hold us lends us stature in the world; and it is for that reason that we are prepared to speak.

"We have heard this with regard to instruction in the knowledge of the future, O Lord: 'While the conquest of the world is incomplete, the discus may not rest from its labors.' For that reason, this flaming and terrible weapon of Yours tarries at the gate of the city incomprehensibly, as if held in restraint.

"The concepts enemy, friend, enemy's friend and friend's friend are simply distinctions found only in the literature, O Lord, since you govern them all as Your subjects. Even so, you must now subdue some opponent. One who would rise up in vigorous opposition in one's own house is like a harsh disease in the bowels. You have only conquered the outer region. The purification of the inner region has not, as yet, occurred. Though Your forces have conquered all there is to conquer, Your brothers remain unsubmissive to you. Your own family swerves from its duty, but certainly poses no obstacle for a Lord such as Yourself.

"One who is great and brilliant is stopped only by another who shares his nature. This is illustrated by the example of the sun in the presence of the special sun- crystal. Even weak relatives, having gained zealous followers, can overthrow a king, just as a staff, when fitted with an axe-blade, can overcome its mightier cousin, the tree.

"These brothers of yours will not be conquered easily, for they are powerful and arrogant. The youngest among them is their leader — Bāhubali, who is clever and strong. Those brothers, all full of vigor and heroism, number ninety-nine; they all insist, 'We are committed to honoring none other than Ṛṣabha, the foremost teacher, our Lord.'

"So You must resist Your remaining enemies, which are like fires or hidden tumors, O Lord. And You should be particularly careful not to overlook the clever one. O Lord, let this earth be blessed solely with your beneficent rule. Let not a bad king rise up among them, and make the earth fall into the evil state of having two kings. While you are king, O Lord, the word of another king holds sway nowhere. When a lion is present, how may fawns pay heed to the command of the king of the deer? O Lord, let Your brothers follow you, made rid of their jealousy, for the following of an elder brother who is also the foremost figure of his era is prescribed in the law books.

"Therefore, let messengers be sent, and let them speak gently, but with a strategic purpose, and thus bring them into obedience to Your commands. If that fails, let them speak harshly. If a rival is inappropriately puffed up with pride and does not conform himself to Your will, then he, alas, will cause not only his own destruction, but also the destruction of those princes who have accepted him; isn't that so? He is merely a beast who shares two things with a rival — his kingdom and his wife — for these are not generally shared.

"What more, then, remains to be said? They must approach you and bend the knee, or they must go to the Jina Ṛṣabha, the protector of the world for refuge. There is no third way. Let their path be one of these two. Either let them enter your audience hall, or take themselves to the forest to commune with the deer. Your own brothers, as all those not obedient to You, burn like firebrands. Only those who are obedient to You are an extraordinary pleasure to the eye. After your brothers have bowed their heads before You, their envy calmed and longing for Your favor, then let them prosper."

When the chaplain, learned in the law books, thus advised him, the Emperor, though he accepted his chaplain's opinion, yet immediately gave vent to his anger. Hurling a glance foul with fury, as if throwing the *bali* offering into the air, casting up a frown which resembled the flame of the fire of anger clouded in smoke, spewing forth a stream of poisonous anger directed at his brothers, and flaring up with untruthful speech, Bharata, enraged, spoke harshly:

"What! What! Are you telling me that my evil-souled brothers are unsubmissive! Watch, then! For I shall dash them into pieces with the violent meteor of my staff, which will fly up against them! Such hatred as they bear me, without cause, is totally without precedent; it has never been heard of nor seen before. No doubt they expect they are beyond danger due to their relationship to me. Their pride in their martial abilities is the consequence of the intoxication of youth. Its antidote is heat inflicted by the flaming discus weapon.

"Those wicked bastards wish to enjoy the earth, given to me by our father, without paying tribute. In that case, let them conquer my land with all the pride of their soldiers. They must accomplish their fealty to me by falling before my royal couch, or on the field of battle, with their limbs fallen into the embrace of sharp arrows. How little do they, who are given over to pleasures of the senses, compare to Us, who have conquered all there is to conquer! Nevertheless, We shall give them their share if they submit to Us.

"I will not share the earth with them to enjoy under any other circumstances. How is it, then, that the discus rests while they remain unconquered? And even Bāhubali, who is clever, knowledgeable and devoted to his kinsmen, shares in this hostility of which even great men dare not speak!

"What is the use of having obedient vassals when Bāhubali is not among them? Is not the enjoyment of another city like poison without Apodāna, his capital? What is the use of turning my adversaries into allies by my terrifying weapons if Bāhubali remains unsubmissive to my orders? What is the use of these warriors among the gods, for whom extraordinary boldness is their very life-juice, when that haughty Bāhubali is engaged in unparalleled competition with me?"

When he who wielded the discus spoke in such a rage for undertaking battle, the chaplain again approached in order to speak with him:

"Though you declare that you have conquered the world, yet are you overcome by the force of your anger! Why? Surely it is to be conquered by one who has first conquered his passions! Quit this immature behavior. Let those youths travel their fruitless path. My Lord, darkness cannot reside in one who has conquered the senses, the six-fold enemy. He who would not rescue himself when sunk in anger's deep darkness is surely not able to escape from uncertainty about whether or not to act. Is a king who is ignorant of his own soul any more able to investigate what is needful or what is to be avoided? Is he not like the king who, having his own dominion, yet fails to undertake the conquest of his enemies? Just so, the self-subdued, who desire to conquer the earth, do, in fact, conquer it, because they put an end to the wrath of those who would do them harm. For people who have vanquished the different senses, learned well the wealth contained in the sacred texts, and who desire to attain the next world, forbearance is the best means to victory. When this task may be accomplished by writing, excessive exertion is fruitless. Who would take a hatchet to young grass, when it may be split by a fingernail? Just so, you should subdue your numerous brothers in a respectful manner by the employment, in a deferential manner, of a number of ambassadors.

"This very day, let messengers bearing letters be sent out simultaneously, and having gone, let them say to your brothers, 'Come to the Emperor. Look to your oldest brother! Service to him, which consists of giving what is desired, is like service to the wish-granting tree of heaven. The emperor, your elder brother, deserves your veneration and should be honored by you in every way! His sovereignty does not shine in glory with you so far from him, just as the orb of the moon does not look so radiant without the host of starts nearby. Universal dominion exercised in the presence of his virtuous kinsmen is surely a cause for joy; in the absence of them, however, it causes no pleasure.'

"This is the message. But another message must filter through the sense of the letter. Clever messengers must be entrusted with these letters and the requisite gifts. Noble king, such an action causes fame and is conducive to prosperity. If your brothers do not, as a consequence, become obedient, then a further step will be considered.

"You must do this in order to prevent any ill-report of You. For surely, while fame is lasting in this world, acquisitions are not."

With that talk, Bharata, the holder of the discus, calmed down and left off his anger. Surely, the emotions of great men are to be steered into submission.

"Let Bāhubali, who is strong of arm, and whose will is not to be subjugated, be for now. I will examine his two-faced behavior by means of the other brothers."

Bharata's mind was clear when engaged in activity. Having made this determination, he charged responsible emissaries with his message and sent them to his brothers. The ambassadors went to the princes, as they had been instructed, saw them each in accordance with propriety, and delivered their Lord's message to them as circumstances dictated.

The princes, hardened due to their heightened intoxication with sovereignty, addressed the messengers together in order to declare their independence:

"We esteem the King's statement as true. In the absence of our father, we, the younger brothers, are to honor our older brother. But our father and teacher, who perceives all things, is still visible and present. He is our authority. Indeed, this sovereignty of ours is granted us by him. Consequently, we are not independent, but hold as paramount the guidance received at the feet of our father. There is nothing that Lord Bharata can either give or withhold from us.

"Nevertheless, we are delighted and well-pleased by this invitation to share the wealth with the holder of the discus."

The princes treated the messengers well, in accordance with the respect due to Lord Bharata, presented gifts to them, and sent them off with their replies. Having honored the messengers with their gifts, and handing over to them a verbal message for the emperor, the princes went to their teacher and father and conveyed to him Bharata's machinations. And having gone to him with a retinue appropriately limited so that they could approach him, they saw their father, lofty as a great mountain, rising up on the peak of Mt. Kailāsa. Throwing themselves down in order before him in a proper manner, the princes reported this command to him who hated killing:

"We have obtained our birth and the highest prosperity from you. We strive only after your favor, O Lord, and seek nothing else from you. This man only speaks of the favor of his father with a loud voice. But we have obtained prosperity on account of your favor, and are conversant with its very essence. We are fond of honoring you, long for your favor, and are servants of your words; let happen to us what will, we desire nothing else.

"Even so, Bharata desires to elicit from us our reverence on a permanent basis, whether out of arrogance or jealousy, we do not know. Our heads, spoiled by the pleasure of repeatedly bowing before you, are most certainly not resolved upon another object of reverence, O Lord.

"Does the royal swan, who enjoys the waters of Lake Mānasa, that are colored gold with the pollen of lotuses, take delight in the waters of any other lake? Does a bee, even at the point of death, betake itself to the *tumbi* plant, when he has been caressed by the fragrant flower on the hair of a celestial nymph? Does the *cataka* bird, drinking up from a new cloud the water of the sky, clear as a pearl, also desire to drink water from a dry lake?

"Our heads are tinted with dust from bowing to your lotus-like feet, and we are unable to bow before wicked people, either in this world or the next. We have come to you to undertake the consecration due to heroes, which is free from fear, and which is firmly opposed to any act of reverence to any other person. Tell us the path which is proper and salutary for us, that we may be fit to abide in houses firm in devotion to you. O Lord, let us attain to a path like yours, by which we may overcome the fear of loss of honor caused by subjection in existence after existence. For ascetics thrive happily in the forest along with lions, and have overcome the fear of humiliation which arises in the loss of honor."

The noble Ṛṣabha then instructed them sternly, rebuking them, and with a loud voice, causing them to stand on the eternal path:

"How are you to be made subject to another? For you are proud, are comely in body, and endowed with virtues, courage and youth, resembling the finest of elephants. What use is a transient empire and of what value is this worldly life that must pass? And what, pray tell, is the value of the power of lordship, that corruption which is nothing more than the insanity of youthfulness? What is the use of armies that can be subjugated by others with their own strong forces, and what use are riches and livestock which will, in turn, be carried off by another? What point is there in exciting the fire of desire, kindling it, so to speak, with riches? Leave off the pleasures of the senses, the enjoyment of which is like enjoying food laced with poison. Even when you have enjoyed them for a very long time, they eventually cease to give pleasure and become wearisome burdens. Moreover, my sons, is there any sensual pleasure that you have not tasted? And the taste of the pleasure of the senses, has it left you satisfied? Fie! upon such a kingdom, where friends are weapons, sons and relations are enemies, and the earth is a wife common to all! Let Bharata, that tiger among princes, enjoy the soil of the Land of the Bhāratas. So long as it is blessed with good fortune, you have no grounds for impatience. When this ephemeral kingdom is to be abandoned in due course even by him, why, then, do you fight over this impermanent thing? Abandon your rivalry, then. Resolve yourselves, instead, upon the great fruit of liberation, the unwithering flower of compassion on the great tree of *dharma*.

"You possess great self-respect, and your asceticism is the protection of that self-respect. It is only honored by others, and does not require the humiliation of according honor to others. The undertaking of religious mendicancy is the guards, virtues are the servants, and compassion is the beloved queen. This excellent dominion of austerity has indeed a commendable retinue."

Having heard the Lord's elegant discourse on disregard for the world, the princes, who had come to him, left their homes and went to the forest, and there sought refuge in the life of wandering religious mendicancy. Immediately those youthful princes took on the appearance of new bridegrooms, having, as it were, the new bride, Dīkṣā (Initiation), shown them by their father. And they made this bride their own, just as a groom takes possession of his newly wedded wife, in ceremonies of love making, pulling at each other's hair, for as these princes married her, and thus attained to the steadfast, proper pleasures of that state, they began by uprooting the hairs on their heads in five handfuls, as the sign of becoming true monks.

Having undertaken severe ascetic penances, those princely sages shone like the rays of the sun during the hot season, occupying all the quarters of the sky with their own brilliance. They made their bodies, which were, so to speak, shot through with the external marks of asceticism and aflame with its inner qualities, emaciated through the practice of very arduous asceticism. Firm in conduct which looks on all things in the universe with equanimity, which is characteristic of the conduct of the Jinas, they engaged in intense asceticism which was embraced by knowledge and purity.

Those lords of that era ascended the supreme summit of indifference to the world. Not concerned with the marks of royalty, they made the marks of asceticism their own. Embraced by the mistress of asceticism, and longing for the mistress of liberation, they forgot about the mistress of earthly dominion, and became devoted to complete knowledge.

Having studied the collection of the twelve *aṅgas* and the *āgamas*, the sacred texts, these highly intelligent princes ornamented themselves with abundant subjects for meditation. Thinking, "By the study of religious texts the mind is focussed, and that, in turn, leads to the conquest of the senses," those steadfast brothers attained to the wisdom of these religious texts. They became thoroughly familiar with right conduct by means of the *Ācārāṅga*. On its account, they came to rule over purity of conduct, free from transgressions. Having learned the well-written *Sūtrakṛtāṅga* in its entirety, both with respect to its style and meaning, they attained to the state of preachers and guides in their intentness on religious activity. They immersed themselves in the oceanic depths of the 100 chapters of the *Sthānāṅga*, and immediately were able to distinguish among the seven jewels of reality. They studied the *Samavāyāṅga*, which is a complete collection dealing with various matters such as the categories of substance, etc., and developed great wisdom. Those steadfast ascetics correctly ascertained the various answers to questions contained in the fifth *aṅga*, entitled *Vyākhyā-prajñapti*. In accordance with what Ṛṣabha taught, they first learned thoroughly the *Jñātādharmakathā*, which is a collection of religious tales, and then taught it flawlessly to those who desired to know it. Having studied the entirety of the seventh *aṅga*, the *Śrāvakācāra*, they instructed hearers in the conduct of householders. They next acquired knowledge about the ten sorts of ascetic sages who attain liberation during the span of years between the *nirvāṇas* of successive *Tīrthaṃkaras*. These sages must weather horrible afflictions nearly impossible to endure. These tranquil and eminently learned ascetics learned about such things as the ten classes of Opapadika gods and their five sorts of unexcelled mansions from the ninth *aṅga*. Having taken up a question for consideration from the "Topics of Controversy," they all together expounded the arising of pleasure, pain, and so forth, among embodied beings. They bound themselves with an oath to eradicate the fruition of good and bad *karma*, which they understood well from the *Vipākasūtra*, and performed asceticism tirelessly. They acquired knowledge of differing religious systems through the *dṛṣṭivāda*, and, rooted in the deepest love for the teachings of the Jina, extended the highest order of devotion to the Jaina texts. Having understood the essence of all the religious texts, which is located in the *dṛṣṭivāda*, they then gradually studied the contents of the older fourteen *Pūrvas*. Consequently, having understood the meaning of all the texts, so that they literally perceived matters through the eyes of these texts, they gained purity in the conduct of their asceticism through the excellence of their understanding of the meaning of those texts.

The action of asceticism produced pain among them, as if she were jealous that they were silent with her and, at the same time, conversational with the Goddess of Learning. Those wise conquerors of the senses undertook powerful extended and unbearable asceticism, both of an external and an internal nature. Ascending to the summits of mountains, those victorious ascetics bore the burning hot rays of the summer sun, which are very difficult to endure. They stood in rocky areas on the tops of mountains, their feet planted on scorching hot slabs of rock, with their arms suspended at their sides. The earth, at this time, was covered over with hot dust. The forests were burnt by fire. The river beds were dried up. The skies were darkened by smoke. They resided in burned out mountain groves during the extraordinarily hot summer season, bearing the scorching heat by means of their harsh discipline.

These practitioners of *yoga* passed their nights at the bases of trees at the approach of the monsoon season, which darkened the sky with rain clouds. During the rainy season, when rain clouds pounded the earth with thick sheets of water, as pestles pound the husks off rice, those great sages passed their nights without either motion or fear. Those great figures prevailed over the rain-filled days, thick with clouds, dwelling in the inner rooms of meditation, and wrapped in the thick outer garment of fortitude.

In winter, lying down in open spaces, covered over by a mass of snow, they gained thinness of body. Naked, their clothing destroyed, they did not take to fire for warmth, but prevailed over the winds of winter, their limbs fully equipped with fortitude. During the three watches of the night during the winter season, those steadfast princes lay as they pleased, covered over by a mass of snow which clothed their limbs.

Having recourse to discipline that was hard to bear during each of the three seasons of the year, the steadfast ascetics, firm in their resolve, bore the discipline for a long time. Generating heat by ascetic conduct of an intensity unheard of, with an interior brilliance, they resembled the ocean in their profound depth, and with the wave-like movements of their bodily limbs. Those honored and wise princes did not desire the material things that they had once enjoyed and abandoned, considering them to be as worthless as a garland once worn and now wilted. Considering the life of the body to be as ephemeral as clouds, evening, dew, waves or foam, they steadfastly cultivated devotion to the eternal path. Disgusted with the realm of birth, death and rebirth, and gone out from their dwellings, they possessed the firmest resolve upon the Jaina path, which is the means to liberation. With their mental powers made strongly focussed on the proper subjects for meditation, they conformed their activities of body, speech and mind to the teachings of Ṛṣabha, believing nothing to be superior to that.

When the eternal *dharma* had been eloquently declared by Jina Ṛṣabha, they were thrilled, and desiring to attain liberation, girded themselves and strove for that goal. Their faith was born of extraordinary affection for the *dharma* and its fruit, and they embodied the proper notion of the great vows of mendicancy, which are difficult to observe, in their unexcelled purity of conduct. They practiced these six vows — non-violence, truthfulness, refraining from theft, celibacy, avoidance of possessions, and nightly fasting. Resolute in their conduct of combat against the senses and *karmas* due to these vows, and confessing their transgressions with respect to body, speech and mind, they obtained the highest purity for the length of their lives. Becoming liberated from all activity that might entail violence to living creatures, being without defilement or property, and abandoning all bodily supports, they did honor to the Jaina path. Liberated from all kinds of possessions, and firmly-rooted in the *dharma* arisen from the Jina, they did not desire property, which is said to be of two kinds, even to the smallest extent. They passed their time free from illusion, rooted in the conduct of the *dharma* even while in their own bodies, abandoning all desires in favor of the proper understanding of contentment.

Houseless and wandering, they remained in whatever place they happened to be when the sun set, and there cultivated the highest level of non-attachment. Due to their preference for dwelling in solitary places, they stayed in villages for only one day at a time, and not beyond five days in larger cities. With their abodes in isolated dwellings, such as abandoned houses, cremation grounds, and so forth, they shared the dwelling of true heroes, abandoned by the seven kinds of fear. Courageous and governed by a mental disposition of simplicity, they resorted to dwellings on mountain tops, or in natural caves or forests, on a daily basis. They dwelt on the edge of the forest, inhabited by lions, bears, wolves, tigers, hyenas, and other such animals, all possessed of terrifying roars. Unperturbed, they dwelt on the table-lands of mountains, which were alive with the echoes of the harsh, reverberating roars of the tigers. Having cast off fear, they sojourned in the forest, where they encountered the harsh-sounding roars which emanated from the throats of young lions. These brothers, rich in austerities, lived in forests pervaded by the low murmurs of the owl, over which hosts of flesh-eating Ḍākinīs roamed in the vicinity of dancing clouds. All the directions were besieged by the ominous sounds of jackals. They also inhabited the great cremation grounds of the ancestors. Those man-lions, whose refuges were mountain caves, stood like lions, assembled together with hearts free from all apprehension, in accordance with the teaching of the Jina. They inhabited the forbidding forest regions, which teemed with injurious animals, and practiced meditation in the dark of night. They frequented the forest haunts of the elephants, whose tusks broke the trees there and left the terrain uneven. In those forests, they inhabited caves where fierce lions dwelt, and which reverberated with the great sound of the wild elephants.

United in the practice of *yoga* and study, and zealously seeking the right understanding of the sacred texts, they never slept at night, but were ever awake. Fond of the *Vīrāsana* yogic posture, they passed the nights either in that posture or in the *palyaṅka* posture. Having abandoned all attributes, renounced the body and been completely purified by poverty, the resolute, nude princes strove to attain the path to liberation.

They were indifferent and without any expectations. Following the path of the wind, they roamed this earth, which is studded by a multitude of towns and villages. They wandered over the entire earth and showed malice to no one. In showing pity to all living beings, they showed the compassionate feelings of others towards their sons. They were knowledgeable of the distinctions between animate and inanimate things, and discerned the concrete manifestations of the objects of knowledge. They gave up all censurable activity; their eating and dwelling places were blameless.

For the sake of purity of the three jewels — right knowledge, faith and conduct — they renounced whatever was censurable in body, speech and thought, for the remainder of their lives. With great diligence, they protected living beings, plant-, earth-, water-, wind- and fire-bodies, from all calamities. They were tranquil, their minds were not depressed, and they were graced with supreme indifference. They undertook the means to liberation, protected by the three jewels of right faith, knowledge and conduct, and did not crave the gratification of mundane desires. They followed the commands of the Jina. Their minds were terrified by the thought of going through the cycle of birth, death and rebirth, the eternal cycle of *saṃsāra*. They were radiant, and grasped the knowledge of the sacred literature, by which one perceives the highest truth. While yet in the body, they attained an eternal state by means of the light of knowledge.

They ate completely pure food given to them by another, measuring a single handful in a day. Thus they caused the true path, the means to liberation, to be manifest for a long time. Even though it might result in bodily death, they did not desire food prohibited in the scriptures, which is categorized in the following ways: of doubtful purity, acquired through exchange, prepared specifically for an ascetic, purchased, etc. Joined together in the ascetic life, the resolute princes undertook to beg in a limited area. This begging activity was pure due to the moderate number of houses visited. Taking no pleasure in food, they accepted food which was neither cold nor hot, nor astringent, nor oily, nor salty, with the sole intention of maintaining the body. They ate only for the sake of supporting the body. They held onto life only for the sake of *dharma*. The stain of sin was removed from them who valued highly the extraordinary acquisition of penance. They were not pleased to acquire food, nor distressed at the lack of it. Always regarding all things impartially, they perceived praise and blame, happiness and misery, and honor and contempt with equanimity. Maintaining their silence, they wandered about for food as a cow wanders a field, eating the tops of grass in the fields; even if they obtained nothing, they did not break their vow of silence. Their limbs were withered by great acts of abstinence, yet they strove to maintain the body. Even so they were not led to desire impure food. Those heroes went forth to beg for food and, having eaten appropriate food quickly and retraced their actions mentally to undo any errors of conduct, returned to pass the time in the ascetic groves.

Their bodies became emaciated due to the heat generated by religious austerities. Those lords of ascetics had a vow of constancy, and they did not falter in their attachment to the practice of those austerities. The undertaking of severe austerities caused languidness in their limbs; that languidness, however, was merely an assertion of their firmness in perfecting their meditation on the truth. There was no breach of their fasting by disruptions for a long time. Any disruptions simply went away frustrated, unable to overcome the princes. Their superior splendor, resulting from the heat born of the fire of asceticism, surpassed the brightness of refined gold.

They obtained the highest interior purity, their bodies brilliant and heated by the fire of asceticism. From the blazing fire that was their asceticism, they obtained the highest radiance. True it is that the shine of gold when it is heated is brightest of all. And those princes, their bodies ablaze from the fire of their ascetic acts, obtained the greatest inner purity. For when the body, like a crucible, is heated with asceticism, the soul, like gold, becomes pure. Their bodies nothing but skin and bones, the princes kindled purity of meditation. Surely every external act of penance and asceticism is for the purification of the inner and outer self.

In them the *siddhis,* which are the virtues and spiritual accomplishments born of *yoga* (such as the ability to become of atomic size, etc.), became manifest. Certainly completely pure asceticism brings forth great fruits.

Delight in asceticism was the well-made fire. The actions were the oblations. They who acted according to the proper rules of conduct for monks were the proper sacrificers. The ritual verses were the words of the Self-Existent Ṛṣabha. Lord Ṛṣabha is the lord of the great sacrifice. Compassion is the gift for the petitioner. The fulfillment of the desired objective is the fruit. The end is the cessation of action.

Rightly having in mind this oblation derived from Ṛṣabha, they, being well-versed in the sacred texts, performed the unexcelled worship of asceticism. Thus, being in mutual agreement, they brought to pass that superior action of the homeless ascetics. This is the natural state of the very great.

What more remains to be said? As long as they observed their duties without transgression, they, who had abandoned the unnatural condition of royalty, made the realm of asceticism entirely their own. Thus, having gained wisdom from Lord Ṛṣabha, the primeval male, those superior royal princes, plunged into the waters of his words as royal swans plunge into Lake Mānasa, and had their delusion dispersed. No longer desiring to do obeisance to King Bharata, they abandoned sovereignty and became religious mendicants. Those most excellent sages of the Pūru clan, whose steadfastness was deep and abundant, were attentive in the practices of those dedicated to the houseless state. May they, who pursued the path taken by Ṛṣabha, lord of ascetics, their minds fixed on the sole object which is salutary for the entire world, give us peace.

They bowed to the arranger of the world, Ṛṣabha, lord of the animate and inanimate, and clinging to the supreme religious state, thought that they were obedient to no one less than he who was honored by the heavens. May they be worthy examples for us, for their asceticism was abundant and satisfying, they made the treasure of liberation their own, they were born of the soul of the self-restrained Ṛṣabha, and are the foremost of those devoted to the Jina. Lord

Bharata was neither able to lead them into submission, nor to enjoy the earth by sharing it with them, for they resorted to the powerful conqueror, Ṛṣabha, their father and teacher, for the better condition of liberation. May they, who are rich in honor, be the kindling wood which burns up our *karma*, and carry away evil for us.

Chapter 35

Now when the youthful Bāhubali, abounding in the pride of his strength of arm, was to be conciliated, Emperor Bharata's mind was somewhat agitated. "So," he thought, "Our brothers do not welcome Our joy. They think their inviolability is due to their blood relationship. At the moment, Our brothers think that there is safety in numbers, and have, therefore, opposed Us, turning away from obeisance. The affliction of an external enemy who does not acknowledge Us is not so great by far as an extremely haughty group of kinsmen within Our very family. They smolder, their faces inflamed with the fire of evil speech, and, fanned by the winds of opposition, burn like firebrands.

"Let the other princes, whom We have spoiled and let run wild since boyhood, be in opposition to Us, if that is their wish. But young Bāhubali — intelligent, knowledgeable in custom, courteous and clever — pray! Has even he, benevolent though he is, gone into opposition to Us? And how is he now to be conciliated? For he is powerful, and rich in self-respect, and his own arm, when upraised in the field of battle, is always the means to victory.

"Certainly, he possesses great power in his arms. Drunken with pride, he is like a great maddened elephant, and is difficult to catch without conciliations. That proud one is not brought into obeisance by the usual means of communication. It is as if he were an evil spirit that has taken over with no one learned in the science of magical utterances to exorcise it.

"The distinction between him and the remainder of the young warrior princes is great. And can a lion be held down by nets after the fashion of common animals? He cannot be split off from the others — he is too politically adroit for that. Nor is he to be subdued by force. Nor can he be bought off. And this is certainly not a matter for peaceful negotiation. Bāhubali's splendor is even enhanced by Our affection, and flames just like the sacrificial fire, whose flames are kindled by the dripping oblation of clarified butter. A peace mission directed at one who is violent by nature is as useless as applying skin cream to the hide of an elephant.

"His disposition is, by and large, to be inferred from the behavior of the other princes, who have turned away from my commands, abandoned the delights of kingship, and set their faces toward the forest. Let us, still, examine further his intentions by means of conciliatory approaches. If, however, he should prove intractable, We shall consider what else to do later. Concealing incurable hostility within a kinsman's deceit, he may engulf the entire clan like a digestive fire arising and seizing the bowels. Anger born in one's own inner circle is an obstacle for a king, as the fire produced from the rubbing together of two sticks is for the mountain. Therefore, We must respond quickly to this strong prince, who clings to his contrary behavior. There is peace for Us only when he, like an inauspicious planet, is quieted."

Having resolved matters along these lines, Bharata despatched a skilled and trustworthy ambassador, fully apprised of the situation, to Bāhubali. The ambassador was followed by a coterie of his own dependents, as if by a second affectionate self, which brought along its own provisions. The ambassador reflected, "If Bāhubali speaks in a manner favorably disposed, I shall then speak without boasting. If he speaks of waging war, I shall attempt to ward off conflict. Should he make a treaty and offer tribute, well, such is only our inner desire. If he remains unreconciled and desirous of conquest, I shall make a display of bravado and depart quickly."

Calculating the well-being of his own side and the ruin of the other, he took care not to be made of two minds by the divisive effect of other advice, and kept his own counsel. He slept alone and secretly on the journey, for fear of breaching counsel, and observed land appropriate for undertaking battle while he traveled the long distance. He crossed over several countries, rivers, and territorial boundaries in the course of his journey, and, after many nights' travel, he reached the city of Podanapura. Then, having come to lands outside the city that bore a rich and beautiful crop, he beheld a spot which bore a veritable forest of fully grown rice, and became very happy.

He beheld tufts of rice that had sprouted up bearing abundant fruit, carefully maintained by the common people. Seeing this, the ambassador considered the populace to be unhostile, and intent on their own concerns. He heard the sound of the scythes clashing with one another as the farmers were reaping in the fields. The sound of the scythes resembled the sounds of the *tūrya* drum, and were enjoyed by the tillers and their families as they danced, their scythes upraised. In one spot he saw parrots extracting with their beaks the seeds from the ears of rice, which lay in clusters on the retaining mounds of the paddies; and those ears of rice looked to him like so many women who had been enjoyed by their lovers. He saw the women who guarded the rice fields against bird and animal predators, shooing off the parrots with inarticulate sounds, flapping their breast coverings, which were as beautiful as the parrots' wings. The entire sky, garlanded with rice grains, was perfumed by these women, whose exhaled breath rivalled the fragrance of the sweet-smelling rice. With the droplets of perspiration falling from their large breasts, the women looked as if they were making themselves beautiful by putting ornaments of pearls on their chests. Their hair partings were flecked with particles of lotus pollen, and they made for themselves fancy chignons, bound with casually crafted garlands of blue lotuses. Beads of perspiration, caused by their toil, beauteous as the rice grains, flowed down the sides of their faces, which were fatigued by the heat.

He beheld sugar cane plantations, from which emanated the noises of the cane-crushing machines and the ovens for making jaggery. It was as though the cane was crying out in fear of being cut down. And in a neighboring field he saw milk cows stooped over from the burden of their large udders. They were fondly mothering a herd of calves, which caused their milk to flow. Beholding Podanapura's beautiful outlying areas, Bharata's emissary considered himself to be a man whose aim was accomplished, since he had obtained the pleasure of viewing this scene.

The environs of the city captured his imagination. Water flowed from irrigation channels, and watered surrounding fields bearing millet, sugar cane and rice. He beheld the outlying lands of that city, with their ponds, wells, tanks, pleasure gardens and abundant lotuses. Passing through the city gates with reverence, he considered the numerous merchant shops to be a hoard of precious stones heaped together. Looking about, he admired the royal courtyard which, filled with the turgid rut of elephants and saliva of horses gifted by other kings, was as though sprinkled with water.

The ambassador's presence was communicated by the keepers of the main door, and he was ushered in to see Prince Bāhubali, who was seated on his throne. Beheld from afar, Bāhubali appeared as a blazing mass of splendor. With a broad chest and a high-peaked prominent crown, he was like a single pleasure-mountain for his mistress, the Goddess of Victory. He had a very broad turban bound round his head, elevated above the flat surface of his brow, as if he had, with a great *éclat*, received the marriage turban from the Goddess of Victory. He sported a long, staff-like arm, by which all the accumulated fame of noble warriors was equalled. It was like a balancing stick which supported the burden of the earth. He wore the beauty of the lotus in his face, and the lustre of the blue lotus in his eyes. He had no lower-caste persons in his vicinity. He possessed an undulled mind. He had a mind and a chest which were both very broad, both of which were ever available to accommodate the Goddesses of Learning and Fortune. He had caused the assemblage of virtues, the fruit of which is great and which acts as a protecting armor, to enter into his own limbs and into the minds of the noble. He was anointing the sky with a bright outer covering of shimmering ornaments, as if with the not insignificant lustre of his valor. His face shone like a moonstone, he had ruby-colored pleasing feet, and a diamond-like upper body. He was like a single emerald-green pillar brought forth by the Creator to preserve the world's stability. Brilliance permeated his entire body, as did strength befitting his regal status. He seemed to be comprised of atomic particles made only of splendor. Seeing this, the emissary moved a little ways off out of respect for him, who was the abode of such radiance. Then, approaching the feet of Prince Bāhubali and bowing his head which had been bowed at a distance already, he was bade enter by Bāhubali with all due hospitality.

The emissary, obeying Baharata's command, sat down in an appropriate chair, and Bāhubali addressed him, scattering the rays of his smile in all directions:

"Now, after so long a time, we have come to the Emperor's mind. Tell me, kind sir, is the world of Our Lord the Emperor well or not? For he has many cares. Is the right arm of the Lord of Princes skillful? For he has not completed even yet the conquest of his enemies. It is said that he has acquired all the earth and brought all the kings into subjection. Is there anything left to do or not? Speak!"

Prince Bāhubali spoke calmly let forcefully and briefly. Then he granted the messenger leave to speak.

Now the messenger, bringing together, so to speak, both sound and meaning amid the rays emanating from his teeth, commenced to speak in a stylish manner:

"Your intention is easily discerned in your speech, which is like a mirror, for the meaning in it is clear even to an unpolished person such as myself. We are, in fact, a messenger of King Bharata, and move at his pleasure. We are dull-witted in the dilation upon matters of virtue and vice.

"Noble Prince, the emperor has declared what is proper for those whom he cherishes. Therefore, judge the worth of that pronouncement, not according to the quality of the messenger, but, rather, according to the stature of the declarer. The speech of your teacher and father should be accepted. What he says is beyond dispute. Because of its authority, you must now conform to Bharata's command.

"Bharata is the foremost among kings, the first of the Solar Race. He has trod over the entire earth, and made the gods bow before him. Leaping all alone beyond the town of Gāngādvāra in his chariot, he made the sea a wounded and trembling enemy. His arrow's burning fire blazes in the ocean's waters and has drunk both the wealth and pride of the gods in heaven. He pulled the gods into subjection by fastening a noose of arrows around their necks. How can they fail to bow before him in a great multitude? His arrow's flight covered a distance of twelve leagues, and made the ocean-bound abode of the deity Magadha the target of its violence. Bharata's triumph was proclaimed by the gods on Mount Vijayārddha, for he conquered their Lord by his arrow's unerring flight. The gods, led by Kṛtāmala, submitted to him. But enough about how the aerial deities on both sides of Mt. Vijayārddha praised his victories.

"Having conquered the gaping darkness, he entered the northern face of that mountain with his victorious forces. With the aid of his general, he gained victory by those forces, surrounding even the foreigners who resisted his commands and seizing their wealth. He was anointed by the most excellent gods at once, and his fame became like lotus flowers which grow on the peaks of the highest mountains.

"Those twin deities, the Rivers of Heaven, attended him with respect and with riches, for he had carved his fame into the peak of Mount Vṛṣabhādri. Lakṣmī was made a servant, and the gods were bound in servitude by Bharata, under whose command all the jewels were gathered together. Indeed, the 14 jewels of the emperor yield wealth.

"He whose armies of conquest have conquered the entire earth roams over all countries, forests, borders and ocean shores. He is worthy of honor, and now celebrates possession of the discus. Honoring you with a proper blessing, he appoints you a king. He rules over our realm, which is comprised of all the oceans and continents which he traverses — over everything and everyone except his beloved brother Bāhubali.

"Behold his accomplishments; behold his dominion; behold the enjoyments and the insignia of royalty, which all the brothers will savor equally, with the resulting pleasure distributed among them. Though its men, demons, gods and flying creatures are all submissive to him, the realm does not shine in its full splendor while you are averse to bowing before him. When a relation does not honor the King out of foolish pride, that intransigent rogue sears the King's heart sorely.

"Approach the impatient King and honor him with your prostration. Obeisance to the King who desires it brings forth concord, does it not? The discus is subject to no orders but his alone, and it chastises the enmity of those who ignore his commands, which always bear authority. Behold the sovereigns of several districts, cut down to size by his thundering staff, lacking the nerve to transgress his commands. Approach him and make complete his heart's desire, O Valiant Prince. Let all the world be united through your reconciliation."

When the messenger had finished speaking, the clear-sighted young prince smiled gently, and replied with strong words pregnant with meaning:

"You have described well the noble deeds of your Lord. For that is considered true eloquence which well serves the speaker's purpose. And you have shown your originality in accomplishing your chosen task by displaying conciliation and at the same time inciting to division and war. You truly are the intimate of a Lord who is like no other; otherwise how could you display so cleverly his inner thoughts? Your Lord sent you to me because you have so often proven yourself. You are unusual, but that is wasted on me. For it villainy to behave thus.

"The display of force, the proclaiming of one's own virtues, and the highlighting of others' faults characterize the conduct of a scoundrel. A malicious person willingly points out his own virtues and others' faults, and covers up his own faults and even others' virtues.

"An ignorant man abides in the evil of the barren behavior of the scoundrel. The wise man abandons this evil, for it is like a vine which attempts to support itself by clinging to the air. Such a vine is despicable; it abounds in tasteless fruits, and sears the world with pain. I consider it a vine of suffering. Conciliatory words spoken first and accompanied by gifts are brought to nought by words of division and war that follow, for a person is justly made angry by such talk of division and war. Proper employment of these strategies leads to success in one's aims. Improper use of them leads to utter failure. Surely, when even a friendly man is heated in anger, the conciliatory approach of which you speak, which aims at total pacification, is like the sprinkling of water on clarified butter. Similarly I consider this sort of giving to a powerful man; how can you extinguish a blazing fire when you do nothing but offer it more and more sticks as fuel? There is softness in heated iron, but not in the wise man heated in anger. A stick is used on an elephant that can be pacified, but not on a lion. It is the man who is incompetent in the use of these stratagems and mixes them up who fails because of the defectiveness of his diplomacy, and not someone like me. You must have thought that We could not be subjugated by peaceful means, and so you decided to be insolent. What a fool you are!

"King Bharata is not to be praised merely because he is older. Is an aging elephant a fit match for the young of the lion? Affection and respect exist among siblings who are on friendly terms with one another; but among those where this is not the case, this peaceful condition between them is destroyed. The adage that the eldest is to be reverenced may hold in other places or at another time. What recourse other than reverence is there for a man with a sword placed at his head? O messenger, our heart burns at the gratifying of another's pride. There is but one blazing sun. Is there another more splendid than this?

"Our father divided kingship between Bharata and me by proclamation. Bharata is called King of Kings. Now he is like a pimple on a goiter! Let that King of Kings wallow greedily in his riches, as he wishes. We rest upon our own good government, and not merely upon that king. He has summoned Us and tried to make Us bow to him under some pretext or other, as though We were a child; but that portion of the earth he offers Us appears to Us to be no larger than a clump of *aśoka* trees.

"Wise men prize any fruit that is the result of the efforts of their own tree-like arms, but despise the fruit condescendingly dropped from another's look of favor, even though it were world dominion. A man, even if he is a prince, who desires wealth attached to the strings of another's commands, brings the title "king" into disrepute, like the lizard which calls itself a snake! Are not the trappings of royalty a burden to the bestial prince who allows his prosperity to be sullied by another's contempt? One who clings eagerly to life and possessions acquired at a loss of honor is like a two-tusked elephant whose tusks are broken. How can he destroy others? The man who bows his head in loss of honor, may yet retain his royal parasol, but he forfeits its splendor and its shade. Sages are of equal status because they have abandoned outer trappings and pleasures; but what man on earth, if he would be a king, would give up his pride? A man who is proud of his descent is not fit to be governed by another's commands. Loss of life, or even the hermit's life in the forest, is preferable. Let those who are steadfast protect their honor by destroying their enemies. Glory always adorns the man who has earned respect.

"You have exaggerated nicely the Emperor's prowess. And how do I know that? Because your words are like any other description that means to praise or blame. Skillful speakers make even a quite lifeless thing flourish by means of their rhetoric. Does not even a domestic animal become a lion when its praises are sufficiently sung? All that you have spoken seems to Us to be mere words. There is no similarity between setting forth to conquer the world and the mere gathering of grains of wealth. That Lord parades around in circles collecting taxes, as if he were begging alms. Yet you have elevated him to the highest eminence from a state of beggarliness.

"Now, that the Emperor did conquer the gods when he conquered the world, you must take on faith. But consider this well: did he not sleep on *darbha* grass, and fast, and rain his arrows down while the water was stilled by magical utterances when he conquered Magadha? And making his discus wander about by means of his long staff of rule, and drawing the princes under his sway, alas, he does mere potter's work!

"The dust of his offense soils himself, his family, and past and future generations, and it has been tainting the members of his own party, and even their families, for a long time. What is the point of praising so immodestly the unmanliness of one who, by using spells and magical utterances, endeavors to draw the princes into his orbit? O messenger, it galls us greatly that you praise his martial abilities, when the foreigners' forces made his army waver uncertainly in water. Let that warrior's son have a care for his incorruptible wealth of fame, for strong men who bury their wealth in the earth have gone to ruin.

"What is the use of jewels which don't cover even the amount of earth measured by a fist? Yet princes have gone straight to destruction for such things. This man is the sort who is weighed in a balance against a heap of jewels piled on by his vassals. Sovereignty, alas, is not of such a quality.

"Clearly he desires to possess the land Our father granted Us. Would it satiate his greed if We acquiesced? O messenger, that respected Lord has no shame, for he desires to take from Us the family land Our father bequeathed Us. Will he next desire his brother's wife? A man who is free and desires unhindered conquest should offer something other than his wife and family and the land conquered by the strength of his own arm.

"We have spoken enough. Either he or We, with valor in our arms, must enjoy the earth, which is marked by a single royal parasol. We have had Our fill of leisurely but pointless conversations with servants. His valor and Ours will be revealed in the touchstone of battle. Therefore, let the matter be resolved between us in violent combat. Convey this, Our single certain message, messenger!"

The ambassador, dismissed by Prince Bāhubali, who had revealed his pride, went off quickly, charged with telling his lord to gird for battle, making all due preparations. Then Bāhubali arose, along with his vassals, heaps of jewels falling off his crown, resembling hundreds of hurled firebrands, thoughts of battle to the fore.

The heroic expressions of the warriors in Bāhubali's army were heard by many, indicating that battle was imminent:

"At last, this battle has now come for our Lord. And are we able to be without debt to him, since he has been so beneficent to us? Lords who protect the earth also protect their dependents. And what if these men of straw fail to seize the opportune moment? We must give up the body. We must procure the treasure of fame. We must obtain the Goddess of Victory by conquest. The thrill of battle is no small consequence."

"When shall I, with every limb pierced by arrows, obtain repose on the field of battle, resting in the shade of a hail of arrows which dull the sun's heat? Having burst asunder numerous deployments of the enemy armies by means of my arrows, I shall, at some time or other, lie down on a spacious bed of arrows. How soon shall I sit on the elephant's shoulders, momentarily stupefied, but then revived when the elephant's flapping ears drive away my battle fatigue? With my speech stammering and my bowels oozing out, strung on the bolt which is the elephant's tusk, how soon shall I be the object of the sidelong glance of the Goddess of Victory? When shall I lift her on a swing supported by the garland of my bowels hanging from the elephant's tusk and balance her?"

In battalion after battalion the valiant warriors, delighting in war, spoke in this manner, and donned their helmets and seized their weapons.

Now the day became exceedingly anxious and went to its demise somewhere, as if it were frightened by the threats emanating from the warriors' contracted eyebrows. The hot sun was a red circle, as though sporting a lustre which was the reflection of that in the faces of the angry soldiers. For a moment, the scattered mass of flashing sunbeams appeared all at once with a reddish lustre, as though it were painted by the leafy sprouts born of the earth of the forest on the slope of the western mountain, behind which it was setting.

For a moment, the sun appeared to be clinging to the mountaintops with its rays, as if, fearful of falling, it were dependent on the extension of a hand by the formidable peaks to support it. But the sun seemed drunk, and because of this imagined impropriety, the Western Mountain did not grasp the sun, who had lost its lustre when it fell from that region of the sky. Has the sun gone to look for the day? Has it entered the Lower World? Is it hidden by the peaks of the Western Mountain? Thus people wondered, for they could no longer see the sun. Earlier, the sun dispersed the nocturnal darkness and held the mountain fast with its hand-like rays. Now, without lustre, at day's end, it seemed to fall. Actually, foolish people who saw it disappear understood it to be falling, when it was simply roaming eternally on its horizontal circular path around Mount Meru.

The Virgin Quarters of the sky were besieged by darkness and bore colorless countenances, as if tormented by the sadness of the sun in this predicament. The lotus plant, its flowers withered, and afflicted with pain from separation from the sun, seemed to be grieving because of the mournful buzzing of the bees about it. The forests of the Western mountain, spread over by the heat of twilight, were as if encompassed by the jagged flames of a forest fire.

Lady Twilight, who was fond of the sun, was nevertheless abandoned by it, and was seen in the sky as reddish in color, as though she had cast herself into a fire in despair. With the lustre of vermilion, she glowed softly in the Western region, like rows of coral gardens floating on a sea of sky. Her color, red as the China Rose flower, spread out along the Western horizon, resembling the fire that kindles the mental anguish of female *cakra* birds. She shimmered red in the West, and was, for an instant, perceived as the concentration of all the passion of ladies hearts in a single spot. The world highly esteemed the Twilight, who bore aloft her red rays, and followed after the Lord of the Day as if into death.

The male *cakra* birds abandoned the female *cakras*, who followed after their mates in an agitated state of mind. Now, then, who may avoid destiny? Was it the sun's transgression? Or was it more a matter of the destined time which caused the pairs of *cakra* birds to become separated?

Without the sun, darkness quickly pervaded the sky; generally speaking, in the absence of the sun's brilliance, darkness prevails. The night, covered by darkness, was clothed in dark blue and bedecked with stars, and appeared as a woman wearing luminous pearls set off to meet her lover.

In a world covered with thick darkness, people with opened eyes did not see the city at all. It was as if they were defiled with delusion. The people were thoroughly shrouded in darkness and were inwardly bewildered. Consequently, they were greatly inclined to go to bed, since it was impossible to see. Lamps were prepared and shone in every house with trembling brilliance, their flames like needles to pierce the thick darkness.

Then the moon arose, as if purifying the world with milk, and its rays drove off the darkness, causing the world to rejoice. Promoting the fulfillment of joy, it rose up like a good king, governing with affection all its territory. Just as a heard of elephants seeing the lion dragging off a deer's carcass in its mouth, flees, so the massive darkness, seeing the deer in the maw of the moon, fled. The multitude of stars spread across the sky and sparkled around the moon, as though a rapid flow of bubbling water had been made to stream forth. As the young swan, seeking for grasses to nibble, plunges deep into a pond, so the moon traversed the sky with its companions, the stars, nibbling away at the darkness. Having dispelled the darkness and bathed the world with its beams, the frosty-rayed moon spread over everything, as if coating it with ambrosia. But even having driven the darkness a long way off, the solitary moon was possessed of a stain, for innate darkness is very difficult to overcome, even for the noble-minded.

With the destroying of their darkness, as though they had been touched by the hands of a physician, the quarters of the sky spread out their light with a cool lustre, with gentle visages, as it were. So, when evening arose, its stars clearly visible, the women shared the air on the palace roof with their lovers. The women were garlanded, and had ornaments in their ears; their delicate limbs were anointed with trickling sandal paste, and they shone with glittering ornaments. They were live vines that fulfilled one's every wish. And as, by the rays of the moon, the ocean rose up to high tide with crashing waves, so in the minds of the lovers arose the desire for sexual union.

Charming lovers, the most excellent rays of the moon and sandal paste — these intoxicants have spread the beginnings of love in the hearts of the beautiful young women. And now the God of Desire, born of the mind, marches against the houses of the king's beloveds, threatening the entire world with his triumphant weapons, the moon beams, taken from the hare-marked moon. Wine is neither drunk freely, nor smelled, nor even held in the hand; the young women experience longing simply because passion possesses them.

One woman, sitting on her lord's lap, is agitated, as though intoxicated; she is, alas, threatened by the arrow of bewilderment loosed by the bodiless God of Desire. Another woman, casting pride aside, but now with all constraints abandoned, spurns the counsel of her female companion, and goes to her lover's lodgings, made bold by the Bodiless God. Yet another woman, afflicted by the words of her friend and go-between, suffers severely like the female *cakra* bird, her eyes bathed in tears, when he who is dear as life has not come.

The God of Desire composes, so to speak, an overture for all these lovers by means of the bewitching sounds of the women's songs, accompanied by the low, murmuring hum of his bow string of bees. Nor has He neglected the newly-married woman, who was enraged that her husband inadvertently mentioned the name of his mistress when referring to her, but has now taken her on his lap. Another betrayed lady is not calmed down by the moon's rays, nor by the roots of the *uśīra* plant, nor by wet breezes, for within her rages a terrible fire of passion. Another woman, with beautiful hips, though afflicted by the God of Love with his burning arrows, takes heart and desires no remedy. Yet another lady makes a rival endure harsh words as she sees that rival being led by her lover to a place suitable for making love, "Queen bee! Tell that lotus, you err now to call me your beloved; the word no longer suits me. Has she robbed you of your sense of shame as well as your heart that you now dare to make love to me? Go, run after her, who boasts of your love. You can only regret the love you shower on a wrong object." And for his part, as he hears his beloved utter these words in the presence of her friend, do you think the young man doesn't come and throw himself at the angry damsel's feet?

One lady said to her friend, "The rays of the moon are as if torturing me, the sandal paste as if burning me. The fire of desire is kindled by the breeze stirred up by the fans. Having conciliated him, bring him to me or lead me to him.

Since the lord of my life has many lovers, my life is dependent upon you for support." The woman, suffering in this way at the hands of the God of Desire, was reconciled to her lover through the offices of her female companion, and though recently separated from her lord, was again embraced by him, restrained in the tight embrace of his strong arms.

The bell-covered girdles of the women lovers, with their soft tones, proclaimed "Let everyone delight as he pleases in the realm of the Mind-Born God," as if making a general public pronouncement. Did the God of Desire, perhaps, whisper at the base of the woman's ears, or was it merely the confused uproar of a swam of bees buzzing around the lotus flowers tucked behind their ears? Among the multitude of lovers, there was an outbreak of violent embraces, rubbing of the decorative coloring on the women's breasts, and impetuous hair-pulling. After intercourse, the eyes of the lovers were of an impure reddish hue, and the lower lip was a little bit reddened from having repeatedly uttered moans of ecstasy. At the end of love-making couples lay on beds fragrant with flowers, the covers fallen away from and exposing the pubic regions.

A few of the warriors made a feast of the love-making, even though their desire was sluggish due to having feasted heartily in honor of the impending battle. Some of the more determined warriors did not succumb to the embrace of their lovers, for their desires could only be fulfilled by the joy of union with Lady Glory. Some soldiers, whose lives were committed to conquest, did not even take to the bed, thinking that they could only enjoy their lovers after conquering the enemy's army. The foremost among the warriors, though their desire was great, forsook the beds of their lovers because of their greater desire for the joy of lying on a bed of arrows. Yet other warriors engaged in heroic speech with their lovers, and, with their faces already turned toward battle, did not even notice the shimmering starry night. Some soldiers were of two minds — though their minds were zealously desiring battle, they, nevertheless, also experienced a strong taste for union with their ladies. So they enjoyed the commencement of love-play, harsh with the biting of lips, and looked forward to the commencement of battle, harsh with the clash of swords.

The love-sick women carried away the minds of their lovers, gratifying them in love-play with kisses and eager embraces. Even at the end of the lovers' intercourse, the artifices usually undertaken at the beginning of it were satisfying — glances from the corner of the eye, suppressed laughing, whispered talking, becoming fiercely angry without reason, ardent passion and expressively-arched eyebrows, and feigned deceptions which ill-concealed true love.

The night turned away, as if blushing to see them falling to earth, hungry for sexual union. The Lady of the Western region stood with a face like a pendulous moon, as if cautioning the lovers, "Enough, now! You two, lords of your house, have dallied for quite some time and are exhausted!" The sun, having separated the *cakra* birds from one another when it set, now rose up all around with its heat, as if anguished at what it had done.

And so day began. The darkness of night melted away, and the many-rayed sun embraced the Eastern region with its bundle of rays. The nocturnal darkness was driven off by the fresh, newly-arisen sun. All that remained was for the sun to embrace the Splendour of the new day.

The hot-rayed sun spread its light uniformly on the mass of lotuses, with a reddish hue reflecting the love of the *cakravāka* birds, and made off with the light from the moon. The hot sun opened the door of darkness and revealed the heavens, opening the eyes of the world, as it were, with its rays. Thus, having arisen very early in the morning and caused the lotuses to blossom, the sun, with its glowing heat, emulated the soldiers desirous of conquest.

Then the prince's sweet-voiced morning musicians, desirous of joining their Lord with consciousness, even though he had, in fact, already awakened on his own, chanted a hymn.

Chapter 36

Now, the ocean-like army of the victorious Bharata set forth, obscuring heaven and earth with its size, and agitated by the angry wind of the messenger's speech, like the ocean struck by the winds of a storm. The great kettle-drums of war reverberated with sounds so strong that even the celestial beings intent on the use of the sword panicked. The forces of King Bharata, divided into infantry, cavalry and elephant corps, set out from the gates of the city. Platoons of chariots moved about in front of and behind the flanks of the army, and the aerial gods were overhead.

King Bharata, possessed of this full, six-limbed army, arose and set out with his vassal princes, desirous of vanquishing his younger brother. The gathering of great war elephants, with their battle regalia, appeared to be a collection of mountains roaming about and engaging in combat with their trees. Rutting elephants stood on all sides, cascading streams of juice from their temples onto the earth; indeed the earth resembled a range of mountains with waterfalls. The lofty war elephants, their limbs decorated, appeared to be shimmering mountains covered over by the soft heat of morning. As Lord Bharata reviewed his forces, the elephant divisions, caparisoned in armor and sporting the auspicious marks of victory, gave the impression that several mountain ranges had arrived on the scene. The elephant drivers, dressed in the exalted, shining dress of heroes, were mounted on elephants' shoulders, and appeared to be the amassing of Pride itself.

The horsemen were fallen into rank, their sword-tips touching their shoulders and their arrows having sharpened tips. It was as though these men embodied their own valor along their upper arms. The great-limbed archers, with various kinds of arrows firmly placed in their quivers, resembled a forest of large branched trees with snakes emanating from their hollows. Charioteers, furnished with their standard weapons, stood in numerous chariots like helmsmen on their boats in the ocean of battle.

Helmeted and armed warriors guarded the feet of the lead elephant with drawn swords, their blades razor-sharp. Other warriors, armed with a multitude of quivering weapons, trembled like a portentous wind attended by meteors and gathering clouds. Still another warrior, taking up in his hand a sword with a dreadfully sharp point, and seeing the heroism in his own countenance, observed his own valor reflected in the sword blade. One warrior was waving a sword held firmly in his hand, and appeared as if he desired to measure out with it the extent of regard his master would have for him this day. The forces of those attached to the King Bharata set out, in divisions of infantry, elephants, cavalry and chariots.

The vassal princes had their heads turned towards the jewel-like beams of the sun. It was as if the *Lokapālas*, the protectors of the world, had descended to earth. The princes gathered around Bharata, the Lord of the Earth, indicated to him in a proper manner the collected might of their armies in the distance, and then set out.

The warriors calmed their wives, whose hearts were distressed at hearing of the undertaking of this new battle, and set off with words of prayer on their lips. Then the dust of the earth, kicked up by the horses' hooves and leaping into the air, momentarily obstructed the view of the ladies of the heavenly realms. When the dust was thrown up into the sky, causing it to be covered over by thick darkness, light emanated from the emperor's discus, causing the warriors to focus on it as their proper object of concentration.

The Lords of the Earth fortified their resolve on the march by means of the speech of the soldiers, which was full of bravado, and even by means of the gossip of the common folk, which was of a similar flavor. Prince Bāhubali stood close at hand, ornamenting the battlefield with his presence; and Bharata, that tiger among princes, approached unhindered.

People spoke in this vein: "How can we possibly know what may befall these two brothers? Generally speaking, for their partisans, the battle is not for peaceful ends. This monstrous battle is begun by Bharata. True it is that princes in their lust for empire will behave according to their own whims. They who are joined to the crown are unable to hold these two brothers in check, for are they not the very ones who have come fully-armed to make war? So this Prince Bāhubali, great in dignity and valorous of arm, stands face to face with battle because he has, assuredly, provoked his brother, who bears the discus weapon. Nevertheless, a wise man realizes that possession of a mightier army is not the surety of victory. Can not a single lion conquer even an entire herd of elephants? And the emperor is not generally taken for an ordinary man, for he receives the protection of thousands of bowing deities, who feed on the nectar of immortality. Therefore, let there not be war between these two, for its sole result is the annihilation of people. Rather, let the divinities, if they are close at hand, forge peace."

Thus some people, in an impartial manner, lauded both sides. Others, tainted by favoritism, praised the excellence of their own side.

Thus, the Lords of the Earth, diverted by the considerable gossip of the common people, quickly reached the place where stood the foremost among heroes, Bāhubali. Opposing warriors in Bharata's presence usually esteemed his pride in his martial abilities, and trembled, for they could not subdue him. Thus, in the presence of Emperor Bharata's army, the army of Lord Bāhubali, desirous of conquest, was agitated like the ocean's waters, and overwhelmed the heavens with its ebullient noise.

Now, the resolute commanders in both armies, their energy rivalling that of an armored elephant, deployed their forces, intent on combat. Meanwhile, the counselors and ministers deliberated on the situation and said, "War between these two, like the clashing of two inauspicious planets, is not conducive to peace. These two are without the smell of death about them. There will be no injury whatever to either of them. But the likelihood of the loss of large numbers of lives is great." Having decided this, these ministers obtained the assent of the two princes to speak, and exhorted them to a righteous battle: "Leave off this fighting, for it is without cause, yet causes the destruction of human life. In a battle like this there is much unrighteousness and a great loss of fame. A test for supremacy is possible in a completely different way. And in that contest between you, you must both bear defeat without anger or victory without pride. This is the correct way between brothers."

The two agitated princes, thus addressed by all the vassals and ministers who had expressed these objections, determined, with heavy hearts, to undertake the suggested mutual combat. "Whichever one of you gains victory in close combat of water, eye and arm, let him, reliant on his own abilities, be lord of the coquette, Jayaśrī, the Goddess of Victory." The joyful, deep-sounding drums proclaimed these tidings, which inspired joy, and summoned all the army commanders together in one place. The princes who adhered to Bharata's party encamped themselves on one side, and those belonging to Bāhubali's on the other.

In the midst of these princes stood the two princely brothers, shining, as if for some reason or another, the two mountains Nīṣadha and Nīla had come together. Of the two, Lord Bāhubali, dark-haired and resembling a lofty rose-apple tree with bees buzzing around it, shone with the lustre of the sky-blue Garuda stone; while Bharata, the King of Kings, shone with the lustre of heated gold, even in separation from his crown, and resembled the high-peaked King of Mountains.

The valorous Bāhubali sported the steadier, unblinking, calm eye, and quickly obtained victory in the battle of glances. Checking the agitation of Bharata's irresistible, ocean-like army, the princes respectfully granted the victory to the younger prince.

Then the two arrogant princes, like two of the elephants that support the sky, entered into the water of the lake, and splashed one another with their long arms. Like the streams of water clinging to the lap of Himavat, Lord of Mountains, clear columns of water rained down on the broad manly chest of Bharata, desirous of conquest. A large quantity of water loosed by Lord Bharata toward the towering Bāhubali did not reach his face at that distance, and descended harmlessly near him. Lord Bharata was also unable to obtain that victory, and his defeat was proclaimed loudly by Prince Bāhubali's forces.

Then the two firm princes, courageous as lions, assented to close combat, and ascended into the arena. Great was the battle of their arms, for each possessed great pride in his arms' strength. There were many tight embraces and holds, and there was much flapping of arms and bounding around.

The Emperor Bharata, whose splendor was like his blazing crown, was lifted up with ease by his younger brother. The staggering ruler instantly felt what it was like to be spun around like a fire-brand.

The younger lord conquered the older, the tiger who had conquered the land of the Bharatas. But Bāhubali did not throw Bharata to the ground on account of the respect due him. Just as if Nīla Mountain were to carry Hima Mountain, with its great shining slopes, so Bāhubali placed his arms around Bharata and lifted him up.

Then, the favored Bāhubali, along with his allies, let out a loud cry. But the princes allied with Bharata bowed their heads in shame. Suffering a state of highest humiliation, the emperor became visibly bewildered in the very sight of his princely allies. Contracting his eyebrows, brightening like the reddish sun at its arising, and blazing with anger, the Emperor instantly became terrible to behold.

Then the Lord of Treasure, blind with anger, remembered the discus weapon, which had cut off the entire world of his enemies, for the purpose of defeating his brother. Simply being called to mind, the discus leaped immediately toward Bāhubali, circumambulated him and, making dull the brightness of the sun, came to rest before that prince who could not be killed. Then the Emperor was very repentant, and was chastised by the nobles, who scolded him, saying, "For shame! Enough of this violence!"

The resolute Bāhubali, having lifted up Bharata with his hand as if weighing him, proclaimed the greatness of his deed with a loud voice, and brought him down to a debased status on the undebased earth. Then Bāhubali was approached by the princes and was honored by them with shouts of victory, and he thought to himself how great he was. But then he reflected, "What shameful things my elder brother does for the sake of this kingdom which will perish! Fie on this sovereignty which tastes bitter when it is gained and which disappears in an instant. It is difficult to be rid of, though it deserts one, just like an unfaithful wife. People, attached to the pleasures of the senses, never stop to consider how grotesque are the sense objects, how harmful, transient and tasteless. What wise man would hanker after the poisonous pleasures of the senses, for once caught by them a person goes from one misfortune to another. Preferable is poison which may or may not kill you in this very life; the pleasures of the senses kill you forever. Even the wise man needlessly goes to disasters on account of the sense objects, which give momentary pleasure, but whose essence is astringent at the time of ripeness. Who would partake of the objects of sense? For they are like the astringent ripe *kancheera* fruit, of extraordinary taste at first, yet taking away one's life in the end. Slashing swords, blazing fires, Indra's thunderbolt, and great snakes are in no way the causes of affliction that sense objects are. Ignorant men whose object is sensual enjoyment, and who long for the acquisition of wealth, obtain possession of oceans, violent armies, fearful forests, rivers and mountains. Those whose goals are the objects of the senses traverse an ocean of sea monsters, and are buffeted by the noisy thunderbolt in the form of the blows of the monsters' long arms. Those who are allured by sensual pleasures enter the field of battle without fear, where the sky is covered by a hailstorm of arrows, to obtain them. Such insensate people roam in wildernesses, where even the forest-dwellers roam with fear in their eyes, afflicted by the hope for sensual enjoyments. Alas, those tormented by the dangerous graspings after sense objects cross over rivers with formidable whirlpools stirred up by aquine predators. Fearless people, bewildered by the speech of deceivers who claim the knowledge of the science of medicine that cures aging, would climb even the most difficult mountains to find the cave that holds that supposed cure.

This old age, violently seizing the hair and turning it white under the pretext of aging, embraces us like an unwanted mistress. In general, those eager for transient enjoyments do not know the distinction between good and evil. How great a difference can there be between sensual indulgence and death among aged men? Man's falling into old age is like the arising of a severe feverish chill, with the body's limbs trembling, causing him to topple to the ground. Among men, aging and the enjoyment of spirituous liquor quickly accomplish decay of the body and slipping of the mind, as well as slurring of speech. This hitching post of life, which, when it is strong, sustains the lives of men, is uprooted violently by the malevolent elephant, Time. The strength of this body is unstable, like the elephant's ear, and this tattered hut of a body is destroyed by disease as a real hut is by rats.

Alas! Lord Bharata's mind is obstructed by delusion, and he thinks constantly about ephemeral matters such as the kingdom."

Then Bāhubali, that destroyer of deceit, having observed the debased condition of his elder brother for a bit, expressed these sharp words to him:

"Hear me, O tiger among men! Leave off your astonishment! You have resorted to this ill-intentioned and excessive violence in your delusion. The discus, which you ordered against my invisible, mountainous body, fell like a thunderbolt against an unpierceable diamond mountain.

"You have certainly obtained virtue and worthy fame by this empire you have coveted, for you have shattered the vassals which are your brothers. You were praised as 'Son of the Creator, most excellent, bearer of the discus, uplifter of your family.' For that reason you think this wealth of princes, which you have just now conquered, is indestructible and not to be enjoyed by others; but it is, in fact, afflicted by sin.

"Never mind this mistress of yours, the Glory of Dominion, which you so highly honor. She is not proper for me. O vigorous Lord, no bondage ever causes delight to good men. What wise man would touch this glory of yours? It is like some thorny vine, bearing fruit, yet also defiled by your enemies. We must avoid this completely, as if it were a cluster of poisonous thorns. Let us two, rather, desire to engage in the wealth of asceticism and penance, free from thorns, dependent only upon ourselves.

"Let us forgive any transgressions that have been committed. For my part, I have demonstrated my insolence, and have utterly fallen away from good conduct."

This cascade of words, issuing from the mouth of Bāhubali like thunder from a cloud, gladdened the fevered mind of Bharata, the King eager for conquest. Bharata reviled himself, saying "Alas! I have committed an outrage," and repented of his own evil deed.

Bāhubali did not retreat from his determination, but rejected Bharata's pleas to stay and become emperor. Oh! How steadfast are the mindful! Rejoicing, Bāhubali threw down the treasure of the territorial dominion at the feet of his powerful brother, and honoring the feet of his teacher and father, took upon himself initiation into the ascetic life of the Jainas.

Embraced by the vine of initiation, all his clothing cast aside, he was like a tree denuded of its leaves, embraced by vines. With his father's consent, the learned and restrained Bāhubali wandered about alone and performed *yoga* in a standing posture until the rains came. Maintaining a praiseworthy vow, fasting amid the forest's spreading vines, standing among snakes slinking from the openings of anthills, he was a fearful sight. His feet were covered by the expanded hoods of young, hissing cobras, as though covered with poisonous sprouts. With vines descending through his hair down to his shoulders, he emulated the paradisal sandal tree with its multitude of black snakes. The flower-covered vine of spring embraced him tightly, enveloping him with its branch-like arms, as though it were a laughing companion. The flowers picked off that vine by the hand of the Vidyādharīs withered, and resembled beautiful ladies bowing at the feet of their lord. Engaging in the most strenuous ascetic activity, Bāhubali seemed to be a lover emaciated by longing for his mistress, Emancipation.

Asceticism withered not only his body, aflame as it was by the heat of self-generated austerities, but also his *karma*, which does not confer happiness. He was overcome by no affliction whatever, even though he engaged in excessive ascetic penances. The steadfastness of the very great, because of which they are not shaken from their purpose, is beyond conceiving by ordinary men.

Bearing all things patiently, composed, detached, and shining, he overcame the burdens of the earth, and afflictions of cold water, wind and fire. He prevailed over the pairs of afflictions — hunger and thirst, cold and heat, gadflies and gnats — for the sake of success in his movement along the Jaina ascetic path. He undertook the excellent vow of nakedness, and was not overwhelmed by the mischievous senses. The restraint of the state of chastity, which is nakedness, is the highest ascetic activity. Bāhubali endured both discomfort and pleasure patiently. For those not attached to desires, pleasure and pain surely do not represent obstacles. He was not tempted by women, for he had attained the state of being totally indifferent to pleasures, and he looked upon the impure body of a woman as no more inviting than a leather doll. He paid no heed to footwear, a bed or a chair, but bore easily the afflictions resulting from walking, lying down and sitting. This foremost among men who knew the highest truth was free from desire and forsook happiness, and bore physical and verbal abuse to his person, since he was to give up the body. He did not desire to maintain the body by eating and gathering food on begging rounds. In this manner did he endure, silently, the afflictions of mendicancy. Making no discrimination between pleasure and pain, undertaking the purificatory activity of abandoning the body, and exhibiting supreme patience, he put up with dirt and the touch of thorns all over his body. His intellect firm, he endured the torment born of these diverse bodily afflictions, which is difficult to endure, and meditated on the body, that abode of diseases. Steeped in wisdom, he cast away the pride that comes from mundane knowledge and which is an affliction to true wisdom, and boldly bore the afflictions rising from that knowledge until he attained omniscience.

He was not eager either for honor or precedence. He took no pleasure in honor, nor any delight in deferential treatment. Contented as he was, he did not succumb to any of these afflictions, and suffered neither from ignorance nor lack of perception. On account of his conquest of these afflictions, extensive damage was visited on the *karmas* which imprisoned his body. Indeed, the destruction of the *karmas* is the consequence of the supreme victory over these afflictions.

He easily overcame anger with forbearance, pride by abstaining from haughtiness, and deceit with sincerity. Having put amorous passions to flight, he easily conquered the five senses. Asceticism and penance are the calming of desire's fire, which flames up when kindled by sensual enjoyments. Conquering desire, he eradicated in himself the characteristics of a living being bound by *karma* — eating, fearing, copulating, and desiring possessions. Thus, breaking the courage of the interior enemies all at once, he, knowing the soul, and knowing all that there was to know, conquered the self by means of the self.

That steadfast, great and wise mendicant was vigorous in his dedication to the observance of the fundamental virtues (*guṇas*), which are enumerated as follows: the vow of the mendicant; the five rules of conduct, called *samitis*; the proper curbing and obstruction of the senses and their activities; the state of nudity; acquiescence to periodic plucking out of the hair from one's head; and, among the essential religious duties, bathing in scarcely-frequented places, lying down only on the earth, refraining from cleaning the teeth, and eating a single meal of boiled rice daily. He neglected none of these modes of virtuous conduct. Clinging to supreme purity of vow, he was illumined by beams of light like the sun by its fiery rays. He laid aside the three encumbrances of speech, wealth and passion, and attained the superior state of painlessness, wherein his stability was increased by the ten *dharmas*; thus was he on the path to liberation. Clinging to the fortress of the three restraints (*gupti*), restraint of speech, thought and action; brilliantly equipped with the blazing sword of knowledge, fully-armed with the rules of proper conduct (*samiti*) for moving, speaking, begging, taking and abandoning material objects, he became desirous of conquering his enemies.

Since he was ever awake and increasingly attentive, the treasure of the three jewels — right knowledge, right belief and right conduct — was not in danger of being taken from him by dull-witted thieves. Having restrained his speech by taking the vow of silence, no idle chatter emanated from him. His stronghold of the mind was well-guarded from attacks by the senses. The light of knowledge was made manifest in the great abode of his mind. And in the light of that lamp of knowledge every object in the world became an object for his contemplation. He reflected upon the true nature of everything by means of *mati* and *śruta* consciousness, and the universe became as clear to him as a small seed held in the palm of his hand. With his brilliance enhanced by the conquest of the afflictions, hostile to the senses which he had utterly conquered, and with his enemies, the passions, destroyed, Bāhubali embraced asceticism as his dominion.

His supernatural spiritual powers, which were born of meditational discipline, were manifest through the force of his ascetic endeavors, and his power was clearly capable of shaking the three worlds. Then his eminence in the four-fold knowledge, which was expanded through the subsiding and destruction of each of the *karmas* which obstruct the qualities of the soul, became manifest. On account of the manifestation of perceptual knowledge, there arose a storehouse of knowledge. By means of *śruta* knowledge arose knowledge of all the religious texts, commentarial literature, etc. Having proceeded to the highest level of *avadhi* knowledge, he gained knowledge of all material forms. And then his expansive mind engaged in the understanding of the thoughts of all others, called *manaḥparyāya* knowledge. His ascetic purity was preeminent on account of his purity of knowledge. Surely, knowledge is the root of the great tree of asceticism and penance.

Made exceeding thin by the pitch-peak of his more formidable asceticism, he blazed forth like the sun with its blazing heat. He underwent every one of the stages of asceticism in the Jaina mendicant's life, which are called *ugra*, *ugrogra*, *dīpta*, *tapta*, *ghora*, *mahā*, and *uttarāṇi*, undertaking each stage in the order of increasing severity. This superior sage, liberated from all material impediments, shone forth by means of these perfect ascetic endeavors as the sun does by its rays.

How wondrous! Having given up all imperfections, there was manifest in him, who engaged in this sharp penance, the collection of eight modifications, brought about by the force of his asceticism. His very presence was beneficial to the whole world, and even his belching, spitting and sweating had the supernatural quality of a powerful medicine. Even though he fasted, there arose, on account of the power of his fasting, the supernatural spiritual power related to lifejuices in him. The spiritual power related to strength arose though the power of his asceticism. He was then both an unfailing refuge, and one whose very presence kept other peoples' houses prosperous. Considering that the state of indifference to opposites properly pertains to the soul, that conquering ascetic, who was supreme among those knowledgeable in the ascetic discipline, subdued his mind and directed it in the constant exercise of meditation. Indeed, he now undertook these specific activities derived from proper meditation: supreme forbearance, supreme gentleness, highest sincerity, true purity, abandonment, asceticism, complete poverty, restraint of the senses and celibacy. Practitioners of *yoga* consider the highest accomplishment to rest in the perfection of meditation.

He meditated upon the precepts called the *anuprekṣas*, which are completely pure and twelve in number: he meditated on how nothing in the world is permanent; on how there is nothing to save a person; on the painful nature of the world of birth, death and rebirth; on how a person is ever alone; on how the soul is different from material objects; on how the body is impure; on how attachment to the senses leads to the influx of *karma*; on how good action can prevent the influx of *karma*; on how one can rid oneself of karmic bondage; on the real nature of the world; on how difficult it is to obtain the truth; and on the special greatness of the doctrine of the Jinas. He then undertook the level of meditation called *Dharmadhyāna*, or righteous meditation; in this stage he meditated upon the authority of the Jina's teachings, death, ripening of karmic actions into fruits, the structure of existence, and the thinning out of *karma*. In that lamp, which is the light of mediation, he could see the pieces of karmic matter instantly shattered, like so many specks of lampblack. Light emanated from his body and was diffused in all directions; it spread through the forest, which appeared as though it were permeated by the splendor of an emerald.

All the species of common animals were motionless and in a state of repose at his feet; they were not oppressed by other, more savage, animals, for they, too, had become extremely gentle in his presence. Even animals who are hostile by nature sat down, free from hostility. Elephants, lions and other animals sat near the feet of Bāhubali and praised his might. The tigress, who had only recently given birth, kissed the aged jackal on the head, and even bade all the jackal's offspring to share the milk that flowed from her teat. Elephants, in the company of their leaders, sat next to the lions, their natural enemies. The young of lions, eager to drink from a breast, resorted to the female elephants. The lions caressed the throats of the young elephants with their sharp claws; the elephants emitted low, melodious sounds of contentment, and the lions were encouraged in this activity by the elephant leaders. The female elephants, desiring to cleanse the ground in Bāhubali's vicinity, carried water by means of cups made from folded-over lotus leaves held in their trunks. The elephants placed at his feet the lotuses that they brought in their trunks, and honored the sage Bāhubali. Oh, is not asceticism peace-inducing?

The sage was radiant with the dark blue bodies of snakes at his feet, as if he were garlanded with blue lotus blossoms placed down by worshippers. The dark-blue serpents arose from the anthills, their hoods entirely expanded, and emitted a brilliance that resembled an offering of dark pearls made at the sage's feet. The vines of the forest, brilliant with blossoms hanging from the tips of their branches, resembled devotees bowing before Bāhubali and honoring him with an offering of flowers. The trees of the forest, the tips of their branches stirred by the wind and their flowers blossoming repeatedly, appeared to want to dance constantly because of their joy. Certainly the serpents danced, emitting an inarticulate singing which sounded like a swarm of bees, with their hoods expanded, their bodies contorted, and radiant with the beams emanating from their pearl-like hoods. And the peacocks, the haters of snakes, danced for a while as the serpents watched, to the beat of the *Diṇḍima* drum, which made a sweet sound resembling the male cuckoo. And that forest became a place of tranquility by means of the majesty of the tranquil Bāhubali. Indeed, diligence among the great begets tranquility even among those not tranquil by nature. Birds chirped with placid sounds at the edge of that forest, as though they were proclaiming that this ascetic grove was an exceedingly tranquil place.

And as that forest abode became tranquil through the power of his asceticism, no harm of any kind befell any creature. Even the wild beasts had the darkness in their hearts removed by the great power that was born of his asceticism, and they became freed from any feelings of aggression or hostility.

Those beings who travel among the clouds perceived the presence of this lord of sages, absorbed in his meditation, because their movement became unstable; so they descended to him and caused him to be worshipped over and over again. At once, there was a trembling in the place of the gods, the eaters of immortal nectar, who had bowed their heads; this trembling arose on account of his great majesty, which was born of the heroic energy of asceticism. The Vidyādharīs, approaching at some point in order to frolic in the area, caused the vines clinging to all of Bāhubali's limbs to be removed.

With a force of asceticism born of the force of right meditation, Bāhubali leapt directly to complete purity from stains, and lifted his face up in pure concentration. Honored by Lord Bharata at the end of a year's fasting, he experienced the most excellent light of truth called "*kevala*," or omniscience, which is imperishable. The arising of this omniscience required the worship of Lord Bharata, for Bāhubali had great affection deep in his heart for his brother and he thought, "On account of us Lord Bharata was beset by difficulties." Lord Bharata did adoration to the clear light of meditation manifested by that practitioner of *yoga* according to prescription, both before and after omniscience arose in Bāhubali. When Lord Bharata worshipped Bāhubali before his Omniscience, that devotional activity had as its object the wiping away of Bharata's own sins; his later devotion, exceeding the former, was purely out of regard to the arising of *kevala* knowledge in Bāhubali. Who is competent to describe the great worship Lord Bharata did to his own younger brother, who had attained the state of omniscience? Any one of these reasons by itself would lead to pre-eminence in devotional activity: the fact that Bāhubali was his younger brother; the fact that Bharata was naturally devoted to religion; the fact that the two brothers were united through previous births, and the fact that they bore each other great love. Now, then, what good action can fail to be nourished by all of them taken together? The supreme emperor Bharata did obeisance to that Indra among *yogins*, Bāhubali, accompanied by his councilors, vassal kings and the palace chaplain.

What more need be said? Bharata's offering was made with jewels. The waters of the River of Heaven washed Bāhubali's feet. The devotional lamps were the lustre of the jewels. The offering of uncooked rice grains was made with pearls. The oblation was made with the *piṇḍa* ball of rice and curds, really immortal nectar; the incense was made with fragments of the red sandal tree, and the worship with flowers was done by means of clumps of flowers taken from the trees of the gods, the pleasingly-colored coral tree, and such like. All the receptacles, filled with jewels, were placed at the spot where fruits are placed. The Lord of Jewels thus performed his worship, which consisted of the giving of jewels.

When Bāhubali attained omniscience, the abodes of the gods trembled. At that, the gods, recipients of hundreds of sacrifices, rose up and performed adoration of the highest quality. Then the sweet-smelling wind, capable of shaking the trees in the gardens of heaven, blew gently, fetching the mists from off the river of heaven, the Ganges. And thunder sounded forth in a low rumble along the path of the clouds. A heap of flowers from the wishing tree of heaven fell from the sky. Bāhubali's jewelled umbrella was fashioned by the artificers of the gods, and his celestial seat, composed of the most excellent of jewels, shone forth. On either side of him, fly-whisks waved spontaneously upwards. Then the assembly hall which arises around a *kevalin* magically came into existence, and manifested great splendor. Worshipped by the gods, that King of

Yogins, who possessed the spiritual gift of omniscience, was served by numerous sages, who were like stars dependent upon the moon. Bearing a superiority which arose through the destruction of *karmas*, he who was honored by the nectar-eating gods roamed over the entire earth as a preacher of the Jaina *dharma*. Thus did that omniscient sage, who pleased the world with the nectar of his own speech, attain to the clear, unmoving Mount Kailāsa, which was sanctified by the presence of Ṛṣabha, his teacher and father.

Bāhubali is renowned for his conquest of Bharata by means of a battle with water, wrestling and a battle of glances, in the assembly of all the princes. Yet he set forth to become a monk, regarding the burden of lofty empire as though it were nothing more than grass. May that foremost among those who endure the last body protect you.

The Goddess of Victory abandoned Bharata, who was accompanied by the blazing discus weapon, and approached the self-restrained Bāhubali before the eyes of all the warrior princes. And she became a receptacle of shame, discarded by Bāhubali forever. May that mighty-armed prince, who took to the path of the teacher, his father, protect us.

Desiring an encounter with the Goddess of Victory, who is not to be tied down to one man, Bāhubali was victorious in the presence of all the princes of the earth by means of a greater strength and majesty. Yet, that son of the first orderer, whose renown is spread through all the houses of the world, undertook, instead, asceticism for the sake of glory.

Glorious is Lord Bāhubali, the strength of whose arms was formerly revealed in his fight with King Bharata in the presence of the warriors. Merely thinking on the syllables of Bāhubali's name purifies all living beings.

The venomous, fiery poison vomited forth from the mouths of cobras always becomes ineffective when it reaches the feet of Lord Bāhubali, who is surrounded with creepers loosened by the finger tips of the Vidyādharīs. Lord Bāhubali, respected by the entire world, is victorious.

His toenails appeared to glitter because of the lustre of the gems in King Bharata's lofty crown, which was placed before them when the emperor bowed to the sage. Though he was surrounded by anthills full of snakes, Bāhubali was not shaken in the conduct of his meditational discipline, but was driven along by the force of his steadfastness.

The hair of his head, curly at the tips and black like a swarm of bees, hung down on his arms, covering the top of his arms; the splendor of this sight rivalled that of a mountain with its peak covered by a thick raincloud. May this Bāhubali protect us!

A Note on the Translation

Due to the length of the passage, I have foregone footnotes and attempted to concentrate on making the narrative as readable as possible. This does not allow me to indicate one or two marvelous plays on words: yet, others, I believe, will be apparent. I have omitted a twenty-three-verse long *suprabhātam*, or morning hymn, that closes chapter 35 for two reasons. First, the text is surely lengthy enough for this volume; second, I have not yet been able to render the hymn entirely to my satisfaction.

Finally, I would be remiss not to offer my thanks to Professor Edwin Gerow, my Sanskrit professor at The University of Chicago, now at Reed College; and Professor M.D. Vasantha Raj, recently-retired as Chairman of the Department of Postgraduate Studies in Jainology and Prakrits at Mysore University, India.

Twelve Chapters from *The Guidebook to Various Pilgrimage Places, the* Vividhatīrthakalpa *of Jinaprabhasūri*

Translated by John E. Cort

Introduction

The *Vividhatīrthakalpa* ("Guidebook to Various Pilgrimage Places") has been rightly hailed as an important source for both medieval Indian history and geography. In the 63 chapters of this compendium the author gives us valuable information about nearly four dozen Jaina pilgrimage places in the early 14th century.

I have translated 12 chapters of the text. These chapters fall into two groups. The first nine chapters cover four of the five *pañca tīrthīs*, or five major places of Jain pilgrimage, and the continent of Nandīśvara, which is the seventh of the many continents that the Jains believe circle Mt. Meru, the mountain that serves as a kind of cosmic fulcrum. I have given further information about these sites and about the institution of pilgrimage in Jainism in my appendix to my translation. I have also included a biographical note about Jinaprabhasūri.
Several of these chapters, especially those on Giraṇāra, exhibit a fascination with alchemy, reminding us that in medieval times Jaina holy men were renowned as magicians and wizards. In some instances, Jinaprabhasūri seems to indicate that the gold and other wealth derived from alchemical practices are to be used for the benefit of the Jaina congregation, but for the most part the descriptions and treasure maps are presented with no attempt at justification within the context of Jaina practice or ethics. These passages also indicate that as interesting and diverse a collection of ascetics were to be found at holy sites in the 14th century as are to be found there today.

The other three chapters describe two pilgrimage places in North Gujarat. These provide examples of the detailed descriptions Jinaprabhasūri gives of contemporary Jaina centers. They were also chosen for inclusion for sentimental reasons: I lived in Patan for 21 months while conducting fieldwork on contemporary Śvetāmbara Mūrtipūjaka Jaina practice and belief, during which time I visited Śaṅkheśvar half-a-dozen times.

Chapter 1

Śatruñjaya

May the god Nābheya, who adorns the temple atop the peak known as blessed Puṇḍarīka, be your prosperity. I will tell in brief the greatness of the blessed Śatruñjaya *tīrtha*; it was formerly told by the enlightened Atimuktaka to the seer Nārada, so that I and others may contemplate it. Those pious people who desire the destruction of sin should listen. 1-3.

The ascetic Puṇḍarīka attained liberation on Śatruñjaya on the full moon in Caitra along with 50 million [*sādhus*]; therefore it is known as Puṇḍarīka. The 21 names by which it is known, and which are sung by gods, men, and seers, are: Siddhakṣetra, Tīrtharāja, Marudeva, Bhagīratha, Vimalādri, Bāhubali, Sahasrakamala, Tāladhvaja, Kadamba, Śatapatra, Nāgādhirāja, Aṣṭottaraśatakūṭa, Sahasrapatra, Ḍhaṅka, Lauhitya, Kaparddinivāsa, Siddhiśekhara, Śatruñjaya, Muktinilaya, Siddhiparvata, and Puṇḍarīka. 4-8.

Ḍhaṅka, etc., are the five peaks which have deities, and are distinguished by their quicksilver mines, gem mines, caves, and herbs. Ḍhaṅka, Kadamba, Lauhitya, Tāladhvaja, and Kaparddī are the names which have been mistakenly accepted by people over time. 9-10.

[Its height] is 80 *yojana*s in the first spoke, 70 in the second, 60 in the third, 50 in the fourth, 12 in the fifth, and 7 cubits in the last spoke. Thus the authorities explain its height in the descent of time. It was 50 *yojana*s at the base, 10 at the top, and 8 tall when Yugādīśa practiced austerities. 11-13.

Ṛṣabha and countless others — kings of *tīrtha*s, *siddha*s, and great seers — preached here in former times. The future Jina-leaders, starting with Padmanābha, will preach here in order to praise and purify the worlds. 23 Arhats, from Nābheya through Mahāvīra, excepting only Nemi, preached here. 14-16.

Earlier in the present descent, at the time of Ṛṣabha's enlightenment, the purifying emperor Bharata commissioned a temple measuring one *yojana*, with an image of Ṛṣabha made of moon-stone, and 22 small temples with images of gold and silver. Here shines a row of temples containing plaster images of the 22 Jina-kings, each with his own footprints. And here King Bāhubali built a tall temple of Marudevā, which includes a *samavasaraṇa*. 17-21.

In this descent the first *gaṇadhara* of the first Arhat and the first son of the first Emperor attained liberation here. The two great seers, the *khecara* kings Nami and Vinami, attained liberation here along with 20 million great seers. The kings Draviḍa, Vālikhilya, etc., attained liberation here along with 100 million *sādhus*. 30 million royal seers — Jaya, Rāma, and others, — and 100,090 *munis* — Nārada, and others, — attained liberation here. And here princes — Pradyumna, Śāmba, etc. — attained liberation along with 85 million *sādhus*. The kings born in Ṛṣabha's lineage from Ādityayaśas through Sāgara attained liberation here, along with hosts of followers, uncountable numbers of them such as 1.4 million, etc. The descendants of Bharata — his son Śailaka, Śuka, etc. — attained liberation here along with innumerable millions of millions. The five Pāṇḍavas, who established an image of the Arhat [Ṛṣabha], attained liberation here along with Kuntī and 200 million *munis*. The second and sixteenth Jina-lords [of the present descent], Ajita and Śānti, each stayed here for a four-month rainy season, fixed in one place. After coming on a pilgrimage at the command of Nemi, the *gaṇadhara* composed here the *Ajitaśāntistava*, which removes all ills. 22-32.

Countless images and countless temples have been energetically established here at this great *tīrtha*. 33.

By the devotion of bowing down to images commissioned by Bharata at small tanks and in caves, one will enjoy only one more rebirth. 34.

Samprati, Vikramāditya, Sātavāhana, Vāgbhaṭa, Pādalipta, Āma, and Datta are remembered as those who restored its temples. 35.

Even the faithful residents of Videha remember it, or so it is said that Indra told Kālikācārya. 36.

The tank Anupamā used to be here, where the tank of Ajita is; Jāvaḍa installed an image here. The wise king Meghaghoṣa, grandson of Kalki, will build the temples of Marudevā and Śānti here. King Vimalavāhana, at the preaching of Duṣprasahasūri, will arrange for the last rebuilding of it. Even when the congregation is destroyed, this, praised by the gods as Ṛṣabha Peak, will last until Padmanābha's congregation. 37-40.

Even plants and animals dwell here free from sin. They are pure-minded due to the glory of the *tīrtha*, and go to a good birth. Thinking upon it destroys men's fear of lions, fire, oceans, vicious animals, kings, poison, war, thieves, enemies, and death. Meditating as though one were in the lap of the plaster image of Ādyajineśitṛ commissioned by Bharata conquers all fears. 41-43.

The merit gained by fierce asceticism and celibacy is attained by living on Śatruñjaya. The merit attained by spending millions for feedings of desired foods at other *tīrtha*s is attained by performing one fast at Vimalācala. All the *tīrtha*s in the triple world, the earth, midspace, and heaven, are praised as being seen at Puṇḍarīka. 44-46.

Birds of ill-omen never gather here, even though there is food and places to roost and gather. 47.

Giving food to a pilgrim here earns millions of auspicious merits, and there is infinite merit for the pilgrim who returns home after doing the pilgrimage.

There are millions of merit for the one who, without having seen Vimalācala, gifts to the congregation; having seen it, there is endless merit. 48-49.

When this one is praised, then all the various *tīrthas* where arose the enlightenment and liberation of the great souls are also praised. The festivals of birth, renunciation, enlightenment, and liberation occurred separately or together at Ayodhyā, Mithilā, Campā, Śrāvastī, Hastināpura, Kauśambi, Kāśī, Kākandī, Kāmpilya, Bhadrila, Ratnavāha, Sauryapura, Kuṇḍagrāma, Pāpayā, Candrānana, Siṃhapura, Rājagṛha, Śriraivataka, Sammeta, Vaibhārā, and Aṣṭāpada Mountain. In making one pilgrimage here there is 100 times as much merit as in making a pilgrimage to all of them. 50-54.

There is 100 times as much merit in installing an image as in doing *pūjā*, 1000 times in building a temple, and endless times in maintaining [a temple]. He who has built an image or a temple on this peak shall enjoy the wealth of Bhāratavarṣa, and then go to heaven. 55-56.

A man who performs asceticism with the Namaskāra Mantra, etc., by thinking upon Puṇḍarīka will attain the fruit of the highest asceticism. A mortal who is pure in the three organs [thought, word, and deed] and thinks upon this *tīrtha* will attain the fruit of the austerity that begins on the sixth and ends with the month. Even today, one who performs the highest fast on Puṇḍarīka Mountain, goes to heaven easily, even though he be without virtues. He who gifts here an umbrella, fly-whisk, jar, banner, or serving plate is reborn as a wizard; he who donates a chariot will become an emperor. He who with purity of devotion donates ten flower garlands, even though he be an enjoyer of worldly pleasures, will attain the fruit of a four-month fast. Gifting twice equals the fruit of a six-month fast, gifting thrice that of an eight-month fast, four times that of a ten-month fast, and gifting five times equals the fruit of a twelve-month fast; the fruit increases just as the donation is increased. The merit attained on Vimalācala just by the bathing worship [of a Jina image] is not attained at other *tīrthas* even by gifting gold, land, and ornaments. By offering incense, one attains the fruit of a one-month fast. He who gifts proper food, etc., to *sādhus* here attains the fruit of the Kārttika month fast. He who performs lustration worship here [of a Jina image] with mantras at the three times of the day, who fasts in Caitra and Kārttika, and meditates on "Praise to the Arhats," will be reborn as a *tīrthaṅkara*. 57-67.

The shrines of Pārśva and Mahāvīra shine in the city of Pādalipta, and in the lower section there is the great temple of Neminātha. Blessed Vāgbhaṭa, the lord of mantras, spent 20,700,000 and had the temple of Yugādīśa renovated. 68-69.

Seeing the brilliant image of the first Arhat immediately upon entering the *tīrtha* gives the fast-breaking food of the nectar of immortality to the eyes. 70.

In the year 108 of the Vikrama era Jāvaḍi spent much wealth to have an image installed here. They say that the gem called Jyotīrasa, which was mined from the slope of the jewelled peak of brilliantly shining Mammana, was used by him to make [the image]. Śeṭh Jāvaḍi, who lived in Madhumatī town, heard of the glory of Śatruñjaya from Vajrasvāmī. He was distressed that there was only a plaster image, since he was fond of offering scented water. So he thought upon Cakreśvarī and went to the mine on Mount Mammana. He commissioned a stone image, placed it on a cart, and set out along with his wife by a pleasant footpath for Vimala Mountain. But no matter how far the cart travelled along the road during the day, at night it would return to the starting place. He became distressed and thought upon Kaparddī; discerning the reason for the occurrence, the pious man and his wife fell prostrate in the path of the cart. The god was pleased by his rashness, and so placed the cart and the image atop the mountain. What is difficult to accomplish for the pure? At the same time that the main image was set up there, the image on the altar was cast down. With a cry from the plaster image, the mountain burst in pieces. Lightning flashed from the former image; it was deflected by the image installed by the *śeṭh*, and after cleaving the staircase and splitting the mountain, it departed. Jāvaḍi was pleased at having thus established the image on the temple peak, and so he danced wildly with his wife, his hair erect with pleasure and jangling like armor. Eighteen ships returning from foreign lands arrived at the coast, and the Śeṭh by spending their money made a donation here. Thus Jāvaḍi, who caused the installation of the first Arhat, Puṇḍarīka, and Kaparddī, is known as one who enjoys the state of being a guest in heaven. 71-83.

The original image of Puṇḍarīka is here on the right hand of the Lord; the other one, established by Jāvaḍi, shines on the left hand. 84.

Countless millions of millions in the Ikṣvāku and Vṛṣṇi lineages attained liberation here; thus it is known as "the forehead ornament of millions of millions." The five Pāṇḍavas and their mother Kuntī attained liberation here, so plaster images of the six teach here on the *tīrtha*. The *caitya*-tree Rājādana rains milk here by the wondrous merit of the Blessed Congregation, just as a bundle of moonrays rains nectar. Animals, with tigresses and peacocks foremost, attain the world of the gods by abandoning food and bowing to the footprints of Ādīśa. 85-88.

The incarnation of Satyapura is to the left of the temple of the Mūlajina. The Aṣṭāpada temple is located to the right behind the Sakunī temple. The incarnations of Nandīśvara, Stambhanaka, and Ujjayanta, which increase the merit of those in the future, are found without difficulty. Nābheya, worshipped by Vinami and Nami, shines in the temple which rises up to heaven. 89-91.

Śreyāṃsa, Śānti, Nemi, Ṛṣabha, Mahāvīra, and other Jinas adorn the second peak. Worshippers believe that [the evil fruits of] their own past and future deeds are cut off by doing *namaskāra* here in the temple of the blessed Marudevī who cuts off rebirth. The *yakṣa* king Kaparddī, a wishing tree to those who bow down, erases the manifold obstacles of troupes of pilgrims. 92-94.

Kṛṣṇa propitiated Kaparddī *yakṣa* at the instruction of Nemi in a cave in the mountain and fasted for eight days, for the protection of the three images. It is said that even today Śakra goes there. 95-96.

There is a cave to the north of the image of Ṛṣabha established by the Pāṇḍavas, and even today there is a small pond there. Images are seen there due to the instructions of the *yakṣa*, and Ajita and Śānti also each stayed there for a rainy season. To the east are their two temples, and near the Ajita temple is the tank Anupamā. 97-99.

The temple of Śānti, cooling to the eyes and which is a thunderbolt to the delusions of rebirth, is near Marudevī. Two mines of gold and silver are thirty cubits and seven fathoms to the east of the Śānti temple. One hundred cubits to the east is a well, which is filled with quicksilver at a depth of eight cubits. Gems and gold are located near it, placed there by Pādalipta Ācārya for the renovation of the *tīrtha*. 100-103.

One should perform three fasts to the east of the image of Vṛṣabha, and thirty bow-lengths down from Ṛṣabha Peak. If the offerings are done correctly, Vairoṭyā will manifest herself. In the middle of the night lift the slab at her command, and enter it. As a result of fasting all the magical powers will be attained there. From attending to the worship of Ṛṣabha, there one will become the enjoyer of just one more rebirth. 104-106.

A stone cistern sits five hundred bow-lengths to the east. A wise man should perform offerings correctly. From the merit of two fasts, he will find a quicksilver well by pulling up a slab. 107-108.

Dharmadatta, the son of Kalki, will be an Arhat. He will enjoy [the fruit] of establishing a Jina image every day. He will restore Śatruñjaya, and his son Jitaśatru will be blessed by the prosperity of a rule of 32 years. Jitaśatru's son Meghaghoṣa will restore the temple of Śānti and Marudevī here at the command of Kaparddī *yakṣa*. Nandisūri, Ārya Śriprabha, Maṇibhadra, Yaśomitra, Dhanamitra, Vikaṭadharmma, Sumaṅgala, and Sūrasena will restore it, then Duṣprasaha, and finally Vimalavāhana. 109-113.

Whoever oppresses pilgrims to this place, or steals goods, will from the weight of his sin fall into a fierce hell along with his descendants. One who performs pilgrimage, *pūjā*, protection of wealth, praise of pilgrims, or hospitality here is praised along with his lineage even in heaven. 114-115.

One cannot omit to praise the religious buildings undertaken by Vastupāla, and made by Pīthaḍa and others. The wise minister Vastupāla, elder brother of Tejaḥpāla, foresaw the destruction by the barbarian minister, and so after arranging for the making of extremely immaculate images with Mammāṇa gems, established images of the first Arhat and Puṇḍarīka in the main building. In 1369 of the Vikrama era the image established by Jāvaḍi was thrown down by the barbarians, due to the strength of Kali. In 1371 of the Vikrama era, the good blessed Samara restored the main image. 116-120.

Blessed be those who have been, are, or will be leaders of congregations. May they be blessed with wealth for a long time. 121.

Following the *Kalpaprābhṛta*, first a Kalpa was composed by blessed Bhadrabāhu, then by Vajra, and finally by Ācārya Pādalipta. This "Śatruñjaya Kalpa" of Jinaprabhasūri, which gives what is desired, is abridged from them. Those who speak, meditate upon, recite, or hear this Kalpa with devotion will be liberated in their third rebirth. 122-124.

O lord of peaks Śatruñjaya! How can even wise people describe in brief your qualities? Due to the influence of this *tīrtha*, there is auspicious mental modification of men who come on pilgrimage. A pious man eliminates sin by placing on his limbs dust from the carts and the feet of the horses, camels, and men in a congregation who go on pilgrimage to you. Doing *namaskāra*, etc., to you results in as much decay of karma as a one month fast elsewhere. O abode of Nābheya! O you whose glory is praised by Indra! You should be praised, O land of perfection, with mind, speech, and body. 125-129.

May the merit acquired by ignorant me from composing this Kalpa be for universal joy. Whoever honors this Kalpa, or has it set down in books, completely achieves his desired success and magical powers. 130-131.

The king of kings has been pleased by [my] beginning this, and so this Kalpa will always be victorious as the Grace of the King. 132.

This is completed in 1375 of the Vikrama era, on the seventh day of the bright half of Jyeṣṭha month, a Friday. 133.

Thus the Blessed Śatruñjaya Kalpa of Blessed Jinaprabhasūri is concluded.

Chapter 2

An abbreviated account of Raivatagiri

After bowing my head to Blessed Nemijina,
[I will tell] the Kalpa of the Lord Raivata Mountain,
just as was told by the pupil of blessed Vajra and by Pādalipta. 1.

Nemi took his initiation on the stone seat near the Chatraśilā. His enlightenment occurred in Thousand Mango Grove. His teaching occurred in Hundred-Thousand Garden. His liberation occurred on the lofty peak Avalokana. Kṛṣṇa commissioned three temples in the vicinity of Raivata, adorned with golden, jewelled images, for the three beneficial events of the Living Lord, and also [a temple] of Ambādevī. Indra carved the mountain by means of his thunderbolt into a silver temple with a golden altar, and made a jewelled image in lifelike color in the ornamented pavilion on Ambā Peak. Śiva did the same in the bench pavilion of Avalokana Peak. The doorkeeper is Siddha Vināyaka. A likeness [of Neminātha] was established by Kṛṣṇa immediately after [Nemi's] liberation; [Kṛṣṇa] learnt the location of the liberation from Nemi himself. The seven Yādavas — Kāmamegha, Meghanāda, Girividāraṇa, Kapāṭa, Siṃhanāda,

Khoḍika, and Raivata — became *kṣetrapālas* due to their fierce asceticism, which was like play for them. Meghanāda has correct faith, and stands firm in devotion to Nemi's feet. Girividāraṇa arranged for the restoration of five golden benches.

There is a cave 107 paces north of Ambā. Perform three fasts along with proper offerings, and a slab will lift up; and in the middle there is an image of Girividāraṇa. Go fifty paces, bow to the eternal image of the Jina commissioned by Baladeva, and then go fifty paces to the north, where there are three gates. Enter the first gate by crouching down, and go 300 paces. Perform five fasts, and the fearful form of a black bee will appear. Crawl seven paces face downwards into the seat-pavilion made by Kubera *yakṣa* at the command of Indra. Worship Ambādevī, and establish her in a golden net. Stand there, and praise the Main Lord Nemi Jinendra. Perform worship with just one verse, and go in the second gate. Go forty paces below the well Svayaṃvara, and then 700 paces beyond the middle gate where there is a well. There again praise the Main Lord, who is established there as a most excellent swan. Enter the main door of the third gate at the command of Ambā, and of no one else. Take the road of the golden bench, and there is a cave twenty hands in front of Ambā. Do three fasts at the command of Ambā. Uncover a slab which is twenty hands away, where there are seven holes. There is a quicksilver well five box-lengths down, which opens on every new moon. Do three fasts there along with worship and the correct offerings, at the command of Ambā; then it can be grasped.

Perform three fasts on Old Peak, along with worship of offerings by the easy path, to attain Siddha Vināyaka. Then you will attain the powers which you desire. Stay there for one day and they will become manifest.

Crouch down and go one hundred paces from the Rājamatī cave: there are a quicksilver well, a black-spotted creeper, a jewelled image of Rājīmatī, Ambā, and various herbs. Three slabs are known to be there, Chatraśilā, Ghaṇṭaśilā, and Koḍiśilā. Chatraśilā is in the middle, with a golden creeper in the middle.

There are 24 [Jina images] made of silver and gold in the middle of Thousand Mango Grove, and 72 [Jina images] in the Hundred-Thousand Garden, where there is also known to be a cave with 24 Jinas.

Go ahead from Kālamegha 308 paces to the north from the Suvarṇavālukā River, and enter a mountain cave. After bathing in the water and performing a fast, the seeker can open the door. Inside the first door is a gold trove. Inside the second door is a jewel trove, made by Ambā for the sake of the congregation.

There are five Kṛṣṇa storehouses. Another is near Dāmodara. There is known to be silver and gold dust 20 fathoms down in the lower part of the collyrium slab.

For the one who knows the lore of this,

there is an auspiciousness-giving pumpkin, and the mastery of the power of quicksilver.

This description by Blessed Vajra
is for the restoration of the congregation. 1.

Place the powder from Ghaṇṭaśilā
in the middle of a frying pan of vegetables,
mixed with millions of seeds,
then use it as eyeblack
to attain powers. 2.

The Abbreviated Raivata Kalpa, based on the explanation given in the *Vidyāprābhṛta*, is concluded.

Chapter 3

Blessed Ujjayanta Stava

I praise Girināra, Lord of mountains; it is purified by Blessed Nemi, and famous by the names Raivata, Ujjayanta, etc. This country is known in the worlds as Surāṣṭra; this mountain is the ornament on the forehead of the beautiful woman who is the earth. 1-2.

Ṛṣabha, etc., adorn the Khaṅgāra fort. Pārśva adorns the lowland area known as Tejalapura. On the peak of the two *yojana* high mountain a row of Jina temples shines like a white mass, like a stainless autumn moon beam. A beautiful temple of Lord Nemi shines on top, beautified by a pure lake and golden pillars and offering pots. 3-5.

Here the footprints of the God, son of Śiva, when seen, touched, or worshipped, drive away the host of sins of the wise. 6.

The Lord, after renouncing great kingship like an old straw, shook off dear friends and undertook the great vow. He attained enlightenment here, and desiring the welfare of the people of the world discovered liberation. 7-8.

The minister blessed Vastupāla made a temple of the three beneficial moments here, which produces amazing and good things. People who do the bathing of Nemi in the best of pavilions which is full of Jina images shine like Indras. 9-10.

The tank Gajendrapada adorns the peak. It is full of water for bathing the Arhat, like nectar, fit for bathing. 11.

Images of Ṛṣabha, Puṇḍarīka, Aṣṭāpada, and Nandīśvara were commissioned by Vastupāla here in the Śatruñjaya-incarnation [temple]. Ambā is here, riding a lion, golden colored, with her sons Siddha and Buddha, her hands holding lovely mangoes and a drum; she removes the obstacles of the congregation. 12-13.

Good people who see the peak Avalokana, which purifies the lotus feet of Nemi, attain the fulfillment of their deeds. 14.

Śāmba, the son of Jāmbavatī and Kṛṣṇa, and the glorious Pradyumna performed difficult penance atop the mountain. 15.

Various sorts of herbs blaze up brightly here at night, and on top shine Ghaṇṭākṣara and Chatraśilā. Thousand Mangoes, Hundred-Thousand Garden, and other dense groves are graced by the songs of peacocks, koil-birds, and bees. There is no tree, creeper, flower, or fruit which is not seen here by the experts. Thus [say] those who know the tradition. 16-18.

Who does not exclaim praise inside the cave Rājīmatī, where Rathanemi, having descended, went from the wrong path to the good path? Performing *pūjā*, bathing, gifting, and performing asceticism here are causes of the pleasure of liberation for good people. People, even from being lost, or going off the road onto this mountain, see the worshipped Jina who dwells in the temple being bathed and worshipped. Ratna came here from Kasmira at the order of Kuṣmāṇḍī, and installed a stone image in place of the plaster one. 19-22.

What mathematician can count the number of streams, waterfalls, tanks, mines, and even plants? 23.

Hail to the great *tīrtha*, appearing as though anointed [by milk], the savior, the peak adorned with temples, Mount Raivata. 24.

May Giriṇāra, the land which shines with gold and silver, which has been praised by Jinaprabha, the praiser of the gods, be joyful to you. 25.

Thus is the Blessed Ujjayanta Stava.

Chapter 4

Ujjayanta

In Surāṣṭra there is a beautiful mountain named Ujjayanta. Climb its peak and praise Nemijina. After performing *pūjā* with bathing, adoration, scent, incense, lamps, etc., and prostrating, the person who desires wealth will see Ambikā Devī. The *kṣetrapāla* is seen at mountain tops, tunnels, caves, springs, doorways, manifestations, wells, etc., as was said by the former teachers. 1-3.

The place of Nemināth, the destroyer of the pride of lust and the destroyer of bad rebirth, is known in the world by the name of Nirvāṇaśilā. There is a downward-facing cave on its northern slope, at ten bowlengths. There is a *liṅga* in a section [of the cave] four bowlengths inside its door. There is a liquid there which smells like animal urine. After forty minutes it splits a copper plate and makes it into silver, flashing white like the moon and blossoms of jasmine. 4-6.

To the east, within a bowlength, there is a stone cow. Twelve bowlengths straight to the south is seen a divine superior elixir, vermilion colored, manifest. By contact with fire it splits all iron. 7-8.

On Ujjayanta there is a river named Vihalā, and an image of Pārvatī. If touched by elixir, its fingers show the gate to Pārvatī. Śakra-incarnation is on the northern slope of Ujjayanta Mountain. There is a row of stairs, and the earth is pigeon colored. At five *gavyas*, bind up and burn rice balls to get the best silver which destroys the disease of poverty, and rescues one from the forest of suffering. 9-11.

A tiled floor is seen on the peak Viśālaśṛṅga. There is silver near it on the peak Kavvaḍahaḍhā. The monkey Suddāra is in the Ujjayanta Raivata Forest. Pull on his left ear, and he will open the door to the best cave. Go inside 100 cubits, where a golden colored tree is seen, oozing blue sap, which certainly is *hiṅg*. After taking that, the liberated one should touch the left foot of Hanuman, who shows the best door by which no human can go. 12-15.

The temple known as Kohaṇḍi is seen atop Ujjayanta Peak. Behind that is a peak, on both slopes of which there is salty earth. Placing that along with linseed oil on a deformed limb purifies a deformed limb. Ambikā when propitiated takes away both bad birth and disease. 16-17.

Vegavatī is the name of the red colored river which flows there. Excellent silver is obtained from it by mixing purified and heated rice balls [with the water]. 18.

Jñānaśilā is on Ujjayanta; it has golden colored earth. Gold is obtained by [mixing it] in the embers of *khair*-wood with rice balls and goat urine. At five *gavyas*, bind up some myrobalan with a ball made of earth and clay from Jñānaśilā, and *hiṅg* will become gold. 19-20.

The peak named Tilavisāraṇa is located near the best of mountains. Press strongly on a bound-up slab there to find 200,000 gold coins. 21.

The river which is full of *laḍḍus* in the golden *tīrtha* is known as Sena. It purifies copper and turns it into gold; there is no doubt about this. 22.

There is a divine peak named Mayukagṛha situated in the middle of Billakkhaya city, and above it is the elixir well Gaṇapati. Perform a fast to cause the worshipped Gaṇapati to move, and find the superior elixir *sāmasevī*, which makes a deformed limb firm. On this there is no doubt. 23-24.

The *tīrtha* Sahasrāsrava is beautiful and true because a *karañja* medicinal tree is located there. It is in the shape of stones, with two sections. One section is mercury. Grind [it with] urine in a small crucible, heat it, and it becomes silver, which saves one from the forest of sorrows. 25-26.

The best elixir arises behind the peak of the mountain Avalokana. It turns brass the color of a parrot's wing into gold. 27.

Atop Pradyumna Mountain is the place named Ambikāśrama. There also the golden yellow earth becomes the finest gold. 28.

On Ujjayanta is Jñānaśilā, at the base of which is yellow clay. Say a *sāhāmiya* prayer to obtain bright white gold. Climb the first peak of Ujjayanta, descend 300 bow lengths to the south, and you will come to a cave named

Pūikara. Uncover the cave, look about, and enter it carefully. Twelve fathoms inside there is divine elixir, like rose-apple fruit. Mix a 100th part of it in a dish with lac, and let it penetrate into silver; suddenly it makes a lovely bazaar gold. 29-32.

There is a place of asceticism to the east from the Kohaṇḍi temple, going toward the north. A stone image of Vasudeva is there. Ten cubits to the north of that is seen an image of Pārvatī. She shows the cave with her fingers which chastise transgressions. Enter nine bowlengths to the north, and a well is seen on the right, which is essentially musk sap, the color of yellow fool's gold. 33-35.

Jñānaśilā on Ujjayanta is famous. There is a stone there. On its northern slope is a cave, facing down to the south. Ten bowlengths into its southern portion there is vermilion colored earth. There is a *śatavedhī* elixir which dissolves copper, without a doubt. 36-37.

On the peak of Vṛṣabha, Ṛṣabha, etc., is a gathering of stones. When they are smeared with the dung of a bull elephant, there is a penetrating elixir in the middle. 38.

Ninety bowlengths to the south of the Jina temple is *jalukacarī* earth. [Mixed with] animal blood, it pierces copper to make gold. 39.

Vegavatī is the name of the river in which are stones the color of red arsenic. When heated, they instantly exude a fivefold penetrating substance which pierces copper. 40.

Thus is the Kalpa of Ujjayanta, for certain. The one who does *bhakti* to the Jina, and prostrates his body to Kohaṇḍi, should attain his desired pleasures. 41.

The Kalpa of the Great *Tīrtha* of Blessed Ujjayanta is concluded.

Chapter 5

Raivatagiri

In the west, in Surāṣṭra, on the king of peaks Raivata Mountain, there is the temple of blessed Nemināthа with its high tower. It is said that formerly a plaster image of blessed Neminātha was there. Once the two brothers named Ajita and Ratna from the country of Kasmira which adorns the northern direction became congregation leaders and came to Giriṇāra. In an excess of zeal they bathed the image with pitchers full of saffron juice. The plaster image of blessed Neminātha melted away. They grieved at what they had done and renounced food.

After they had fasted for 21 days, the blessed goddess Ambikā came to them. The congregation leader was raised up. When he saw the goddess, he said, "Victory!" Then the goddess said, "Grab ahold of this image, but do not look at its backside." The congregation leader Ajita towed the jewelled image of blessed Nemi with a single rope, and led it to a golden bench. On the threshold of the first temple the congregation leader raised it up and in the fullness of his great joy he saw its backside. It stayed right there and could not be moved. The goddess rained down flowers. He said, "Victory!" This image was established by the congregation leader on the full moon of Vaiśākhā in the newly made temple which faces west. Ajita performed a great festival with bathing, etc., and returned to his own country with his relative. In this age of Kali, recognizing that people have sinful thoughts, Ambikā Devī has covered over the lustre of the shimmering jewelled image.

Formerly, in Gujarat, Jayasimhadeva killed King Khaṅgāra and installed Sajjana as chief magistrate. A new temple to Nemi Jinendra was commissioned in 1185 Vikrama by him [Sajjana]. The golden mango lake was commissioned by the good Bhāvaḍa, the chief ornament of the Malava country. The footpath was commissioned in 1220 Vikrama by the magistrate of Saurāṣṭra who arose from the blessed Śrīmāla clan and was established in his position by the Cālukya Emperor Kumārapāla, that lord of men. Dhavala in the meantime from his sentiment expanded the drinking station. Hundred-Thousand Garden is seen on the right side by people climbing the steps.

In Aṇahillavāda Paṭṭana, those adornments of the Poravāḍa lineage, the sons of Āsārāja and Kumāradevī, the supports of the kingship of blessed Vīradhavala the lord of the country of Gujarat, the two brothers who bear the names Vastupāla and Tejaḥpāla, were ministers. Tejaḥpāla commissioned on Giriṇāra an excellent fort, monastery, drinking station, temple, and a beautiful garden, named Tejalapura after himself. He commissioned a temple to Pārśvanātha, named the Āsarāja Vihāra after his father. He commissioned a tank, named Kumārasāra after his mother. To the east of Tejalapura is the fort Ugrasenagaḍha; the temple of the chief Jina, Yugādinātha, shines there. It is famous by three names: Ugrasenagaḍha, Khaṅgāragaḍha, and Jūnagaḍha. Behind the fort to the south are the places Cauria, Vedī, Laḍḍu Sarovara, Paśuvāṭaka, etc. To the north is the pavilion Daśa-daśāra; it shines with a hall of great pillars, at the gate of the mountain, where are the fifth Viṣṇu and Dāmodara on the shore of the river Suvarṇarekhā. After a long time, the minister Tejaḥpāla convened the congregation on Mount Ujjayanta near Kālamegha and addressed it. The minister Vastupāla commissioned the Śatruñjaya-incarnation temple, the Aṣṭāpada-Sammeta pavilion, and the temple of Kaparddī *yakṣa* and Marudevī. The temple to the three beneficial events was commissioned by Tejaḥpāla. The Indra pavilion was renovated by the minister Depāla. The tank Gajendrapada is there, adorned by the mark of the elephant footprint of Airāvata. People come there and perform the funeral libations to sorrow by cleansing their limbs. The Thousand Mango Grove is near Chatraśilā. There occurred the beneficial events of renunciation, enlightenment, and liberation of the lord, the lamp of the Yādava clan and the joy of Śivā and Samudravijaya. By climbing to the mountain peak, the temple of Ambikādevī is seen. From there is Avalokana Peak. It is said that Nemisvāmī seated there can be seen from the ten directions. Then [there are images] on the first peak Śāmbakumāra and the second peak

Pradyumna. Jina images made of gold and jewels are seen in temples in various places on the mountain, and are bathed and worshipped daily. Golden earth and various elixirs which split metals are visible there, shining. At night herbs are seen glowing, as if by day. Various trees, creepers, leaves, flowers, and fruits are found at every step. The sound of continuously falling waterfalls, the *khalahala* of intoxicated koil birds, and the buzzing of bees are heard.

Thus is expounded the remainder of the Kalpa of the great *tīrtha* of Ujjayanta. It was written by the *muni* Jinaprabha, just as it was heard.

The blessed Raivataka Kalpa is concluded.

Chapter 8

Mt. Arbuda

After bowing to the Arhats Nābheya and Nemi, I will briefly tell the Kalpa of the great mountain Arbuda. First I will tell of the arising of the goddess, the blessed mother, from whose residence this mountain is famous on earth, just as it was heard. 1-2.

Ratnaśekhara was king in blessed Ratnamāla city. He was distressed because he was childless, and sent out his soothsayers. They saw a poor woman carrying wood atop her head, in a pile that looked like the king's fort. They told the king that her son would take his place. The king ordered this woman along with her foetus to be killed at night by the men. She was thrown into a pit, but she came out of it, pretending that she needs must attend to bodily matters. She gave birth, and, frightened for her son, set him free in a grove. She was led back to the pit and killed by the men, who were ignorant of what had occurred. A doe, impelled by merit [from a previous life], fed milk to the boy at dawn and dusk. While he was growing up in this way, a new coin appeared in the mint due to [the power of] Mahālakṣmī. The coin showed the four feet of the doe and the child. A rumor of the child's birth spread among the people: "Someone is a new king." The king heard this, and sent his warriors to kill the child. They saw him one evening at the town gate. They were afraid to kill him, so they set him free in the path of an oncoming herd of cows. As he was sitting there, by chance a bull was in the front [of the herd]. He dispersed the herd, and placed the child between his four legs. The king was told of this, and on the advice of his minister, joyously considered the child as his own. In time, he became king with the name Śrīpuñja. 3-12a

Śrīpuñja's daughter was Śrīmātā. She was endowed with beauty, but had the face of a monkey. She remembered her former life: "Formerly I was a female monkey, running on the branch of a tree on Arbuda. Someone struck me on the jaw, and — pardon my language — my headless body fell into a well at the base of the tree. My present body is human because of the greatness of that desire-granting *tīrtha*. But since my head is still the same, today I am monkey-faced." Śrīpuñja sent his men to throw her former head into the well, and she became human-faced. She practiced austerities on Mt. Arbuda. One day, a yogi who was travelling through the air saw her, and became infatuated with her beauty. He descended from the sky, and smitten with love, he said, "O Beautiful One, what would it take for you to choose me?" She said, "If by any magic between now and the cry of the morning cock you can make twelve beautiful steps here on the mountain, then you will be my choice." He had that done by his servants within two watches. By her own power, however, she made an artificial cock crow, and thus prevented the marriage. But he did not desist, even though he knew of her deceit. He was prepared for marriage by his sister. On the riverbank she said to him, "Put aside your trident, and approach to marry me." He did so, and she set horrible dogs on him to immobilize his legs, and then killed him by stabbing him through the heart with his own trident. In this way she maintained her virginity, and in her next birth attained heaven. Śrīpuñja had a temple built there on the mountain. Six months later, the snake named Arbuda moved beneath the mountain. From this shaking of the mountain, all the temples lost their spires. 12b-24.

But more popularly it is said:

Formerly this mountain was Nandivardhana, the son of Himādri. Due to the resistance here of the snake Arbuda, it became known as Arbuda. 25.

There are twelve villages atop it, known for their wealth. The ascetics are known as Goggalika-s, and there are thousands of Rāṣṭrika-s. 26.

There is no tree, vine, flower, fruit, cave, or mine which is not found here. Fluorescent herbs shine here at night, and there are both fragrant and sap-filled trees. The Mandākinī River shines here, bringing bliss to the thirsty; its pure waves splash spontaneously, and it is adorned by the blossoms of trees on its bank. [The mountain's] thousands of high peaks shine, over which even the chariot horses of the sun stumble a bit. Caves such as Caṇḍālī, Vajra, and Tailebha are seen here; they accomplish all ends. Places are adorned with wonderous tanks, metal troves, and waterfalls with ambrosial waters. When the high sound of a koil bird is heard, a stream is visible from the tank Kokuyita which makes a "khalahala" sound. 26-33.

Here are the worldly *tīrtha*s of Śrīmātā, Acaleśvara, Vasiṣṭha's Āśrama, Mandākinī, etc. 34.

The rulers of this great mountain are the Paramāra kings. They live in the city of Candrāvatī, an abode of Śrī. 35.

The pure-minded magistrate Vimala made here the temple of Ṛṣabha with a brass image. He worshipped the divine Ambā, not out of any desire for a wealth of sons, but in order to establish the *tīrtha*. The general saw a sprout made of cowdung garlanded with flowers near a *campaka* tree, and so he took this land near the Śrīmātā temple. He appeased the anger of the Gurjara king at the feudatory lord Dhāndūka by his devotion, and at his command brought the latter from Citrakūṭa Mountain. In Vikrama 1088 he expended much wealth to build the Vimalavasati temple. Here Ambikā Devī, worshipped by many rites, destroys unrestrained the obstacles of a congregation coming on pilgrimage. In one night a stonemason made a fine horse from stone in front of the temple of Yugādideva. 36-42.

In Vikrama 1288 the Nemi temple Lūṇigavasati was built by the moon-like minister. Blessed Tejaḥpāla the royal minister installed an image of touchstone at Stambhatīrtha, which became the collyrium of immortality for the eyes. At the order of blessed King Soma he installed images of his own ancestors and built an elephant stable. 43-45.

O! From the lustrous craftsmanship of the temple, the name of Śobhanadeva (Lord of Beauty), the crest jewel of architects, became true. 46.

The younger brother of this mountain is Maināka. He is protected from the thunderbolt by the ocean, and in turn all his life he protects the general and the minister, those two oceans. 47.

Both *tīrtha*s were destroyed by chance by the barbarians, and were renovated in Śaka 1243 by two men. The restorer of the first *tīrtha* was Lalla, son of Mahaṇasiṃha, and [the restorer] of the second was Pīthaḍa, son of the merchant Caṇḍasiṃha. 48-49.

Emperor Kumārapāla, the moon of the Caulukya lineage, built the Blessed Vīra temple on the high peak. 50.

Fortunate are the people who see this Arbuda mountain, filled with wonders, adorned with herbs, and purified by more than one *tīrtha*. 51.

This Kalpa, strung together by blessed Jinaprabhasūri, this Arbuda Kalpa which is a nectar to the ears, should be studied by skilled people. 52.

Thus the blessed Arbuda Kalpa is concluded.

Chapter 18

Aṣṭāpada, by Dharmaghoṣasūri

Victorious is that lord of mountains Aṣṭāpada,
  which is superior due to the glory of Ṛṣabha's dharma,
the refuge of Vidyānanda, the purifier,
  praised by Devendra. 1.
Victorious is that lord of mountains Aṣṭāpada,
  where resided Ṛṣabha the light of Aṣṭāpada,
which has eight feet,
  chief Aṣṭāpada the remover of thousands of sins. 2.
Victorious is that lord of mountains Aṣṭāpada,
  where the 99 sons of Ṛṣabha—Bāhubali and the rest—
superior ascetics,
  consumed the nectar of immortality. 3.
Victorious is that lord of mountains Aṣṭāpada,

where 10,000 seers,
frightened due to separation from the lord,
engaged in yoga for liberation. 4.
Victorious is that lord of mountains Aṣṭāpada,
where his 8 grandsons and 99 sons
went to liberation with Ṛṣabha
all at the same time. 5.
Victorious is that lord of mountains Aṣṭāpada,
where Indra established at the site of the three pyres
three stūpas with images,
like three jewels. 6.
Victorious is that lord of mountains Aṣṭāpada,
where Bharata made
the fourfold temple Lion Seat
with the image Liberation Seat. 7.
Victorious is that lord of mountains Aṣṭāpada,
where the temple one yojana long,
half that wide, and three kro'sas high
is enthroned. 8.
Victorious is that lord of mountains Aṣṭāpada,
where Bharata made the image of his brother,
the images of the 24 Jinas,
and his own image. 9.
Victorious is that lord of mountains Aṣṭāpada,
where Bharata described the images
of the 24 contemporary Jinas,
each described with its own shape, color, and mark. 10.
Victorious is that lord of mountains Aṣṭāpada,
where the Emperor [Bharata] built the stūpas
with images of the 99 brothers,
and the stūpa of the Arhat [Ṛṣabha]. 11.
Victorious is that lord of mountains Aṣṭāpada,
where Bharata made the 8-footed,
8-yojana long 'sarabha
to kill the lion of delusion. 12.
Victorious is that lord of mountains Aṣṭāpada,
where many millions of great seers,
the Emperor Bharata, and others
succeeded to liberation. 13.
Victorious is that lord of mountains Aṣṭāpada,
where Subuddhi told how the seers in Bharata's lineage,
with Sagara's sons at the forefront,

went to liberation and perfection. 14.
Victorious is that lord of mountains Aṣṭāpada,
where Sagara's sons contained the ocean
by making an ocean-moat
which protects [Aṣṭāpada] on all sides. 15.
Victorious is that lord of mountains Aṣṭāpada,
where Jaina [mountain] rests on the Ganga
with its unceasing rolling [waves] on all sides,
as if to bathe its own sins. 16.
Victorious is that lord of mountains Aṣṭāpada,
where even Damayantī, by giving a tilaka to the Jina,
received on her forehead a permanent tilaka
which matched the fruit [of her deed]. 17.
Victorious is that lord of mountains Aṣṭāpada,
where Rāvaṇa was stepped on by Bali's foot,
and having as a result thrown the mountain into the ocean,
cried out in anger. 18.
Victorious is that lord of mountains Aṣṭāpada,
where the king of Laṅkā
received from Dharaṇendra the power of infallible victory
by performing the Jina festival with an instrument held
in his hand. 19.
Victorious is that lord of mountains Aṣṭāpada,
where the Gaṇabhṛt praised the Jina images
—four, eight, ten, and two—
in the four directions of west, etc. 20.
Victorious is that lord of mountains Aṣṭāpada,
for on this mountain people who have praised the Jina as
they can
—exactly as Vira said—
attain unshakable welfare from their own power. 21.
Victorious is that lord of mountains Aṣṭāpada,
where by studying the lotus-text spoken by the Lord,
the godlike Puṇḍarīka
came to know the ten Pūrvas. 22.
Victorious is that lord of mountains Aṣṭāpada,
where, after praising the Lord Jina,
the Gaṇa-leader Gautama
initiated 1,500 ascetics. 23.
Victorious is that lord of mountains Aṣṭāpada;
this long-standing poem made with eight feet,
like the Aṣṭāpada mountain,

ennumerates in great detail the great tīrtha. 24.

Thus the blessed Kalpa of the Great Tīrtha Aṣṭāpada is concluded.

It is the work of blessed Dharmaghoṣasūri.

Chapter 24

Nandīśvara

After worshipping the feet of Jinas, which were worshipped by the King of Gods, I will tell the all-purifying Kalpa of Nandīśvaradvīpa. 1.

Nandīśvara is the eighth continent, resembling heaven. It is encircled by the ocean Nandīśvara. 2.

It is 1,630,840,000 *yojanas* in circumference. 3.

This is an enjoyment land of the gods, with various arrangements of gardens. It is made beautiful by the congregation of gods intent on worshipping the Jinas. 4.

In the center stand four collyrium colored mountains of collyrium, in the directions in order, starting with the east. 5.

They are 10,000 *yojanas* on the ground and 1,000 *yojanas* high, the height of a small Meru. 6.

In the east there is Devaramaṇa, in the south Nityodyota, in the west Svayaṃprabha, in the north Ramaṇīya. 7.

There are Arhat temples 100 *yojanas* long, half that wide, and 72 *yojanas* high. 8.

Each of the four gates is 16 *yojanas* high, 8 *yojanas* in the entrance, and 8 across. 9.

They are known by the names of the sky-dwelling gods, *asuras*, *nāgas*, and birds, with which they are connected. 10.

In the middle [of the temples] are jewelled seats 16 *yojanas* long and wide, and 8 *yojanas* high. 11.

Above the seats are divine umbrellas made of many jewels, which are much longer and higher than the seats. 12.

Ṛṣabhas, Vardhamānas, Candrānanas, and Vāriṣeṇas, each one made of gems, and with their own families, are seated in the lotus position; there are 108 images of each of the eternal Arhats. 13-14.

There is a *nāga* and a *yakṣa*, holding pots, at each image, and behind each image is an umbrella-holding image. 15.

In [the temples] are incense, jars, garlands, bells, the eight auspicious symbols, banners, umbrellas, gateways, baskets, trunks, and seats. 16.

There are 16 full pots as adornments, and the earth there is gold and silver dust and sand. 17.

In accordance with the size of the temples there are silver chief-pavilions, pavilions for the purpose of performances, assembly halls, and jewelled seats. 18.

At every step there are pleasing *stūpa*s and images, pretty temples and trees, divine Indra banners, and lotus ponds. 19.

There are 16 images in each of the four-doored *stūpa*s, so there are 2,508 in total. 20.

In the four directions from each collyrium mountain are fishless pure lakes, lotus ponds 100,000 *yojana*s long, 1,000 *yojana*s deep [or 1,000 up the slope], 100,000 *yojana*s across. Their 16 names are, in order: Nandiṣenā, Amoghā, Gostūpā, Sudarśanā, Nandottarā, Nandā, Sunandā, Nandivardhanā, Bhadrā, Viśālā, Kumudā, Puṇḍarīkinī, Vijayā, Vaijayantī, Jayantī, and Aparājitā. 21-24.

500 *yojana*s beyond each of them are great gardens, 500-*yojana*s wide and 100,000 *yojana*s long, known for their *aśoka*, *saptacchadaka*, *campaka*, and mango trees. 25-26.

In the middle of the lotus ponds are crystal Dadhimukha mountains, which have the shape of grain sacks. They are distinguished by their ornaments, verandas, and groves. 27.

They are 64,000 *yojana*s high and extend down 1,000. They are 10,000 wide at bottom and top. 28.

Between each lotus pond are two Love-Making (Ratikara) mountains; so there are 32 Love-Making mountains in total. 29.

On these Dadhimukha and Love-Making mountains are temples of the eternal Arhats, just like on the collyrium mountains. 30.

In the four intermediate directions of the continent are four Love-Making mountains, 10,000 *yojana*s long and wide, and adorned with a height of 1,000 *yojana*s. They are made of many divine gems, and have the shape of a drum. 31-32.

On the two Love-Makings to the south are Śakra's [capitals], and Iśāna's are similarly on the two to the north. 33.

In the eight directions are the capitals of the eight great goddesses. They are 100,000 *yojana*s wide and long, and adorned with Jina temples. 34.

In order they are: Sujātā, Saumanasā, Arcirmālī, Prabhākarā, Padmā, Śivā, Suci, Añjanā, Cūtā, Cūtāvataṃsikā, Gostūpā, Sudarśanā, Amalā, Apsarā, Rohiṇī, Navamī, Ratnā, Ratnocchayā, Sarvaratnaratnasañcayā, Vasu, Vasumitrikā, Vasubhāgā, Vasundharā, Nandā, Uttarā, Nandottarakuru, Devakuru, Kṛṣṇā, Kṛṣṇarājī, Ramā, Rāmā, Rakṣitā, beginning with the east. 35-38.

The all-wealthy gods along with all their retinues perform the *aṣṭāhikā* at the temples on the beneficial days of the blessed Arhats. 39.

Śakra performs the *aṣṭāhikā* in the four-doored Jina temple with the eternal images on the mountain in the east. 40.

Śakra's four directional guardians perform the *aṣṭāhikā* according to precept in the temples of the eternal images of the Arhats on the four crystal Dadhimukha mountains in the great tanks located in the four directions from that mountain. 41-42.

Iśānendra performs it on the collyrium mountain to the north, and his directional guardians perform it on the Dadhimukha mountains in those tanks. 43.

Cāmarendra does the festival on the collyrium mountain in the south, and his directional guardians on the Dadhimukhas in the tanks. 44.

Balīndra does the festival on the collyrium mountain in the west. His directional guardians [do it] on the Dadhimukha mountains in those tanks. 45.

By performing the worship of Nandīśvara on Kuhū *tithi*, and fasting starting on the annual Dīpāvali, they attain protective auspiciousness/wealth. 46.

He who worships Nandīśvara on every *parva* by singing praises, hymns, and recitations with devotion to the temples, surely will cross over his sin. 47.

Thus the Nandīśvara Kalpa is written by Jinaprabha Ācārya, in verses which were given by the former teachers. 48.

Thus is the blessed Nandīśvara Kalpa.

Chapter 26

Ariṣṭanemi of Aṇahilapura

After bowing to Ariṣṭanemi,
I will make famous the Kalpa of Ariṣṭanemi,
refuge of the Brāhmaṇa Gaccha and
garland of Anahilapura town. 1.

It is said that formerly in Kannauja city there was a very wealthy and very rich merchant named Yakṣa. Once in the course of trading he took his wares in a caravan of bullocks and departed for Gujarat. Gujarat was a dependency of Kannauja; it had been given as dowry to Mahanigā, daughter of the king of Kannauja. Yakṣa stayed on the banks of the Sarasvatī in Lakṣārāma. It is said that this is the original site of Aṇahillavāḍaya town. The monsoon fell upon the merchant while the caravan was there. It began to rain. In the month of Bhadrapada the entire bullock herd wandered off somewhere. No one knew where. He looked for it everywhere, but couldn't find it. He worried ceaselessly that it was all destroyed. Then the blessed Ambādevī came to him one night in a dream. She said, "Child. Are you awake or asleep?" Yakṣa said, "Mother! How can I sleep? My bullock herd and all my belongings have disappeared." The goddess said, "Good man. There are three images here in Lakṣārāma at the base of a tamarind tree. Dig down three fathoms and retrieve them. One image is of blessed Ariṣṭanemi Svāmī, another is of blessed Pārśvanātha, and the third is of Ambikā Devī." Yakṣa said, "Goddess! How can I know where it is among a multitude of tamarind trees?" The goddess said, "You will see a circle of metal and a heap of flowers. That is the location of the three images. If you uncover and worship the three images, the bullocks will come to you of their own accord." He got up at dawn, did the worship as he had been told, and found the three images. He worshipped them according to the proper rite. At that moment, as though unexpected, the bullocks returned. The merchant was happy. He built a temple there and consecrated the images.

Another time blessed Yaśobhadrasūri, the ornament of the Brāhmaṇa Gaccha, came here at the [start of the] monsoon season, while walking towards Khambhāta from Aggahāra village which is adorned with 1,800 *upāśrayas*. The people requested that he stay, saying, "Lord! You cannot go on if you bypass this *tīrtha*." So the *sūri* worshipped the images with praises. The banner raising festival was performed on the day of the full moon of Mārgaśīrṣa. Today the banner raising is still performed on that day every year. The banner-raising festival occurred in Vikrama 502.

Pattana was established by Vanarāja, the pearl of the Caukkada [Cāpotkaḍā, Cāvaḍā] dynasty in Vikrama 802, in Lakṣārāma in the region under the rule of King Aṇahilla. Seven kings of the Cāvaḍā dynasty reigned: Vanarājā, Yogarājā, Kṣemarājā, Bhuyagaḍa, Vajrasiṃha, Ratnāditya, and Samantasiṃha. Then eleven kings of the Cālukya dynasty reigned in that town: Mularājā, Camuṇḍarājā, Vallabharājā, Durlabharājā, Bhīmadeva, Karṇa, Jayasiṃhadeva, Kumārapāladeva, Ajayadeva, the younger Mularājā, and Bhīmadeva. Then reigned the kings in the Vāghelā years: Lavaṇaprasāda, Vīradhavala, Vīsaladeva, Arjunadeva, Sāraṅgadeva, and Karṇadeva. Then in Gujarat came the rule of the sultans — 'Ala-u'd-dina, etc. But Ariṣṭanemi Svāmī is still worshipped in the same way today.

May this Ariṣṭanemi Kalpa,
  be excellent to us.
It was written by blessed Jinaprabhasūri
  who heard it from the mouths of those who know former things.
  Thus the Ariṣṭanemi Kalpa.

Chapter 27

The Pārśvanātha at Śaṅkhapura

It is said that once Jarāsandha, the ninth Prativāsudeva, went west from Rājagṛha City with his entire army. He was engaged in war with Kṛṣṇa, the ninth Vāsudeva. Kṛṣṇa also left Dvāravatī with all his retinue to face him, and came to the border of his country. Lord Ariṣṭanemi blew the conch Pañcajanya there, and so the city Śaṅkheśvara [Lord of the Conch] was founded. Jarāsandha grew fearful at the sound of the conch and so worshipped his *kuladevatā* Jarā. She caused old age (*jarā*) to beset the army of Viṣṇu. Keśava was perplexed and worried at seeing his own army struck down by sicknesses of coughing and (short)-breath, and asked Lord Ariṣṭanemi Svāmī, "Lord! How can my army be freed of this affliction? And how can I get the blessedness of victory in the palm of my hand?" The Lord looked at the unseen with his *avadhi jñāna*, and said, "An image of Pārśva the future Arhat is worshipped in Pātāla by the serpent gods. If you worship it as your personal god, then your (army) will become free from affliction and you will obtain the blessing of victory." After he heard this, for seven months and three days — or, according to another opinion, three days — Viṣṇu worshipped the serpent king by fasting in the proper manner. Then the Nāga king Vāsuki appeared. Hari with bhakti and respect asked for the image. The Nāga king gave it to him. It was brought with full festival, and Kṛṣṇa established it as his personal god. Thrice-daily *pūjā* in the proper manner was begun. Viṣṇu sprinkled the entire army with the water from the lustration (of the image), and the army was freed from the oppressions such as old age, illness, and suffering, and became fit. Jarāsandha was defeated. The image was victorious in removing all obstacles and creating all wealth due to the proximity of Dharaṇendra and Padmāvatī. It was established in Śaṅkhapura. Over time it became concealed. Then it reappeared in the Śaṅkha well. Today it is worshipped in the temple by the entire congregation of the faithful. Even the Turkish kings proclaim its glory.

This *kalpa* of Jineśvara Pārśva,
  whose image is located at Śaṅkhapura,
the *tīrtha* of desires,
  has been written by me in accordance with a song. 1.
Pārśvanātha, Lord of Śaṅkha, Lord of lords,
  a wishing tree of auspiciousness:
may this God forever place wealth
  in the bodies and homes of good souls. 2.
Thus the blessed Śaṅkhapura Kalpa.

Chapter 40

Kokāvasati Pārśvanātha

After bowing to Pārśvanātha
  who is served by Padmāvatī and the Nāga king,
I will tell the story
  of Kokāvasati Pārśva. 1.

One day Abhayadevasūri of the blessed Praśnavāhaṇa Kula of the Harṣapurīya Gaccha left Harṣapura on tour and came to blessed Aṇahillavāḍa Paṭṭana. He remained outside of town with his mendicant family. One day blessed Jayasiṃha, lord of men, mounted his elephant and came to the royal park. There he saw Abhayadeva's unwashed and dirty clothes and body. The king dismounted his elephant, praised Abhayadeva, and gave him the name Maladhāri in recognition of his difficult asceticism. The king then requested that he come into the city. He gave him an *upāśraya* next to the ghee market. The *sūri* stayed there.

Some years later the blessed Hemacandrasūri, widely famous for composing various books, was on Abhayadeva's *paṭṭa*. He went to the ghee market to give a sermon every day during the four month rainy season retreat. One day in the ghee market temple someone from the ghee market association started a *bali* offering for ancestor worship. Hemacandrasūri arrived to give the sermon. The gathering forbade him, saying, "No sermon can be given here today, for there shouldn't be a sermon at the site of a *bali* offering." The *sūri* replied, "I'll have to give at least a short sermon today, or else there will be a break in the sermons of the rainy season." But the people of the association were not persuaded. The *ācārya* returned to the *upāśraya* angry and embarrassed at what had happened. A wealthy layman named Mokhadeva Nāyaka came to know of the guru's depressed state of mind. He sought land near the ghee market to build a new temple in order that such an insult against the faith should not occur in another temple, but could find none. Finally he obtained land from a merchant named Kokā. In opposition the ghee market assembly offered to give three times the price. The *sūri* came with the congregation to Kokā's house. Kokā honored him and said, "I gave the land at the proper price, so build the temple in my name." The *sūri* and the laymen accepted this. The temple Kokāvasati was built near the ghee market. Blessed Pārśvanātha was established in it, and thrice daily *pūjā* was begun.

Later, during the reign of blessed Bhīmadeva, Paṭṭana was looted by the king of Mālavā, and the image of Pārśvanātha was broken. Rāmadeva Āsadhara, a descendant of the wealthy Nāyaka, began to restore it. Three pieces of marble were brought which had flaws. Three images were made from them, but the guru and the laymen were not happy. Rāmadeva vowed, "I will not eat as long as the Pārśvanātha image has not been carved." The guru also began a fast. On the eighth day Rāmadeva received an instruction from a god, that he would find a wooden plank covered with flowers, with a stone slab as many hands beneath it as it was far from the temple. He dug up the earth and found the slab. A new image of Pārśvanātha was carved. In Vikrama 1266 Devanandasūri performed the *pratiṣṭhā* to establish it in the temple. It became famous as Kokā Pārśvanātha.

Merchant Rāmadeva had two sons named Tihuṇā and Jājā. Tihuṇā's son was Malla. His sons are named Delhaṇa and Jaitasīha; today they perform *pūjā* daily to Pārśvanātha.

Once Delhaṇa was given a dream by blessed Śaṅkheśvara Pārśvanātha. "I will be present in Kokā Pārśvanātha at dawn at 4:00 a.m.. Those who perform *pūjā* to that image at 4:00 a.m. will be doing *pūjā* to me." Kokā Pārśvanātha when worshipped in this way by the people fulfills [requests] like Śaṅkheśvara Pārśvanātha. People's *pūjā*, *yātrā*, vows, etc., done in connection with Śaṅkheśvara

Pārśvanātha are also fulfilled here. Thus is [the story of] the miracle working image, 33 fingers high, of Kokā Pārśvanātha, which is attached to the Maladhāri Gaccha.

May this short Kalpa
of Kokāvasati Pārśvanātha
who adorns Aṇahila Paṭṭana
destroy the obstacles of the people. 1.

Thus is the Kalpa of Kokāvasati Pārśvanātha.

Chapter 49

Mt.Aṣṭāpada

After bowing to Ṛṣabha
who is like the world-engendering eight-legged Śarabha
with a golden body
I will recite in brief the Kalpa
of Aṣṭāpada Mountain. 1.

On this Jambudvīpa continent in the middle of the southern half of Bhāratavarṣa there is a city called Ayodhyā, which is nine *yojanas* wide and twelve *yojanas* long. It is the birthplace of the Jinas blessed Ṛṣabha, Ajita, Abhinandana, Sumati, and Ananta. Twelve *yojanas* to the north of it is the excellent mountain called Aṣṭāpada, also known as Kailāsa, which is eight *yojanas* high and made of pure crystal. It is also famous among the people as Dhavalagiri. Even today, when one stands atop Uddaya Hill near Ayodhyā, one can see the whiteness of its range of peaks if the sky is clear.

The great Mānasa Lake is also there. There are many fine trees and full waterfalls. Clouds travel in the vicinity. It is filled with the noise of intoxicated peacocks and other birds, and made beautiful by *kinnara* and *khacara* women. Just seeing it takes away the hunger and thirst of people such as *caraṇas* and *śramaṇas* coming here for *caitya-vandana*.

The residents of Sāketa play various kinds of games in the valleys. Ṛṣabha Svāmī was established in *paryaṅka-āsana* by fourteen devotees on this peak. He attained *nirvāṇa* with 10,000 homeless mendicants on the morning of Māgha dark 13th in the Abhijita *nakṣatra*. Śakra and others performed the cremation of the body of Svāmī there. The pyre of Svāmī was in the east, that of [the mendicants of] the Ikṣvāku lineage in the south, and [that of] the rest of the *sādhus* in the west. Three *stūpas* were built by the gods on these three pyre sites. Emperor Bharata built a temple one *yojana* long, half that wide, and three *krośas* tall called Lion Residence out of gems and precious stones on the site of the cremation of Svāmī. It has four crystal gateways. There are sixteen sandalwood pots made of gems on either side of each gateway. At each gateway there are sixteen arches made of gems. There are sixteen *aṣṭamaṅgalas* on each gateway. From these gateways there are four expansive pavilions. Ahead from these pavilions are four assembly halls. In the middle of the assembly halls there are four gathering halls. In the middle of each gathering hall is a lion throne made of gems. Ahead of each assembly hall are jewelled benches. Atop them are *caitya-stūpas* made of gems. Ahead of each *caitya-stūpa* in each direction are immense jewelled benches. Atop each of them is a *caitya*-tree. Facing each *caitya-stūpa* are beautiful images in the *paryaṅka-āsana* of the eternal Jinas Ṛṣabha, Varddhamāna, Candrānana, and Variṣeṇa, measuring 500 bow-lengths and made of all sorts of gems. Ahead from each of the *caitya-stūpas* are *caitya*-trees. Ahead from each *caitya*-tree are jewelled benches, and atop each of them is an Indra Banner. Ahead of each Indra Banner is a Nandā lotus pond with a stairway and archway, full of pure cool water, adorned by multicolored lotuses, beautiful, like a Dadhimukhadhara lotus pond. In the middle portion of the great *caitya* Lion Residence is an immense jewelled bench. Atop it is a colorful god-seat made of gems. Atop that is a multi-colored canopy. Under the canopy on the side is a hook made of diamonds. Hanging from the hooks are garlands of large pearls shaped like pots and mangoes. Amidst the garlands are stainless garlands of gems. Amidst the garlands of gems are garlands of diamonds. On the walls of the *caitya* are round windows made of multicolored gems in which hang chains holding burning incense.

On each god seat are images made by Emperor Bharata of the 24 Jinas — Ṛṣabha, etc. — made of diamond, each bearing its own form, identification, color. Sixteen images — Ṛṣabha, Ajita, Sambhava, Abhinandana, Sumati, Supārśva, Śītala, Śreyāṃsa, Vimala, Ananta, Dharma, Śānti, Kunthu, Ara, Nemi, Mahāvīra — are made of gold. Those of Munisuvrata and Nemi are made of lapis. Those of Candraprabha and Suvidhi are made of crystal. Those of Malli and Pārśvanātha are made of cat's eye. Those of Padmaprabha and Vāsupūjya are made of ruby. The nails of each image are made of diamonds and moistened by red dye. The edge of each nail appears as if sprinkled with juice of red gems or lac, hence they are called moistened. The surfaces of the navel, hairline, tongue, palate, *śrīvatsa*, nipples, hands, and feet are made of refined gold. The lotus-eyes, pupils, facial hairs, eyebrows, body hairs, and head hairs were made of *ariṣṭa* gems. The lips are made of coral gems. The teeth are made of crystal. The head bumps are made of diamonds. The insides of the nostrils are golden, and colored red by the anointing. The eyes, colored red by the anointing, are made of *aṅka* gems.

Behind each [Jina] image is another image, made of diamond, holding pearls, branches, noose, cup, *koraṇṭa*, dish, garland, and staff made of crystal and gem, and holding aloft a white umbrella. Fan-holding images made of diamond, waving jewelled fans are on either side of each [Jina] image. Standing in front of each image and honoring it are two *nāga* images, two *yakṣa* images, two *bhūta* images, and two *kuṇḍadhara* images, made of diamond, with their hands folded in obeisance and shining limbs. On the god seats are twenty-four diamond bells, twenty-four jewelled mirrors, twenty-four standing lamps made of gold, with bouquets of flowers in diamond baskets, hair-brooms, small tablets, ornamented baskets, holding standing incense burners, lamps, diamond auspicious lamps, diamond pitchers, diamond platters, receptacles of refined gold, diamond sandalwood pots, diamond lion seats, *aṣṭamaṅgalas* made of diamond, golden oil pots, golden incense burners, and golden lotus holders. All of this is in front of each image.

The *caitya* is adorned by a moonstone tree. It is surrounded by diamond pillars, which are wonderously decorated with wolves, bulls, crocodiles, horses, men, *kinnaras*, birds, bearded creatures, antelopes, deer, oxen, elephants, and creepers. It has a beautiful banner and is adorned with a golden flagpole. There is the sound of tiny bells. A lotus king pot sits atop it. It is marked by decorations in finest sandalwood paste. There are dancing women with multi-colored moving limbs and uplifted breasts. Both sides of the gateways are adorned with a pair of pots smeared with sandalwood paste. Garlands scented with incense hang at an angle. The floor is made with five-colored flowers. It is full of *apsaras* holding incense-holders with camphor, aloe, and musk; it is also filled with *vidyādharīs*. It is adorned by sweet *caitya*-trees and jewelled benches in front, behind, and to the sides. It was prepared with copious diamonds according to the proper rites at the instruction of Bharata. He made images of his 99 brothers out of divine diamond, with an image of himself in attendance. Outside the *caitya* he made a *stūpa* of Lord Ṛṣabhasvāmī, and one *stūpa* for each brother. He made an iron protector man so that men and women should not commit *āśātanā* while coming and going. One cannot proceed past him. The peaks of the mountain were torn by firm diamond to make the mountain unclimbable. One *yojana* inside Bharata made eight stairways in the shape of girdles, so that it is impassable by men. From this it became famous by the name Eight Steps (Aṣṭāpada).

Many years later the 7,000 sons of Emperor Sagara opened the earth with firm diamonds and made a 1,000 *yojana* [wide] moat for the protection of the *caitya*. They filled it with water by breaching the bank of the Gaṅgā with firm diamonds. When [the bank of] the Gaṅgā was broken, Aṣṭāpada seat, villages, towns, and cities were flooded. Prince Bhagīratha, the son of Jahnu, used a firm diamond to open a river pathway to the eastern ocean at the command of Sagara. It went through the Kurus, to the south of Hastināpura, to the west of the Kośala country, to the north of Prayāga, to the south of the Kāśī country, to the south of the middle of Vatsa, and to the north of Magadha. In this way the *tīrtha* of Gaṅgāsagara was born.

Ṛṣabha Svāmī's eight grandsons and 99 sons led by Bāhubali became *siddhas* with Svāmī on this mountain; thus its miraculousness was demonstrated by 108 becoming immersed in excellence at one time.

Blessed Varddhamāna Svāmī himself said, "The man who climbs this mountain by his own power and performs *vandana* to the *caityas* will attain liberation in this lifetime." After hearing this, Lord Gautamasvāmī, a storehouse of attainment, climbed this excellent mountain. He did *vandana* to the *caityas*, and saw ascetics with limbs emaciated from asceticism, striving at the base of an Aśoka tree, while he himself was strong in body. "Oh! I must not be misunderstood," he said, and so he composed the Puṇḍarīka Teaching to ward off uncertainty. Puṇḍarīka himself, with robust body but purified sentiment, went to Sarvārthasiddhi. Kaṇḍarīka, with his weakened body, went to the seventh hell. A striving Sāmānika became determined when he heard this Puṇḍarīka teaching from Gautama. He entered into Tumbavana and was conceived in the womb of Dhanagiri's wife Sunandā, and became the ten-*Pūrva*-holder Vajrasvāmī. Gautama Svāmī descended from Aṣṭāpada and gave *dīkṣā* to 1,503 ascetics from Kauḍinya, Dinna, and Sevāli. The Kauḍinyas and the others in these lineages climbed the first, second, and third lower levels after they heard the words of Vīra, "whoever performs *caitya-vandana* in this *tīrtha* attains liberation in this lifetime." They could not go further, but they were amazed to see Gautama Svāmī climbing unimpeded; they were enlightened, and took *dīkṣā*.

Millions of various *maharṣis* became *siddhas* on this mountain, with Emperor Bharata at the fore. Subuddhi was the chief minister of Emperor Sagara. In the presence of Jahnu and the other sons of Sagara he heard from Ādityayaśas the examples of how the *rajarṣis* born in the lineage of King Bharata went to Sarvārthasiddhi and to liberation during the first five million of the ten-million *sagaropama* years.

Vīramatī, in accordance with the preaching of the gods, placed *tilakas* made of gold inlaid with diamonds on the foreheads of the images of the 24 Jinas on this mountain. She was born as a pigeon, a twin, and a god, and then in her birth as Damayantī the *tilaka* on the forehead was successful in removing the darkness [of ignorance].

Bāli Maharṣi was firm in *kāyotsarga* on this mountain. Then Daśagrīva, who remembered a former enmity and grew angry as he descended in his vehicle, opened up the earth's surface. He entered into it, and in his enmity uprooted Aṣṭāpada and threw it into the Salt Ocean. Then he lifted up the mountain by calling to mind 1,000 spells. The *rājarṣi* [Bāli] knew of this from his *avadhi jñāna*, and pressed down on the mountain peak with his toe to protect the *caitya*. The sound of fierce vomiting came from the ten mouths of the contracted body. Thus he became known as Rāvaṇa. Then he was freed by the compassionate *maharṣi*, bowed to his feet, did *kṣamā*, and returned to his own place.

There [on Aṣṭāpada] the Lord of Laṅkā performed before the Jina. The *vīṇā* broke due to a divine spell. In order that the flavor of the performance not be broken, [Rāvaṇa] cut a tendon from his own arm and restrung the *vīṇā*. Dharaṇendra, who had come to praise the *tīrtha*, was pleased at the daring devotion exhibited in the sound of the limb-*vīṇā*, and gave Rāvaṇa a spell with the power of unfailing victory.

Gautama Svāmī entered the southern gateway of the *caitya* Lion Residence on this mountain. First he performed *vandana* to the four images of Sambhava, etc.; then he circumambulated to the western gateway and [did *vandana*] to the eight [images] of Pārśva, etc. ; then at the northern gateway to the ten of Dharma, etc.; finally at the eastern gateway to the two of Ṛṣabha and Ajita.

This *tīrtha*-gem is unattainable;
[but] those good souls who with purified *bhāva*
remember its unapproachable crystal grove,
or see in water the reflection
of its *caitya*, banner, and pot,
receive as much fruit of lofty *bhāva*
as the fruit from pilgrimage
and doing *pūjā* and anointing. 1-2.

Those who bow down and glorify
this *caitya-stūpa* along with its images
which was made by Lord Bharata
are blessed with the abode of Śrī. 3.

Benefit shines
in the good souls who in their own mind
contemplate this Aṣṭāpada Kalpa
composed by Jinaprabhasūri. 4.

The meaning which was sung in brief earlier
in the Aṣṭāpada Stava
has been publicized at length
here in this Kalpa. 5.

Thus the blessed Aṣṭāpada Kalpa is concluded.

GLOSSARY

ABBREVIATIONS

TSPC = *Trisaṣṭiśalākāpuruṣacaritra* of Hemacandrasūri.

VTK = *Vividhatīrthakalpa* of Jinaprabhasūri.

CHAPTER 1

On Śatruñjaya, see also Burgess (1869b, 1873), J. Jain (1980), Kanchansāgarsūri (1982), and Weber (1901).

Nābheya = "Son of Nabhi" = Ṛṣabha.

Atimuktaka = Younger brother of Kānsa, and a Jaina *sādhu*. See Weber (1901:298) and TSPC V,157.

Nārada = a Jaina *sādhu*. See TSPC V,154-5.

Spoke = *ara*. Time revolves in an endless cycle, with each descending (*avasarpiṇī*) and ascending (*utsarpiṇī*) half-cycle consisting of six spokes. Enlightenment and liberation are possible only in the middle two spokes. The third spoke of the present *avasarpiṇī* began during the life of Ṛṣabha, the first Jina. The fourth spoke ended three years after the death and liberation of Mahāvīra, the 24th and last Jina.

Descent of time = *avasarpiṇī*.

Yugādīśa = "First Lord of the era" = Ṛṣabha.

Siddha = enlightened and liberated soul.

Padmanābha = first Jina in the coming *utsarpiṇī*.

Arhat = Jina.

Nemi = 22rd Jina of the current *avasarpiṇī*.

Emperor = Cakravartin. According to Jaina universal history, there are 12 Cakravartins in each cycle of time. See Cort (forthcoming).

Bharata = Ṛṣabha's eldest son, and first Cakravartin of the present *avasarpiṇī*. See TSPC I.

Bāhubali = son of Ṛṣabha. See TSPC I,273-326.

Marudevā = Ṛṣabha's mother.

Samavasaraṇa = the platform in the shape of a cosmic axial mountain atop which each newly enlightened Jina gives his or her first sermon. See Norton (1981).

Gaṇadhara = the mendicant leaders of the congregations established by each Jina.

First *gaṇadhara* of the first Arhat = Puṇḍarīka. See TSPC I,356-358; and Weber (1901:249).

First son of the first Emperor = Ādityayaśas. See Weber (1901:250).

kheca = *vidyādhara* = wizard.

Nami and Vinami = two *vidyādhara* kings. See Cort (1987:239).

Draviḍa and Vālikhilya = two sons of Ṛṣabha who "fell out with each other and made war, but afterwards they were reconciled and undertook pilgrimages to Śatruñjaya" (Weber 1901:250).

sādhu = general term for all Jain male mendicants.

Muni = male mendicants of the lowest rung. In common usage, *sādhu* and *muni* are synonymous.

Jaya = the 11th *cakravartin*. See TSPC IV,365-367.

Rāma = the 8th Baladeva. See TSPC IV,107-352. According to the Jaina universal history, among the 63 Great heroes (*śalākā puruṣas*) in each cycle of time there are 9 Vāsudevas, 9 Baladevas, and 9 Prati-Vāsudevas, who occur in sets of one each. The Vāsudeva and Baladeva are half-brothers, while the Prati-Vāsudeva is their opponent. See Cort (forthcoming).

Pradyumna = son of Kṛṣṇa by Rukminī. See TSPC V,188-218.

Śāmba = son of Kṛṣṇa by Jāmbavatī. See below, chapter 3, and TSPC V,214.

Sagara = the 2nd Cakravartin. See Fick (1888) and TPSC II,63-220.

The Prakrit *Ajitaśānti Stava* of Nandiṣeṇa is a favorite Jaina hymn.

Rebirth = *avātara*.

Samprati = grandson of Aśoka, considered by the Jainas to have been a devout Jaina and great builder of temples.

Vikramāditya = legendary king. See Merutuṅga (1899-1901) and Weber (1901:304).

Sātavāhana (or Śālivāhana) = Jaina king of Pratiṣṭhāna. See Merutuṅga (1899-1901:14-16).

Vāgbhaṭa = prime minister of the Caulukyan Emperor Jayasiṃha Siddharāja. See Merutuṅga (1899-1901:129).

Pādalipta = a miracle-working Jaina *ācārya*, author of the *Nirvāṇa Kalikā* and other works. See Tripuṭī (1952:230-246).

Āma =8th century king of Kannauj. See Chatterjee (1978-84:I:169).

Datta = Dharmadatta = son of the future King Kalki. See Weber (1901:307).

Videha = another continent where liberation is possible. See Caillat and Kumar (1981:28).

Kalikācārya = famous *ācārya*, who reputedly lived in the early centuries B.C.E. See Brown (1933).

Jāvaḍa = see verses 71-83, and Weber (1901:304-306).

Meghaghoṣa = see verses 109-113.

Kalki = future king. See Weber (1901:307).

Vimalavāhana = forecast to be the last Jaina king of this era. See Weber (1901:308).

Duṣprasahasūri = forecast to be the last Jaina *sādhu* of this era. See Weber (1901:308).

Congregation = *tīrtha*. The Jain religion will disappear among humanity, but the memory of Śatruñjaya will be kept alive by the residents of the heavens.

Ādyajineśitṛ = Ṛṣabha. According to Jaina biology, even plants have souls which transmigrate.

Congregation = *saṅgha*, the fourfold congregation of male and female mendicants and male and female laity (*sādhus*, *sādhvīs*, *śrāvakas*, *śrāvikās*).In the life of each Jina there are five benificial events (*kalyāṇaka*): conception, birth, renunciation, enlightenment, and liberation. (See Fischer and Jain 1978:I.) These are the places where the five events in the lives of the 24 Jinas of the present *avasarpiṇī* occurred.

Namaskāra Mantra = the most sacred hymn of the Jains. See Jaini (1979:162-163).

Wizard = *vidyādhara*.

"Praise to the Arhats" = namo'rhadbhyaḥ.

Pādalipta = Pālītāṇa, the town at the base of the mountain.

First Arhat = Ṛṣabha.

108 Vikrama era = 52 C.E.

Cakreśvarī is the *yakṣī* goddess who presides over the teachings (*śāsana*) of Ṛṣabha. Kaparddī is the *yakṣa* god who presides over Śatruñjaya. See Shah (1987:63,98).

Root Lord or Main Lord = *mūlanāyaka* = the principal image of a temple.

split the mountain = there are two ridges atop Śatruñjaya, separated by a shallow valley.

Ikṣvāku = the lineage of Ṛṣabha.

Vṛṣṇi = the lineage into which Kṛṣṇa and Nemi were born.

caiyta-tree = see Shah (1955:65-76).

Rājadāna = the tree atop the mountain behind the main temple of Ṛṣabha, known as the Rāyana tree.

Ādīśa = First Lord = Ṛṣabha.

Mūlajina = Root or Main Jina = Ṛṣabha.

incarnation = *avatāra*. Representations of other *tīrthas* are known as *avatāras*; from worship of them one approximates to having performed the pilgrimage.

Satyapura = Jaina *tīrtha* in Southern Rajasthan. See VTK chapter 17.

Stambhanaka = Jaina temple in Cambay. See VTK chapters 6 and 59.

Śakra = Indra = the king of the gods.

Śānti= the 16th Jina. See TSPC III,199-336.As part of the rite of consecrating a new or renovated temple, members of the congregation drop money, gems, and other wealth down a hole over which the main image is then cemented down. This gift is a provision for any future renovation of the temple.

Vṛṣabha = Ṛṣabha.

Vairoṭyā = ancient snake goddess, and one of the Jaina goddesses of magic (*vidyādevī*).

Magical powers = *siddhis*.

Enjoyer of one incarnation = one will be reborn only once before attaining liberation.

Vastupāla and Tejaḥpāla = 13th century ministers of the Vāghelā kings. See VTK chapter 42 and Sandesara (1953).

Pīthaḍa (also Pethaḍa) = layman of Māṇḍavagaḍha who, in 1264 C.E., led a *saṅgha* pilgrimage to Śatruñjaya and established a pavilion and an image of Śāntinātha (Dosi 1955:4).

1369 Vikrama = 1313 C.E.

Kali = the fourth and most degenerate age according to Brahmanical cosmology, here equated with the fifth spoke of the descent of time.

alpaprābhṛta = Kapadia (1941:93) notes that this is the only reference to this text which had come to his attention.

Bhadrabāhu = Jaina *ācārya*, died 357 B.C.E., 7th in succession from Mahāvīra. See Triputi (1952:119-137).

Vajra = Jaina *ācārya*, 13th in succession from Mahāvīra. He lived from 31 B.C.E. to 57 C.E. See Tripuṭī (1952:284-303).

1375 Vikrama = 1319 C.E.

Jyeṣṭha = June-July.

CHAPTER 2

The successor to Vajrasvāmī was Vajrasenasūri (38 B.C.E. — 90 C.E.). See Tripuṭī (1952:301-307).

Living Lord = Jivantasvāmī, a title applied to the Jina while still living.

Ambādevī = Ambikā, the *yakṣī* goddess who presides over the teachings of Neminātha. There is a temple to the Hindu goddess Ambājī above the Jain temples on Girnar, atop the first peak. See Burgess (1869a:48-49).

Siddha Vināyaka = a form of Gaṇeśa. See Weber (1901:295).

Kṣetrapāla = local protector deity.

Correct faith = *samyakdṛṣṭi*, i.e., is a Jain.

Baladeva = Balabhadra, half-brother of Kṛṣṇa and the 9th Baladeva.

Kubera = the lord of the underworld and of riches.

box-length = *samudga*.

Rājīmatī = Nemi's fiancée. See TSPC V,255-261.

Vidyāprābhṛta = See Kapadia (1941:92).

CHAPTER 3

one *yojana* = a distance somewhere between 2½ and 9 miles.

Śivā = Nemi's mother.

Beneficial moments = *kalyāṇakas*. See above, notes to chapter 1.

Puṇḍarīka = see above, chapter 1.

Aṣṭāpada = see below, chapters 18 and 49.

Nandīśvara = see below, chapter 24.

Ambā = the *yakṣī* goddess who presides over the teachings of Nemi. Nemi (Rathanemi) was in his own wedding procession — the wrong path — when he heard the cries of the animals in their pens which were to be slaughtered for the wedding feast, and decided to renounce the world — the good path.

Ratna = see below, chapter 5.

Kuṣmāṇḍī= Ambā

CHAPTER 4

Bowlength = *dhanus* = four forearms (*hasta*) ≈ six feet (Monier-Williams 1899:509).

gavya = According to Monier-Williams (1899:351,466,1294), 1 *gavya* or *gavyuti* equals 4,000 *daṇḍa*s (staff, fathom), one *daṇḍa* equals 4 *hasta*s, and 1 *hasta* is approximately 1.5 feet. 5 *gavya*s therefore = 5 x 4,000 *daṇḍa*s x 4 *hasta*s x 1.5 feet = 120,000 feet ≈ 22.7 miles. Clearly that is not the distance intended here.

cubit = *hasta* (forearm) ≈ 1.5 feet.

Kohaṇḍi = Ambikā.

sāhāmiya = *sāhammi* (Skt. *sadharmi*), co-religionist?

fathom = *daṇḍa* (staff) ≈ 6 feet.

CHAPTER 5

Vaiśākha = May-June.

Jayasiṃhadeva = Caulukyan emperor of Gujarat, whose capital was at Aṇahilla-vāḍa Paṭṭana in North Gujarat. His reign was from 1094 to 1143 C.E.

Khaṅgāra = see Merutuṅga (1899-1901:95-96) and Majumdar (1956:68-70).

1185 Vikrama = 1129 C.E.

Kumārapāla succeeded Jayasiṃha. He reigned from 1143 — 1175 C.E.

1220 Vikrama = 1164 C.E.

Vīradhavala (d. 1238 C.E.) of Dholkā was a minister under the weak Caulukyan Emperor Bhīma II (died 1242 C.E.); his son Vīsaladeva established the Vāghelā dynasty. (Sandesara 1953:26-34).

Yugādinātha = Ṛṣabha.

Sammeta = Sammeta Śikhara, the mountain in Bihar where 20 of the 24 Jinas of this era attained liberation.

Marudevī = the mother of Ṛṣabha.

lamp of the Yādava clan = Nemi.

Śivā = Nemi's mother.

Samudravijaya = Nemi's father.

CHAPTER 8

On Abu, see also Jayant Vijay (1954).

Ambā = "Mother," the most important goddess of Western India, whose main temple is slightly less than 20 miles southeast of Arbuda. She is often worshipped by women who desire to have sons.

1088 Vikrama era = 1032 C.E.

Yugādideva = Ṛṣabha.

1288 Vikrama era = 1232 C.E.

Lūṇa = elder brother of Vastupāla and Tejaḥpāla, who died young. See Sandesara (1953:27,37).

Stambhatīrtha = Cambay. See VTK, chapters 6 and 59.

In verses 48-51, *tīrtha* refers to an individual temple, not a pilgrimage place.

1243 Śaka era = 1322 C.E.

The temple of Mahāvīra built by Kumārapāla is at Acaleśvara.

CHAPTER 18

Dharmaghoṣasūri = This famous *ācārya* of the Rāja Gaccha lived in the 12th century. According to Triputi (1952:513-514), he gave sermons in the royal courts of Nāgora, Śākambharī, and Ajamera, and many royalty considered him as a personal guru. He defeated the Digambara Guṇacandra in a public debate in the court of King Arṇorāja of Śākambharī. At his teachings, both kings and laity (including Pethaḍa) renovated Jaina temples. His followers formed the Dharmaghoṣa Śākhā (branch) of the Rāja Gaccha.

krośa = either 6,000 or 12,000 feet.

Bharata's brother = Bāhubali.

śarabha = "a fabulous animal supposed to have eight legs and to inhabit the snowy mountains; it is represented as stronger than the lion" (Monier-Williams 1899:1057).

Damayantī = for the Jaina story of Damayantī/Davadantī and Nala, see TSPC V,97-148.

Tilaka = forehead mark, made out of devotion and respect.

Rāvaṇa = king of Laṅkā, and the 8th Prati-Vāsudeva. See TSPC IV,107-352.

Bali = warrior turned Jaina *sādhu*. See TSPC IV,128-136.

Dharaṇendra = *nāga* lord of the underworld.

Gaṇabhṛt = Gautama Svāmī, the chief disciple of Mahāvīra.

Pūrvas = the "former" texts, now lost. See Jaini (1979:49-50).

CHAPTER 24

On Jain cosmography see Caillat and Kumar (1981); on Nandīśvaradvīpa see Shah (1955:119-121 and 1987:22-23) and Fischer and Jain (1978:II:19).

King of Gods = Indra.

Ṛṣabha, Vardhamāna, Candrānana, and Variṣeṇa are the four eternal Jinas. In every era, "names of these Tīrthaṅkaras are always repeated and they flourish in any of the fifteen karmabhūmis" (Shah 1987:100).

aṣṭāhikā = eight-day festival, performed thrice annually in the months of Kārttika (November-December), Phalguna (March-April), and Āṣāḍha (July-August).

Kuhū = new moon.

parva = the three annual 8-day festivals.

CHAPTER 26

Gaccha = mendicant lineage.

Brāhmaṇa Gaccha = The Tripuṭī Mahārāj (1952:275) write, "A Brāhmaṇa Gaccha arose in Varamāṇa village near Ābū," but are otherwise silent about this *gaccha*. On Varamāṇa and this Gaccha, see also K.C. Jain (1972:273-275).

Bhadrapada = September-October.

Khambhāta = the modern Cambay.

Aggahāra [Skt. Agrahāra] = a village of Brāhmaṇas. The connection between the Brāhmaṇa Gaccha and Aggahāra village would seem to indicate that this was a *gaccha* of mendicants who were born into Brāhmaṇa families. Aggahāra may be Varamāṇa.

upāśraya = mendicant rest house.

Mārgaśīrṣa = December-January.

502 Vikrama era = 446 C.E.

802 Vikrama era = 746 C.E.

For a slightly different list of the seven kings of the Cāvaḍā dynasty, along with the years of their reigns, see Merutuṅga (1899-1901:19-21). On the Cālukyas, see Majumdar (1956); on the Vāghelās, see Sandesara (1953).

CHAPTER 27

On Śaṅkhapura/Śaṅkheśvara, see Bhadragupt Vijay (1982), Cort (1987), and Jayant Vijay (1942).

Dvāravatī = Dvārkā in Okhāmaṇḍal at the western tip of Saurāṣṭra. It was Kṛṣṇa's capital.

Ariṣṭanemi = the 22nd Jina, and cousin of Kṛṣṇa.

Pañcajanya = Kṛṣṇa's conch.

For the story of Nemi's blowing of Kṛṣṇa's conch, which is here transferred to North Gujarat from Kṛṣṇa's arsenal in Dvārkā in order to provide a derivation for the name of Śaṅkhapura, see Brown (1934:46-47).

kuladevatā = lineage deity.

Viṣṇu = Kṛṣṇa.

Keśava = Kṛṣṇa.

avadhi jñāna = "a limited ability to become aware of things which lie beyond the normal range of the senses, as in clairvoyance, the'divine ear,' and so on" (Jaini 1979:121).

Pātāla = the underworld.

Pārśva = the 23rd Jina, and therefore at the time of the story not yet a Jina.

serpent gods = *pannagas*.

Nāga = another kind of serpent deity.

Padmāvatī = queen of Dharaṇendra, and the *yakṣī* associated with the teachings and congregation established by Pārśva. See Cort (1987).The image was efficacious not on its own, but because Dharaṇendra and Padmāvatī responded to the faithful prayers addressed to the image.

congregation = *saṅgha*.

good souls = *bhavya*, those souls with the possibility of attaining liberation, used generally to refer to Jains. See Jaini (1979:139-141).

The second verse is in Sanskrit.

CHAPTER 40

Nāga king = Dharaṇendra, the husband of Padmāvatī.

Abhayadevasūri, Praśnavāhaṇa Kula, and Harṣapurīya Gaccha = "Harṣapura was founded during the reign of King Allaṭa of Chiṭṭor and named after Queen Hariyadevī. In the Jain congregation, the *ācāryas* of the Praśnavāhaṇa Kula of the middle branch of [followers of] ācārya Priyagranthasūri stayed there, from which the mendicant congregation of the *gaccha* of the Praśnavāhaṇa

Kula became known as the Harṣapurīya Gaccha. Among them in the 12th century of the Vikram era there was ācārya Vijayasiṃha. The Harṣapurīya Gaccha became known as the Maladhara Gaccha in the time of King Karṇadeva due to [Vijayasiṃha's] disciple Abhayadevasūri." (Tripuṭī Mahārāj 1952:567-568).

Family = *parivāra*, the group of mendicants who travel under the guidance of one leader.

Maladhāri = dirty.

sūri = *ācārya* = the highest position in the hierarchy of mendicants.

paṭṭa = seat, position of authority within a mendicant lineage.

Hemacandrasūri Maladhāri, disciple of the great Agamic commentator Abhayadevasūri, and author of commentaries on *Nandisūtra*, *Anuyogadvāra*, and Haribhadrasūri's *Viśesāvaśyakabhāṣya*. He should not be confused with his younger contemporary Hemacandrasūri, called Kalikālasarvajña (Omniscient One of the Kali Yuga), author of the *Yogaśāstra*,*Siddhahema*, *Abhidhānacintāmaṇi*, *Triṣaṣṭiśalākāpuruṣacaritra*,*Vītarāga Stotra*, and many other works.

bali = offering of food to a deity. It is a distinctly Brahmanical rite. Jainas have long preached against the utility of ancestor worship. See Jaini (1979:302-303).

Thrice daily *pūjā* = at morning, midday, and evening. See Hemacandra, *Yogaśāstra* III.122-123 (pp.580-584), Babb (1988), Cort (1989:504-507), and Humphrey (1985).Bhīmadeva II ruled 1178 — 1242 C.E.

wooden slab (?) = *gohalia*.

1266 V.S. = 1210 C.E.

pratiṣṭhā = the rite by which an image is formally installed in a temple.There is still a temple of Kokā Pārśvanātha in Patan today.

CHAPTER 49

Śarabha = aṣṭāpada (see above, notes to chapter 18).

golden = aṣṭāpada.

Ajita = second Jina of this era.

Abhinandana = fourth Jina of this era.

Sumati = fifth Jina of this era.

Ananta = fourteenth Jina of this era.

Dhavalagiri = White Mountain.

kinnara = divine musician.

khacara = *vidyādhara* or wizard.

caranas = "a kind of Jaina mendicant who has the power to travel in the air" (Sheth 1963:322).

śramaṇas = "strivers" = Jaina mendicants.

caitya-vandana = the rite of praising an image of a Jina in a temple. See Williams (1963:187-198), Cort (1989:348-357).

Sāketa = Ayodhyā.

paryaṅka-āsana = the lotus posture. See Bhattacharya (1974:138-139).

Śakra = Indra = king of the gods.

aṣṭamaṅgala = representation of the eight auspicious objects: *svastika*, *śrīvatsa*, *nandyāvarta*, powder vase, throne, full pot, mirror, and pair of fish. See Shah (1955:109-112).

Indra Banner = Indra *dhvaja*.

Dadhimukhadhara = the lotus ponds on Nandīśvaradvīpa; see chapter 24.

śrīvatsa = diamond-shaped symbol on the chest of every Jina image.

koraṇṭa = branch(?).

kuṇḍadhara = type of *nāga*.

āśātanā = an expiable moral fault. See Williams (1963:225-229).

siddha = liberated soul.

Varddhamāna Svāmī = Mahāvīra.

Gautama Svāmī = the chief disciple of Mahāvīra.

attainment = *labdhi*. See Jaini (1979:142-144).

bhāva = internal state of the soul. See Glasenapp (1942:40-43).

Sarvārthasiddhi = the highest of the 14 heavens, from which one will be reborn just once more before attaining liberation. See Caillat and Kumar (1981:26,102).

Sāmānika = type of god.

ten-*Pūrva*-holder = knower of ten *Pūrva*s, the "Former" texts which are now lost. See Jaini (1979:49-52).

dīkṣā = initiation as a mendicant.

twin = in the first three spokes of the current downward cycle of time, people are born as twins. See Stevenson (1915:273-274).

kāyotsarga = "abandonment of the body," a form of standing meditation. See Williams (1963:213-215).

Daśagrīva = Rāvaṇa.

Rāvaṇa = "the roarer, the vomiter."

kṣamā = ritual pronouncement that one's evil actions may bear no fruit. See Shāntā (1985:415).

Aṣṭāpada Stava = chapter 18.

Verse 5 is in Sanskrit; the rest of the chapter is in Prakrit.

Bibliography

EDITION USED

Vividhatīrthakalpa of Jinaprabhasūri. Ed. Jina Vijaya. Santiniketan: Singhi Jaina Jnanapitha, 1934. (Singhi Jaina Series 10.)

EDITIONS CONSULTED

Vividhatīrthakalpa. Ed. D.R. Bhandarkar and Pandit Kedarnath Sahityabhusana. Calcutta: Asiatic Society of Bengal, 1923-1942. (Bibliotheca Indica 238.)

_____. Hindi translation by Agarcand and Bhanvarlal Nahta. Mevanagar: Jain Svetambar Nakoda Parsvanath Tirth, 1978.

OTHER SOURCES CITED

Babb, Lawrence A. 1988. "Giving and Giving Up: The Eightfold Worship among Svetambar Murtipujak Jains," in *Journal of Anthropological Research* 44, 67-86.

Bhadragupt Vijay, Muni. 1982. *Jay Śaṅkheśvar*. Mehsana (Visvakalyan Prakasan Trust).

Bhattacharya, B.C. 1974. *The Jaina Iconography*. Second edition. Delhi (Motilal Banarsidass).

Brown, W. Norman. 1933. *The Story of Kālaka*. Washington (Smithsonian Institution, Freer Gallery of Art).

_____. 1934. *A Descriptive Catalogue of Miniature Paintings of the Jaina Kalpasūtra as Executed in the Early Western Indian Style*. Washington (Smithsonian Institution, Freer Gallery of Art).

Bühler, G. 1898. "A Legend of the Jain Stupa at Mathura," in *Indian Antiquary* 27, 49-54.

Burgess, Jas. 1869a. *Notes of a Visit to Somnath, Girnar and Other Places in Kathiawad, in May, 1869*. Bombay. Reprint Varanasi (Kishor Vidya Niketan), 1976.

_____. 1869b. *The Temples of Śatruñjaya*. Bombay (Sykes and Dwyer).

_____. 1873. "Papers on Śatruñjaya and the Jains. V. Śatruñjaya Hill," in *Indian Antiquary* 2, 354-357.

Caillat, Colette, and Kumar, Ravi. 1981. *The Jain Cosmology*. Trans. R. Norman. New York (Harmony Books).

Chatterjee, Asim Kumar. 1978-84. *A Comprehensive History of Jainism*. 2 vols. Calcutta (Firma KLM Limited).

Cort, John. 1987. "Medieval Jaina Goddess Traditions," in *Numen* 34, 235-255.

_____. 1988. "Pilgrimage to Shankheshvar Parshvanath," in *Bulletin of the Center for the Study of World Religions* 14:1, 63-72.

_____. 1989. *Liberation and Wellbeing: A Study of the Svetambar Murtipujak Jains of North Gujarat.* Unpublished Ph.D. dissertation, Committee on the Study of religion, Harvard University.

_____. Forthcoming. "An Overview of the Jaina Purāṇas," in untitled volume on the Purāṇas edited by Wendy Doniger.

Dośī, Kulcand Haricand. 1955. *Bhārat Jain Tīrthdarśan.* Bombay (Jain Dharmik Siksansangh).

_____. 1981. *Pāṭaṇ Tīrth Darśan.* Patan (Hemcandracarya Jain Sabha).

Fick, Richard. 1888. *Eine jainistische Bearbeitung der Sagara-Sage.* Kiel.

Fischer, Eberhard, and Jain, Jyotindra. 1978. *Jaina Iconography.* Two volumes. Leiden (E.J. Brill).

Glasenapp, Helmuth von. 1942. *The Doctrine of Karman in Jain Philosophy.* Trans. G. Barry Gifford. Bombay (Bai Vijibai Jivanlal Panalal Charity Fund).

Gode, P.K. 1953. "Identification of Kutulakhana Mentioned by Jinaprabhasuri in his Vividha-Tirtha-Kalpa," in his *Studies in Indian Literary History*, Vol. I (Bombay: Singhi Jain Shastra Siksapith and Bharatiya Vidya Bhavan), 43-47.

Hemacandrācārya. 1931-62. *Triṣaṣṭiśalākāpuruṣacaritra.* 6 vols. Trans. Helen Johnston. Baroda (Oriental Institute).

_____. 1977-86. *Yogaśāstra* with *svopajñavṛtti.* 3 vols. Ed. Muni Jambu Vijay. Bombay (Jain Sahitya Vikas Mandal).

Humphrey, Caroline. 1985. "Some Aspects of the Jain *Puja*: The Idea of 'God' and the Symbolism of Offerings," in *Cambridge Anthropology* 9:3, 1-19.

Jain, Jyoti Prasad. 1978. "Prastāvnā," in Agarcand and Bhanvarlal Nahta (trans.), *Vividha Tīrtha-Kalpa*, pp. 7-35.

Jain, Jyotindra. 1980. "Spatial System and Ritual Use of Satrunjaya Hill," in *art and archaeology research papers* 17, 47-51.

Jain, Kailash Chand. 1972. *Ancient Cities and Towns of Rajasthan.* Delhi (Motilal Banarsidass).

Jaini, Padmanabh S. 1979. *The Jaina Path of Purification.* Berkeley (University of California Press).

Jayant Vijay, Muni. 1942. *Śaṅkheśvar Mahātīrth.* Ujjain (Vijaydharmsuri Jain Granthmala).

_____. 1954. *Holy Abu.* Trans. U.P. Shah. Bhavnagar (Yashovijaya Jaina Granthamala).

Kanchansagarsuri, Acharya. *Shri Shatrunjay Giriraj Darshan in Sculptures and Architecture.* Kapadwanj (Agamoddharak Granthmala).

Kapadia, Hitalal Rasikdas. 1941. *A History of the Canonical Literature of the Jainas.* Surat (the author).

Kuruvā, Caulā. 1986. *Gujarāt nā Jain Tīrth-dhāmo.* Ahmedabad (Pramila Publishers).

Law, B.C. 1939. "Studies in the Vividha-Tirtha-Kalpa," in *Jaina Antiquary* IV:4, 109-123.

Majumdar, A.K. 1956. *Chaulukyas of Gujarat.* Bombay (Bharatiya Vidya Bhavan).

McCormick, Thomas. Forthcoming. "The Jaina Monk as Center of Pilgrimage." In E. Alan Morinis and Robert H. Stoddard (eds.), *Sacred Places, Sacred Spaces: The Geography of Pilgrimage.*

Merutuṅga. 1899-1901. *The Prabandhacintāmaṇi.* Trans. C.H. Tawney. Calcutta (Asiatic Society).

Monier-Williams, M. 1899. *A Sanskrit-English Dictionary.* Oxford (Oxford University Press).

Norton, Ann Wood. 1981. *The Jain Samavasarana.* Unpublished Ph.D. dissertation, Department of Fine Arts, New York University.

Ratna Prabha Vijaya, Muni. 1941. "Late Seth Mansukhbhai Bhagubhai," in his *Sramana Bhagavan Mahavira,* Vol. I, Part I, 1-22. Ahmedabad (Grantha Prakasaka Sabha).

Sandesara, Bhogilal J. 1953. *Literary Circle of Mahamatya Vastupala.* Bombay (Singhi Jain Shastra Siksapith and Bharatiya Vidya Bhavan).

Saurāṣtra Tīrth Saṅgh Yātrā. 1939. Jamnagar (Jamnagar Jain Osval Volunteer Core).

Shah, Umakant P. 1955. *Studies in Jaina Art.* Banaras (Jaina Cultural Research Society).

_____. 1987. *Jaina-Rupa-Mandana,* Vol. I. New Delhi (Abhinav).

Shāntā, N. 1985. *La voie jaina.* Paris (O.E.I.L.).

Sheth, Pandit Hargovinddas T. 1963. *Pāia-sadda-mahaṇṇavo.* Second edition. Banaras (Prakrit Text Society 7).

Stevenson, Mrs. Sinclair [Margaret]. 1915. *The Heart of Jainism.* London (Oxford University Press).

Suśīlsūri, Acarya Vijay. 1975. *Cha'rī Pālit (Pāltā) Tīrthyātrā Saṅgh nī Mahattā.* Ed. Upadhyaya Candan Vijay and Upadhyaya Vinod Vijay. Botad (Sri Jnanopasak Samiti).

Tripuṭī Mahārāj (Munis Darśan Vijay, Jñān Vijay, and Nyāy Vijay). 1952. *Jain Paramparā no Itihās.* Ahmedabad (Sri Caritra Smarak Granthamala 51).

Weber, Albert. 1901. "The Śatruñjaya Māhātmyam." Ed. James Burgess, tr. Krishna Sastri Godbole. In *Indian Antiquary* 30, 239-251, 288-308.

Williams, R. 1963. *Jaina Yoga.* London (Oxford University Press).

Appendix 1

Jinaprabhasūri

Jinaprabhasūri was born around 1261 C.E. in the village of Mohilvāḍī in Gujarat in a family of the Śrīmālī merchant caste. His childhood name was Subhaṭapāla. Gujarat at that time was still under Hindu rule; not until the very end of the 13th century did the last Hindu dynasty fall to the army of'Ala-u'd-din Khilji, the Tughlak Sultan of Delhi. Subhaṭapāla took *dīkṣā* (mendicant initiation) as a Śvetāmbara Jaina *sādhu* at the age of 8 from Jinasiṃhasūri, leader of the Laghu Kharatara Gaccha, and was given the name Śarmatilaka. He quickly became a prize pupil of Jinasiṃhasūri, and in 1284 he became an *ācārya*. He was given the new name of Jinaprabha, with the customary title of *sūri* added to his name to indicate his status as an *ācārya*. He eventually succeeded to the position of head of the Laghu Kharatara Gaccha, and died in Delhi in 1333 or shortly thereafter.[1]

Jinaprabhasūri travelled widely, even though the first quarter of the 14th century was a time of great social change and unrest in northern India. In the course of his travels he wrote small treatises on the Jaina pilgrimage places and centers which he visited. These eventually were compiled to form the *Vividhatīrthakalpa* also known as the *Kalpapradīpa*. The colophons to individual chapters indicate that they were composed between 1308 and 1333 (Gode 1953:44-45). His sources for the different chapters varied, as will be seen from the colophons of the chapters translated here. In some cases he used other written sources (see chapters 1, 2, 24), in some he copied down the oral traditions concerning a place (chapters 5, 26, 40), in at least one case his description is based on popular songs (chapter 27), and in some he used a variety of sources (chapter 8). His descriptions of Aṇahillavāḍa Paṭṭana in chapter 40 and of Uddaya Hill outside of Ayodhyā [2] in chapter 49 both sound like they are based on personal experience. He also incorporated texts by other writers into his book verbatim, as in the case of the "Aṣṭāpada Mahātīrtha Kalpa" (chapter 18) of Dharmaghoṣasūri. As befits a compendium written over many decades, some of the chapters in the *Vividhatīrthakalpa* are in Sanskrit and some in Prakrit [3]; some are in prose while others are in verse. Jinaprabhasūri also used the three genres of hymn, story, and descriptive account.[4]

Jinaprabhasūri spent the last years of his life as a member of the court of the Tughlak Sultān Mahammad Shah. He accompanied the Sultān when the latter shifted his capital from Delhi to Daulatābād in the Deccan. Jinaprabhasūri was honored by the sultan in Daulatabad in 1332; he was given a residence, the Bhaṭṭāraka Sarāī, and the sultan also constructed a meditation hall and a temple to Mahāvīra.[5] At the same time the Sultān also arranged for Jaina laity to settle in his capital, and another time granted the right of unimpeded travel throughout his dominion to both Śvetāmbara and Digambara Jainas. Jinaprabhasūri was presumably an important mediator between the Jaina merchants and the Muslim rulers, in which role he prefigured the great Hīravijayasūri of the Tapā Gaccha,who enjoyed a special relationship in the 16th century with the Mughal Emperor Akbar.[6]

Notes

1. Information on Jinaprabhasūri's life is from J.P. Jain (1978:11-13).

2. We know from the colophon to his commentaries on the *Bhayahara Stotra* and *Ajitaśānti Stava* that he was in Ayodhyā in 1309 (Gode 1953:44).

3. Of the chapters translated here, chapters 1, 3, 8, 18, and 24 are in Sanskrit, and the other seven in Prakrit.

4. In addition to the *Vividhatīrthakalpa*, Jinaprabhasūri wrote commentaries on three popular hymns (*Ajitaśānti Stava*, *Bhayahara Stotra*, and *Uvasaggahara Stotra*), on the *Kalpa Sūtra*, and on the *Yati Pratikramaṇa Sūtra*, the independent *Vidhimārgaprapā*, and is credited with having composed over 700 hymns.

5. See VTK, ch. 51.

6. Such a relationship between Jaina holy men and rulers existed frequently in Indian history; see, for example, the role of Hemacandrasūri in the 12th century courts of the Caulukyan Emperors Jayasiṃha Siddharāja and Kumārapāla (Cort 1989:71-74).

Appendix 2

Pilgrimage, sacred geography and cosmography in the Jaina Tradition

The patterns and networks of pilgrimage in a religious tradition constitute one clear way in which the members of that tradition define their universe. As is seen in the chapters translated here, the *tīrthas* (pilgrimage places) of the Śvetāmbara Jainas include sites that from an outside perspective belong in the separate categories of geography and cosmography, but are here not distinguished as such. Some of the sites — Śatruñjaya, Giranāra, Śaṅkheśvara, Aṇahillavāḍa, and Arbuda — are within the known geography of India, and Jinaprabhasūri's accounts indicate that he visited these places himself. Aṣṭāpada is geographically locatable, as the Jaina equivalent of Mount Kailāsa in the Himalayas; but a reading of the descriptions of this *tīrtha* quickly shows that the *tīrtha* as understood by the Jainas only slightly overlaps with the mountain known by modern geographers. With Nandīśvaradvīpa, we clearly have arrived in the realm of cosmography. Jaina cosmography posits a series of circular continents and oceans centered on the axial Mount Meru; Nandīśvaradvīpa is the seventh of these continents.

Medieval and contemporary Śvetāmbara accounts of their sacred geography start with depictions of five major pilgrimage places, known as the *pañca tīrtha*. These are Śatruñjaya and Giranāra (also known as Ujjayanta and Raivata) in Saurashtra, Abu (Arbuda) in southern Rajasthan, Sammeta Śikhara in eastern Bihar, and Aṣṭāpada in the Himalayas. All of these are mountains. Śatruñjaya and Aṣṭāpada are associated with events in the life of the first Jina or Tīrthaṅkara of this age, Ādinātha, (also known as Ṛṣabhanātha), Giranāra with the life of the 22nd Jina Neminātha, and Sammeta Śikhara is the site of the final liberation (*nirvāṇa*, *mokṣa*) of twenty of the Jinas. There are many descriptions of these *tīrthas* in medieval literature, and they are frequently depicted in paintings, scrolls, and sculpture. This framework of five *tīrthas* is translated onto local geography, and the *tīrthas* nearby a larger *tīrtha* are called *pañca tīrthīs*, even though the number oftentimes is greater than five. *Pañca tīrthī* means, essentially, "small tīrthas." For example, the *pañca tīrthī* of North Gujarat are Carup, Metrana, Bhildi, Kamboi, Taranga, Simandhar Svami in Mehsana, Valam, Canasma, Gambhu, Bhoyani, and Pansar (Dosi 1981:38-57); and the *pañca tīrthī* of Śankheśvar are Radhanpur, Sami, Mujpur, Vadgam, and Upariyala [1] (Bhadraguptvijay 1981:31).[2]

Pilgrimage is a ubiquitous practice among Śvetāmbara Jainas. Since the *tīrthas* are all famous because of the temples, and more especially due to the images (*mūrtis*) enshrined

within the temples, these *tīrthas* are visited only by those Jainas who permit image worship, the Mūrtipūjaka branch of the Śvetāmbaras. But *tīrtha* has a broader connotation within Jainism than just a pilgrimage place. Jaina authors distinguish between immobile (*sthāvara*) *tīrthas*, such as the places described by Jinaprabhasūri, and mobile (*jaṅgama*) *tīrthas*, in particular Jaina monks and nuns. Thus pilgrimage to one's mendicant guru is as popular as pilgrimage to a place, and pilgrimage among the Sthānakavāsis and Terāpanthis is restricted to pilgrimage to mendicants.[3] Jaina authors further distinguish between spiritual (*bhāva*) *tīrthas* such as the teachings of the Jina and the Jaina scriptures, and physical (*dravya*) *tīrthas* such as those described here.[4] Most pilgrimage is performed by small groups of either family members or neighbors. Such a pilgrimage might be a one-day visit to a nearby temple, the annual three-day *darśana* of all the temples in Patan on the first three days of the new year, a four or five day trip to Śatruñjaya and nearby *pañca tīrthīs*, or a several week long bus tour of the major *tīrthas* of North India. Jaina mendicants are not allowed to reside permanently in any one place, but must always spend eight months of the year on the move. The travel of the mendicants can be seen as lifelong pilgrimage.

Jainas for many centuries have also performed large congregational pilgrimages, known as *cha'rī pālaka saṅghas* ("congregations which uphold the six *-rīs*"). These most frequently occur at the end of the four month rainy season retreat (*caturmāsa*, *comāsu*), during which the mendicants must stay in one place. Oftentimes at the beginning of their eight months of wandering, the mendicants will travel to an important *tīrtha*, accompanied by a large group of lay persons. For the duration of the pilgrimage the laity take temporary vows to observe six mendicant-like restrictions: (1) eating only once a day; (2) sleeping on the ground; (3) walking barefoot (or at least on foot); (4) having deep faith in Jainism; (5) avoidance of 'living' food, i.e. food the eating of which involves much karmic harm ; and (6) celibacy. The restrictions are summarized in a Sanskrit verse, where each provision ends in *-rī*; hence they are known as the six *rīs*.'[5]

In addition, there are six duties (*kartavya*) incumbent upon each pilgrim: (1) gifting, (2) austerities, (3) wearing pure clothes, (4) playing devotional music, (5) singing hymns, and (6) offering reverence (*bhakti*) in the temples visited. [6]

Such a group pilgrimage is usually sponsored by a wealthy layman, who upon the successful completion of the pilgrimage receives the title of *saṅgha-pati* (congregation leader), which then becomes the inherited family name of Sanghvi. A *cha'rī pālaka saṅgha* might be a small undertaking of one day to a nearby *pañca tīrthī*, or a large undertaking to a major *tīrtha* such as Śatruñjaya or Abu by hundreds of mendicants and thousands of laity lasting many weeks. [7]

Notes

1. Another list is given by Dośī (1955:45-48): Rādhanpur, Vīramgām, Pāṭaṇ, Cārūp, and Kamboī.

2. See Dośī (1955) for lists of the *pañca tīrthī* of Saurashtra and Marwar, and Kuruvā (1986) for those of Ahmedabad (two sets), Kacch-Bhadreśvar (two sets), Śatruñjaya, Barodā, and Girnār.

3. See McCormick (forthcoming).

4. See Suśīlsūri (1975).

5 Quoted by Suśīlsūri (1975:27). He does not give a source for this oft-cited verse.

6. The six are *dāna*, *tapa*, *ucita-veśa-bhūṣā*, *gīta-vājintra*, *stuti-stotra*, and *prekṣaṇa*. Suśīlsūri (1975:32-39).

7. For descriptions of two large *cha'rī pālaka sanghas*, one from Ahmedabad to Śatruñjaya in 1935, and the other from Jamnagar to Giraṇāra and Śatruñjaya in 1939, see Ratna Prabha Vijaya (1941:18-22) and *Saurāṣṭra Tīrth Saṅgh Yātrā*. Ratna Prabha Vijaya says that the 1935 pilgrimage consisted of about 400 monks, 700 nuns, and 15,000 laity, and was accompanied by about 1,300 bullock carts, 200 big tents, 900 small tents, 200 servants and cooks, 200 watchmen, and 100 volunteers. The pilgrimage cost its patron, Seth Maneklalbhai Mansukhbhai, between 500,000 and 600,000 rupees.

Appendix 3

A Note on the translations

Jinaprabhasūri was a keen observer who provides us with many valuable insights into India and the Jains of the early 14th century, but he was not a scintillating stylist. I have endeavored to make these translations enjoyable while at the same time avoiding the translator's sin of improving upon the originals. Half of the chapters translated are in prose and the other half in verse; I have translated all of them into English prose with the exception of chapter 18. This is the one chapter in which the verse genre is not that of narrative but rather that of a praise-hymn, and so I have rendered it in the form of an English poem.

Jinaprabhasūri was writing for a Jaina audience, and so his text is full of allusions and references which he did not need to spell out. But even scholars of India have at best only a limited knowledge of the Jaina worldview, and so I have provided brief notes to explain most of the references in the text. Providing a full explanation would have resulted in the notes outweighing the translation, so in most cases I have given only a minimal definition, and provided a few references for the curious reader who wants to learn more about the Jainas.